THE PARADOX:
THE SOLDIER AND THE MYSTIC

Daughters of the Empire 1

Suzette Hollingsworth

ROMANCE

BookStrand
www.BookStrand.com

A SIREN-BOOKSTRAND TITLE
IMPRINT: Romance

THE PARADOX: THE SOLDIER AND THE MYSTIC
Copyright © 2012 by Suzette Hollingsworth

ISBN: 978-1-62241-176-4

First Printing: July 2012

Knight, Ian. *Marching to the Drums: Eyewitness Accounts of War from the Kabul Massacre to the Siege of Mafikeng.* London: Greenhill Books, 1999.

Cover design by Jinger Heaston
All cover art and logo copyright © 2012 by Siren Publishing, Inc.

ALL RIGHTS RESERVED: This literary work may not be reproduced or transmitted in any form or by any means, including electronic or photographic reproduction, in whole or in part, without express written permission.

All characters and events in this book are fictitious. Any resemblance to actual persons living or dead is strictly coincidental.

Printed in the U.S.A.

PUBLISHER
www.BookStrand.com

DEDICATION

To Amy Brazil
a psychic sage
who gave me a dream with her vision

To Susan Bartroff
whose creativity, kindness, wisdom, and friendship are treasured

To Virginia Hashii
who first told me that I was a writer
and to Sherrie Holmes, editor extraordinaire, who made me one

Thank you for giving me an image of myself

Additional thanks to Gehan Hanafi, Advertising and Promotion Manager at Shepheard's Hotel in Cairo, Egypt, for her courtesy and professionalism.

And to Harvey Gover, faculty librarian at W.S.U. and *U.S. Long-Distance Librarian of the Year,* 2008, for nurturing the spirit and soul as well as the mind

THE PARADOX: THE SOLDIER AND THE MYSTIC

Daughters of the Empire 1

SUZETTE HOLLINGSWORTH
Copyright © 2012

Chapter One

"Fold!" he boomed as he viewed his hand with disgust. Val Huntington took another swig of whiskey and threw his cards on the table. Quickly he placed his winnings in a leather pouch in one swift movement as he simultaneously pushed his chair from the table in an almost undetectable motion. "I shall take my leave of you, sir, and thank you to bathe before our next encounter. It will make for a less memorable occasion, which can only be to your advantage."

"Eh, the night's young, gov'nor," his greasy companion growled encouragingly as he hurriedly retrieved the small amount of money left in the center of the table, his eyes moving greedily over Val's leather pouch, still visible. A stiff grin forced its way into his expression, revealing teeth darkened by tobacco.

"And so it is," Val agreed. Assuming a nonchalance of manner, Val cloaked the intensity with which he watched the burlesque man seated across from him.

When he observed a brief flash of anger in his opponent's eyes, unable to hide an unnatural eagerness to relieve him of his winnings, Val placed his hand deftly on his pistol under the table, watching for any signs of trouble.

"There are finer pleasures to be had than wasting my time with a stinking soldier."

"Beggin' yer pardon"—the hulk of a man seated opposite Val frowned. Momentarily his unshaven face assumed a contrived humility—"I were honorbly discharged," he mumbled with a forced politeness.

"Right." Val made no effort to conceal his amusement. "Discharged."

Val surveyed the illustrious establishment in which he found himself. It was dark and dirty, and his companion smelled like...like...well, it defied description. Possibly there was a dead camel somewhere that could match it, but that was questionable at best.

It was even damp in here. *Damp.* How was that possible in the desert?

There were a dozen card players left in the room, all having had too much to drink, and most as dirty as their surroundings. He felt a smile forming on his lips as he pictured the elegant setting and companions of his stylish London club, mentally comparing the conjured image to his present circumstances. With the reflection, melancholy encroached upon his mood, but he refused to surrender his amusement. His might be a morbid, unnatural smile, but it would be a smile nonetheless. After what he had seen in his life, he would be damned before he would let a mere gaming hell dampen his spirits.

Involuntarily Val reached to his neck with his free hand to straighten the Ascot knot, the cravat that had been all the rage when he left London. Instead, his hand found the emblem of the 7th Dragoon Guards, the *Princess Royal's*, reminding him that he wore only his officer's uniform.

If only there were something reminiscent of a more dignified and civilized existence. He glanced at his shining black Hessians and reflected that his boots might be the whole of it.

Clippity-clop-clop-clop. He could hear the sound of horses hooves on gravel forming a lonely cadence. He could almost hear the moon and know its fullness. In his London club he wouldn't have been able to hear someone in the next room much less the sauntering of a steed outside the building.

Most noticeable was the absence of laughter. The room's inhabitants— he could not truthfully call them *companions*—were lost in their own small worlds contained in their hands and their whiskey glasses. There was none of the friendly banter that occurred between friends to whom the socializing was the most important aspect of the card game and the club setting.

Ah, well. War takes some of the frivolity out of life.

Bloody hell. Val cursed under his breath, interrupting his own thoughts. *Why the devil am I in this den of jackals?* He reminded himself that he didn't need the money, and he probably wouldn't be around to spend it if he had. This was the last place an officer of Her Majesty's military forces should find himself.

Do I have a death wish? He laughed out loud at his own joke. The Crown had already taken that well in hand, and there was no need to offer any assistance. He wondered that England was so anxious to dispose of her young men.

Still, being here in this hell hole is death with dishonor, while my other option is death with honor.

Though somehow he failed to perceive the difference tonight.

"Those…uh…*pleasures* you speaked of can still be found when we're done playing, m' lord," the gorilla seated opposite him pleaded cajolingly while pulling violently at his beard, distorting his face as he spoke. Attempting to return the officer's interest back to the card game yet again, he dealt five cards to each of them in a maladroit fashion.

"Ah, perhaps for you, but I am in the prime of my life, and restless for a sweeter companion than yourself, Mr. Snipes." *The nearby tombs should be able to meet that requirement.*

"There'll be time enough for all what pleases ye, m'lord."

"Not likely. And I could be dead tomorrow," he prophesied, resolute. "No time like the present for a soldier."

He gazed into a rusting gilded mirror hanging crookedly on a faded and cracking plastered wall across from his playing table. As he sensed the heavy blanket of melancholy enshroud him even further, he instantly saw its reflection in his darkly brooding features. He had been oft described as devilishly handsome in the London circuit, but the image staring back at him did nothing to support that view, he concluded with disinterest.

"Aack! You'll kill a squadron of stinkin' Egyptians tomorrow like you always do and live to be an old man," the giant countered as he spit on the ground.

"Not if the British Empire has anything to say in the matter, Mr. Snipes." Val laughed morosely. "I will likely be a red stain on the horizon, having made no other impression on this earth, and be replaced by some other young sot."

"You were born under a lucky star, m'lord, and that's a fact," Snipes proclaimed with a wavering grin and no small amount of envy, attesting that he was anxious to relieve the officer of the fruits of his good fortune.

"Glad to hear it. That's a welcome, if surprising, bit of news." Rising from the table, Val swung the leather pouch into his pocket in one fell swoop. He cautioned himself that his swift and decisive movement was in direct contrast to his swaying stance, a contrived effort to appear far more inebriated than he was. He did not wish Snipes to consider him threatening enough to require the full extent of his attentions.

He quickly assumed a vague and indifferent expression as he stumbled. Rather than sitting down, however, he merely balanced himself with his hand on the back of the chair, placing himself in a stronger strategic position. He did not intend to relinquish the advantage, but it was hoped that an advantage would not be needed.

"We're not finished playing, m'lord." Val's hopes vanished as swiftly as his expectations were met. Snipes drew his pistol, his smile simultaneously fading into a hard expression. "You put me money back on the table. *Now*." The large man laughed as he gave the appearance of one who thought how easily this would be accomplished. Val knew himself to be an amiable gentleman under the worst of circumstances. No doubt a man of Snipes's size and resolve considered him an easy target.

"*Your* money? May I remind you that you lost this coin in a fair game, Mr. Snipes," he replied in a low voice.

"*Fair?*" Snipes scowled at his lordship. "Me hates quality what acts like they're the same as everyone else, like they don't have it ten times better." He muttered under his breath while shaking his hair out of his face like a dog just emerging from the water. His hair and beard were long, not from style but out of neglect. He wore mismatched separates, tan trousers and a black coat. On some men this was a stylish look, but the coat was too short for his size, and he wore a low-cut vest, which further emphasized his girth. The one recipient of his attention was a well-oiled moustache, long and drooping.

A startling manner of appearance which might have added to the appeal of a warmer individual fell sadly short of the mark on the man before him.

"I couldn't agree more, Mr. Snipes. That I should have the effrontery to stroll in here and drink and talk with everyone as if they were the same as myself. Unforgivable, to be sure." This was not the first time he had observed the resentment of his attitude of equality. Officers never fraternized with soldiers. It was an unwritten code.

"Since yer a gent who can sport the blunt and 're only here for jawjammin'"—waving his gun toward the seat, Snipes wiped his mouth with the back of the hand holding the gun—"'Ows about we be all sociable-like?"

"Since we are being so frank, Mr. Snipes, might I point out that your conversation is even less skilled than your card playing. I suggest we call it a night and end on a friendly note." Despite his suggestion, Val's voice held an ominous tone.

"Never you mind me skill, m'lord. I'd liefer win the blunt, but I'll take it either way." Snipes growled. Muttering under his breath, he added, "Damn Quality what never quits jabberin' when they's in their cups!" He spit on the floor in a gesture of irritation, his present expression evidencing a deeply felt resentment that there were men who didn't need the funds but merely played for sport, men who could afford such intangibles as honor and friendship.

Snipes motioned begrudgingly to Val to have another drink from the bottle Val himself had paid for.

"*Most generous of you,*" he mumbled, shaking his head as the bottle was thrust toward him. He was merely a trifle disguised, but he had had enough to drink, acting as if it were his last night on earth. He frowned, hoping his celebratory behavior wasn't a premonition—or a warning. Despite the drink, he had beaten almost everyone he had played, further adding to the sense that the pendulum must no doubt swing the other way.

"No more stallin'. I said to put me coin on the table, m'lord." Snipes's voice grew louder.

"I am a reasonable man," Val replied slowly as he placed his earnings back on the table and moved his chair closer to his companion's, deliberately walking clumsily toward it. The ancient mirror revealed clouded gray eyes flashing from beneath arched black eyebrows, promising that which the earl already knew—he was indeed closer to his sword-wielding ancestors than to the effete gentlemen of the London club he had frequented.

"Somehow I thought so," said Snipes, eyeing the coins greedily, his mouth watering. He took his free hand and wiped his mouth with it again. In the split second he let his eyes wander to the leather pouch, as fast as lightning Val knocked the gun from Snipes's hand. Val had spent numerous hours under the tutelage of one of London's best boxing instructors, Mr. P. Argyll Dunlevy. The aforementioned Mr. Dunlevy would have had a tear of contentment come to his eye had he been able to witness his pupil's step forward and right uppercut burying itself in Snipes's ribs.

Val grabbed Snipes's arm and pulled it behind his back, swiftly pulling Snipes's knife out of his belt pocket and holding it to his gargantuan neck. "Don't ever," he growled through barred teeth, "pull that on an officer of the Queen again." The rage that had been controlled to this point now burned through his body. Blood began to trickle down Mr. Snipes's neck as a prelude to what was to come.

"No! No! Course not, m'lord! I didn't mean it! I was just jokin' wif ye."

"I suggest you keep a check on your sense of humor. Joke again and you'll hang as a deserter, you bastard." As Val felt his hand tighten on the knife, the terror crossing Snipes face was evident even in the cloudy mirror, confirming the giant's conviction that he would be stabbed right then and there, a course Val was seriously considering. "And you'll be grateful to die by hanging instead of at my hands."

"I will! I will!"

"Are you laughing now, you sorry son of a bitch?" Val boomed.

A few interested players glanced their way, but no one moved toward them, and most did not even look up from their hands or their whiskey glasses. Apparently a murder in their vicinity was not noteworthy, he mused.

"Yes! Yes! I mean no! No! M'lord," Snipes begged. "Please don' kill me. I 'ave a wife."

"So you found a woman without a sense of smell, did you? How fortuitous," he muttered, distracting his captive with idle banter. Suddenly, with no warning, Val executed a left to his opponent's nose, snapping the man's head back, followed by a right cross to the point of his chin, which

The Paradox: The Soldier and the Mystic 11

rolled the gorilla's eyes back up into his head. "I commend you, sir, for your tireless efforts in what must have been an arduous and lengthy search."

Once again, only the diffused reflection in the rusting gilded mirror bore witness to the momentary flame in the young officer's eye, which bespoke the desire to finish his opponent.

But self-mastery had been developed to an art in the soldier and gentleman, and, sweeping up his winnings, he headed toward the door without a backward glance.

You're too soft, Ravensdale. You're no soldier, he muttered to himself with disgust even as he set his course. The sound of snores coming from the fallen giant interrupted Val's resolve as he reached the door. He admonished himself for not turning in Snipes as a deserter weeks ago, but the man would have hung, and plenty of English would die in the quest for territory for the Crown. One more man here or there really didn't make any difference to the cause.

He frowned. The fellow was a worthless bastard.

Still, he was merely a petty thief. He doubted that Snipes had ever killed anyone, on or off the battlefield. The sleeping giant was a waste of human flesh, but he had done nothing to warrant hanging.

Val forced himself to glance back. If Snipes was going to threaten British soldiers, it was his responsibility as an officer to remove the loose cannon from the vicinity, one way or another. He resolved to turn him in the next morning, giving the misfit a few hours to exit Cairo without the aid of the hangman's noose.

Leaving one hell hole, he entered another one, the back streets of Cairo in the dark of night. The heat was oppressive despite the late hour, exaggerating the smell of the open drains running down the middle of the streets.

"*Merhaba!*" Val motioned to a torchbearer to light his way as there were no street lights. The middle-aged native man hurrying toward him wore a simple calf-length tunic over bare legs, from which worn sandals were visible. Extending from the turban on his head was a hanging fold, which provided the dual advantage of disguise and diffusing the noxious vapors.

Val wished he had just such a veil. The smell of the open drains mixed with the smell of smoke and burnt cooking oil, not to mention the fragrant body odor of the torchbearer himself, threatened to compromise his focus on his surroundings.

He needed to keep his wits about him. It was a dangerous place to be at night where footpads and thieves would kill for nothing more than the clothes one wore. He remembered his glistening boots and cursed his ignorance, not for the first time. He wished that he could jump on his horse and ride home, but he hadn't dared bring the stallion, who would not have been safe. If his boots were a temptation, the horse was his ticket to hell.

Oh, I forget. I am already there.

And yet, one man's heaven was another man's hell, so the reverse must be true. Even in the stinking back streets in Cairo in the dead of night, he relished the experience. Despite all that had occurred, he was filled with the wonder and excitement of discovering a foreign land.

They walked along narrow streets more closely resembling crooked alleys until he reached his destination without incident. It had only been necessary to wave his gun at lurkers in the shadows two or three times.

"*Ma'assalama.*" The torchbearer gladly took his offered coin, scurrying off with a wide grin on his face, the coin clutched in his fist.

Val returned to his quarters, never intending to seek other diversions as he had indicated. Instead, he gingerly removed an old book from underneath his bed and inspected the hieroglyphic scribblings with interest. He took out his notebook and calligraphic pen, opened both books to the spot where he had last worked, and began to write.

Pausing from his work for a moment, Val thought of his soldiering companions and wondered which of them he would never see again after the morrow. Being an officer, he knew the plan of attack. They would start out tomorrow morning toward *Tel-el-Kebir*, followed by a brief rest before they initiated their attack in the middle of the night on sleeping Egyptians. It was unquestionably to be a bloody and terrifying battle. The Egyptians were fighting for control of their home and their country. They were like cornered animals, and they were proud and brave men, nationalists, who viewed death as favorable to the loss of freedom.

After Val had pictured his fellow soldiers and officers, he pondered his own existence and wondered if this was the last evening *he* would ever spend on this earth. No one would read or care about his last scholarly treatises.

The Paradox: The Soldier and the Mystic 13

Educated at Cambridge to be cannon fodder. Simply another pawn in Britain's quest for new territory. His tombstone would read, *Valerius Gregory Christopher Huntington, 5th Earl of Ravensdale, January 11, 1854-August 25, 1882, died in the line of duty, serving the Crown at Tel-el-Kebir, Egypt.* Val shook his head. Was the campaign worth the loss of human life, the contributions these young men on both sides might have made had they lived?

Val snorted. *Contributions?* What did he have to offer? He was twenty-eight years old and had never produced anything of any interest to anyone. No one cared to see his translation of ancient Egyptian text. No one was interested in the five ancient languages he read. The four living languages he read and spoke fluently were of some interest if he could but learn to apply them for imperialism and material gain.

Unless it can be converted into gold for Britain's coffers, there is no value to my existence on the planet.

Val shook his head in disgust at his own philosophizing. *It is my duty, and I have to fight. My family's honor depends upon it.*

He was born twenty years too late. Being a scholar and possessed of a classical education was now quite outmoded and unfashionable. Best to do away with him and make room for someone who had something to contribute to this industrial machine. Involuntarily, he somberly recollected the many balls and soirées during which he had bored gushing young ladies to death.

If the truth be known, he bored everyone to death. The thought pained him, though he was, by now, well acquainted with his social status. He was a linguist, a soldier, and an earl, and the only interest anyone had in him were the latter two roles. It was quite true, Britain had the right of it. *His main value was in being someone who could die for the Crown.* Though he might be dead tomorrow, there wasn't anything he would rather be doing, so he went back to work.

Val had a bad feeling about the morrow. Victory for the British, a swift demise for the 5th Earl of Ravensdale and for all his future descendants who would never see the sun rise over their family estate.

Chapter Two

Slowly they covered the rectangular plot with fresh earth. Their eyes were fixated on the ground, as if they were afraid to look elsewhere. The older miss placed her hand on top of the small child's hand and held it momentarily, a personal ritual of sorts. As she did so, she closed her eyes briefly. Her entire body revealed the slightest tremble for an instant, almost undetectable.

A small, pale, reddish-blonde head bent very close to the ground as if she hoped to see beneath the earth's surface. The child then turned her tiny ear toward the ground, looking up with a question written all over her face.

"Nothing is happening, Lita," the child whispered in obvious dismay, her large blue eyes troubled. "Didn't we do it right?"

Miss Alita Stanton's expression revealed a depth of character beyond her years. She bent down to kiss her sister's forehead. "You performed your task perfectly, Julianne," she murmured with sincerity.

Julianne studied the ground, making no effort to hide her disappointment. "But when will it grow, Lita?" asked the child.

"In the summer. Just wait, love. You'll see what magic will happen."

"*Magic*? What kind of magic?"

A thrill of anticipation rippled through Alita as she motioned to the pond. "There will be white lilies framing the pond. Add to that the heavenly scents of jasmine and honeysuckle. The clover that now caresses our feet will be framed by everlasting pea and sweet william. All one ever need do is to plant the seed and life...*happens*..."

"And will there be froggies, like last year?" Julianne asked excitedly.

"Most definitely. Frogs will jump from lily pad to lily pad."

"Why do the froggies jump?" Julianne's already overly large blue eyes grew wide with wonder.

The Paradox: The Soldier and the Mystic   *15*

"Why indeed?" Alita felt a smile tugging at her mouth. She tapped her lavender ruffled parasol on the ground. "I suspect to cast a spell, but I don't know. Why do you think they jump, Jules?"

"Are they dancing a ballet? A froggie ballet?"

"A froggie ballet!" Before Alita could respond, a guttural laughter burst through their subdued whispers. "You girls talk such nonsense," snorted Harvey, Alita's younger brother.

"Why *do* they jump, then, Mr. Knows Everything?" demanded Julianne.

"They jump to get somewhere!" Just as explosively as he had burst through their confidences, pink frocks, and blonde curls, reminding Alita of a deafening combustion she had once witnessed in her father's laboratory, he turned back to his easel, dabbing color onto his painting with energetic strokes. He clearly had vastly more important things to do than to converse with females, at the same time feeling that it was his responsibility to instruct them.

The girls could not help but join in their brother's regalement, adding giggles to his hearty laughter. Alita rose from the ground and removed her gardener's apron, uncovering a summer gingham dress bordered with wide stripes of creamy white, pink, lavender, and dark brown. She smoothed her dress, fitted at the waist with a wide pink sash, accentuating the balloon sleeves.

She delighted in her feminine ensemble, complete with a large straw hat trimmed with brown velvet ribbon and pink- and cream-colored blossoms. She twirled her parasol mischievously while anticipating some further commentary from her brother.

"Alita, you mustn't encourage Julianne in untruths," he advised thoughtfully, meeting her expectation without delay. He might be eleven years of age and Alita sixteen, but there could be no doubt in her mind that Harvey believed himself to have far more sense than his older sister and was yet again in the unfortunate position of finding it necessary to point that out to her.

"You don't believe that frogs can dance, Harvey?"

"You are hopeless, Alita! You're such a...a...*girl*."

"Ma-ma is a girl, Harvey," Alita replied calmly, feeling no insult. Her eyes did not waver from her brother's, who put his paintbrush down and placed his hands firmly on his waist, his legs far apart. He had not long graduated from knee trousers to the long pants he now wore in a blue tweed cheviot, which were held on his slim frame by suspenders. With his sapphire-blue eyes and coal-black hair, Alita was pleased to recognize that every day he more closely resembled his father, the only deviation being that his hair was curly like his mother's.

"But Ma-ma talks sense, Alita! Why can't you talk sense? Especially for Julianne's sake? You are good at everything, but you care about nothing!"

"*I care about nothing?*" she repeated with emphasis. "This is astonishing news!"

"Nothing important, that is," he mumbled, stubbing his toe into the ground. "You're the smartest girl I know, even better at mathematics than me—without trying! All you and your girlfriends talk about is Belgian lace ad nauseam and your coming out on the marriage mart, when you will each find your husbands and live happily ever after."

"You listened to our private conversation?" Alita exclaimed with pretend indignation. "A gentleman would never do such a thing. I am gravely disappointed in you, Harvey!"

"Well, *no*, Lita. I was just walking by, right where I was supposed to be, and you females are so loud…" He blushed, clearly embarrassed, but Alita did not relent, feeling no shame in pressing her advantage.

"If I should discuss horses, boxing, or swordplay with my friends, then might I earn your approval, dear brother? Is that as important as mathematics?"

"Well, yes. I mean…*no*. Dash it, Alita!" Staring at her for a long while and then beginning to sputter and giggle, Harvey's lips formed a broad grin. "That's what I mean! You have the brains of a scientist and—"

"And she looks like an *angel*!" Julianne interjected.

"Certainly not! Possibly I am the angel's sister!" she exclaimed, twirling Julianne, almost dislodging a small cap on the child's strawberry-blonde hair which fell almost to her waist, a gift from her auburn-haired mother and blonde grandmother much envied by her older sister.

"Quite so! Brains, beauty—and what do you talk about, Alita? Froggie ballets?"

"What's wrong with ballet?" Julianne demanded as she regained her balance and stuck her tongue out at him, clearly affronted by the unfounded insults to her sister and her favorite art form. The little girl felt behind herself in a most unladylike manner, her toes almost touching, to see if the small bustle pad support which created ruffles down the back of her pink cotton dress was still in place.

Alita glanced at her idyllic surroundings. She had to admit it was one of the prettiest gardens in London, and she had designed and supervised its creation almost all by herself over the past three years. The landscape was comprised of bold flashes of color only slightly louder than the surrounding sweet fragrances. Bleeding hearts, Canterbury bells, and lilac bushes outlined the garden filled with heirloom roses, hollyhocks, sweet peas, morning glories, and lilies. Climbing antique roses in yellow and lavender embraced a wrought-iron arbor granting entry to the garden.

A small pond was in the center of the garden, home to each a black and a white swan. A bench was situated along a stone walk-way, and on the other side of the pond was a gazebo, which would soon be drenched in the delicate scent of honeysuckle and a dark purple wisteria hanging overhead. Peering out from English ivy was a white-marble birdbath, a sundial, and statues of cherubs and angels.

Drinking in the sight of the garden, she could hear a harpsichord playing a Bach fugue in the background as clearly as if it were there. And yet, according to her brother, she should be doing something of much greater importance, she thought with sly amusement. *He is his mother's son.*

"Do not distress yourself so, Harvey. You take on too great a burden. Enjoy your sisters instead of attempting to enlighten them. It is a hopeless endeavor." She moved to pat her brother's hand, serene in the face of his condemnation. "You know, dear brother, there exists another world we do not see."

"Another world? Like with dragons and knights?"

"In a manner of speaking." She motioned to his painting. "Do the great masters paint an exact duplication of the landscape around them?"

"Well...yes...maybe...I don't know..."

"No, when one views the sublime works of art, one has the sense of an untold story. Isn't that true, Harvey?"

"A mystery!" Julianne clapped her hands.

"I guess," replied Harvey. "But what has that to do with your made-up fairyland that doesn't exist?"

"Not made up. *Real.* The physical realm is not the only reality. In fact, it is only a very small part of the real world."

"You really should grow up, Alita." He puffed up his chest. "There is only one world."

"A touch of white here and feathered strokes of blue here would create more of the effect you want, Harvey." She pointed to a spot on the painting. Harvey studied his inexpert rendition and then his sister. He immediately followed her advice and returned to his painting.

"How do you see it, Lita?" As Julianne and Alita began to walk about the garden hand in hand, Julianne's face lit up with curiosity. "The 'nother world?"

"You don't see it with your eyes, Julianne."

"Not with your eyes!" she blurted out. "How can you see without your *eyes?*"

"Shhh! You'll awaken the sleeping fairies, Jules." Alita giggled. "We all see the other world differently, in different ways. You have your own special way, Julianne. You see it with your imagination. Everything transforms into something else for you."

"Like what, Lita?"

"Like dancing gumdrops, singing teakettles, and magical frogs."

"'Magination is best!" Julianne clapped her hands, smiling.

"Would you like me to show you how I see it, Jules?"

Julianne nodded emphatically, her hair swishing back and forth.

"If I show you, we can't speak of it to anyone except Ma-ma and Papa. It's a great secret."

"Not even Harvey?" Julianne asked, her eyes wide.

"Not even Harvey." She tapped her forehead with her index finger. "This is how Harvey sees the world, through his brain. He only views the world one way. We are girls and not so limited as that." Alita made a sweeping motion with her arms.

"Because we're special?" Julianne giggled.

"Boys are special, too, just…more apt to travel in a straight line. They miss many splendid sights.

"Close your eyes, Julianne," Alita whispered. She took her sister's hand and walked to a holly-berry bush out of Harvey's line of vision as he continued to work on his painting. She took Julianne's hand and held it one inch from the bush, the tiny hand suspended in midair. "Do you feel anything?"

"Feel what?" asked Julianne. "How can I, Lita? I'm not touching anything."

"Do your fingers feel different when I hold your hand close to but not touching the bush?" She moved her hand closer then farther away.

"No," whispered Julianne.

"Keep your eyes shut." Alita led Julianne to the pond, where they sat down on the clover. She held Julianne's hand over a lily pad. She pulled Julianne's hand away from the lily pad, then close. "Feel your hand. Focus on it. Does it feel any different?"

"No." Suddenly Julianne's mouth dropped, and her eyes shot open. "I did feel it, I did! It's all *tingly!*" she exclaimed.

"Shhhh!" cautioned Alita, giggling, unable to hide her excitement at Julianne's discovery from the ripples of water illuminating her reflection, unruly wheat-blonde ringlets peering out from underneath her straw hat. Alita held her finger to her too-full smiling lips, overlarge for her face, as were her eyes, her imperfections accentuated by the pond mirror.

"Each flower and tree feels different. You can travel all about the garden and feel the different energy patterns of each plant. You can name it in your mind."

"What is it? Can it hurt you?" Julianne whispered, her eyes wide with fear even as she covered her mouth with her hands. "Is it *evil spirits?*"

"No, silly. It has a healing power—it's the life energy of the plant reaching out to you. Every living thing has a language. Most people just don't know how to hear it. Fortunately, understanding is not always necessary. One feels calmer without naming it or knowing why."

"Why is it so hard to hear it, Lita?"

"That I cannot answer, Julianne, since I do hear it. But I do know that the greatest problem in all the world is that people do not know how to receive what is already there. "

Chapter Three

"Do the animals have a language, Lita?" Julianne demanded, never one to leave any stone unturned. Alita could see that the wheels in her sister's mind were spinning uncontrollably.

"When Sir Galahad is barking, is he talking to you, Julianne?"

"Yesssss…But I don't know what he is saying."

"Precisely. But just because you don't understand doesn't mean he isn't *speaking*. Only today you learned a new language, Jules. And you're only six years old! Think how many more you could learn by the time you grow up."

"How did you find out 'bout this, Lita? Who told you?" Julianne demanded, standing beside the pond momentarily and swishing the pink ruffles of her dress back and forth with one hand.

"No one. I just felt it." Alita paused and twirled her parasol from a sitting position beside the pond. The answer was not entirely clear, even to her. She touched her finger to her lips again, their sign that it was a special secret just between the two of them. "There are so many things going on around us all the time, but most people don't see or feel them. And they don't want you to see these other worlds either."

"Why?" Julianne asked. "Why don't they want me to talk to the plants and animals?"

"Because it is not written in a book somewhere that it can be done, I suppose." Alita shrugged.

"Then let's get Papa to write it down in a book! Then we can talk to *anyone,* and no one will care."

"A brilliant thought, Julianne," Alita concluded with heartfelt sincerity.

Julianne appeared deep in thought. "Can Ma-ma speak the plant's language?"

"Hmmm…I don't think Ma-ma has tried, so I don't know."

The Paradox: The Soldier and the Mystic

"She hasn't *tried*? That doesn't sound like Ma-ma! She tries *everything*."

"That is true, Julianne. Ma-ma has a high calling and does very important work." It was a mystery how she came to be the daughter of two of the most accomplished people she knew. Her father had been instrumental in ushering in the industrial revolution with his inventions. Her mother, Lady Elaina Lancastor, the daughter of the Duke of Salford, had shocked Victorian England by denouncing a life of leisure in the highest spheres of polite society, her birthright as a daughter of a peer of the realm, and joining with Florence Nightingale as a nurse."

"Do you want to be a nurse when you grow up, Lita?" Julianne asked, her large aqua-blue eyes upturned.

"My dream..." Alita sighed softly. "My only unrealized dream is to have a husband and a family of my own to love." She felt the familiar mix of happiness and anxiety as she pondered the greatest wish of her heart.

"But, Lita. Don't you want to be famous like Papa?" Even this six-year-old had an inkling of that which was well known in London society, that her parents, Elaina Lancastor and Dr. Jonathan Stanton, born into a preindustrial world dominated by agriculture, royalty, and serfdom, had changed the world irrevocably and dramatically by their existence. Dr. Stanton was himself instrumental in bringing the world into the industrial age with his inventions.

"And Ma-ma," Alita added. "She has made many contributions to the field of nursing and is in the royal court of political hostesses—she is possibly the *queen*."

"Do *you* want to be queen, Lita?" Julianne giggled.

"Societal achievements are of no moment to me, Jules." She shook her head before tossing a blossom into the pond.

Julianne stared at her, skepticism written across her face.

"Outside of making the match of the season!" She pinched her sister's cheeks, and they both fell back, giggling.

"There is no hope for advancement in any arena of study without a thorough understanding of mathematics," Lady Elaina had pronounced. She had the brains for math and science, she knew. Other people touched mystery through these subjects, but it was not her venue. Her lack of interest in academic pursuits was a constant source of aggravation to Lady Elaina,

who had staged battle on par with Waterloo with her own mother for the right to study mathematics. She sat up and began making ripples of water in the pond with her parasol.

"*But, my darling, don't you have any ambitions?*" Alita smiled with amusement as she replayed in her mind Lady Elaina's aghast expression, now superimposed on the pond's ripples of water. Alita had gurgled with laughter. "Mother, do you place mathematics as a higher ambition than the growth of the soul? Or to learn to love fully? If so, I am content to set my sights low." Alita had not added that the last thing she would want to do was to be away from her children when her situation allowed her to be near them.

Lady Elaina had sat in stunned silence, mouth opened, as if she could neither believe her daughter's viewpoint nor respond to it.

"Ma-ma doesn't have time to talk to the plants." Julianne shook her head slowly in understanding. "But we do, don't we, Lita?"

"Yes, Jules, we have time to talk to every living creature in the garden." Alita put her finger to her lips again for emphasis. "But remember, it's our secret."

"What does Ma-ma do all day?" Julianne's face glowed, clearly reveling in the arrangement. "Vol...volunt...volunteeeerink at the hospital?"

"She heals sick people. And Ma-ma is working to obtain the vote for women. It is truly her life's purpose. We must pray that she succeeds."

"Why does Ma-ma want to vote? Can't Papa do it for her?"

"Ma-ma always has her own thoughts on things." She tapped her index finger on her forehead. "Julianne, you love your brother very much, don't you?"

The child nodded her head emphatically.

"Would you wish Harvey to speak for you in all matters and to never be permitted to open your mouth?"

"*Harvey?* No! He would mess everything up! He doesn't know what I want!"

Alita nodded quietly, knowing this to be a moment of epiphany for her sister. Suddenly she looked up toward the house. She saw no one in sight.

"What is it, Lita?"

"It's Miss Kristine come to visit."

The Paradox: The Soldier and the Mystic 23

There was still no one visible, but Julianne's face fell. "You always run off when we're playing and say that someone needs you, Lita." She pouted accusingly.

"And someone always does, don't they, Jules? Remember when Mrs. Mulroney fell?" Alita kneeled on the ground beside her sister. "And we were having so much fun playing dress-up when we suddenly had to leave, didn't we? If we hadn't taken a carriage to Mrs. Mulroney's house and found her, she might have died—or at the very least, suffered a great deal."

"Kristine isn't going to die." Julianne pouted, as if she wished it might happen, or at the very least, that she would go away forever. "You would rather play with her than me."

"That is definitely not true, Jules." Alita felt her heart ache at Julianne's dejected expression even though she knew her devotion to her sister was complete. "I have learned to obey even when I don't understand. *Especially* when I don't understand. The message would not be sent if I weren't supposed to act on it. I hold alertness and obedience as virtues most dear."

"Fun is a virtue!"

"Definitely fun is a virtue!" Alita gurgled, standing up and twirling Julianne round and round. "And we shall embroider after dinner together. Would you like that, Jules?"

A few moments later, Miss Kristine Tutt presented herself to the small garden party, having eyes for no one but Alita. The elegant brunette might have been Marie Antoinette playing shepherdess at the Petit Trianon in her "Little Bo Peep" pink satin ensemble, complete with staff. The gown flowed over her shapely hips like a cascading waterfall into a lace-flounced ruffle and pleated border. A circle of lace and bows formed a reverse collar along her back. Bows gathered at the sleeves just below her elbows. She wore a wide-brimmed straw hat with a pink satin band and a large magnolia blossom in the front of the headdress. Alita sighed happily as she gently hugged her friend and kissed the air so as not to muss her gown.

"Oh, you are a picture, Krissy!" It took one's breath away just to gaze upon her! She wished a special someone might have his breath taken away just to gaze upon her, but that was not a possibility. She was as thin as a rail! And just about as shapeless. She swung her gingham skirt about her, suddenly feeling like a toddler in Kristine's presence.

"My mother thinks it is too old for me, but I don't agree at all." Kristine looked down at her own dress and began smoothing the satin. "I think I have the figure for it."

"Indeed you do. You are quite *perfect*, Krissy." She sighed longingly. Lady Elaina would never let her wear such a formfitting outfit—even if she had any curves to reveal.

"Julianne, can you help me with my next painting?" Harvey simultaneously approached his sisters, propping a new canvas on the easel, even as Alita winked at him in gratitude.

"Harvey, you can't vote for me!" Julianne admonished, shuffling her feet as she walked toward him.

"I don't wish to, Jules," he replied, taken aback.

"Yes, you do! You always tell me what to do."

Kristine and Alita sat on a bench under a second arbor near the pond, their heads close together. The always-bubbly brunette was even more animated than usual. "There's to be a small dinner party at my home on Saturday next, with cards and dancing. And there will be *gentlemen*. You simply must come, Alita."

"I'll ask Ma-ma and Papa, dear Krissy. And who is to be invited?" Alita felt a decided interest.

"My mother is comprising the list. The first son of an earl. A well-to-do cousin from Staffordshire. And best of all, are you acquainted with Richard Stanhope?" Kristine caught her breath, followed by a wistful expression.

"Richard Stanhope...Yes, I think I am." Alita had not met Mr. Stanhope. Focusing all of her concentration, she contemplated his name while maintaining the social smile she had learned to project at such times. She held her hand lightly over Kristine's in a practiced gesture as she repeated Richard Stanhope's name to herself. "Give me a moment, Krissy. I'm trying to recall where I met him."

In startling fashion, a random mix of thoughts and feelings encompassed her. She felt a wave of energy rush over her, followed instantly by a scent of expensive men's cologne. She knew at once that she was encountering Richard Stanhope.

And what she saw there, she could not like—a great ego, few scruples, and a lack of compassion for the feelings of others. The absence of motivation outside of the drive to satisfy his own desires, and no hesitation

The Paradox: The Soldier and the Mystic

to do so. Charisma, intelligence, and the ability to charm. Alarmingly, she saw no values to curb him from satiating himself at the expense of others— no room for anything but Richard Stanhope in his picture and for those whom Mr. Stanhope found momentarily amusing or satisfying.

"Well? Alita?" Kristine demanded impatiently. "You have a dreadful habit of suddenly going silent. It is quite rude."

"You must make allowances for those who are slow of thought, unlike yourself, Krissy." Alita feigned an expression of contemplation, stalling for time. "And anyway, you know that Ma-ma is selective in social gatherings and does not permit us to attend without a family member present. I am attempting to place him."

Kristine rolled her eyes, Alita's strict upbringing being too well known to her.

"And what is Mr. Stanhope's appearance, Krissy?" Alita forced her countenance to remain nonplussed despite the churning of her stomach at entering the mind of such an unscrupulous person. She held her hands tightly in her lap, attempting to calm herself.

"Now I know that you haven't seen Richard, or you wouldn't ask." Kristine almost fell off the bench as she clasped her arms around herself. "He's tall and blond, with brown eyes, positively dreamy and...*perfect*. I never thought to see a boy smile like *that*..."

"It's a meeting of the minds, I gather?" Alita cocked one eyebrow at her friend.

They both hunched closer and giggled. Harvey cast a disapproving eye in their direction.

"And what is Mr. Stanhope's personality, Krissy?" Alita persisted breezily, forcing an expression of interest.

"Oh, charming. And he is a famous dancer, and well...everything divine."

"Hmmm...Yes, I believe I recall Mr. Stanhope." She sniffed.

Kristine studied her friend with surprise. Alita knew well that her socially polished friend was acutely attuned to the subtle slights utilized by her sex when wishing to communicate effectively in the accepted ladylike manner.

"What is it, Alita?" demanded Kristine, her curiosity peaked. "What could you possibly find to dislike in Richard Stanhope?"

"An elegant gentleman, certainly." Alita strove to make her frown *almost* undetectable as she lowered her head to momentarily cover her eyes with her hat, pretending to study her lace-gloved hands. She paused for emphasis before returning her eyes to Kristine's.

"Elegant...And?"

She cleared her throat.

"Alita, I *demand* that you tell me!"

"If memory serves...a bit on the boorish side."

"*Boorish?*" The insult was complete. "How could you possibly find six feet of charm topped with wavy blond hair and dark brown eyes boorish?"

"That will grow old after a time, Krissy. Beauty fades. And then what does one have?"

"I'd be willing to endure the deprivation."

"Certainly, if the gentleman were possessed of other more substantive qualities. A sense of humor, for example." Alita waved her hand nonchalantly. "I had always pictured you with a beau with a sort of madcap cleverness. Your perfect match would show a great deal of enthusiasm for life. You're such a lively girl, Krissy."

"A *sense of humor?*" asked Kristine incredulously. "What an odd criteria, Alita. I hadn't considered the matter, but I suppose I have enough wit for the both of us."

"And what are Mr. Stanhope's interests?" Alita nodded, somberly indicating that Kristine had answered her question. "If he doesn't like museums, balloon rides, theatre, and concerts—if he doesn't appear animated when you speak of such things—I wouldn't even consider him as a prospective beau. You know, Krissy, if a gentleman can't show interest in pleasing you at the outset of the acquaintance, then how devoted to you will he be in twenty years, when he has fewer incentives?"

"*Museums?*" Kristine stared at her friend in obvious disbelief. But Alita knew that her words had left an impression both of the gentleman in question and of a few simple but revealing methods of evaluation of prospective suitors.

"Who else shall be at the party? I mean, which *girls*?"

"And why might this be of interest to you, Alita?" Kristine inquired, casting a sly glance.

The Paradox: The Soldier and the Mystic   27

"One desires to anticipate one's competition." And a burst of giggles came forth again.

"I have to invite Veronica Monroe." Kristine's expression became somewhat twisted. "So selfish."

"No, not selfish. I assure you that Veronica's heart is not unkind. I would say merely lazy."

"And is laziness not a fault?" Kristine insisted.

"It's what she likes." Alita shrugged. "This is her lifetime to sit on a pink pillow and eat marshmallows."

"*It's what she likes?*" Kristine burst into laughter. "Honestly, Alita, you say the most peculiar things. Have you been studying world religions again? We only have one lifetime."

"Oh? All the more reason to sit on a pink pillow and eat marshmallows if one can accomplish it!"

Chuckling, Kristine appeared to find nothing in that to argue with.

"Let's return to the gentlemen, dear Alita. And who is your dream beau? Now it's your turn. Fair is fair."

"I haven't met him, Krissy, or I assure you that you would know!" Alita smiled wistfully, leaning back into the bench while turning sideways to look at her friend.

"Of *all* the young men we know, not one whom you could marry?"

"No. That is to say…I have a picture of him in my mind."

"A vision? Like the psychics have?" Kristine gurgled.

"Of c–c–course not!" She swallowed hard. "I just *know*. I know exactly what he'll be like." In point of fact, she drew a complete blank where she most wanted to see!

"Tell me, you foolish girl! Honestly, Alita, why does it take so long for you to say anything?"

"Well…" Alita sighed. "He'll be tall and handsome, blond if possible, and a fabulous dancer."

"Oh, it's shallow for me but good enough for you, I see," drawled Kristine.

"It's my lifetime to be shallow," replied Alita demurely with a shrug of her shoulders.

They burst into peals of laughter before Alita continued. "But seriously, Krissy, my beau will be polished, debonair, and charming. A favorite in society. He'll be cheerful and eager to enjoy himself and others." She shook her head as a feeling of resolve overtook her. "He won't be serious, forlorn, or melancholy. I can't tolerate the Lord Byron types!

"I rather like them. They're so...*passionate*."

"Passionately exasperating! Nor will he be hunting or boxing-mad. Athletic, possibly, but not his horses and swordplay to the exclusion of all else."

"So you wish for a scholar like your father?"

"Smart, but not *too* smart." Alita shook her head adamantly. "I don't wish to have a husband who speaks incessantly on subjects of no interest to anyone—like ancient history or Latin. Some men get positively obsessed with the most boring subjects imaginable."

"So he can't be an athlete, scholar, or historian."

"Decidedly. It would ruin many a pleasant evening. He'll be able to speak on many topics of interest in conversation—but not *too* many." She raised her eyes to the heavens. "Please, please, don't let him be a scientist or a suffragette!"

"The list grows longer. Why would you possibly object to the vote for women? Honestly, Alita, you are so old-fashioned. It is 1880, after all! These are very modern times we live in."

"Certainly I don't object. I simply have no need of it." *And no wish to speak of it for hours on end.*

"Most assuredly," Kristine agreed. "You'll be dancing the night away with Prince Charming in the enchanted palace. What need would you have of a voting poll at such a time as that?"

"Precisely." The two resumed their giggling.

Alita Jane Celeste Lancastor Stanton was born in London, England March 19, 1864. Born to privilege, wealth, education, and beauty, Miss Alita Stanton was the Victorian cover girl in search of a titled husband. Alita identified so strongly with the society into which she was born—and desperately wished to be accepted by it—that she might have been a Victorian paper doll except for one inescapable trait. She knew what other people were feeling and thinking. It was her gift, and she could no more separate herself from it than she could forget her own name.

The Paradox: The Soldier and the Mystic

Despite the extraordinary contributions of her exceptional parents, both of whom stepped outside of the sphere into which they were born, Miss Alita Stanton had no wish to follow suit or to be different from anyone. She wanted to be inside the sphere. And she might have been, except for a light that would not be extinguished. Miss Alita Stanton had the *sight*.

Chapter Four

The day of the ball! The day she had been longing for since she was six years old, and it had finally arrived! After two years of preparations, Alita had been presented at court to Queen Victoria in the year of our Lord eighteen hundred and eighty-two.

The Queen's Ball was that evening in the State Ballroom of Buckingham Palace.

Jittery with excitement, Alita fell back on her four-poster canopy bed, sheer wisps of lavender chiffon floating in swags above her head. The movement of the chiffon in the morning breeze tantalized her, bringing to mind couples dancing gracefully across the ballroom.

As if she could have thought of anything else. Who would she dance with? What if no one asked her to dance? Would she become tongue-tied when she was introduced to dashing young men instead of the boys she had played with and grown up with? What would she say? Could she talk and dance at the same time? Heaven forbid she should trip.

Still lying in her bed, she glanced about the room, the morning light landing on the blue and white hydrangeas on her writing table. She loved this room, which she had decorated herself. The furniture was an almost-black walnut, which she had covered in lilacs in her mind's eye and in reality, lavender chiffon draping over the windows and the canopy bed. Buttercream walls, wood floors, and white and blue hydrangeas everywhere completed her vision.

She giggled as she reflected how the world outside her bedroom door was an entirely different world—quite literally. Traversing the rest of the house, a three-story Gothic-revival Victorian only two houses down from Apsley House at the Grand Entrance to Hyde Park, it did not take long to discover that Lady Elaina's favorite color was red or that she had grown up in a castle. The exterior of the home was painted in a gold-toned moss green and trimmed in white, only hinting at the medieval influences of the interior.

The Paradox: The Soldier and the Mystic 31

Even with its gabled roof, towers, angled bay windows, shingled insets, and covered 180-degree front porch, stepping inside was like traveling back in time to the Knights of the Round Table.

Throwing back her bedding, Alita stood up and studied herself before her cheval oval mirror, her blonde hair pulled back from her face and flowing over her shoulders in curls.

Her hairstyle was too "young" and not at all sophisticated. She liked her unusually vivid green eyes, but they were definitely too big for her face. As were her lips.

Why can't my lips be thin like the rest of me? How she longed for the thin lips that were in fashion!

She turned sideways, frowning at her own reflection. *Frightfully thin.* Her small bosom was attractive enough, though not sufficient to be fashionable. And yet, she had begun to think she would never have breasts at all and therefore could not help but feel gratitude!

Even worse were her hips, which especially required padding. She pursed her lips. How she longed for a fuller figure like her mother's. Her waist was small as was the style, but nothing else conformed. She had the appearance of one who might be blown over with a feather.

Recognizing a *tap-tap* that she knew to be her mother's, Alita forgot her inner criticisms and happily ran to her bedroom door. Opening the door wide, she threw her arms around her mother, dressed smartly in a fitted-satin, striped street suit, with its crisp tailoring almost manly in appearance were it not for rows of gathered black Spanish lace at the neckline. Even her auburn coiffure arranged atop her head was astonishing, swept back from her face and cascading down the back of her head in interlocking, endless curls.

"You were magnificent, my dear," Lady Elaina exclaimed as she flung herself into the room.

Alita smiled wistfully. Whereas she blended into the background, preferring to listen and observe, her mother had the gift of bursting onto the scene in a flame.

"Honestly, Ma-ma, I amaze myself that I was able to move!" Alita blushed. She took her mother by the hand and led her to a small wing-backed couch embossed in buttercream satin, where they both situated themselves.

"You're so thin and lithe, Alita." Lady Elaina shook her head in wonderment. "Your gown would have weighted down an ocean barge! There was enough material in it to cover all the windows in our home with extravagance!"

"The dress I could manage—but the headdress! Oh, Ma-ma, I believe I still have a headache..." she murmured, rubbing her head.

"Now perhaps you will thank me for not allowing you to overdress or to wear a tight corset as so many of your friends do. Follow the fashion if you will, but *simplify*."

"One girl fainted at the presentation from her corset being too tight."

"I saw her. My goodness! She was perfectly slim as it was. What difference would another inch make? Why is beauty always defined as one inch smaller?" Lady Elaina arose from her seat and rummaged through the vanity until she found what she was looking for.

"If that were the case, then I should be the fashion," murmured Alita.

"Ridiculous!" Returning to the couch, Lady Elaina handed the lavender compress to Alita, commanding her to place it on her eyelids for her headache. "It's a wonder that your neck did not snap from the weight! All that was lacking was for you to balance an elephant on your shoulders!"

"As difficult as all that was, the curtsy was the most challenging," Alita admitted, holding the compress to the side of her head.

"I have no doubt! The curtsy was no modest bending of the knees," Lady Elaina acknowledged with a shake of the head, now situated once again. "As was required, it was a full court curtsy in which you bent your knee near to the floor and held it there for interminable seconds as you executed your bow—all while keeping your teetering headdress from tumbling forward." She poured tea for both of them from the tea set only just delivered and handed a cup to Alita before seating herself with her own cup.

"I was trembling in trepidation that the feathers in my headdress would fly out!" Alita giggled, taking a sip of tea. "Or worse, that I would *fall*!" She wondered herself how she had managed it all. She had spent months preparing and practicing. In the end, she had somehow executed her movements without mishap. She was announced, walked across the lengthy Throne Room, and curtsied to the ground before the queen. Her nose might have touched the carpet. She had then walked backward against the long train—somehow avoiding being tangled up in the dress or in the yards of material comprising the train—and curtsied again, necessitated because one was forbidden from *ever* turning one's back to the monarch. All the while she balanced the lopsided headdress on her head and miraculously kept the fan and flowers that she was carrying from slipping through her perspiring hands.

"Well, the worst is now over," pronounced Lady Elaina.

"I must admit that I had expected Queen Victoria's court would be more the thing, Ma-ma. I imagined that I would leave feeling myself to be in the height of fashion—and instead, I felt merely relieved. It was not modish or even entertaining, to be quite honest."

"Queen Victoria's court has never been smart, and only diverting in the worst possible way," stated Lady Elaina with finality. "Since the closing of Almack's, the place to see and be seen is in the company of Prince Edward and the Marlborough House set."

"That is where I shall be seen, then," remarked Alita mischievously.

"*That* you shall never be, young lady. A very fast crowd indeed."

"That would never do," agreed Alita with a sly smile. "Besides, it is almost as prestigious to be seen at the exclusive soirées of the political hostesses."

"Very true."

"Your being in the top echelon of that prestigious group, Ma-ma," Alita added, giggling. She was delighted, and somewhat astonished, if the truth be known, that her mother was afforded the freedom to be herself. "Your scandalous opinions are now sought after."

"Yes, the actions which were used to gain me censure now add to my influence!" Lady Elaina observed.

"In *some* circles at least..." Alita added upon reflection.

"I can never understand why so many women of my acquaintance have difficulty forming an opinion on *anything* and instantly change it to suit the men's opinions."

"They want to belong, I suppose." Alita barely sighed. *Desperately.*

"Unfortunately, society's current fascination with Lady Elaina Stanton cannot finalize your initiation, Alita." Lady Elaina turned instantly toward her. "All I can do is to provide the required sponsorship. You must now earn your place in the ton on your own terms, if indeed you wish such a place.

Society is relentless, unforgiving, and requires the same price from all—one's soul."

"Ma-ma, you never paid that price. You have always been true to yourself...*Unlike myself*," she added softly.

"Whatever do you mean, Alita?" Lady Elaina asked her, startled.

"No one must know," she whispered. *"No one can ever know."*

"I know. Your father knows. Your sister knows, though she doesn't know she knows. Your brother suspects. And we all love you. *So much."* Lady Elaina took her hand. "It is part of who you are, Alita. It is your gift. It is not something to be discarded but embraced."

"You cannot be serious, Ma-ma. Have you ever thought what might happen?"

"Currently, there is a great fascination with the psychic world."

"It threatens everything dear to me." Alita shook her head. "It is fine for the eccentric widow or the middle classes to purport to have certain gifts. But I would lose any chance I have of a respectable marriage were it to be made known."

"Society makes all the rules, however inconsistent and illogical"—Lady Elaina nodded reluctantly—"and is completely unforgiving of the slightest deviation. And yet, one cannot always predict society's reaction. Besides, you don't have to name your gift to utilize it, as you well know. Be yourself, dear. You are so precious."

"I can be myself to a point. I hope I have not misjudged that point." Alita stood and moved to the window, still holding her teacup, where one of her favorite plants was situated, the bee orchid. She smiled at the little flower, which interspersed a note of whimsy into these weighty events that would shape her future. Turning to her mother again, she asked, "But what of your presentation, Ma-ma? Surely it was as challenging?"

"Oh, yes! In addition to the same acrobatic demands, the emotional stamina required was intense." Lady Elaina's expression grew stern as she set down her teacup. *"You,* my dear, had only to face the Queen of England! *I* had to stand before the far-more terrifying patronesses of Almack's!"

"And await their verdict?"

"You cannot know their influence and the horror which gripped a young girl's heart in their presence! You see, they had something to prove while

The Paradox: The Soldier and the Mystic   35

the Queen of England does *not*. They were not above reminding one that they could refuse entrance into Almack's."

"And, as a consequence, entrance into London high society," murmured Alita softly. She touched her finger to her lips, then to her little flower, before returning to sit beside her mother.

"*Precisely*, my dear. In a society in which women are disenfranchised, there are those who enjoy exercising an unnatural amount of power over others. That is why the vote..." She cleared her throat and waved her hand in a circular motion. "The *season*. Your grandmamma, not to put too fine a point on it, was evaluated by *all* of the original patronesses—Lady Jersey, Lady Castlereagh, Lady Cowper, Lady Sefton, Princess Esterházy, and Princess Lieven."

"*All* of them?" Alita forgot to breathe as her eyes were glued on her mother, sitting forward on the couch.

"In one room." Lady Elaina smiled smugly. "She could have taken on another dozen."...

"And she only a vicar's daughter on her first trip to London." Alita fell back into the couch, touching her palm to her cheek in obvious amazement.

"I, on the other hand, was unable to succeed in society." Lady Elaina's smile faded slightly.

"But you did succeed, Ma-ma, until you entered Florence Nightingale's School of Nursing to become a nurse. It was—and is—unheard of. You *are* the daughter of the Duke of Salford, after all."

"Yes, I learned what cruelty was." Momentarily, Lady Elaina's expression revealed the devastation of being shunned by everyone she had formerly known. "And even that, as unforgivable a transgression as it was, was not my greatest social faux pas!"

"Oh yes, I know, Ma-ma! It was one scandal after another with you, each more shocking than the last!" She giggled, taking her mother's unencumbered hand. "But now you are firmly established in society as one of the most sought-after political hostesses in London, on par with the Duchess of Buccleuch. "

"Do not forget Lady Palmerston, formerly Lady Cowper, one of the original patronesses of Almack's!" Lady Elaina interjected, chuckling. "The woman has reigned for fifty years!"

"I prefer your parlor, Ma-ma. It has a different *flavor*."

"Indeed." Lady Elaina sighed. "But we both influence the titled men who vote in parliament. That is the relevant point." She pursed her lips resolutely. "But that is not to our purpose at the moment. Now it is time for you to move on to the inexplicable delights of the season, my darling."

"Oh, tell me, Ma-ma, tell me!" Alita squeezed her mother's hand tighter.

"A day in the season begins with a ride in Hyde Park, followed by breakfast, shopping, and morning calls to close friends." Even though she had described the London season a thousand times before, Lady Elaina humored her daughter. "After lunch, calls are made to new acquaintances. After dinner, soirées or the opera, followed by a whirlwind of balls and dances! In a season, you will easily attend fifty parties, an equal number of balls, and at least half as many dinners and breakfasts, not to mention the sporting events!"

"What is it, Ma-ma?" Alita asked, noticing the sudden agitation in her mother's expression.

"Dearest, I have news which cannot be delayed much longer."

"Yes, Ma-ma?" Alita moved forward.

"I have just been informed that your grandmamma has arrived. I understand that she is directing the servants in putting away her belongings."

"You left Grandmamma *alone* with the servants?" she exclaimed in a whispered breath, rising suddenly from the couch as if she had just been informed of a fire in the next room.

"She insisted, and one does not argue with the Duchess, least of all her own daughter. We will be well-advised to add a bonus to the salaries this month." Lady Elaina cleared her throat, suddenly comprehending her error.

As Alita headed toward the door, Lady Elaina added solemnly, "I advise you to stay and situate yourself prettily on the settee in your sitting room, displaying a quiet boredom."

"*Boredom!*" Alita laughed effortlessly as she turned to face her. "How could I ever be bored today?"

A few seconds later, Marvella Lancastor, the Dowager Duchess of Salford, swept into the room unannounced, with nothing more than a light tap upon the door with a cane. Even as mouths were opening to offer admittance, she was already in the room. Her pale blue-gray eyes surveyed the room, her opinion easily discernible.

Her white-blonde hair was arranged simply and elegantly atop her head, with none of the flamboyance that her daughter favored in hairstyles.

That Her Grace made up for in her attire. She wore her finest visiting toilette consisting of a form-fitting dress and jacket in Oriental sapphire embossed in a floral pattern, emphasizing an hourglass figure the envy of many a younger woman. The full white ruffle of her blouse extended from the neckline to below the waist. She wore blue kid gloves and a large round hat of blue plush, felt trimmed, with blue ostrich plumes. She carried a white cane with a gold handle in an Egyptian motif.

Alita ran to her grandmother, bubbling over with happiness.

"Show some refinement, my dear child." The Dowager Duchess of Salford scowled. "There is no occasion upon which to be less than ladylike!"

"Please forgive me, Grandmamma." Alita smiled with docility at her grandmother and kissed her cheek. "I am simply so happy to see you."

"Very proper that you should be," Marvella replied reservedly. "And will you be so pleased today at Buckingham Palace that you shall hop about?"

"No, Grandmamma," Alita answered demurely.

"Good. Gentlemen are much more impressed with quiet reserve than with bouncy movements and lively opinions." Marvella raised her eyebrows disapprovingly at her daughter.

"Yes, Grandmamma."

"It is so refreshing." Marvella sighed, looking at her daughter. "When you were her age, Elaina, you never acquiesced or agreed to anything, no matter how sensible. If I had told you to avoid a bee's nest, you would have gone toward it just to spite me."

"Oh, no, mother." Lady Elaina shook her head. "Not to spite you. I would have gone toward it to learn for myself."

* * * *

Marvella stared at her daughter blankly, still clearly lacking in comprehension these twenty-five years later. Her granddaughter she understood, or so she thought, Lady Elaina mused.

As for Alita, Lady Elaina knew that she loved her grandmother very much. Marvella Lancastor was everything Alita wanted to be, beautiful, elegant, a successful mother and wife, and well-received in high society. A perfect woman for her time. Alita well knew that her grandmother's understanding was limited, but Marvella's way of coping with life's difficulties was to focus on that which she wanted and to ignore the rest.

"Rest a bit, Alita." Lady Elaina kissed her daughter's cheek. "You have a busy day ahead of you. I will attend to your Grandmamma."

Not budging an inch, Marvella turned to face her daughter. "Elaina, I understand that you have hot running water now. What is it called?"

"Indoor plumbing, Mother."

"This isn't a home." Marvella shook her head in disapproval. She moved away from the door to sit in the couch. "It's a science laboratory."

"Yes, and we're all part of the experiment." She moved to her mother and patted her hand. "Don't worry, Jon will explain it to you over dinner."

"Certainly not, Elaina Genevieve!" exclaimed Her Grace adamantly, her voice rising in pitch. "I should hope that I raised you better than that. Most improper dinner conversation."

"Politics, then?" Lady Elaina goaded, knowing that the duke had been partial to this topic, as was she. Just as quickly, she wished she had not been so quick with a retort. Her grief seized her as her heart ached for her father.

"Politics runs a close second to indoor plumbing as a most inappropriate topic for dinner conversation." Her Grace shook her head in disbelief. "It is a wonder that Alita has turned out so well."

Alita smiled, watching the proceedings with interest but remaining silent as was proper.

"Yes, I marvel at that myself." Lady Elaina shook herself and came out of her reverie, returning to the door and placing her hand on the doorknob. She smiled back at her mother, "Come, Mother, I'll show you how the plumbing works."

"But don't you have servants to draw the water?" Marvella viewed her daughter with suspicion, as she always had, as if Elaina were asking her to renounce her station in life and give her jewels to the poor. "Of what possible difference could it make?"

"Mother, there are some things that are much nicer without a servant's assistance, which are truly not their business."

The Paradox: The Soldier and the Mystic 39

There could be no argument on this point, and the dowager duchess stood to follow her daughter reservedly but with some apparent interest.

At this moment, the maid appeared in the doorway, her hand raised as if to knock. All eyes turned upon her, Alita's maid stated shyly, "Miss Kristine Tutt is here to see Miss Alita." She curtsied before adding, "Miss Tutt appears to be quite upset."

"At this hour?" demanded Lady Elaina.

"Oh, something is terribly wrong." Alita's face grew alarmed as she rushed to throw on her morning gown, motioning to her maid to assist. She turned to her mother. "I'll be in the parlor with Krissy. Ma-ma, would you mind asking Mrs. Hill to bring tea?"

Lady Elaina nodded her immediate agreement, and Alita hurried to her friend.

Chapter Five

"Whatever is the matter, my dear Krissy?" Sniffing into a lace handkerchief as Alita reached the drawing room, Kristine was showcased in a circle of light streaming in through five twelve-foot rounded windows separating the room from the garden. Sensing intense grief, Alita ran to her, taking her free hand.

Leaning against a white marble fireplace, Kristine's reflection was mirrored in a life-size gilded mirror over the fireplace, and even in her obvious grief she was dazzling against such a setting. While Alita had thrown on a flowing blue cashmere Watteau wrapper, Kristine was elaborately dressed in a walking suit of green satin cascading from her hips. Three layers of six-inch ruffles began mid calf and extended to the floor. Large velvet buttons in a darker forest green accented the side of the dress from waist to floor, and she wore a small matching cape tied with a satin string, and a matching green bonnet ornamented with pink velvet roses.

"I have a letter from my brother," Kristine moaned, withdrawing her hand while she dropped into a crimson satin winged-back couch underneath a six-tiered gold chandelier in the middle of the room, the letter falling beside her on the couch.

"*Robert.*" Alita caught her breath in trepidation.

"Yes." Kristine barely nodded. "He fought in the desert battle of *Tel-el-Kebir* in Egypt."

Alita lowered herself slowly onto the couch, dreading the news that could only be terrible from Kristine's demeanor. She knew that Kristine's father had fought in the first Afghan invasion in 1839, and that another of her brothers, Randall, had fought in the Second Afghan invasion only just ended. Thankfully, neither had died. Alita's heart fell as she sensed that news of death was in the letter. It appeared that the Tutt family's luck had run out.

The Paradox: The Soldier and the Mystic 41

At this moment there was an unwelcome light knock at the door. Mrs. Hill entered with tea and cakes, no doubt since the eldest daughter had not yet had breakfast. Alita hurriedly thanked Mrs. Hill, who seemed happy to depart, and she poured the tea herself. Kristine stared straight ahead, not touching her cup, saying nothing.

Barely able to stop her hand from shaking, Alita picked up the discarded letter and frantically began to read.

It was a black, moonless night of impenetrable darkness. Imagine, if you will, being a stranger in a vast desert, moving toward the enemy camp. The only sound was the unrelenting and foreboding pulse of thousands of boots hitting sand: 14,000 British soldiers moving toward 26,000 sleeping Egyptians in their fortified camp.

We might be heading toward our death under cover of night, but for once we had escaped the heat and the relentless swirling flies. The poisoned water, unpalatable food, and effects of dysentery were with us ever.

It was the twenty-fifth day of August, the year of our Lord, eighteen hundred and eighty-two, a night that will haunt me for as long as I live. This was the unpromising start to the bloody battle of Tel-el-Kebir.

Alita read furiously. As she read, dots of light, a reflection from the chandelier overhead, twinkled across the page as if mimicking the march across the desert. Ordinarily she would have had no difficulty focusing her mind on Kristine's distress, a skill which she had painstakingly developed, but for some reason, the visual scene of the letter claimed her mind. She could see it as if she were there, a vast stretch of desert sand, an army of tens of thousands men with guns, horses, camels, mules, and ammunition. Momentarily Alita studied Kristine with grave concern. She had never seen her friend more distraught. She scanned the letter furiously for the cause.

We struck camp and ate our last meal before battle in near silence. Our water bottles were filled with cold tea to hide the taste of the water— miserable fuel for fighting men. I am not the only Englishman who shall never again have a taste for tea. God in His mercy has allowed me to forget what we ate.

Despite our circumstances and the odds, or perhaps because of them, intensity was high: there was both excitement and dread in the air. Many of our party were but mere lads, wild for the fight. Others were more solemn with the reflection that this pitiful meal in a foreign land was the last meal for some of us. As we ate and stared at each other, one wondered who among us would be together the following night.

Everyone thought it, and no one spoke it. We knew a ferocious battle lay ahead, we knew that our chances at victory were slim, we knew that it was our duty to fight anyway, but we did not know which of us would live to tell the tale.

Alita closed her eyes. Many of the men she could see and feel preparing for battle were now…*dead*. How they could be so alive to her and yet now gone? The very idea caused her to tremble. This was a place she had never wished to visit.

"Krissy, tell me. What happened?" *Please, dear God, not Robert.* This letter was proof that he was still alive at least at the time of writing. Had he lost a limb? Was he dying alone in a hospital of a disease? Something *terrible* was in the letter, she knew it.

"Read it, Alita," Kristine replied without emotion. Slowly she raised the cup of tea to her lips and drank mechanically, as the hand on a clock might move forward with perfect precision. Alita's eyes jumped to the page at the same time she was fearful of the answer she would find there.

Our dinner complete, the advance began. The unrelenting rhythm of the boots on sand sounded strangely like the drum cadence prior to an execution. The last rays of the sun set, and darkness enveloped us, forming a sort of unnatural tomb. Never was there a clearer omen.

The escalating strain was a revolting torture. Even the ankle-biters among us knew that we must gain control of our emotions for there to be any chance of success. We were even afraid to breathe for fear it would be heard by the enemy—one imagined that every sound, every breath, would somehow discharge an army of weapons now faced at oneself alone, blasting one off the desert sands once and for all.

The Paradox: The Soldier and the Mystic 43

She felt the battle growing nearer, and terror flowed through her veins. The rage and ferocity of the Egyptians, fighting for the control of their invaded homeland, gripped her heart. Trepidation for the safety of her countrymen and her friends overcame her. Anxiously she read on, desperate to find answers. She had the strange feeling that the answers which she both dreaded and craved would leave her with only more questions.

The moment of our advance was then upon us. The last words of optimism and "Glory for the Queen!" were uttered, and finally the whispered orders to fix bayonets.

And then came one of the unforeseen misfortunes of war. Unexpectedly our heady hopes of a much-needed advantage were dashed. A solitary bugle call in the Egyptian camp revealed that our presence was known. Attempting concealment was a lost cause at this point.

As if to bring the point home, with startling abruptness the Egyptians closed in upon us, a burst of rifle fire showering out of the darkness. Everything was in their favor: they were sheltered, and we were in open desert. Officers and fellow soldiers were killed instantly, dropping and dying all around us, when only a second previous they had been the virulent picture of brilliant health.

I looked up, and even in the darkness I saw, lit against the gun blasts, the Egyptian camp's bugler robed entirely in white. He was carrying a brass-hilted sword and moving like the wind. I might have thought he was an angel of God if he had not been bent on killing me. His determination to put a period to my life did nothing to place him in my favor, if the truth be known.

This Arabian Avenger fulfilled my worst nightmare. He came from nowhere, and suddenly he was about four feet above me as if suspended in midair, ruthlessly slicing at me like a primordial beast.

The image of the ferocious white-clad Egyptian, splattered with blood, claimed Alita's very soul. She knew inexplicably that he would impact her life in some astonishing turn of events. The association was so convoluted that she could not grasp its form.

She read on to discover that Robert had miraculously survived the attack. "But, Krissy, Robert is alive. This letter is evidence of that." Alita did not add that she felt him to be alive still.

Kristine's expression was unmoved.

"Furthermore," Alita added as she skipped to the last paragraph, "Robert states most exuberantly that Britain has won! Tel-el-Kebir broke the back of Egyptian resistance, Urabi has surrendered, and British troops have entered Cairo in triumph. I gather that control of Egypt has effectively passed to the queen. This will secure the future of the Suez Canal for the English." She could not eat at her mother's table and not be well-informed in the political arena.

"Robert is not the only person to fight!" Kristine lashed out uncharacteristically. Can you not tell from this letter that many men died?"

"*Of course*, I know, but…"

"Colin has been killed," she whispered. Kristine struggled for breath, giving the impression of one who was asphyxiating. And then the flood burst, tears pouring down her cheeks.

Alita sat stunned for some moments before she could find her words, the letter dropping into her lap.

It is too horrible to be true.

"I am so, so sorry," she finally managed to whisper. She had been trying so diligently to connect to the scene that she had ended up wide of the mark, and the obvious had escaped her.

Colin O'Rourke had been an unlikely match for the beautiful and sought-after brunette. His looks were not outstanding, but he was highly intelligent, with a lively wit and a gift for amusing himself and others. He was a superb dancer with impeccable manners—when he chose to utilize them. One never knew what Colin would do next. Colin had courted Kristine with wild abandon, riding for hours to find her favorite wildflower, sending her ridiculous poems which sent her into fits of laughter, and presenting himself at the park wearing a pink bonnet and cloak so as not to be detected by Kristine's chaperone.

Colin had been Kristine's perfect match. And here he was, dead on the battlefield at twenty-three years of age.

Alita went numb. Where there had been so much life, there was now nothing but a memory.

The Paradox: The Soldier and the Mystic 45

"Oh, why must England be plagued with assisting every backward country to right itself? Can these barbarians do nothing to help themselves?" Kristine wailed.

Alita glanced at her porcelain teacup covered in pansies. It was lavender and yellow with a gold rim, and the jasmine leaves floated in the cup to form a heavenly scented tea. And her countrymen longing for a drink of pure, undoctored water. She looked at her friend who would have found delight in their beautiful tea setting only the day before and for whom nothing, absolutely nothing, was real or mattered now except her beloved Colin.

"If I could, I would kill every Egyptian myself." Kristine gritted her teeth and clenched her fists as she spit the words.

Feeling the full impact of the darkness encroaching upon her friend's soul, Alita grew suddenly alarmed. "But, Krissy dear, the war was on Egyptian soil. Egypt did not come to Britain and attack our people. What else could they do but defend their own country?" She knew from her mother that Egypt had been protecting herself continually against European invasion for almost a century, starting with Napoleon Bonaparte who landed in Egypt with thirty-eight thousand troops in 1798.

"*How dare you!*" Kristine shot Alita a look that registered betrayal. Her hands were shaking as she picked up her discarded letter, as if this might bring Colin back, tears falling down her cheeks. Returning her eyes to Alita, her teeth barred, she hissed, "Colin was *good*. He died because of *them*."

"He was good. *Very* good," Alita murmured, sadness engulfing her. She searched frantically for some way to comfort her friend. She closed her eyes. Alita thought of Colin and realized with a stark suddenness that he had experienced a particularly gruesome death. She saw again the white-clad Egyptian.

Is it Colin from the afterlife? Without warning, someone called to her. Frightened by the possibility that it was a departed soul, Alita fought the connection. She placed her hands palms down firmly in her lap.

And then it came, the scent of blood and decaying bodies and organs, of human and animal waste. It smelled inconceivably worse than her mother's hospital, and without the accompanying antiseptic smells. As her stomach began to churn, she fought the need to regurgitate with great effort and might have failed had she eaten any food.

She began to shake. Involuntarily she transported into a dream state, so powerful was the image. She saw Colin hurry to Robert's aid. The thundering Egyptian turned his attentions toward Colin, his gigantic sword gleaming in the moonlight as it sliced the air.

Another soldier rushed like lightning toward the scene, only a few seconds behind the attacker. Both men converging upon Colin and Robert were mighty, fearless warriors.

Colin's protector took the form of a black panther in her vision. The *Black Panther* left a trail of men in his wake as he ran to Colin's side, slashing them right and left as he moved. Despite his enormous speed and skill, the *Black Panther* arrived too late, just as the Egyptian stabbed Colin, blood gushing forth from Colin's mouth.

As she accessed the anger and remorse that filled the *Black Panther's* being, Alita found herself choking and gasping for air. But the warrior was silent. He did not scream, nor did he curse. His pale silver-blue eyes, all the more eerie offset against black hair, focused intently on the Egyptian he had watched kill Colin.

Without hesitation, and with the warrior's reflexes, the *Black Panther* attacked the bugler. The Egyptian was yelling something, but it could not be heard in the noise of battle. The combat that ensued as the darkness of night surrounded them was fierce and lengthy until the *Black Panther* delivered his fatal blow. The Egyptian fell backward, and his cloak fell off with the fall, uncovering his face. As he looked up into the *Black Panther's* eyes, a wave of horror and recognition struck the victor. He leaned to the ground, not caring if he would be struck down, and held his friend's head in his hands, tears streaming down his face. The Egyptian died in his arms as he whispered a name Alita could not discern, followed by an utterance of *"friend"* and *"Mother Egypt."*

The life he had taken would never return, and the realization was rich with meaning for the *Black Panther*. This dead man in his arms had children, precious children whom he had just robbed of a father. Their faces flashed before his eyes, their laughter turning to ice.

He had killed out of rage and hatred, for revenge, not for any just cause. Not even for a false idealism. He had bought into the spirit of things and acted as if he had the right to kill in order to assert his country's will on a people who refused to submit. He had sympathized with his dead friend's

The Paradox: The Soldier and the Mystic   *47*

cause and he had killed anyway, disregarding his own conscience. He knew no sense of honor for his part in this battle. *He wanted to die.* He prayed that he would die.

The enormity of his misery made Alita feel as if her heart would break and her head would burst. She swayed, clutching her heart. Never before had she entered into emotions of such a magnitude that there was the very real possibility they might engulf and destroy her. And yet she could not pull back, did not know how to pull back, did not *wish* to pull back.

Fear overtook her. He was in great danger of being killed on the battlefield. Being an accomplished killer, possibly his instincts would take over, defending him against attack.

Did he live? Alita frantically focused all her energy toward finding the answer to this question so important to her now, *critical* to her existence, she knew not why.

Suddenly a wave of relief swept over her, and she began to swoon.

"Alita, Alita!" Kristine shook her, momentarily taken out of her own grief. "Why do you ignore me? What is wrong with you?"

"Not now, Krissy!" *I have to know.* Alita braced herself against her chair, fighting her dizziness. Ordinarily she was guarded in what she revealed to her friends of her abilities, but she had just emerged—*did not wish to emerge*—from the most powerful trance she had ever experienced. If only Krissy would be quiet! "I have seen the *Black Panther.*"

"The black...*what*?"

"Shhh! He is confused..."

"How *could* you? Today of all days!"

He lived.

Suddenly, a wave of relief swept over her, and she began to swoon. Sobbing from the encounter, her entire body began to shake. "He thought he knew his enemy, and then he saw the face of his friend in his enemy. He lost two friends on this day, one of them was Colin, and he blames himself for the deaths of both. The *Black Panther* is retreating to treat his wounds. He goes to a dark place where he will stay for a time."

"A dark place? Alita, what did you say about Colin?"

"Enemy and friend are one and the same." Her teeth were chattering now, even as she was sweating. She forced herself to speak, the purity of his convictions now intermingled with her own. "He does not have the heart for his duty…"

"Alita, have you gone mad?" Kristine exclaimed. "How can you talk this nonsense when Colin has died? Have you heard nothing I have said?"

"Oh, Krissy," Alita replied faintly, patting the tears in her eyes. "I am so sorry. Believe me. The pain and suffering was incomprehensible. It was *terrible. I was there.*"

Chapter Six

Something about descending the Grand Staircase at Buckingham Palace, merely walking down some steps, made one feel that there was a great significance to the moment. And there always was.

One was utterly present with each step, aware that kings and queens had preceded one. If every architectural structure had the power of rendering its occupants completely present, how might the connecting moments of a life change the outcome? A mere moment of enlightened observation had initiated one on a different path and changed everything more than once.

Even as these thoughts danced through her head, Lady Elaina was struck by the grandeur of the rooms though she had seen the palace many times before.

Gasp! Her daughter's constricted breathing returned her to the task at hand. She glanced at Alita, an expression of complete dread washing across her daughter's face. Lady Elaina smiled to herself at the absurdity of it as she contemplated her daughter's trepidation and quivering hands despite her obvious beauty.

The young never saw themselves as they were. Youth was always beautiful, but they invariably focused on their deviations from perfection.

Alita was as nervous as if she were going to her own wedding rather than to a ball! True, this ball would determine the future lives of many in attendance. Even so, it wasn't like Alita to look upon a social event with anything other than expectant jubilation.

"Calm down, darling. If the presentation went well, what could possibly go astray here? You cannot fail to please. Enjoy yourself."

"Yes, Ma-ma." Alita swallowed.

"You look so lovely, dearest. You are positively an ethereal vision in white." Even though white was required for the presentation to the queen, and thus most girls chose outlandishly colorful gowns for the ball, she was proud that Alita had chosen an antique ivory silk with a small circular train surrounded by Belgian lace. Covered buttons ran down the back of the dress, which was lower cut to form a "V" above her hips and from which two bouffant puffs formed. She wore elbow-length gloves, white pearls around her neck, and delicate pearl-and-diamond earrings dotted her ears. A myriad of curls were placed artistically on her head and laced with pearl droplets and the palest peach-tone rosebuds, offsetting her emerald-green eyes.

"You will stand out like a swan amongst the peacocks," the Dowager Duchess of Salford murmured, flanking Alita.

"Or amongst *the parrots*," Lady Elaina mused.

"Oh, Grandmamma, I should say not! Everyone looks positively *radiant*!" Alita giggled. "For myself, I merely wish to look nice without bringing undue attention to myself."

"Not bring attention to yourself?" retorted Marvella. "You must *always* bring attention to yourself, Alita—but without appearing to do so, of course." She swatted her daughter with a silk Chinese fan. "Slow your pace, Elaina!"

"Yes, Mother." Without warning, Lady Elaina felt some consternation, knowing that her own confident, purposeful manner had nothing to do with the fashion of the day and everything to do with raised, disapproving eyebrows. She had never belonged in this venue, and it appeared she never would, regardless of her accomplishments. Or perhaps because of them.

Suddenly Alita asked in a whisper, barely audible, as if she were afraid of her own words, "But w–w–what if no one wishes to marry me?"

"Would that it could be so…"

"Ma-ma! Do you mean it?" asked Alita, staring at her mother in disbelief.

"Bite your tongue, Elaina!" added the duchess.

"Indeed I am confident of your success, Alita, and convinced that the establishment of your household will occur all too quickly," explained Lady Elaina, ignoring her mother's admonitions. "I fully expect you to be betrothed in six month's time, my sweet—or sooner."

"However could you know, Ma-ma?" asked Alita hopefully.

"Because you perfectly fit the fashion of the day, my love," Lady Elaina shrugged. "To the current way of thinking, a lady is refined and discreet in

The Paradox: The Soldier and the Mystic   *51*

her manners. She is natural and unpretentious in her language, speaking little of herself and focusing on others."

"She gets that from me," the dowager duchess interjected, raising her chin.

"I merely prefer to listen," Alita defended herself, feeling the color rise in her cheeks. "I am sure if I have something to say, I do so."

"Some of us do so regardless," remarked Lady Elaina, staring pointedly at her mother. "In addition, a lady is kindhearted and would be mortified at the thought of wounding anyone's feelings. She would never ridicule or criticize anyone openly, nor would she have any wish to do so."

"Of course not! How could anyone wish to deliberately hurt someone else or to speak ill of them?" asked Alita, descending the final steps of the staircase carefully.

"Some find the wherewithal, it appears." Lady Elaina shrugged, raising her eyebrows. "And yet, a *lady*, in her heart, feels compassion for the ill-fated and the ignorant."

"It depends on *how* ignorant," mused the duchess.

"I do not comprehend how anyone cannot feel compassion for those who are not as fortunate as oneself."

"Nor I, but look at the state of the world." Lady Elaina nodded. "And yet, a *lady's* manner is one of sweetness and goodness of character…A perfect description of you, Alita dear."

"Oh, Ma-ma, how sweet you are!"

"Indeed I am, for I, too, am a lady for my time, whatever the opponents of women's rights shall say," she emphasized. "Some would add innocence and submissiveness to their requirements, but I find it ridiculous that naivety and servitude should be a stipulation of femininity."

"Do you think I am naive, Ma-ma?"

"Oh no, darling, not at all. Merely wanting in experience."

"Oh *my*. It is…it is…very…*bold* is it not?" uttered Alita as they entered the State Ballroom, the largest and tallest room in Buckingham Palace at forty-five feet high, strikingly ornate with dark Corinthian turquoise marble columns, orange-red velvet and silk, a gold domed ceiling, and crystal lighting. "I didn't quite imagine it to be like this!"

"It is *impressive*, Alita," corrected Marvella. "Not *bold*."

"It is bold. It would seem to swallow one whole," Lady Elaina countered. Her hands suddenly shaking, she wondered at herself as she realized how easily she had forgotten her current status and flown back in time—her disastrous dissent upon London society was twenty-five years ago! Funny how the years melted away, and it seemed like yesterday when one reentered the witches' den. It must have hurt more than she supposed so many years ago.

Suddenly she spotted a tall, dashing young man in a tuxedo with blond-streaked hair and a boyish grin, and her breath caught in her chest at the striking resemblance. *Could it be?* She closed her eyes and shook her head involuntarily, almost tripping on her own feet.

What is happening to me? It felt as if she were engaged in time travel from one second to the next.

"Elaina!" Marvella quipped. "Watch your step! We aren't in a race here!"

"Yes, of course, Mother, though I don't know how much more slowly I can walk and still be moving." She mustered her considerable resolve, and though it seemed an absolute waste of time to take forever to walk across the room, she strove to contain her stride and to take dainty, disinterested steps. She didn't wish to be an embarrassment to her daughter, and she determined to do everything in her power to support her.

"*Move?*" Her Grace reiterated with disdain under her breath, her smile unwavering. She might have been a ventriloquist. "Ladies do not *move*. They float."

Alita said nothing but smiled at her grandmother, taking her arm.

"Yes, Mother. Quite right. We are not human beings with brains and appendages—particularly not brains—we are clouds." With all the extra time this pace afforded her, Lady Elaina glanced at her mother even as Alita suppressed a giggle.

"It is good that you comprehend, Elaina. And a welcome change." The dowager duchess now had a beaming smile plastered on her lips as if to say, *Look who's in charge now*, no doubt reliving her own frightening introduction into society, succeeding without social standing, money, or position.

And the reason they were all three standing here today.

The Paradox: The Soldier and the Mystic 53

"And it is equally good that you are here to guide us, Mother. I know very well where we would all be without you," she remarked with sincerity.

"As do I," the dowager duchess agreed, regal and elegant as she glided across the ballroom. Alita would not be put to shame there! Marvella's hair had been blonde in her youth but was now blonde-white and stylishly arranged. Her pale blue eyes were exquisite against a light-lavender silk gown of the highest fashion and were set off by diamonds, family heirlooms. Though Marvella shared her daughter's curvaceous figure, to that she added an elegance of deportment few women possessed. Certainly she herself was not among that number.

Lady Elaina bestowed her warmest smile upon her mother who had taken an interest in this granddaughter, so much like her and yet so very different. Surprisingly, the quite unconventional side to Alita's personality was unknown to the dowager duchess, while their shared characteristics had forged a common bond almost from the moment of Alita's birth.

She opened her fan with one swift twist of the wrist. There was no need to enlighten her mother on the exceptional talents of her favorite granddaughter. Marvella Lancastor had never been one to approve of extraordinary abilities in the female sex, and it would only distress her were she to learn of it.

Better to allow Alita to bask in her grandmother's love. A child always benefited from being enveloped in love.

Alita spotted her group of girlfriends huddled in one corner, the children of six of London's most privileged families.

"*Good Heavens!*" the duchess murmured disapprovingly but with a decided hint of admiration as she glanced in that direction. "Much too old for a young girl just out," Her Grace pronounced, stating the obvious.

Whereas Alita's dress was elegant in its simplicity, the gown which had captured her attention was not a dress meant for ease of dancing but for show stopping—and that, without question, the brunette had accomplished. Her wine-and-maroon-red satin was form-fitting, daringly low cut, and with a three-foot-long ruffled satin taffeta train. A bow of satin ribbon formed a corsage along the revealed bodice which the young lady showed to advantage. She carried a Louis XV fan behind which she appeared to be whispering. She wore bloodred roses in her coiffure and rubies and diamonds on her voluptuous, bare chest.

"Do you suppose that Miss Tutt is unaware of that fact, Mother?" stated Lady Elaina.

"Tsk! Tsk! *Rubies*! Shameful!" The dowager duchess's lips curled into a smile.

Alita waved at her friends in an understated, ladylike manner. As usual, the girls were whispering and casting glances in their direction, but it struck Lady Elaina that the glances were not those of welcome and approval.

She must be touched in the head to think so. Her memories had cast shadows upon her judgment.

* * * *

Lady Elaina and Her Grace walked reservedly to the punch table for refreshments while Alita hurried to her friends. She stopped frozen in her tracks as several of the girls abruptly ceased conversation and glanced away with her approach. She gasped and released a shaky smile, which was returned with frozen half smiles.

"Randall, would you please procure a glass of punch for me? And one of those little star cookies. I *adore* those! Armand, I would very much like to know the name of that last piece which the orchestra played, if it wouldn't trouble you. You see, I have a bet with Mr. Stanhope, and I shall surely disgrace him with your assistance. Can you let me know the minute Mr. Stanhope arrives?" There were a few young men hovering about Kristine, gaping and gaga with admiration, whom she summarily dismissed.

"Melanie, what is wrong?" Alita asked hesitantly as she approached them, a cold breeze hitting her full in the face. "Why are you looking at me so?"

"Whatever do you mean, Alita? Don't be silly." Melanie laughed nervously. Her expression seemed to waver between confusion and disgust as she glanced at Kristine. "Your imagination runs wild, Alita. I can't fathom what you will say next. Sometimes I don't know what to make of your odd stories."

"Odd stories?" Alita caught her breath. *Kristine had told her*. Clearly Melanie didn't know what to make of her vision at the same time she was inclined to believe Kristine's interpretation.

Of course, she realized with a sudden panic. Kristine was their leader, the society star. Whatever Kristine did, everyone did. She herself had always followed Kristine's lead.

And why would Kristine say something that wasn't true? Especially about her *best friend* she thought as a sob formed in her throat. She knew this would be the question in everyone's mind. If Kristine said it, it had to be true.

She turned to regard Beatrice, whose scrutiny clearly betrayed her jealousy and who somehow appeared dowdy even in all her finery—a very bright green dress worn with yellow roses rather than the white flowers Alita had urged her to wear. Beatrice would be quite lovely if only she could resist attempting to draw so much attention to herself.

"Kristine said that you have been dreaming quite a bit lately, Alita," Beatrice hissed. Alita was well aware that Beatrice had never especially liked her. Matrimony was the only game in town, and Beatrice had been of the mindset that Alita would always outshine her.

"You say things which are decidedly un-Christian, Alita. It is dangerous." Appearing to gain confidence, Melanie voiced her thoughts, her intent sincere if mislead.

"What can you mean, Melanie?" Alita managed to ask as she struggled for air.

"You want to go to heaven, don't you?" Melanie whispered under her breath.

"Of course." Alita nodded, startled by the question.

"Then why," Melanie asked, "are you always talking about other religions? And you aren't saying that those people are heathens, either!"

"You want me to call other people *heathens*, Melanie?"

She was drawn to Dottie's giggling, an apparent attempt to gain Kristine's approval. Dottie adored Kristine and had long been envious of Alita's closeness with her. As Alita's eyes pleaded with no one in particular, she saw Dottie move closer to Kristine.

"Who cares about dreams and other religions?" demanded Veronica. "I certainly don't. And I doubt you do either. Why don't we procure some lemonade and find some comfortable chairs to sit in instead of standing about like gaping toads?" Alita turned toward Veronica, who appeared bored by the proceedings. Brunette like Kristine, she was a little plumper but just as pretty, though lacking Kristine's vivacity. She moved as if her corset were too tight.

Kristine glared at Veronica.

"*What*?" Veronica challenged, having none of it. "Who died and made you queen?"

Alita's heart sank as she realized that, although Veronica had no wish to hurt her, she would not raise a finger to help her either.

Only Charlise's expression remained neutral as she observed the scene unfolding before her. Charlise was a vicar's daughter, so Alita presumed she would side with Melanie, as they generally saw eye-to-eye. Charlise was not well-to-do like the other girls in the group, being the favorite of a wealthy aunt whom she had been visiting since childhood.

"Krissy, I am sorry if I was not attentive to you this afternoon. I…tried…to be." Kristine Tutt was not the same young woman she had been. Colin's death had filled her heart with terror and bitterness, so immersed was she in grief. *How can I be cruel to someone who has already suffered so much?*

Stop it! Stop it! Alita knew that in her inability to disconnect from the pain of others, she was immobilized. Kristine was desperate to unload that unbearable pain somewhere, anywhere. *And I am helping her do it.*

"I shall try to remember your method if ever you have lost someone dear to you, Alita," Kristine added.

The only response her companions would understand was more snubs and artificially polite conversation. To state the truth, that they were breaking her heart, would only give them ammunition. Her very survival in society, everything she held dear, depended on the cold and calculating act she knew to be necessary, no, *critical* to her success.

Every value, every feeling rebelled against it.

"I may be a little different from you, but you are still my friends, and I still love you." Alita knew that she was pleading, but she could not help herself. Tears welled up in her eyes. "This day is *everything* to me—just as it is *to you*."

Kristine and her entourage stared at Alita as she stared back, all in a standstill. Without a word, Charlise Sinclair crossed the invisible line and put her arm around Alita.

The Paradox: The Soldier and the Mystic 57

"This is a dance, for goodness's sake!" Charlise pronounced as she turned toward the other girls. She pulled out her handkerchief and dotted Alita's eyes. "Unquestionably not the time to discuss Alita's dreams. Most inappropriate for well-brought-up young ladies."

Kristine jabbed Charlise, who ignored her, not even turning to look at her.

"But dreams of black panthers. And *visions*," Melanie admonished.

"It seems almost *blasphemous*, does it not?" Beatrice sniffed, knowing that which would matter to Charlise.

"Certainly I don't put any store by odd dreams unless they are in the *Bible*." Charlise turned to face Beatrice and Melanie square on. "But neither will I be party to unkindness shown to anyone, most definitely not to my friends! Jesus said that even the tax collectors are kind to their friends. *We* must be kind to our enemies. And *you*—you, cannot even be kind to your friends! I am ashamed of you!" she admonished indignantly. Alita was startled to see this gentle vicar's daughter's feathers so ruffled.

"But my vision was real, Charlise!" Alita murmured. Now that it was out in the open, she found that she wanted desperately to be believed.

"We'll speak of that later, dear Alita," replied Charlise under her breath, her clear blue eyes pleading with her.

Must I always be invisible to everyone? Struggling to fight her disappointment, Alita reminded herself that Charlise was doing the best that she knew to support her, possibly at great detriment to her own social standing. Charlise was one of those rare Christians who *lived* in love. Love had created an opening for the living God to enter her soul, and love always transformed a willing heart irrespective of beliefs, logic, or theology.

"Let us take a turn about the room, Alita." Charlise's smile could have coaxed a leprechaun away from his pot of gold.

But there was far more at stake here than gold. As Alita longingly beheld her childhood friends, now gathered together on the day she had so long anticipated, she wondered that these girls still felt like her treasure though they would have sacrificed her for a wink.

In an instant, she saw all too clearly the flaw in having only friends who cared as much about societal approval and status as she did.

"I don't know, Charlise. I'm not sure what to do…"

"The walk will revive you, Alita," Charlise added gently, taking her hand. But Alita's knees went weak, and she was unable to proceed. Charlise was nonetheless able to pull her a few feet from the other girls when the orchestra began to play.

"But, Charlise," she whispered, "you had best not side with me. I will only ensure your demise as well."

What is wrong with me? I have someone supporting me, and I am endeavoring to push her away as well! It was as if everything flowed together and she had no sense of herself.

"I don't care a fig for society if I must sacrifice my character to that end. That would be an empty prize for me." Charlise's eyes were penetrating in their gaze, her resolve unwavering even as she patted Alita's hand. "One cannot build one's happiness on someone else's suffering. And besides, Alita..."

"Besides what, Charlise?"

"*I love you, Alita.*" She hugged her friend.

"Oh, Charlise, you are too dear to me for words. I'm sure I don't deserve you. But what about Krissy's suffering? She is suffering, too."

"Oh, yes. Terribly." Charlise's pink lips parted, richly warm against her pale skin. "Love her—as you should—but realize what she is. Kristine is trying to hurt you and will very likely succeed. How does this cruel act help Kristine? Not at all. It provides her with momentary relief. It can never be right to behave with evil intent."

"I can't comprehend how they can do this, Charlise."

"People have different reasons for what they do." Charlise shrugged. "And the devil works in devious ways, often appearing in desirable forms."

"I always strove to be a good friend." Though Alita did not share Charlise's view of the spirit world, the symbolism of her friend's words strangely helped her to regain her footing. To her relief, the room stopped spinning. "Everyone wouldn't turn against me unless...unless I caused it somehow."

"I assure you, dear Alita, that you are a wonderful friend!" Charlise shook her head, her platinum-blonde curls swinging. "This is happening because *they* are not good friends."

"No, Charlise. The cruelty did not originate with me, and I did not cause it, but something in my character permitted it." She was so willing to enter

The Paradox: The Soldier and the Mystic 59

into everyone's world, into everyone's feelings, into everyone's life. In fact, it appeared that *the only person she did not wish to enter into was Miss Alita Stanton.*

Before she was able to embark upon her turn about the room with Charlise, an exquisitely dashing gentleman, obviously desiring an introduction, approached them accompanied by a mutual friend. He was tall and slim with deep blue eyes and blond hair streaked with light brown. His face was shaven and his jaw strong. Surprisingly, his boyish grin and natural, confident manner added to his elegance.

It was the same young man whom her mother had been staring at. *Oh, no. He has come to claim a dance with Charlise.* She wished he would go away. Though she knew it was selfish, Charlise was the only friend she had in the world right now.

I am doomed! She glanced in the floor-to-ceiling gilded mirror opposite where they stood, astonished that she had not noticed it earlier. Charlise was quite the prettiest girl in the room. Charlise's hair was platinum blonde against her own wheat-colored hair, with vividly blue eyes next to her green. Or rather, *red.* They were each about the same height, petite, and delicate in appearance. But while she had worn antique ivory, Charlise was much more elaborately dressed in a Pannier skirt reminiscent of Marie Antoinette. Three flounces flowed from beneath the pannier, forming bows at thigh level. Charlise's romantic satin dress in rose and light pink was long-sleeved and V-necked with a satin rose at the bosom and exquisite Belgian lace along the collar. A sprinkle of dark pink rosebuds in Charlise's platinum-blonde hair created a dazzling effect while she wore a simple gold cross around her neck. When she smiled, her sweetness was completely transparent. Charlise had accomplished the ultimate. She was both striking and *angelic.*

Ordinarily Alita would not have made these comparisons, but ordinarily the two standing together with their arms around each other might have presented a very pretty picture. Today, however, her dismal expression and watering, red eyes created a peculiar sight.

Introductions were made, and Alita nodded, but she didn't hear anything that transpired. She was too preoccupied with the terrifying thought that this gentleman had come to take Charlise away. *What will I do?* Stand here in the middle of the room alone?

"Would you care to dance?" he asked as he turned toward her and held out his hand.

Her eyes flew wide open as she checked the impulse to turn and look behind her.

Charlise nudged her, looking straight ahead.

"Or, if you prefer, may I procure some punch for you, Miss Stanton?" The young Adonis smiled down at her even as he seemed unconcerned by her stupefaction and inability to communicate in the language of her birth. "Or possibly a stroll would be refreshing?"

She opened her mouth to speak, but sadly, no words came forth.

"The three of us might care to take a turn about the room?" Receiving not so much as a one-syllable response from her, he turned to Charlise in the hopeful expectation of an elementary command of the language, a skill that he had clearly eliminated as a possibility in her case.

And rightly so.

His tone was concerned—anyone might have seen Charlise comforting her—but he was not embarrassed or ill at ease, nor did he appear anxious to disengage himself. He was in possession of an orator's golden tenor voice, but the other girls nonetheless moved forward to catch the full conversation, which, as yet, consisted of only him.

"*Three*? What about me?" Francis demanded, the mutual friend who had performed the introductions.

"Francis, do you see Miss Penelope standing next to the punch table? I find her repeatedly glancing your way," the Greek god commented.

"She does?" asked Francis hopefully, surveying his surroundings. He seemed only too happy for the respite from the uneasy situation in which he had involuntarily found himself. He bowed and departed for the punch table.

"I apologize, ladies," the blonde gentleman said with a slight nod of his chin. "It did not seem that you were keen on too much company, and I certainly did not wish to forfeit my blessed position, however undeserved."

"Thank you, sir..." Somehow she found her voice. She hoped that didn't prove to be a mistake. She smiled gratefully at both his thoughtfulness and his compliment, and he looked as if he might melt under her gaze.

He seemed to have difficulty finding his voice as well. "And what is your pleasure, Miss Stanton?"

"I am so sorry, I don't recollect...I didn't quite catch..." She was at a loss to know how to ask for his name, which surely had already been given. As she felt herself blushing, she was acutely aware of an admonishing murmur behind them.

Probably too immersed in her dreams to keep from looking like a fool. She could hear their censure as if it were spoken.

"Alita, *Lord William Manchestor* has asked if you would like to dance?" Charlise smiled demurely as she squeezed her hand a bit too tightly. Charlise's eyes grew wide as she turned to look at her, as if to say, "Look alive, dear girl, this could be the pivotal moment of your entire life!"

"Miss Sinclair, I hope I may claim a dance with you later this evening?" he added politely, reluctantly pulling himself out of his reverie and turning to Charlise. His expression had the appearance of warm civility more than of flirtation and interest, Alita reflected with surprise.

"Thank you, Lord Manchestor. That would be most charming." Charlise curtseyed very becomingly. "I believe this dance is Miss Alita's—unless she would prefer to take a turn with us?" Charlise waved her head toward the dance floor, unnoticed by Lord Manchestor as his eyes were now glued to hers.

"Actually, I d–do think dancing would be m–most enjoyable, my lord." Alita exerted considerable effort in regaining her composure.

"I am delighted, Miss Stanton," he replied as he held out his arm with a slight bow.

"I must apologize for my abominable appearance, Lord Manchestor," she stated shyly as he lead her to the dance floor.

"Ordinarily I would not be so forward, Miss Stanton, but since you introduce the subject, I think I may say that I have never seen a more beautiful young lady. A white rose amongst a field of wildly colored daisies comes to mind."

"But I am all teary eyed!" she exclaimed, suddenly unable to hold her thoughts.

"That does little to conceal your beauty, Miss Stanton, so appealing in its modesty." Lord Manchestor laughed, adding somberly, "And frankly, your tears reveal a side which appeals to me in this world of superficialities. An impenetrable facade of polish is questionable at best. I find you quite...genuine."

Genuine. Of all the things she was, she was not that. She felt her lips form a trembling smile. "I thank you for the compliment, Lord Manchestor, but is it not premature? We have only just met."

He laughed again, seemingly greatly amused. "In the purest sense, yes. In another sense, no."

Looking up at him, she searched his deep blue eyes, but the music had begun, making an in-depth conversation difficult. They enjoyed two dances, and she was grateful for the reprieve from her grief. It was heavenly to be dancing the waltz while held in the arms of such a handsome, solicitous, *grown* man.

Feeling in better spirits, she suppressed the knowledge that it was only a matter of minutes before her friends passed on the distorted story to all the young ladies and matrons in attendance at Buckingham Palace while she was powerless to do anything about it.

She resolved to enjoy herself as best she could. She had been waiting *all her life* for this day, and as long as someone was being attentive to her, she would not dispel that pleasure. She was determined to shelve her despair and to address those feelings at a later time when she could no longer escape them. It would come soon enough.

"Would you care for some refreshment, Miss Stanton?"

He was not in a rush to leave her! Nothing in her world made sense today. She nodded her agreement.

"I confess that I was most desirous of meeting you today, Miss Stanton," he remarked upon returning with punch for both of them.

"I don't understand, Lord Manchestor," she replied, confused. "You can't have known anything about me before this evening."

"I have watched for news of your presentation in anticipation of that honor, Miss Stanton."

Suddenly she emerged from her fog to recall where she had heard the name. "Out of curiosity, Lord Manchestor?"

"Why, yes, initially." He appeared impressed, not for the first time this evening.

"My mother was once betrothed to your father. Is this the association you allude to, Lord Manchestor?" she asked matter-of-factly, surprised that she had momentarily forgotten in the midst of her grave upset. She knew the name but had never put the face to the name until now. If she had had prior

The Paradox: The Soldier and the Mystic 63

knowledge of the face, she would have attended to the task with a devoutness to rival the Lutherans!

And if the father were half as handsome as the son...She felt her lips curve into a mischievous smile. Her mother had done well to have been pursued by—and engaged to!—both her father and Phillip Manchestor, now Lord Montague, the 3rd Marquis of Montague. Gazing into expressive blue eyes framed by sun-streaked hair, she reflected that she did not wish pain on anyone, but this was the nature of courtship. And to have memories such as this...

Wonderment washed over her as the full impact of her mother's defiant nonconformity became real to her for the first time. Lady Elaina had both broken her engagement to a peer of the realm, which was in and of itself outrageous, *and*, as the daughter of a duke, entered a trade position!

The irony was lamentable. Her mother had not cared a whit for society and had won every round. She herself wanted acceptance so very badly and had made a mess of everything. Lady Elaina had more courage in her little finger than she herself had in her entire body.

And her mother was a great deceiver and a phony! The truth suddenly became clear. Lady Elaina had always put forward the notion that she was a social imbecile in her youth! With the oh-so-vivid memory of dancing while being held in strong, muscular arms, there was no doubt in Alita's mind that the apple did not fall far from the tree.

"I am surprised that you admit it, Miss Stanton, particularly since your mother broke the engagement. Most unusual for young ladies to state what they know."

"Yes, it can be detrimental to not feign ignorance when one is female." The truth of that statement was painfully clear to her at the moment.

He chuckled, his expression animated.

"It is intriguing to picture our parents dancing here some twenty-five years ago just as we are," he reflected.

"The same and different." She didn't know why she couldn't hold her tongue. It was as if her life was destroyed regardless, and she was thus suddenly free to be herself and to speak her thoughts. And she couldn't seem to stop! Perhaps if the earth were to open up and swallow her whole, then maybe she would manage to cease prattling on. "That is to say...to think that thousands of events have transpired and yet, here we stand again, some reflection of our parents."

"And our parents' *feelings*." He added, seeming to have trouble keeping his eyes from hers, even as he cleared his throat.

"You will never know the extent to which your kindness is appreciated, my lord."

"My dear Miss Stanton, let me disavow you of the notion that my behavior stems from unselfishness. The benefit is all mine," he stated most sincerely, his piercing blue eyes startlingly intent upon her. "May I be blunt with you, Miss Stanton?"

"Everyone is," Alita responded, feeling her face freeze into an acceptable expression. *It is me who is not afforded that luxury.*

"I had always heard that, if the parents are agreeably predisposed toward each other…if they…have an *affinity* for each other, often the children will as well." His exceptional confidence was suddenly replaced with a shyness that surprised her. "My father had said that your mother's authenticity enthralled him. Now that I have met you, I understand completely."

"Yes, but he did not marry her, now did he?" Alita's heart warmed to this gentleman, even as she took a sip of her punch, some of her natural playfulness returning.

"Of that, I am glad. I like you very well as you are, Miss Stanton."

"Perhaps you protect your own existence, Lord Manchestor?" Alita laughed for the first time since her arrival, leaning back into her chair. "You are some six years older than myself, made possible by the broken engagement."

"Possibly it worked out for the best." Lord Manchestor gazed attentively at Alita, his square jawline adding to the firmness in his expression.

Intervening, another young gentleman came forward and begged a dance from Alita. She graciously accepted but thanked Lord Manchestor before rising from her chair and departing, bestowing upon him a warm expression of gratitude, which seemed to catch his breath for an instant.

She danced several more dances. When she went to the punch table and tried once again to speak with her girlfriends, she was snubbed. Some of the young men had begun to bestow odd glances upon her as well.

The Paradox: The Soldier and the Mystic 65

As she felt herself being sucked into the feelings of her reproachers, she mustered everything at her command to imagine herself as separate, to avoid becoming their feelings.

Wondering if they had succeeded at taking almost everything that mattered from her, she suddenly saw it for what it was. Simple ignorance. Desperation. A lack of feeling for others. Playing out the scripts of their lives. And, most of all, an inability to see her for who she was.

But then, she had been guilty of that as well. She had always rejected herself. So how was she different from her "friends"?

She could excuse herself for attempting to keep her gifts a secret. That was a necessity of survival. But she had never truly wanted them either. With all her heart, she wished to be normal, never more so than today.

"Alita, is everything all right?" While holding her close, Lady Elaina asked attentively after the welfare of each of the girls in Alita's vicinity in her most gracious manner, illustrating proper decorum as she left little doubt about her very clear disapproval of their behavior toward her daughter.

After some brief but meaningful exchanges between Lady Elaina and her mother, the Dowager Duchess of Salford paid her respects as well, complimenting the girls while impressing her own importance upon them.

Indeed, no one was less receptive at receiving a cut than Her Grace.

Alita imitated the pattern illustrated for her and did the same. Behavior that she had been unable to fully muster for herself Alita now mimicked. There was a strength in the combined energies that was far greater than the sum of the parts. Alita fed off that strength, her family standing by her when she most needed it.

She turned to squeeze Charlise's hand and gave her a parting hug and kiss on the cheek. "I won't forget," she whispered. "I will repay you some day."

All three women regally departed from the ballroom, a vision of grace and beauty gliding slowly from view.

Chapter Seven

"Alita, might one inquire what just occurred? In Buckingham Palace no less?" Without further aplomb, the dowager duchess quizzed her granddaughter. Three generations of ladies situated themselves in the lavish side-curtain rockaway white carriage with white velvet interior, elegantly adorned with royal-blue satin pillows. The tassels on the pillows bounced as the carriage commenced movement, creating a rhythmic flash of purple-blue tones against the lamplight streaming in through the etched windows.

"She...has told...everyone," Alita sobbed through muffled gasps.

"She has told everyone *what*? And who is *she*?" Marvella demanded with raised eyebrows.

"I told Kristine—Miss Tutt—of a dream I had, and now...she has told...*everyone*."

"A dream? How absurd. Everyone has dreams." Marvella sniffed.

Lady Elaina said nothing but watched the proceedings attentively.

"Yes, but Kristine was very upset at the time, and she, well, she was predisposed to interpret my words in an...incorrect...light." Alita managed, noticeably struggling to gain control of herself.

"What a little *hussy*!" pronounced Marvella with finality. Lady Elaina knew that her mother would never consider using such language in public and would deny such remarks with her last dying breath, but in the presence of family the duchess had always spoken her mind.

"You do not blame *me*?" gasped Alita, appearing surprised that her grandmother should side with her over a social catastrophe centered around her. Tears welled up in her eyes in gratitude. "But, Grandmamma, I *failed*. I should never have..."

"I knew it from the moment I saw her! This only confirms my suspicions."

"But, Grandmamma, honestly, I was indiscreet. I meant well, of course, but..."

"The little vipers!" Lady Elaina murmured under her breath as her thoughts raced through her mind, and she began to piece a very little of it together. *What had happened?* Clearly some inkling of Alita's secret had been leaked in the form of a dream dramatic enough that it had fueled a malicious distortion!

But that was all unimportant. That Alita's girlfriends had embraced the fabrication and turned against her was the only pertinent information.

"Oh, Ma-ma! It hurts so much. My *friends…*"

"Could you expect anything else from a girl who would wear rubies to her first ball?"

"It is of no significance," pronounced Lady Elaina. "We have all had our say, and now we shall not waste another breath on those girls—I shall not call them young *ladies*—unfaithful friends that they are."

"What shall we waste our breath on if not that, I demand to know?" the duchess inquired.

"How we may best reintroduce Alita into society and make her a smashing success. Her season is now ruined."

"Oh, I knew it! I *knew* it!" Alita burst into sobs. "How could it be otherwise?"

"Let us assess the situation honestly," Lady Elaina continued, determined not to break down herself as her precious daughter sat tortured with grief beside her. "It is my policy to face the truth head-on. It might be more painful in the beginning, but it is one's only hope for a good outcome."

"There is no hope!" Alita gasped.

"Never speak those words in my presence again, Alita!" Lady Elaina commanded, raising her voice to the point that both Alita and the dowager duchess opened their eyes wide and sat very still, Alita's handkerchief pausing in midair. *"Now.* No more crying. Maintain your calm *always.* You may cry in the privacy of your room when you don't have three very capable women blessed with excellent minds in the same carriage. For now, let us put those minds to good use."

"Quite true," agreed Marvella in subdued tones. "There is always hope."

"Yes, Ma-ma." Alita sniffed, finding her voice. "Yes, you are very right."

"The situation is this. It does not take too many jaw-jammers to cast doubt on a girl's reputation," stated Lady Elaina. "Above all, one must not appear peculiar, unless it is exceedingly well orchestrated of course, and one must *never* be unfashionable."

"To be eccentric is reserved for widows and matrons. To be odd is disaster," murmured Her Grace softly, staring at her as if she had never known her daughter before this moment. And perhaps she had not.

"My world is...d–d–destroyed. There is no hope now for a good match!" She had never seen Alita so discomposed, now stammering, barely able to keep from bursting into tears. "No young man would have me. I'll never marry. I'll never have a family. And I'm an...*outcast.*"

"Pish tosh!" exclaimed Marvella, patting her hand. "You charmed many a young man. You had the good sense to be kind to everyone you encountered—unlike your mother, who alienated all of her beaux..."

"Kind?" Alita whispered. "That is apparently out of fashion."

"Elaina never settled for anything but precisely what she wanted, and there was no talking sense to her," Marvella continued on her train of thought while studying her daughter reproachfully. "*Where* Elaina came by her stubbornness I will never know."

"It shall remain one of the great unsolved mysteries of all time," murmured Lady Elaina as she smoothed her pale blue cashmere skirt, her mind racing.

"But *Alita*...Alita is of a different cut and would not be satisfied with a mere laborer." Marvella's eyes settled on Alita, pride evident in those eyes, even despite the day's occurrences.

Alita might be fortunate indeed to win the regard of a mere laborer at this point. But she did not say so. That much honesty did not serve.

"Let us save revisiting my lack of expertise in soliciting marriage proposals from pretentious and cosseted young men for a later time." Lady Elaina nodded distractedly to her mother's commentary, motioning toward Alita with her eyes. "Alita is our only concern for the moment."

"Elaina, you are quite right for once." Marvella's expression gave evidence of a sudden realization. "The past is the past, and Alita's success is all that matters now."

"You may recall, Alita, that I was outcasted by *polite* society when I entered nursing school." She forced herself to keep her countenance serene

The Paradox: The Soldier and the Mystic 69

as she recalled the snubs and uncharitable behavior. "And I married very well, don't you think, dear? If all one can hope for is someone who is intelligent, handsome, wealthy, and world-famous—and, not to mention, whom one loves with all one's heart—possibly things are not so bad?"

"Oh no, Ma-ma, no. No one could be dearer—or better!—than Papa. I should be honored...I did not mean...it's only that..." Alita's lips formed a shaky smile.

Marvella began to open her mouth, no doubt to clarify the importance of social connections, and Lady Elaina was determined to put an end to that. "I was indifferent to my presentation to society, but Alita cares very much. Something must be done."

She knew very well that the only way to quiet her mother was to agree with her, and even that was not always successful.

"Alita, I shall tell you what I have rarely told anyone." Marvella sighed heavily, as if she were struggling with a secret that must be protected at all costs, her pale blue-gray eyes suddenly lucid.

"Yes, Grandmamma?" Alita asked with a sudden interest.

"I myself was not liked by the other girls at my coming out. Yes, I know it is difficult to believe, but there it is. You see," she added in a whisper, as if the words were poison, "I was not in their social class."

"Yes, I know, Grandmamma, you were the daughter of a vicar, which is quite respectable."

"Now I am above them all, of course," she added modestly, "but I was born the daughter of a vicar." She explained this as if she had not heard Alita.

"But why...why didn't they like you, Grandmamma?"

"It is astonishing, isn't it?"

"Possibly because you were too shy," Lady Elaina suggested.

"I don't *think* that was it," Marvella considered, shaking her head. "But possibly. Although I went out of my way to be exceedingly friendly to everyone. I think I know better than to sit in a corner!"

"Why, then, Grandmamma?"

"It was because I was so much more beautiful than the other girls," she smiled broadly as if she still thought herself to be so. "Don't stare at me so, Elaina! I thought you were all for speaking the truth!"

"Indeed," replied Lady Elaina. "The truth shall set us free."

"But they had to come up with another reason to dislike me," added Marvella.

"What was the reason they presented?" Alita asked quietly but with a decided interest.

"My gowns." Her voice resumed its normal pitch, her expression haughty. "I wore dresses created by my sister Jane. No one living before or since has a better eye for fashion than my sister Jane. And yet the other young ladies had the audacity, the effrontery"—she choked on her words—"to comment that my gowns were not sewn by any of the modistes in their employ. They laughed at me outright! And why? Never mind that my gowns were more modish than theirs and actually came into mainstream fashion some years *later*! I was ahead of them all! But that wasn't the point. Or possibly it was."

"What was the point then, Grandmamma?"

"They desired a reason to look down on me so they fabricated one. Their snobbery was based on a lie."

"A...*lie*?"

"Don't you see, Alita? The same thing is happening here." Marvella's eyes narrowed. "They needed an *excuse* to thwart the competition—and they created one."

Lady Elaina stared at her mother in shock, astonished at her comprehension. London flew by outside the carriage window as the seconds ticked by, marked by the glistening of the large diamonds on the dowager duchess's chest. There was a long pause while Alita stared at her grandmother with interest.

"Oh, I don't think..." Alita considered. "And what happened, Grandmamma?"

"I'll tell you what happened, my girl." Marvella smirked. "Your grandmamma showed them all. That's what happened. I did not need the little vipers' approval I usurped them all and made the greatest catch of the season, Richard Lancastor, His Grace the Duke of Salford." Her lips trembled as she reflected upon her late, dear husband.

"But how lonely you must have been..." Alita murmured.

"Lonely?" asked Marvella, confused. "When I had Richard?"

"Mother, do you not see that Alita is of a different temperament? She does not have your... competitive...nature, though it would certainly come

The Paradox: The Soldier and the Mystic	*71*

in useful in this circumstance," she added under her breath. "Alita has always been well accepted by other young ladies, and her friends are important to her."

"It appears that she did not choose well," concluded Marvella.

"Indeed. But the relevant point is that it does not further Alita's cause for her to be distressed or on the outskirts of the social sphere of acceptance." Lady Elaina added, resolute, "We must contrive a way to ensure Alita's happiness."

"Yes," Marvella stated with resolve. "It will be necessary for Alita to embark on a fashionable trip. The gossip will die away, Alita will return more appealing than ever imbued with a touch of mystery, and some other piece of malicious gossip directed at someone else will be in the wind by her next season."

"Precisely so," agreed Lady Elaina with conviction. "She must go to Paris or Venice or some other locale equally in vogue."

"Most definitely," stated Marvella.

* * * *

It occurred to Alita that their minds were in a rare state of unity, rapidly devising a plan for her future while the object of their plotting sat quietly between them.

"She will need a chaperone," Lady Elaina pronounced. "A person of unquestionable reputation and standing, someone who will lend countenance to her every action. Someone with whom it would make sense that Alita should suddenly up and away." Lady Elaina smoothed her pale blue cashmere neo-Greek costume, the gold embroidery of a Greek key pattern catching the light. Only her mother could wear such a dress to advantage. Even the transparent sleeves of white pineapple silk seemed to shimmer in the moonlight.

"*I* shall attend her. No one shall *dare* speak ill of my granddaughter or do her a wrong turn while I still breathe air." Marvella's face grew even more hard and determined, if that were possible. She suddenly feared for anyone who should get in the duchess's way.

"Nothing could be better for Alita than to be accompanied by the Dowager Duchess of Salford." Lady Elaina smiled as if this was precisely the outcome she had hoped for. "I myself cannot ignore my responsibilities, but now that you don't have the duke to care for, it will do you good as well to apply your considerable and unique talents to someone who desperately needs them."

Alita nodded. She perceived immediately the wisdom in the plan, although leaving London and her home was the last thing in the world that appealed to her.

"Very good," stated Marvella smugly as she settled into her velvet cushion. "Where shall we go? Paris? Venice? Switzerland?" Marvella reached for a petit four among the sachets and appointments, which had been left in the carriage by the servants.

With the question of location, Alita suddenly was aware of an odor that did not belong here among the scents of lavender, perfume, and confections—a decidedly masculine scent of leather and musk and…raw energy.

This could not be. She *always* initiated the contact. What was happening to her? She had not attempted to reach anyone, and yet someone was searching for *her*. Of that she was certain.

In an instant, an involuntary trance gripped Alita in its throes. She struggled to avoid slipping away.

Before today she had never been claimed by a dream state, and now twice in the course of a day! She was having some success fighting it when, once again, she saw the *Black Panther*, as if he were hunting her. That first encounter with this beast was the reason she was in this terrible predicament, Alita reminded herself as she fought the vision.

And then she was overwhelmed with the smells, delicious and exotic, of cinnamon and honey, dates and frying bananas, mint tea, saffron, jasmine, olives and cheeses, garlic and cucumbers, frankincense and sweet cicely, and the smell of dry, hot earth saturated with the waters of a mighty river.

And masculine scent.

It was intoxicating, an extravagant outpouring of hospitality and sensual delights, both caressing her with promise and igniting her curiosity.

The force of the invitation was even greater than her considerable reservations, and she felt herself moving toward him. As much as she was grieved by the outcome of her initial vision did she yearn to know the state of the *Black Panther's* affairs. Timidly she searched for this incredible man

The Paradox: The Soldier and the Mystic 73

whom she had seen only in animal form. Curious, Alita strove to view his human form, to no avail.

He came closer. He was a huge predator, his muscles highly developed, his senses keen, and his cunning evident as he prowled in the moonlight. He had lost interest in sustenance and did nothing but roam, traveling as much as sixty miles in a night as he remained in a tortured state.

Instantly he looked up, his silver-blue eyes revealing that he knew he was being watched. There was a large mahogany tree before him, and the deep, dark red tones seemed the perfect setting against his sleek, black hair. He turned suddenly, expecting death in the next instant, looking forward to the relief at the same time he instinctively fought it.

He was the most magnificent creature she had ever encountered, and yet his heart ached for death! He rejected life at the same time his survival instincts embraced it ferociously and without thought.

His image, his character, and the state of his emotions hit Alita like a bolt of lightning. The *Black Panther's* power and skill frightened her in its magnitude. His intelligence astonished her. She had never before encountered such bravery, and the strength of it seemed to fill all of London as her spirit intertwined with his. The *Black Panther's* ability to focus through the most terrifying and disturbing of experiences mesmerized her.

His grief overwhelmed her. With the magnitude of the *Black Panther's* qualities, the characteristic which struck her with the greatest impact was his grief.

And yet, the depth of his convictions entranced her. All at once she felt remorse and shame for her own pain, for wallowing in the fact that she had been outcast by the highest echelon of society. This man had made true sacrifices, had forfeited everything he might have personally wished for in obeying his country's commands, and he was suffering deeply. She had had her lollipop taken away and was standing in the middle of a candy store crying, and he, this worthy, magnificent creature, had had his heart ripped out and was lying in a pool of blood in the desert.

Alita had never been more shaken by any experience or person in her life. She had entered into the minds and feelings of many people, and none before had overtaken her, *become* her.

How had he contacted her? Was he aware of the contact on a conscious level? And why had no one else in her life been able to initiate a communication with her? She had stumbled upon the *Black Panther* accidentally in searching for Colin, but something incredible and entirely unknown to her had been initiated as a result of that happenchance meeting.

In the past she had only observed others. But now something was happening to *her*.

Why? Amidst the war and predictable sights, she had seen something—someone—she never expected to see. His was a spirit very different from others she had known—stronger, steelier, and yet, somehow, softer as well.

The *Black Panther* was a powerful being—but without the heart to use his power. Society had presented him with a path, which he had rejected, but no other path was known to him.

But she could see another path. Shocked with the realization, Alita turned it around in her mind again. Another path, a better path, began to form vaguely in her mind, unclear and yet persistent.

She knew that this unusual man had a great, untapped potential. No one of his acquaintance perceived it. Amazingly enough, *neither did he.* She gasped as she realized with a sudden clarity that the *Black Panther* considered himself to have little of value to contribute to the world. Alita shook her head, awestruck. The *Black Panther* was the most underutilized person she had ever encountered.

Suddenly she saw what she thought to be a vision of the future. She knew not how, as one vision faded into another. Alita looked above the man's head, still in panther form in her mind's eye, and there were tongues over his head, cool, soothing water and tongues. She saw people of different nationalities encircling him and bowing to one another in a sign of friendship and trust.

As Alita returned to the present moment without warning, she longed not to return to her own life. She sought out the vision, but it was gone. Her mouth still watered from the smells even though she was far from hungry. She had never been more centered or more clear, and she yearned to stay in the trance.

"Alita!" the duchess exclaimed, her voice sounding to Alita like a screech, jarring her calm. "Answer me, girl! Where shall we go?"

"I am thinking, Grandmamma. Please give me a moment. There is much to consider." The devastation Alita had only just experienced at the Queen's Ball collided with the content of her trance. In an instant, she understood the

The Paradox: The Soldier and the Mystic 75

meaning of her vision and why it had been given to her. She sorely wished otherwise, but she heard the command as clearly as if the order had been delivered by the queen herself.

She had been untrue to her nature almost the entirety of her life. Granted, the one instance in which she had been entirely faithful to her character, disaster had ensued, she reminded herself bitterly.

Nonetheless, she knew beyond the shadow of a doubt that she was being called to service, surprisingly a service that only she could perform. A day which was supposed to be about her pleasure had turned into something far different.

No! No! Alita pleaded, closing her eyes and shaking her head. *Please, no.* The one thing she did know was how to obey, and she longed to forget that lesson with all her heart.

And then she smelled the corpses, the stench stifling. Her lungs felt as if they were collapsing in her chest. She saw an image of another battle, worse even than Tel-el-Kebir. She knew, somehow, that she had the piece in her hand that would stop this onslaught.

She opened her now-watering eyes, stunned. Someone greater than herself believed in her, of that there could be no question. No doubt her contribution was some very small but necessary piece in a much greater puzzle. She would know when the time came, of that she could be sure. At any rate, she would certainly not ignore a direct order from the heavens. She might be a stupid, hapless girl, but she was not that imprudent.

"Alita, are you all right?" Lady Elaina asked anxiously.

"Yes, Ma-ma," Alita replied softly, not quite sure that she was. She released the air in her lungs, and the hideous smell began to fade as her resolve increased. She could not selfishly ignore another's pain when there was something she and only she could do to help. As strange as the idea sounded as she turned it 'round in her mind, her heart knew it to be true— she was uniquely qualified to assist. When she had completed her task, she would return home and set about reclaiming her dreams of marriage, family, and love. She was compelled to go *somewhere*, why not somewhere where she could do some good?

Alita wrung her hands with the realization that she was moving toward doing something she dearly wished not to do. She took a deep breath and steeled herself.

"Egypt," she said delicately but with finality. "We shall go to Egypt." Miss Alita Stanton rarely spoke in absolutes or in an uncooperative tone of voice, but her answer to her grandmamma was expressed without compromise.

As she heard the words for the first time, Alita felt a sense of surprise and shock, mirroring the expressions on her mother's and grandmother's faces.

For a girl who had only a vague sense of purpose some twenty-four hours prior, Miss Alita Stanton suddenly was a woman who knew her mind very well indeed.

Chapter Eight

"EGYPT!" exclaimed Marvella. "Girl, have you gone quite mad?" she demanded, gaping at her granddaughter as if she didn't know her.

"There is a war in Egypt!" Lady Elaina exclaimed, staring at her daughter in disbelief.

"Britain has won the war," Alita replied matter-of-factly, patting away the tears on her cheeks with her lace handkerchief. Her nonchalance stood in marked contrast to her near hysterics only minutes ago. "The Egyptian army has been reorganized under British officers. Control of Egypt has effectively passed to the queen. Didn't you know this, Mother?" she asked, surprised, a hint of disappointment in her voice, her eyebrows raised.

"I don't believe your information has been confirmed as yet, Alita," Lady Elaina countered, wondering if the shock of the day had overtaken her daughter. She would not have believed the scene unfolding before her if she had not seen it with her own eyes. A moment ago the girl had been a basket beggar. Now there was a hint of condescension in her tone, proposing traversing into a war zone as one might discuss how to boil an egg or darn a sock. "And regardless of the report we receive, it still might not be safe," she added in a shaky voice.

"It is quite safe, Mother, I assure you."

Lady Elaina studied Alita intently, making note of her serenity. She had learned to pay attention to her daughter's hunches. On more than one occasion, Alita had warned her not to administer a particular drug to a patient and to pursue a different diagnosis.

But this proposed journey filled her with extreme misgivings. No, *terror*. Alita was born with a special gift, but she was not omniscient. She was still an imperfect person growing up. She suffered and felt pain. Today was proof of that. She had hopes, dreams, misperceptions, and disappointments.

Lady Elaina knew that Alita accessed the feelings of a person she encountered, but those feelings could only be interpreted within the context of her understanding. Moreover, Alita focused on the person in question and contemplated a specific area of concern. People were like crystals, with countless sparkling facets, worlds unto themselves. A person might have a deadly disease, and Alita would not know it unless she was specifically in tune with that condition. Alita could perceive one's distress or pain, but whether or not she could diagnose was dependent on her focus and on how emotionally joined she was to the subject in question.

Worse, Lady Elaina thought with dread, a person might have a demented, dangerous quality which Alita was not aware of if she were, instead, in tune with the individual's positive attributes.

So how could her daughter know the truths of an entire country with accuracy? If individual people were multifaceted, what about an *entire country* of millions of people?

Lady Elaina's heart sank in her chest. Why not an invaded country that had just been overtaken by a foreign enemy, the race of which her daughter shared?

"Egypt is quite fashionable, as fashionable as Paris or London and certainly more exotic," Alita continued offhandedly. "Everyone has been to Paris. To have been to Egypt could make one a sensation alone. Don't you recall the notoriety attached to anyone who attended the grand opening of the Suez Canal? It was the social coup of the decade."

Alita had long been a malleable child. At the moment, none of that agreeable nature was apparent.

"Besides," Alita added unconvincingly, "I wish to see the pyramids."

* * * *

And the Black Panther. Though Alita wished she could forget her vision, the images had both entranced and disturbed her greatly.

She gazed back at her mother and grandmother staring at her as if she had metamorphosed into an apparition before their eyes. *Has she lost her mind?* their expressions read.

Alita began to wonder that herself.

The Paradox: The Soldier and the Mystic 79

"Alita! Are you listening to your grandmamma?" the duchess exclaimed. "I will *not* tolerate this insolence. And let me be perfectly clear on one other point. I shall *not* go to Egypt."

"Oh?" Alita asked. "You don't think you would enjoy seeing Egypt, Grandmamma? The pyramids and the ancient tombs?"

"No, I most certainly do not. Nor do I wish to cavort with foreigners. Nor do I wish to embark on such a long journey. Nor do I have any interest in historical artifacts—nor history of any type, for that matter." Marvella reflected on her words momentarily before continuing in a softer voice. "Well, I do like to visit Versailles or any museum containing jewelry and gowns, of the *European* style."

"My dear Grandmamma, I did not know. Please do forgive me," Alita remarked with contrition. "I would never ask you to do anything you did not wish no matter how much pleasure it might afford me to have you with me. I will ask my Aunt Jane and Uncle Oroville to attend me."

"You will *what*?"

"Uncle Oroville has traveled the world and has no fear of any foreign waters."

"Excuse me, young lady? Did I say that I *feared* Egypt? I most certainly did not! I merely said that I did not *wish* to go," retorted Her Grace. "It is very important in conversation not to change the meaning of other people's words. I notice that you do that quite a bit, Alita."

"I am sorry, Grandmamma. I misunderstood quite obviously."

"Your Aunt Jane?" Marvella cleared her throat. "Certainly not. She is not suitable. She will lend you no countenance."

"Mother, that is most unkind and *untrue*. Aunt Jane always dresses in the first style of fashion, besides being possessed of a charm and warmth to whom *few* can aspire." Lady Elaina stared pointedly at her mother.

"True," agreed Alita. "And despite Aunt Jane's great sense of style in both fashion and manner, she never considers herself too good to speak to anyone or to help anyone. She extends her kindness and generosity of character to all, whether or not they deserve it."

"Precisely my point. Jane speaks to positively everyone rather than reserving her kindness for the truly *important* people. A quality which is unfortunately shared by *that man* she married! Oroville Lovett," she muttered with a wave of the hand as if the movement had the ability dissolve the marriage. "That vagabond would finalize Alita's descent!"

"Uncle Oroville?" asked Alita. "He is the dearest, kindest person alive. And also among the wisest and most intelligent."

"And so he is," added Lady Elaina thoughtfully, "but Uncle Oroville is also boisterous and jovial and…"

"Happy?" asked Alita. "Every place he leaves, people are happier and are left with a smile on their faces. I shall never understand why being refined necessarily means being dull and quiet and leaving everyone feeling gloomy."

"Until you *do* understand that, my dear, we shall need to keep a particularly close eye on you," stated her Grace uncompromisingly.

They hit a bump in the road, and all three ladies bounced, as if to add emphasis to the pronouncement.

"The fact remains," stated Lady Elaina, "that Oroville Lovett is a retired seafaring man who is more colorful in both personality and attire than a peacock in mating season. Though he might have many friends himself, he is not the type of chaperone for a girl who is on the fringes of society."

Alita shook her head in disagreement, unmoved by the opposition. "Uncle Oroville would be excellent as protection. He fears no one, knows how to use all weapons, and is astute and levelheaded."

"Weapons?" exclaimed Marvella. "Good gracious, girl, now you are purposely planning a trip to a location where you need weapons! Let us all be off to America, then, if we wish to die!"

"Don't be absurd, Grandmamma. Egypt is perfectly safe. It is British-occupied and has been for some years since Disraeli instigated the coup which placed Britain as one of the majority owners of the Suez Canal. Ma-ma says that the Suez Canal Company runs Egypt, don't you Ma-ma?"

"Yes…There was a recent failed attempt by nationalists to recover the country for Egyptians—hence the war—but the country has been run by the Suez Canal Company for some time and continues to be. But the war is strongly indicative of unrest in the country."

"Don't talk your politics to me!" snapped Marvella. "Just deal in the facts! Then why do you need to take along *weapons*?"

"We shan't, of course! But how can it not be to one's advantage to have protection, Grandmamma? It is always preferable to have a gentleman

The Paradox: The Soldier and the Mystic

81

along, don't you always say so?" asked Alita demurely. "Paris is safe, too, but one increases one's safety when traveling with a gentleman and taking all the precautions."

"Alita, dear, you have just been dealt a terrible blow." Lady Elaina seemed to feel that the conversation was running astray. "You have been rejected by your friends, whom you love, on the most anticipated day of your life. Possibly you are seeking to run from your life, from everything which is familiar to you?"

"No, Ma-ma," she replied smoothly, shaking her head vehemently at her mother's misunderstanding. She personally had no desire whatsoever to go to Egypt. "I wish to go to Egypt because there is a purpose for me there, an opening for something greater than myself to instruct me."

"*God forbid,*" Marvella groaned. "You sound like your mother. Indeed we must away quickly." In her strongest tone she added, "This is my final word, Alita Stanton. I am *not* going to Egypt, and *neither are you.* You shall go somewhere where I can accompany you. This is your best hope of getting out of this predicament. I have had just about enough of this nonsense, and it is time to make some serious plans. I don't blame you for this unfortunate situation, dearest, but it is now time to turn our minds to solving it."

"Yes, Grandmamma, I agree that my chances of success are greatest if you accompany me. And I would very much enjoy your company." Alita declared politely with steel in her voice, "But I *am* going to Egypt."

Both Marvella and Lady Elaina stared at Alita in obvious disbelief. In all honesty, it was unprecedented for her to speak in absolutes and to defy authority. She had always been easy to mold and to shape, and both her mother and her grandmother were visibly stunned at this change in personality at a time when she *most* needed to comply.

She surprised even herself. Nothing had been more important to her than her presentation in society for as long as anyone could remember, and suddenly she was acting as if she had another agenda.

Chapter Nine

I have been commanded to appear before the King of Egypt! He ran his fingers over the sharp parchment edges of the note crumpled in his left hand from Sir Evelyn Baring, 1st Earl of Cromer and Consul General of Egypt, who was, for all intents and purposes, the supreme ruler of Egypt. It was a well-known fact that the royal family was merely a figurehead and that Sir Evelyn Baring ran Egypt.

Why have I been summoned? Val Huntington stood outside the British Consulate, officially the Office of the Consul General of Egypt, staring at the heavy mahogany door that separated him from the answer.

Not that he gave a damn, but he was still in the army, and he would prefer not to end his career by dishonoring his family. He might no longer have his personal integrity, but his family honor was, as yet, intact.

How could he think about himself and his questionable *honor* when so many, both English and Egyptian, had died?

Just as the Egyptian he had seen die. No, the Egyptian whom *he had killed*. He had gone to visit Banafrit's children, to look after their needs, and it had provided him with endless self-torture.

But who deserves to be tortured more than myself?

Val shook his head in self-recrimination. The Crown could run a sword through his heart or lock him in prison, but he would not kill again for territory or for gold.

Bloody hell. Val cursed to himself, disturbed by his own thoughts which he could not seem to control. Everything seemed out of control since Tel-el-Kebir.

And now it was as if he was having a conversation in his head with someone.

The likely explanation was that he was going mad, Val concluded.

Don't you know what side you are on, Ravensdale? Don't you know where your loyalties lie? Are you a coward or a traitor?

The Paradox: The Soldier and the Mystic

Suddenly he felt a presence, a breath on his ear, a whisper without words. He turned immediately, drawing his sword, and saw no one.

He felt as if he were awake in a nightmare. He returned his sword to its sheath and leaned against the wall, his heart pounding in his chest. He felt...misplaced. He who had always known himself so well.

Yes, I have many questions. But he seriously doubted that he would find any answers in the British Consulate. Despite his unholy skepticism, Val continued to gaze fixedly at the massive door as if secrets were encrypted in the wood grain even as a few people walked in and out. He couldn't fathom why he had been summoned, and he cared even less, but he was ready to tell someone, anyone, of his resignation.

The consul general would do as well as anyone.

Entering the rambling stone building on Rue Maghrabi, the imposing mahogany door creaked as if it might come off its hinges. The carpet was a sickening mustard color, and the drafty, discolored windows were adorned with dirty velveteen curtains edged with little woolly balls, the purpose of which escaped him. The ceilings were shocking in dark green and gold.

His surroundings did nothing to reduce the incoherence and confusion that he felt. Finding the consul-general's offices, he was greeted with reserve by Lord Cromer's secretary. From the expression on the secretary's face, Val surmised that he must look as if he was suffering from a night of drinking.

If the truth be told, drink had more appeal to him than food at the moment, and he could not remember when he had last eaten.

As he entered the connecting door into Lord Cromer's private office, the methodical neatness and cleanliness of the office was in stark contrast to the exterior. The building was outdated, bordering on dilapidated, but nothing was out of place in Lord Cromer's office.

"Ravensdale." The British Consul General studied the Earl of Ravensdale for some moments without speaking, his face displaying no emotion. "I must say you don't look well. Is your health failing you?"

"Sir Evelyn, you summoned me."

Lord Cromer raised his eyebrows. "First, Ravensdale, let me congratulate you on behalf of the Crown for your victory at Tel-el-Kebir."

Val was certain his expression froze into a stare as he nodded, but this was the only way he could control his temper. And he was not terribly invested in control at the moment.

"You appear to take no pride in a difficult victory, Ravensdale." Lord Cromer motioned to Val to be seated, studying him with a hard, expressionless demeanor.

"That is correct, Sir Evelyn," Val muttered. Pouring sherry into a delicate crystal glass, Lord Cromer offered the glass to Val, which he refused.

"Ravensdale, I have heard through the grapevine that you are an expert on speaking and writing in Arabic, also in ancient Coptic." Lord Cromer frowned. He was generally known to take the direct approach. "Quite an accomplishment. You haven't been in Egypt long."

"An interest of mine," Val acknowledged matter-of-factly. As if to apologize for his gift, he added, "Languages come quite easily to me."

"Indeed." Lord Cromer's expression grew even more serious, if that were possible, as he swirled his sherry. "Ravensdale, you may or may not know that we are putting into place an interim government until the Egyptian government can be restored. There are bloody few people here— on our side—who speak both languages. There are many Egyptians who speak English, but I can't trust them. They think we are the enemy."

"Astonishing." *What was their first clue? The dead bodies strewn across the desert?*

"I need someone I can trust," stated Lord Cromer evenly, even as he raised his eyebrows.

"Ah," remarked Val, noncommittally. *We come to the point.* "Someone who is for British interests rather than for Egyptian interests."

"No, Ravensdale. The two are one and the same. I set the financial affairs of India straight and got the country in working order, and I will restore order in Egypt as well." Lord Cromer leaned back in his chair as he studied Val, everything about him neat and meticulous, from his three-piece suit with its satiny sheen to his short, trimmed hair and perfect moustache to the books behind his desk. Val had always hated the perfect regularity of government officials, so different from the unpredictability of the battlefield.

He looked up to see that the paint on the ceiling overhead was peeling.

The Paradox: The Soldier and the Mystic   *85*

"Restore order? Could you elaborate, Sir Evelyn?" asked Val carefully. One never went on the attack before all the information was in hand.

"My dear boy, we are here to help the Egyptians, to right the wrongs inflicted on them by their own royal family." Lord Cromer's tone was hopeful. "Britain purchased the Suez Canal without bloodshed after King Ishmael backed himself into a corner through extravagant spending and subsequent massive national debt. We saw our opportunity to buy up the debt and did so."

"Ah, yes. Very unwise to amass a national debt which can be purchased by a rich enemy," Val nodded in apparent agreement.

"Enemy?" Lord Cromer cocked an eyebrow. "I don't catch your drift, Ravensdale."

"We were just at war with Egypt," Val offered, "as you pointed out when I arrived."

"I am now speaking of the purchase of the Suez Canal, all perfectly legal and above board." Lord Cromer tapped his pencil on the desk.

"Beyond a doubt." Val smiled broadly. "And yet, some charge that Egypt is the prototype for just such a form of imperialism which utilizes financial means to gain a foothold in countries with desired resources. Loans with impossible terms are the most frequently utilized. Once the smaller nation defaults on the loan, an invasion follows under the guise of protecting *national interests*. In the end, the invading country controls the economic infrastructure of the smaller country and, therefore, controls *everything*."

Lord Cromer's hard expression turned cold.

"Does the scenario sound *familiar* Sir Evelyn?" Val pressed, moving slightly forward in his chair.

"Certainly not," Lord Cromer replied, indignant. "We are here to assist the Egyptian people."

"We are gentlemen, Sir Evelyn. Let us not dance around the truth." It wasn't that Val was ready to exit the army and to go home. He simply didn't care one way or the other. As far as he was concerned, he had nothing to lose. "Or would you care to call it a *friendly visit* with the murder of Her people, the forced entrenchment of our government, and the usurping of the natural resources?"

"I would *not*. I would call it defending British interests with benevolence." Lord Cromer countered flatly.

"Benevolence?" Val chuckled. "Is there such a thing as a benevolent takeover? Twenty wars in eighty years. Twenty wars in this century alone."

"Keep in mind, Ravensdale, that the vast majority of the British people fully support our presence here."

"It is not difficult to rally popular support for the assault on a non-Christian nation of immoral savages," Val remarked offhandedly. "Was it the Zulu King Cetshwayo who said, 'First comes the trader, then the missionary, then the red soldier'?"

"I certainly don't regard the Egyptian people as such." Lord Cromer tapped his fingers on his desk as he studied him with an expression that would have shot fear through a lesser man. "Simply a less developed people requiring our guidance."

"Guidance?" Val laughed outright. In an instant his voice became very quiet, though his tone was harsh. "This was a violent act of aggression. Whether through legal means or not, it makes no difference. There was, in fact, an Egyptian uprising in response to the Crown's takeover of Egypt, and a war ensued. Hence the Battle of Tel-el-Kebir. If not for British interference, the Mahdi would now be in charge, and more significantly, the Suez Canal would not be under British control."

"And what would that outcome mean for the Suez Canal and English commerce?" Lord Cromer's expression grew clouded and his tone demanding. "Disastrous."

"So it is acceptable to usurp a country if they have a resource which we want? I thought we were discussing the poor Egyptians who need our help. Suddenly we come to the real reason we are here. We were frightened, so we took what we wanted."

"I make no apology for placing the security of my homeland above all other concerns," Lord Cromer replied with finality.

"Of course we should be concerned about security—and there are far-more effective methods to advance that goal. I would have expected the human race to be at a higher stage by now. We are clubbing people on the head because they have something that we want." Val studied his hands absently and then returned his full gaze to Sir Evelyn. "It's not about solving the problem. It's barbarism. A truly benevolent country would be helpful rather than opportunistic."

"Helpful? Very true, Ravensdale. I share your concern for the Egyptian

The Paradox: The Soldier and the Mystic 87

people and am determined that we shall be helpful." Lord Cromer stared at Val a long while before responding, appearing to gather his thoughts. "I couldn't agree with you more on this point. We have taken over Egypt's finances, but the plan is to leave as soon as Egypt is able to run herself. And, believe me, I am the man for the job. I proved that in India. In all events, the queen thinks so."

"And what were your methods in India, Sir Evelyn?" asked Val, sighing heavily.

"Low taxation, being sensitive to the needs of the peasant population, and giving the public what they want before they ask for it."

"Giving the public what they *want*? You can't be serious, Sir."

"I am."

"Regardless of how exemplary a job you do, Sir Evelyn, you will be hated by the Egyptian people. This is a foregone conclusion." Val shook his head. "Freedom is a fundamental desire and right of every people. Self-government is an unalienable right. No country is perfect. Britain is not perfect, but do we want other countries to force us to become better? We would blast them off our shores and tell them to mind their own bloody business if they stepped foot on our lands to *assist* us."

"Hmmm," considered Sir Evelyn, placing his finger to his chin as he leaned back in his chair. "On what do you base your opinion of my unpopularity?"

"I keep my ear to the ground," he replied simply. As he studied Sir Evelyn, Val reflected that the British Consul was clearly expedient in all things and unafraid of the truth. Val could not help but like him despite his fury over Egypt's occupation. Even so, he had no intention of revealing names.

"Just as I thought." Lord Cromer moved forward in his chair. "This is why we need you, my boy. Egyptians assume that you don't know what they are saying and they let things slip."

"You want *me* to spy for you?" Val roared with laughter.

"How do I anticipate public opinion? By penetrating the general population and hearing their unguarded words." Lord Cromer pointed his index finger at him. "That's where you come in, Ravensdale. Can you do it?"

"Of course." He nodded. "If I wished to. But it wouldn't make a whit of difference, I can assure you, Sir Evelyn."

"And what would make a difference, Ravensdale?" Lord Cromer studied him.

"Leaving the country! Thievery and occupation is neither good diplomacy nor in the interest of our national security. Can we possibly fathom the ill will we are creating for future generations? We have invaded Afghanistan—*twice*—Egypt, Russia, China, India, and the list goes on and on. How many enemies can we afford in the next century? As industry and weaponry advances, who is to say how many people will die in the next century as a result of the ill-feeling created in this one?"

"You and I will nip that in the bud, Ravensdale."

"With all due respect, Sir Evelyn, as we create better and better weapons, coupled with the hatred we have instilled, it is conceivable that we will have set into motion a destruction of...vast proportions."

"You exaggerate, Ravensdale."

"What is your plan for Egypt, Sir Evelyn?" Val asked pointedly.

"Peace. Prosperity. Stability."

Val noted that "freedom" was absent from the list but listened without interruption as Lord Cromer cleared his throat thoughtfully. "The first task must necessarily be to put Egypt's finances in order so that it can meet its debt obligations. We must, of course, ensure the continued operation of the Suez Canal, which is critical to both national security and British commerce. Then I wish to introduce electricity to Cairo. Let's bring Egypt into the nineteenth century, my boy."

"The extreme poverty which exists in Egypt should make the English entrenchment an easy matter," Val stated off-handedly, but his hands were clenched in anger. "King Ismail literally taxed his people to the point of starvation."

"No, absolutely not, we will never use poverty as a way to exercise control. It is both morally reprehensible and mismanagement." Lord Cromer's expression was genuinely pained as he shook his head vehemently. "Prosperity is the only appropriate tool. Don't you comprehend the facts, Ravensdale? The Egyptian people were beaten, starved, and taxed to death under King Ismail. People didn't even have *bread*. They were living on barley meal mixed with water. It may offend your academic ideas

The Paradox: The Soldier and the Mystic   89

of freedom for people to have full stomachs, Ravensdale, but it won't disturb me in the least to put an end to suffering."

Val was convinced of Sir Evelyn's sincerity and drive. Sir Evelyn Baring would plow forward with or without his assistance.

"And the fact is that I'm the best you've got." Lord Cromer tapped his pencil on his desk, his lips forming a smile. "Any number of men could be placed in Egypt who would care less about the peasant population or the efficient running of the country—the former King of Egypt being a notable example. And power does not interest me, nor wealth. Merely efficiency and productivity. I am a simple magistrate, nothing more. This is my talent."

Val studied Sir Evelyn's awards on the walls momentarily, unconvinced of the simplicity of his character, before responding. "What is it you wish to know? Let me oblige you, sir, and then I shall be on my way." Val stretched his long legs out before him, his muscular frame being too large for the chair.

"Ravensdale, you have shown me your hand quite clearly. Truth is your master." Lord Cromer tapped his pencil on his gigantic oak desk as if to prove that he was a mere pencil-pusher with a talent for administration. His voice contained a tone of finality. "I desperately need someone who can discern the truth and will tell me without fear or reconstruction. You are a rare find in this regard. And your sources are good if somewhat biased."

"Biased from the English perspective but not from the Egyptian's. A terrorist from one perspective is a freedom fighter from another."

"Where we may differ in ideology, your skills and the information which you can collect for me is invaluable. In the end, we are both working for the Egyptian people and wish their greatest good. This is also evident to me."

"And if I refuse?"

"You would be court-martialed and sent home in dishonor."

"As I suspected," stated Val, shrugging his shoulders as if it were a matter of no moment with him. "I could always resign," he added.

"That won't be the official entry," stated Lord Cromer, smiling warmly. "Let's not start off on the wrong foot, Ravensdale. Your country needs you for a bit longer. That's the bottom line. It won't be long before you can go home. In the meantime, we all have a duty to fulfill, and as it happens, your unusual skills can actually be of use here."

Val raised his eyebrows.

"Have you found a great deal of interest in your knowledge of the Egyptian language on the country estate?" Lord Cromer laughed, smiling for the first time.

As Val considered his options, his gaze rested on the velvet pillows adorning Sir Evelyn's battered couch, new and untouched. They were out of place amongst all this deterioration, a rich royal-blue color, the purples and blues fighting each other for control. A slight breeze entered through the window, and the tassels wavered a bit. The breeze brought a scent of frying meat, and for the first time in weeks, he was hungry.

Val watched the tassels move with the wind. His reaction surprised himself. Funny that nothing seemed more important at the moment than staring at velvet decorative pillows.

Astonishingly, he suddenly felt more peace than he had in weeks.

Val reflected that it might suit him to linger in Egypt a bit longer while he considered his course. He would never again act against his conscience, of that he was certain. Better to die.

Easier to die.

Glancing out the window, his eyes rested on beautiful painted papyrus and magnificent carpets for sale on the sidewalk. Not for the first time, he considered that the Egyptians were an amazing people with a rich and impressive history. They claimed one of the most advanced civilizations that had ever lived on the face of the earth. Two of the seven wonders of the ancient world had been in Egypt. Her people were strong, brave, intelligent, and proud. They had suffered a temporary setback due to the greed and mismanagement of recent leadership. One hundred twenty thousand Egyptians out of a total Egyptian population of only four million people *died* building the Suez Canal. Now, when the canal was starting to make a profit, the canal no longer belonged to Egypt. Val grew determined to assist the Egyptian people in whatever way he could.

"Ravensdale?" Lord Cromer asked.

"Sir Evelyn, I love England, and I have come to love the Egyptian." Val shook his head, feeling the full weight of his inability to make a meaningful contribution to any endeavor he had yet undertaken. He might not have hope, but no one could say he was without discipline. "I doubt that I can be of any service here, but I am more likely to assist being in the thick of things

The Paradox: The Soldier and the Mystic 91

as not."

"Good, my boy." Lord Cromer grinned. "Cairo is a fascinating city, and we are now in peaceful times. Even as we speak, a new office is underway for the Consulate bringing jobs and income to Cairo."

"A *new* office? In these times?" Val looked around him.

"Yes," Lord Cromer nodded. "Britain has purchased a fifty-acre park along the Nile's east bank for the sum of £2,580. An excellent investment in valuable real estate. The building is progressing quickly."

"I have no doubt of that," murmured Val.

"The consulate building will provide both offices and living quarters. More economical that way. You shall reside there as will most of the staff." Sir Evelyn's expression grew suddenly stern. "One thing you must remember, Ravensdale, is though we both work for Egypt, you report to me. Your loyalties can be ascertained fairly quickly with the information presented and how accurate it turns out to be. Will you help me? Will you help Egypt?"

Val sighed. The war was over, and the English occupation of Egypt had begun.

Chapter Ten

It hit her like a bolt of lightning. She could only see his back, his features were not clearly visible to her, and he was at least one hundred feet away.

The Black Panther.

It could not be. But she knew beyond a shadow of a doubt that it was, even as her body felt an instant tremor and her eyes opened wide.

She caught sight of him outside the newly erected British Consulate office in Cairo, where she had heard the gardens were particularly beautiful. The walking roads to the office park were a maze—quite literally—and she was already feeling the full effect of the orchestrated confusion even without his sudden appearance.

Who is he? Involuntarily she covered her mouth with her hand as if to suppress a scream. It was the person in the world she most longed to know.

And most dreaded to find.

Why is he here? None of that mattered. None of that was relevant. She caught her breath even as the realization hit her. *I have found him.*

His appearance did nothing to settle her spirits. He was tall and muscular, his coal-black hair brushed back away from his face, with the exception of a lock of hair that fell forward across his forehead—possibly because he was traversing the lawns at an unholy pace. Despite his speed, even from a distance she could see that he scrutinized his surroundings with watchfulness, as if every moment held life and death.

But it was his spirit rather than his dark looks that told her in an instant this was the man she had come two thousand miles to find. *This is the Black Panther of my vision.* She sensed it in his intensity of movement and in the quiet aura of strength and purposefulness that emanated from him. She had never spoken to him, and she felt as if she knew him better than anyone she had ever known or would ever know.

The Paradox: The Soldier and the Mystic   *93*

A surge of excitement rushed through her. A man who had entered her dreams but whom she had never met was now within her view.

The air vibrated with his presence, causing her to tremble. The Black Panther had overwhelmed her being thousands of miles away. What impact would he have on her from this distance?

What will I say to him? How shall I act? Alita stood frozen as she stared at him. Although this had been the moment she had planned and anticipated for months, somehow she never truly expected to be living it.

I should have thought of this earlier! What if she destroyed everything—once again?

He turned to look at her, and she knew that he sensed her gaze. The minute his pale silver-blue eyes pierced her facade, Alita felt as if she were suddenly bathing in cool water. Almost immediately, a wave of power flowed through her.

Showing little interest in her, he studied her for only a moment before turning his attentions elsewhere. *Oh, no!* He was getting away.

"Sir, sir, please help!" Forcing herself to act, she began waving wildly and almost *shouting*—the Saints forgive her!—for the first time in her life ignoring her upbringing, which had trained her unrelentingly in refined deportment.

She could think of nothing else to do and therefore did the first thing that entered her mind to simply keep him in her vicinity another instant until she could resolve upon a plan.

"Miss, what is the matter?" He rushed toward her without a moment's hesitation, reaching her in seconds. Scrutinizing her, he appeared to draw his conclusions quickly. She caught her breath in her chest.

Here he is, not a foot from me! Her mind was racing for something to say.

She knew everything she needed to say. All the words were there, demanding expression.

And yet I can say none of it.

She shivered as he hesitantly touched her elbow as if preparing to support her. His eyes were a silvery liquid as he studied her. They had a piercing quality, which revealed that he was intensely focused and intelligent. As the sunlight hit his eyes, the depth of his gaze seemed to swallow her. He was devastatingly gorgeous—with an expression that would frighten the dead.

"Miss, are you all right?" he asked, but his disinterest was apparent. When he asked a question, she felt as if she wanted to answer just so his gaze would leave her.

At the same time she longed to stare into those eyes forever.

* * * *

Val considered that the girl expressed some anxiety, but nothing approaching shock. She appeared to be healthy and unharmed. Her hands shook, but her eyes were bright—shimmering, in fact—and her skin…well, it was…*glowing*. She smiled up at him, her lips trembling…

What am I doing? He was supposed to be determining if she were in harm's way or not. Even as he confirmed that she was able to stand on her own, he thought upon closer inspection that she was one of the most beautiful women he had ever beheld. Her eyes were a sparkling jeweled green, and her skin was the color of peaches and cream. She was slim and dainty in appearance, and she wore a peach silk gown trimmed in ivory lace with a matching hat perched provocatively atop her creamy beige curls.

And she interested him not at all. She was exceedingly becoming, true. And altogether too young for his taste. She had a shyness and sweetness of manner, which he found both dull and contrived. A beautiful, protected child who had seen and experienced nothing of the world and who no doubt lived in her fairy-tale world awaiting her prince charming.

Not this fellow, not on your life. In his early manhood he had attended the balls and soirées of the London season, meeting youthful beauties, and he had never been so bored in his life.

But her smile positively sparkled. And *those eyes*…like emeralds in a setting of pearls. He had to admit that she was precisely that which most young men liked to encounter—pure, innocent, hopeful.

Uninformed, delusional, vapid.

"Miss, what is the source of your distress?" he asked stiffly without feigning concern. He resolved to quickly exhibit the minimum civilities required so that he might be on his way and about his business. He had better things to do than to conjure imaginary foes with theatrical females. "I

The Paradox: The Soldier and the Mystic 95

don't recall ever having seen a woman wave quite so frantically," he voiced without smiling, despite not caring one way or the other.

"I was simply so frightened that I would lose you," she replied as she gasped for air, running her hands along her slim waist.

Val raised his eyebrows in surprise, and she took a step back involuntarily. She glanced up at him with a look so open and yet so demure that he was quite taken aback by the overall effect of her unexpected words.

He frankly felt some amazement at her arts. The Earl of Ravensdale was not one to experience surprise, outside of discoveries he might find in ancient texts, but this charming young beauty had almost dropped out of the sky. For just a moment, he forgot that he was in Egypt and twenty-eight years old and felt himself to be young and eager for the games to begin.

Have I abandoned all reason? I have work to do. Sir Evelyn required several reports. There was important information that only he could gather on the other side of Cairo. As much as he hated the idea of British occupation, he had to admit that Sir Evelyn was doing an excellent job of running Egypt—of lowering taxes while at the same time managing the finances, of initiating technological advances, and of reducing poverty. And Sir Evelyn was successful, in large part, by keeping his finger on the pulse of the population—which was the job entrusted to him.

And with the conclusion of his duties, he looked forward to pursuing his one true love—translating ancient text.

"If you should require nothing further, Miss, I shall be about my business." He forced himself to address her politely though he fully communicated in his tone of voice that he would brook no nonsense. He looked about and saw her maid some five feet away, watching quietly. There was nothing here that warranted his presence.

"Indeed I do. Please do not leave…" She turned and nodded to her maid, who retreated several more feet, insuring that her words were not overheard. Returning her eyes to his, her lips parted as she appeared dismayed and unable to find words. Val found himself studying those apricot lips as they opened and closed, offsetting the gold and green in her eyes to perfection.

"Where are you from, Miss? And what brings you to Egypt?" he asked, forgetting himself. In an instant, Val wished he had kept his mouth shut. It surprised him that he had not.

"I live in London." Her expression was delicate but flustered, almost *frightened*. She gazed up at him through long eyelashes. She hesitated, as if this was a difficult question to answer. A wave of something approaching pain washed across her face. Suddenly she appeared resolute. "And I came...I came...to find *you*, sir."

Lord Ravensdale stepped back on his heels. He could not believe his eyes and ears—a beautiful angel uttering advances in a manner that would do any bird of paradise proud.

"This is a line usually reserved for the gentlemen, Miss, but I admit your delivery is far more effective."

"Oh, it is not a *line*, sir, I assure you," she exclaimed, seeming to find her voice while giving an excellent performance of a young innocent in extreme discomfiture. Her countenance was direct, but her voice soft and shy, her wide eyes filled with awe and admiration. "I did come from England to find you. It has been an obsession these many months."

His eyes must have revealed his interest, because she started to stammer.

"Oh...I didn't m—mean..." Suddenly a look of comprehension washed across her face, and she blushed unmercifully. "It isn't *that*. I came for your benefit, not mine."

"Very good of you, Miss," he murmured languidly. *How did she manage the blush*? He smiled with appreciation. He was beginning to enjoy the show immensely. Being both handsome and titled, he had had many a trap set for him. He had to admit that he found the direct approach, accompanied with blushes and coy looks, by far the more enticing.

Val searched his memory in vain for even one other woman who had expressed her intent so sincerely. He glanced around and saw her maid now standing some eight feet away, her eyes to the ground. No hatchet-faced maid for this worldly miss, no, but a retiring, docile child.

The Earl of Ravensdale brought out his full arsenal, purposely producing a slow, lazy smile, which ordinarily would have made young maidens wobbly at the knees, he knew from experience. But she stood firm, her immodest methods and determination in some contrast to her shy mannerisms but evident nonetheless.

If she wishes to get serious, so can I. He had work to do. His eyes surveyed her with a forwardness he rarely allowed himself, and he found that it was a thoroughly pleasant exercise. She wore a form-fitting dress

The Paradox: The Soldier and the Mystic 97

from neck to floor, with the exception of fabric draping along her hips like a waterfall, with bow accents placed tantalizingly along that inviting pathway. Her silhouette revealed an exceptionally slim waist and pleasing bustline. The elaborately trimmed skirt had six-inch pleats all along the bottom of the skirt. A pointed bodice with a cascade of lace down the front of that lovely, small bosom and three-quarter-length sleeves completed the enticing picture.

He could not have been more surprised that she held firm under his sensual glance, making not the slightest movement to slap his face.

She was a woman who knew her own mind.

"Miss…? I am quite certain I have not had the pleasure of your acquaintance, or no doubt I would have remembered," he stated in a sultry voice, which was becoming more natural and less contrived.

"Oh, no, sir," she protested. "I am only presented to society this year, and that was of very short duration. I gather that you have been away from England for some time. My name is Alita Stanton."

"Miss Stanton, I assure you the pleasure is all mine," Lord Ravensdale said as he bowed gallantly, his gaze intent upon her as he surveyed her. He kissed her hand slowly as he looked up at her, making no effort to conceal the invitation in his eyes.

She smiled with some trepidation, once again blushing, all the while appearing quite distracted.

The sincerity of her delivery was bewitching. Though they both knew the truth, she played the game so well that he could not help but wish to enter into it.

She gave the appearance of one who was contemplating a problem of momentous proportions. Miss Alita Stanton was a curious blend of naiveté and uneasiness. But what possible reason for distress could she have?

"But, sir, I am afraid I do not know your n–name," she stammered.

He let out a roar of laughter. He had not believed this temptress could shock him any more. "So, Miss Stanton, you do not know who I am. And yet you have come from England to Egypt to find me?"

"Yes." She nodded self-consciously. She then blurted out without even a modicum of finesse, "I suppose it does sound odd."

"And I am supposed to believe that you did not just suddenly see me and decide to embark on a flirtation?" asked Val, making no effort to hide the glimmer of hope he was sure burned in his eyes. Though he fully expected his blunt delivery to result in a swift cessation of Miss Stanton's advances and her subsequent storming off in anger—one had to play one's cards correctly to avoid humiliating the gentler sex, how well he knew—he found no pleasure in the exchange if he could not engage in a truthful encounter. He saw no harm in putting an end to this masquerade and sending the girl on her way.

Here was her opportunity to go in search of more receptive prey.

"Oh no, sir, no!" She covered her mouth in alarm, as if to suppress a scream. She gasped, catching her breath. But she did not swoon, and there was not the slightest hint of anger in her expression. He liked that about her. It was a rare woman who would have taken no offense at his clarity. "I have come on a most important mission."

"A *mission*, you say? An odd choice of words, Miss Stanton."

"Not at all." She clumsily made efforts to steady herself where she stood as she glanced around nervously. She reached for his arm, and he offered it to her happily when only a few minutes before he would have been reluctant. "It is the correct word, I assure you."

"Do explain yourself, Miss Stanton. You have a devoted audience." And, in fact, he spoke the truth. He didn't know if he had ever been more attentive to a woman.

"If we could but speak privately for a moment." Miss Stanton turned and motioned to her maid, who maintained just enough distance to allow for private conversation as she followed them.

A slow smile came to his lips. The maid knew precisely what was expected of her, even without an interchange of language. This wasn't the first time Miss Stanton had engaged in a private *meeting*, and it wouldn't be the last.

"And, if you could but give me your name, sir, it would provide me with the greatest of relief." She made an obvious effort to steady her breath. "I have been longing to know it these many months and would hate to lose sight of you after this long journey."

Val studied the delicate beauty before him. She was either an excellent actress—or mad. For his sake, he hoped it was the former, though he wasn't entirely sure he cared at this point. Quickly he ascertained the possible

The Paradox: The Soldier and the Mystic 99

outcomes of the scenario before him, each of which was immanently agreeable.

Bloody hell! Odds that were contrary to reason, a game which was impossible to lose. And certainly a situation which did not come his way often.

Next Val considered the young lady before him from a scholastic point of view. This provocative beauty had not fainted of boredom, nor had she stormed off from insult. She had endured with equanimity his direct pronouncements. She seemed intensely interested in him in fact, he thought with an excitement he hadn't felt in some time. Nor was she insipid and predictable, insincerely fawning over him.

An irresistible combination.

"My name is Val Huntington," he stated, his gaze seductively memorizing everything about her. He gently led her to the left toward a path, when she had been inclined to go to the right. Three times out of four one ended up where one started on the grounds. *He mustn't lose this one.*

"Val Huntington, the Earl of Ravensdale? Your family holds the county seat?" she asked in a manner approaching academic retrieval. "I knew that you were an officer in the war, but I did not realize that you had stayed on in Egypt."

"Oh, I wouldn't feel badly about that, Miss Stanton. You seem to know a great deal about me," he replied in his most consoling tone of voice.

"I know no more than any young lady just out would know about the unmarried peerage," she stated with a slight indignation, slowing her pace.

She was not putting forth any effort to hide her intent. *Possibly that was the way she wanted it.* "Stanton...sounds familiar. Would I know your parents?" He reminded himself that she both had a maid and was dressed exquisitely. She was obviously moneyed.

"I wouldn't imagine so," she stated with a wave of the hand, as if she had no time for the niceties. As he watched her, Val thought that he could almost taste those lips. She added with an impatient shake of her head, the light reflecting off her buttery curls, "My father is not a peer of the realm, so you would not have met him in Parliament. At any rate, who I am is of no importance to my purpose."

"You don't say, Miss Stanton," Val drawled, lingering on the words. So, she was a member of the merchant class, a wealthy member from the looks of that expensive gown, which molded to her shape perfectly, out to nab a peer of the realm.

Or to have some fun on holiday while away from the uncompromising scrutiny of London society.

"Lord Ravensdale, may we please sit somewhere and talk? I have traveled a great distance, and I will simply die if I cannot tell you the purpose of my journey." She appeared more and more anxious.

"I beg you not to distress yourself, Miss Stanton," Val replied consolingly, feigning sympathy. "I assure you that I would not permit you to go without *telling* me the whole, so never fear on that subject."

"Oh, thank you, my lord." She sighed, her expression one of relief. She continued to give the impression of having some difficulty in standing, and Val strengthened his hold on her arm. "It does seem as if we are traveling in circles."

"We are, my dear. We are." For once, he didn't mind. Val didn't know when he had ever seen a prettier spectacle. He knew it was contrived, but a part of him wanted to pretend along with her. It had been so long since any woman had had the slightest effect on him, and this was considerably more than slight. "But if you require more *private* quarters, why don't we proceed to the consul-general's office and use his private sitting room? I know for a fact he is gone for hours. We can even lock the door. Unless this offends your sense of propriety?" he asked pointedly.

"No, my lord," she stated without hesitation.

"I didn't think so," murmured Val.

Next they came to the center of the estuary maze only to a find a sculpture of a giant fish facing the Nile. She gasped and almost turned full circle to behold it. "For someone not on a quest of the fanciful, the entire experience of simply walking to the consul-general's office would be somewhat perplexing."

He laughed out loud, not remembering the last time he had done so. "Quite so, Miss Stanton. Though caprice was no doubt the goal of the architect—one of those art-nouveau fairy-flapping types obsessed with moonbeams and talking animals—for the inhabitants of the office, the design has the effect of reducing the number of visitors. The goal of government officials everywhere."

She smiled, but her lips quivered even as she attempted it.

The Paradox: The Soldier and the Mystic 101

"Whatever is the cause of your distress, Miss Stanton?" As they reached the steps of the British Consulate building, framed by two marble lions, Val observed her anxiety mounting. He wanted no part of a liaison that was not entered into without reserve and mutually desired. He stopped in his tracks and faced her. "If the thought of my company is distasteful to you in the slightest, let us abandon the endeavor immediately."

"Oh, no! No! I beg you not to say such a thing, Lord Ravensdale!" Alarm crossed her face as she bit her lip. "It is merely that what I have to say to you is of such vital importance, and when I most need to have my wits about me, an unpleasant memory interferes with my presence of mind. I wouldn't expect a gentleman to understand." She looked up at him through long eyelashes, her eyes sparkling like emeralds floating in a river stream, the sunlight bringing out the golden flecks in her eyes.

"Just a washed up soldier, am I?" Val asked gently, escorting her up the steps. "Ah, you think me ignorant of the concerns of the fairer sex. I have been in the world more than you might think, Miss Stanton."

"Very well then, Lord Ravensdale, I shall explain." Her lips trembled, but the sudden trust revealed in her expression, almost as if she were sure of him, disconcerted him. "You see, I was cast out at the Queen's Ball following my presentation at court, by my dearest friends, no less. Ever since that day, I have had some difficulty maintaining my calm in situations of grave importance to me. It's as if...as if an unnamed fear sweeps over me. I struggle so diligently to control my fear that I lose sight of myself."

"You seem to know your own mind in a way few young ladies do, Miss Stanton."

"You don't understand, Lord Ravensdale." She shook her head.

"I am trying to, believe me." They had reached the front door of the embassy, and he was beginning to feel some anticipation. She stood gazing up at him under the crest of Queen Victoria containing all the floral emblems of the British Isles, as well as those of Upper and Lower Egypt.

"Oh, I do hope so, and I thank you for that, my lord." She smiled so sweetly, and it surprised him that it warmed his heart. He was generally not a fan of *sweet*.

"Believe me, Miss Stanton, the pleasure is all mine." And, strangely enough, *it was*. Even as he opened the door for her to enter and she stepped onto the magnificent Heriz carpet from Persia in the main reception room, he glanced down to see a wave of sadness wash over her face with his words, and he was immediately repentant for his brash response. Whatever her true motive as concerned him, she had been hurt at the Queen's Ball.

"A soldier's friends will die for him," he muttered under his breath. "If indeed silly girls would hurt you over something so self-centered as a presentation, good riddance to bad rubbish, my girl."

"Still I love them, and their rejection pains me," she whispered, walking past the twenty-sixth-dynasty alabaster canopic jars, positioned strangely in view with four watercolor paintings by the famous limerist, Edward Lear.

"It is difficult to have one's love and all that one is be a great inconvenience to those one holds dear," he uttered without meaning to. He saw that the grief in her eyes was genuine, and for just a moment he was captured there.

She opened her mouth to question him, but he did not wish to continue this line of conversation. He was mildly curious to learn how she had managed a presentation at court without a parent of the peerage. She obviously knew someone willing to sponsor her, and he would like to know whom. But they had arrived at Lord Cromer's rooms, and the answers to these and other questions no longer were paramount in his mind.

Again she hesitated, standing in front of the door to paradise.

"What is it, Miss Stanton?" His hopes wavered. "Have you remembered a pressing engagement?"

"*Oh, no!* It's just that…that…"

"Yes?" It felt like an eternity before she spoke again. "Please do tell me."

"I have certain *gifts*…"—she cleared her throat—"which I rely on in instances such as these. And I am distanced from them as well. It makes it more difficult for me to *understand* people. I don't expect you to entirely grasp my meaning, Lord Ravensdale. Suffice it to say that I can't seem to swim out from under my own emotions at the moment, in this case to make contact, so to speak."

"Difficulty in making contact, is it?" As he stared into the depths of her emerald-green eyes, he tried to remember his train of thought. "I know the feeling, Miss Stanton, believe me. But we shall do our best to remedy that."

As they entered Sir Evelyn Baring's plush sitting room, Val motioned to Miss Stanton's maid to remain in the antechamber while inviting Miss

The Paradox: The Soldier and the Mystic 103

Stanton to enter the inner office. He smiled as he observed that she raised no objections, nodding her approval to her maid. It was imperative that the three be seen entering and departing the closed quarters together else Alita Stanton could be ruined, but now that appearances were taken care of, there was now no doubt in his mind that Miss Alita desired a private audience, if there had been any doubt to begin with.

Once in the private chambers, Val locked the door and turned to face her. Swiftly, he turned and locked her into his arms. His mouth came down on hers with an urgency that shocked him, as did his reaction to her lips. He was desperate to entice her to yield to him. He placed his hand on the back of her head, pushing her closer to him.

She did not react initially to his kiss. He knew the moment when she gave into the force between them, timidly opening her lips for him. Her breath mingled with his as his tongue toyed with her lips, teasing her and playing with her. She arched her back and slowly parted her lips, allowing him to take possession of her mouth.

The strength of his attraction surprised him. Oh, it had been so long since he had kissed a woman like this, a stunningly beautiful woman of the world with airs of naiveté. She made everything about him feel alive. He was bathing in his own desire, his body and mind a stranger to him.

"Lord Ravensdale," she gasped, "what are you doing?" Suddenly she began pushing at his arms, though her strength was no match for the tension of his muscles tightly wrapped around her. She turned her head as he trailed kisses along her cheek.

"I thought this was what you wanted, Miss Stanton," Val replied with raw feeling, catching his breath. "Was I mistaken?" he asked, knowing from her response that he had not been.

"Sir, I had no intention—I…I can't say it was unpleasant, but you only distract me from my purpose."

"Not unpleasant?" he repeated in disbelief as he slowly released her. He studied her until he saw what he was looking for in her expression. "You wound me, Miss Stanton. Tell me, how do other kisses compare to that one? For my part, I found it quite unforgettable."

"Lord Ravensdale, I could not say. I have never been kissed before. But I certainly didn't expect my first kiss to be like *that*."

"Miss Stanton, I honestly can't remember when I have been so amused."
Val laughed heartily, slowly releasing her. It had been far too long since he
had known anything but grief. "Please, do sit, Miss Stanton." He motioned
to the sofa. "Make yourself comfortable and tell me your story, so that we
can continue with more pleasant endeavors."

"Lord Ravensdale," she protested, raising her eyebrows as she sat in the
muted plum wingback chair next to the brown leather sofa, clearly forcing
some space in between them, her feet squarely placed on a lavender-and-
blue Persian rug. "I knew that you could be deadly, but I had seen that your
heart was pure, so I perceived no danger to myself. Now I wonder!"

Deadly? A dead bore, more like it. "Please, Miss Stanton, tell your
story, and let us be done with the preliminaries." *It won't take me long to
pick you out of that chair and onto the sofa, but we must play the game in
order if it pleases you, my lady.*

He moved to the cadenza, where he poured himself a glass of sherry.
"Would you care for a drink, Miss Stanton?"

"A small cordial, please," she responded in a subdued tone of voice.

Val felt his lips curl into a slight smile. A young single woman did not
drink alone with a single gentleman. There was something in her manner
that suggested that there were absolutely *no rules* where he was concerned.

He found that he couldn't stop smiling in this woman's presence. He
was not himself. The Earl of Ravensdale was apt to be called melancholy at
best, dangerous at worst.

If she keeps this up, I might have to marry her, harlot or not. As he
glanced back at large gold-green eyes framed by blonde hair the color of
wheat, the idea appealed to him. Then he could have her all to himself.

Bloody hell. He had never in his life thought about marriage. Why
should he do so at a time like this?

She cleared her throat, took a sip, and patted her hair, as if these
inconsequential niceties would uphold the proprieties. She was pluck to the
backbone, Val had to give her that. She set her hat on the Queen Anne table
separating the leather couch and her chair, a move that met with Val's full
approval.

"Oh, it is no use." She sighed heavily. "I have very little hope that you
will believe me, but I can think of no other course than to simply tell the
truth. If you do not believe me, I will have at least done my best."

The Paradox: The Soldier and the Mystic 105

"By all means, Miss Stanton. Do your best, and I shall do mine." He did not believe that her distress was real, but he nonetheless took the opening and moved to sit as close to her as was possible.

"I vow I must maintain my distance." She held her hand up in protest. "I must not enter into your feelings, or I cannot possibly proceed through this."

"Please do continue, Miss Stanton," he repeated in his most reassuring voice, amazed at his reaction to her. He who had been privy to sophisticated military tactics had abandoned his duty within minutes of meeting her and was not long after unable to take his eyes off her. She had maneuvered herself into his company and had his full attention when he wouldn't have believed an hour ago that it was possible.

He tapped his finger on his glass. He knew he could break her spell whenever he chose, but to his surprise, he was enjoying himself too much to do so at the moment.

"Well, Lord Ravensdale." She took a deep breath and a sip of sherry. "It all began when I was in England. I had a dream about you."

"A dream?"

"A powerfully vivid dream."

"Do tell," Val stated, swirling his sherry in his glass, anxious for the coquetries and teasing to be over so that he could return to kissing her. A few stray strands of her blonde hair had fallen about her shoulders in wisps. He reflected, not for the first time, that he had never seen a lovelier girl.

"You were a black panther," stated Alita.

"A favorable comparison," stated Val, his voice low as he stretched his long legs out before him, settling into the leather couch. "I will leave it to you to determine if I am worthy of the name after we have finished our tryst."

"Please, Lord Ravensdale, I beg your attention. My story is not about you and me. It is only about *you*."

"I love it already," he muttered. *It's all about the man.* A very wise ploy on her part.

"Lord Ravensdale, let me assure you that this is not a jest." She appeared to steel herself. "I am deeply concerned about you. This is why I came."

Even better. "And I relish your concern, Miss Alita."

Alita continued with some trepidation. "I saw you on the battlefield at Tel-el-Kebir."

He felt as if his heart had turned to ice in his chest and a dagger run through it. Shooting straight up from the couch, deliberately he bestowed upon her the gaze that could stop grown men in their tracks.

He expected her to run from the room, and at that moment he hoped she would. Deception of any type was abhorrent to him. To his surprise, under his gaze her eyes opened wide and she momentarily covered her mouth with her hands, but she remained intently focused on him.

His mind raced through the possibilities as he considered that she could have learned of his participation in the battle of Tel-el-Kebir if she had researched her quarry, and she had unquestionably done so. But this turn of events surprised him, and he did not find it an amusing tactic. Introducing war into her conversation was tasteless. War was not a gay interlude or a whimsical farce for one's entertainment, certainly not something to be a part of bedroom games.

"I was there," he stated succinctly, placing his face next to hers even as she attempted to shrink into the chair.

"A–a–as I said," she continued, her voice uneven, "You were the Black Panther. You killed many. You killed an Egyptian, a friend, someone you knew with children." Pain washed across her face. "You have since visited these children, trying as best you can to be a father to them."

"Miss Stanton, what are you playing at? I warn you, I am no longer amused." Val punched his fist into the air. That was too much, bringing Banafrit's children into it. He grabbed her by the shoulders and pulled her up, drawing her close. Through gritted teeth he demanded, "Who told you these things? You *will* tell me before you depart, which will be very soon, I might add."

She was trembling now. She had best find her tongue and explain herself, or she would see worse.

"You could kill no more, and guilt about your loyalty plagues you," she whispered, barely able to find her voice. To his surprise, she continued speaking, despite her rising pitch and shaking hands. "In short, you have no idea who you are anymore."

Val's head was spinning. He released her shoulders but kept his eyes glued to her. She sank back down onto the leather couch, grabbing the

The Paradox: The Soldier and the Mystic 107

armrest of the couch, her hands sliding along the leather. He spun around to face her. Despite his strong emotions, Val's military training had taught him to immediately assess every situation from a tactical viewpoint, a strategy that had saved his life more than once. It was now second nature to him even when he might wish his opponent in Hades.

How could she have known? And, more importantly, what did she hope to gain from this ploy? Possibly one of his countrymen might have seen his anguish on the battle-field of Tel-el-Kebir, but to follow him to the home of the orphans he created without his noticing? Unlikely.

Still…possible. He gazed upon a countenance so unnaturally sweet, so sincere, that his conviction of her guilt grew. Could one of the infantry have pieced this together and sold the information to a merchant's daughter? Possibly, for material gain, but out of ill will? He didn't think so. True, his views were unpopular, but he was highly revered for his courage in the rescue and defense of his men.

On the other hand, most of the infantry had very little money, and there were not many opportunities in Egypt to pick up some spare change. There would be an element of shame associated with the transaction—and therefore secrecy—so it would take time and determination to uncover the offender.

He had both.

Val explored the possibilities quickly in his mind while studying her unwavering demeanor. He was inclined to dismiss the idea that she was a tool for someone who disliked him. He suspected that she had her own private motives. Insight into his private life might be a misguided attempt at seeking matrimony to a title.

"Miss Stanton, our discussion is at a close." Furious at her strategy, he determined to extract the truth from her. "Let us complete our business. Why have you come? Have you been hired to torment me by someone who disapproves of me?" He kept his eyes glued to her. He would not give her any reprieve until she confessed.

"No! No! Of course not! Who would…?" Her mouth dropped in surprise.

"Or is greed the motive?" he demanded.

"Certainly not! I do not need your money!" she replied, indignant. "And, if I did, I would not stoop so low as to profit from someone else's misery!"

"If your reason for this charade is not monetary, is it then personal?"

"P–p–personal? Why, *yes*, I mean, *no*, but everything I am saying is completely true, my lord! It is no charade."

"I assure you, Miss Stanton, that I have been to hell and back, and there is nothing you can do to me. Even so, I greatly resent both the attempt and the intrusion into my private affairs."

"You misunderstand me, my lord. I mean you no harm. I only wish to help you and others whose lives you have it within your power to save." Although her hands shook and her large eyes grew even wider, there was warmth in her gaze, which remained fixated on him. "I have come because…because…*I have seen who you are.*"

Val was stunned. He could see clearly that she was shaking from fright, and yet she would not relent from continuing with this bizarre course. "Explain yourself, Miss Stanton," he commanded.

He remembered with what comfort and finesse she had left her maid in the antechamber. Clearly, this was not her first *private meeting*. He did not think her goal was marriage, which was handled quite differently. For the time being, it was necessary to play along in order to learn the nature of her ploy.

"The dream I spoke of…"

"Stop speaking in riddles, Miss Stanton. We are accomplishing nothing with this tactic."

"You are correct, Lord Ravensdale." She sighed heavily. "Absolutely *nothing.*"

And then he started to laugh. This had to be the oddest encounter of his life and yet the most intoxicating. She posed no threat. If her object was matrimony or wealth, she would be sorely disappointed. If her purpose was to discredit him, that was likewise an impossibility. Sir Evelyn, the highest law in the land, knew his views quite clearly and had not yet deported him. True, it was an outcome that Val viewed with indifference, but the point was that there was nothing this merchant's daughter could do to him.

The Paradox: The Soldier and the Mystic   *109*

"I speak the truth," she replied indignantly, her first expression of annoyance. "I have a…a…gift. Or a *curse*, depending on how one looks at it."

"You can see into the future with your dreams?" he asked, chuckling.

"The future? Not usually. No, *never* before."

"Only with me?" he asked, making no effort to contain his amusement.

"Sometimes I am correct, sometimes wrong." She jutted out her chin. "I am an imperfect person with a talent, nothing more."

"And what is that talent, Miss Stanton?"

"I begin to wonder. Well, I see and feel…oh, it *doesn't matter*, Lord Ravensdale! I am *not* wrong where you are concerned. I have never been more sure of anything. Please believe me, my lord, your abilities are extensive." She leaned toward him, which caused him to catch his breath for an instant, breathing in an intoxicating blend of jasmine and honeysuckle, sweet and exotic, confusing and heavenly. "You have a path. A great path."

"Miss Stanton, if you wish to continue our *conversation*, you will not discuss Tel-el-Kebir again." He stretched his legs out in front of him while fixing his gaze on her. "Do I make myself clear?"

"Indeed you do, Lord Ravensdale." Her expression was unreadable. "The relevant point is that your past experiences keep you locked in a circular realm of torment and misdirection. They prevent you from knowing your possibilities. *But I have seen it.* If you will follow your path, you have a great destiny."

"A great destiny." Val laughed out loud as he moved to pour himself another sherry.

And he had no desire to stop laughing. *It had been so long.*

"Yes, my lord."

He returned to sit beside her. Now he had to add to his list of explanations the possibility that she was as crazy as a loon. She had in her possession a strange mix of the facts and absolute nonsense.

Miss Alita Stanton disturbed him. Though it was common for young ladies to research their quarry in advance, Miss Stanton's methods were unusual, and not entirely to his taste, but probably utilized to bestow upon her a certain mysterious air. A signature persona, so to speak. *But to what purpose?* Was it political or personal?

God, I hope it is personal. Val considered the young ingénue before him as he swirled the sherry in his glass, the tactical equal of a general of his acquaintance. As his eyes lingered on her lovely complexion and drank in her sparkling eyes, he let out a slow, uneven breath.

He attempted to return his thoughts to the matter at hand. He would bet on his first instincts. She was looking for some *entertainment* far from home. It was probably just that simple. Unwillingly, his lips formed a half smile. He hated to disappoint a lady.

"I see, Miss Stanton." He was intrigued to hear the entire story before he said good-bye to Miss Alita Stanton forever. "My destiny, as you put it. And what might that be, Miss Stanton?"

"I saw cool, soothing water running through the sky." She took a deep breath. Her utterances began unevenly, but her words gradually gained momentum. "I saw tongues over your head and people of different nationalities bowing to each other in a sign of friendship and trust. I don't know the significance of the tongues, but I know that you are a peace-maker of some type—a person of great influence. It always requires a person capable of great power to bring peace."

"*Great power*? Miss Stanton, do you honestly entertain the idea that I am gullible enough to fall for such obvious attempts at flattery? I am not an egoist. I can perform my part without your obsequious fawning. I am perfectly willing to engage in your afternoon liaison without your pretty speeches. In fact, I prefer it. This is all utter nonsense." He brushed his hand against hers and felt an immediate charge.

"*Liaison*? Surely you don't..." She gasped, suddenly standing and backing up until she bumped into the plum velvet wingback.

"Miss Stanton, please return to sit beside me."

She shook her head vehemently.

"Let us be done with this smoke and mirrors," he implored. He had been quick to anger but just as quick to dismiss it. He reached for her hand, tugging gently until she easily slid back into her seat. Her balance was sadly compromised. Sitting beside her, he took her hand and kissed her fingers lightly. He felt her hand shake inside his.

"You misunderstand me entirely, Lord Ravensdale." She stared at him, her expression aghast, pulling her hand away.

The Paradox: The Soldier and the Mystic   *111*

"Please, Miss Stanton, continue," he begged resignedly. It was her flirtation, and he supposed it was important to her to act out all the parts and to place the pieces of the puzzle in strategic, alluring places before she proceeded to the next step. It was an elaborate and ingenious web she wove, and full of surprises. As much as he hated to admit it, he found the entire scenario extremely...*stimulating.*

"Of course, my lord." She swallowed. "In the further interest of your vocation, I feel compelled to point out that you shouldn't stay here. There is little point." She looked around, motioning to the office with her hands. She focused on the painting of Lord Cromer hanging on the wall, one of the world's most powerful imperialist leaders, portrayed in the painting as unassuming, warm, studious. Altogether an everyday fellow.

"Shouldn't stay *here*. In this room? I find it quite comfortable."

"In Egypt. The person who works here makes a show of wishing to turn over running the country to the Egyptians, but he has no intention of doing so."

Val almost dropped his jaw. This was his sense as well, that he kept working to bring about the self-governing of the Egyptians, but that Sir Evelyn had no intention of making that dream a reality. How could she know this?

"He has done a good job—a necessary job—of repairing the damage done by the former ruler of Egypt and toward eventually restoring Egypt to its rightful place as a world power. But he has no intention of giving up his position." Her expression was pensive. "Britain will be here for many years to come. Your work is beneficial, but it is not consistent with your values nor your goals for Egypt."

"Ah. So, you can see into the future as well, Miss Stanton?"

"The *future*?" She gulped. "I...I..."

"And how long will Britain run Egypt?" he asked as if he were making idle conversation, leaning back into the couch and stretching his legs out before him. He picked up his glass of sherry and swirled the glass as if he were studying its contents.

She pondered for a moment, looking straight ahead as she opened her hands in her lap. "The British occupancy will last something over sixty years. A great leader, an Egyptian, will rise up out of the peasantry and claim back the country for Egyptians."

112   *Suzette Hollingsworth*

"Sixty years?" Val nodded his head, as if he were contemplating a profound statement. He turned toward her, striving to maintain his most solemn expression. "Britain will occupy Egypt for sixty years?"

"Yes." Alita nodded.

"You astonish me, Miss Stanton. And how will this coup d'état be accomplished?" He could not have taken his eyes off her had he wanted to. In controlled tones he added, "I am most curious to know, Miss Stanton."

She grew silent for a while and sat very still, looking so prim and proper sitting beside him on a leather couch, with no maid in sight. Her expression was one of surprise as her lips barely moved in a distant voice. "It will occur through a non-violent revolution. The leader I spoke of will execute an ingenious plan which will return the Suez Canal and all of Egypt to Egyptian control in an extraordinary act of statesmanship. Egypt will be...reincarnated as her former self." Alita nodded slowly, her expression serene. "Rising from the tombs, so to speak."

"Miss Stanton, you actually expect me to believe that England will hand over a valuable, money-making enterprise—not to mention an important military strategic point—without a bloody war?" He was unable to suppress his laughter despite his best efforts. Now he knew she was crazy.

"I don't pretend to understand it, but it will be as I have said," she retorted with indignation. "But the time is not now."

"No doubt."

"And you are not that leader, I am sorry to say."

"Think nothing of it," the earl uttered graciously.

"Please believe me, Lord Ravensdale, your talents are extensive. There is a plan for you. A destiny of magnificent proportions, if you will." She placed her hands primly in her lap. "This is not where your path lies."

"And what do you propose, Miss Stanton?" he asked, raising one eyebrow.

"Return to England," she stated definitively. "There is a position there for you. Something...something to do with other countries."

Val sighed heavily. He was disappointed to learn of her duplicity, but at least he was starting to unravel this puzzle. She wanted him to leave Egypt. And she had the poor taste to appeal to his grief over taking Egyptian lives. *But why?* Had someone hired her? If Sir Evelyn had wanted him to leave, he would have simply dismissed him.

The Paradox: The Soldier and the Mystic 113

There wasn't anyone else. For all practical intents and purposes, the sad truth was that there was no one in particular, outside of a few school chums, who wished him back in England. His family certainly didn't want him back in England where he might place further limits on their purse strings and look into their affairs. *It didn't make sense.*

Val realized that he knew little more than when he started. He had no idea what Miss Alita Stanton was about. Although he hated to admit defeat, particularly in a contest of logical deduction, Val decided that he was growing weary of this battle of the wits. It was time to speed things up or close it down.

"Miss Stanton," Val said in his most sultry voice as he placed his face close to hers, looking into her eyes. "If indeed you traveled from Britain to Egypt to see me, which I strongly doubt, why did you do it?" He had tried commanding her to tell him the truth, and it hadn't worked. He was flexible. He was very willing to try another approach.

"Because I have seen you. It is amazing to behold." As her eyes softened, staring into his, he began to feel the ice in his soul melting. She lightly touched her cheeks with both hands, her eyes shining. "If I ever see you realized in the flesh, Lord Ravensdale, it will be worth the journey of my entire life."

Chapter Eleven

Val swiftly took her into his arms where she sat, bending down to kiss her, his hand cradling her back. "You may certainly see me in the flesh, Miss Alita," he whispered into her mouth, the gentle parting of his lips teasing her. Each kiss warmed her, ignited her.

The raw drive that was the Earl of Ravensdale was focused on her and her alone. The power she had encountered in him was unleashed on her. Nothing else was in his thoughts but her, and it was intoxicating. His tongue entered her mouth, warm and electric. His breath mingled with hers, his lips demanding hers, perfectly molding to hers, claiming her.

She knew the integrity and power of his being, and she was bathing in it. She grew dizzy from the knowledge of his desire, converged upon her, even as her body yearned to be closer to his and sensed there was an answer to be found in melding with his soul. It was as if she were in a magical whirlwind, this amazing man desiring, wanting her.

And she wanted him, too, she realized with a gasp. He groaned and pulled her closer, ravaging her mouth. She was stunned—and delighted.

In that instant she was whole. Safe. And *pure*. How odd that she should feel pure at a time when her thoughts were so improper! She longed to feel the strength of his muscles underneath her palms. She pulled back and looked into his pale silvery eyes framed with dark lashes. His features were harsh, and though he was clean shaven, it was clear that he continually fought a beard. As she studied him, he raised his left eyebrow in an unspoken question, his thick, black hair brushed away from his face except for that one incorrigible lock of hair that fell across his forehead.

He returned her scrutiny. Slowly, a wicked smile formed on his lips. His eyes were his most arresting feature. Until he smiled. Then the angels sang and—heaven help her!—she felt a longing unlike any force she had ever known.

The Paradox: The Soldier and the Mystic 115

"Strangely enough, Miss Alita Stanton, I cannot seem to get enough of you." His voice was deep and masculine, resonating with desire, as he murmured in her ear. He held her body close to his chest, his muscled arms wrapped around her. Alita had never felt so needed in her life. He cradled her head in his strong hands, not caring if he should muss her hair, his tongue gently explored her mouth again, and she felt herself go limp.

He was breathing heavily, and his heart was beating rapidly. She leaned back into the couch until she was in a partially reclining position in a half-hearted attempt to create some distance. He desperately ran his hands along the outside of her hips, as if he were memorizing her body. As he did so, the silk of her skirt rubbed her skin deliciously and created a lovely crinkling sound, as if putting sound to his desire.

Why did a simple touch feel so divine even through the fabric? The crisp linen beige suit he wore moved under her palms, and she wondered what his skin would feel like instead and what he looked like under that suit. Her thoughts were racing, and not where they should be progressing.

"Miss Stanton," he murmured, "I don't believe that our paths will cross again, so I did wish to say good-bye."

Her breath had quickened as well, but her heart fell with his words, suddenly all of these sweet feelings tainted. "You don't believe me," she whispered.

"I honestly don't know what the devil you're talking about, Miss Stanton," Val grumbled, his breath uneven. He brushed kisses across her cheekbone. "And I don't give a damn."

"So you will stay here, in Egypt?" she persisted, exerting every effort to remember her purpose in being here. She knew that she should stop him from kissing her, but she was floating in a heavenly dream.

A dream he had just told her was about to end.

"Of course. I am translating some Egyptian hieroglyphics to English," he whispered hoarsely. "As if anyone cares. Even I don't care at this precise moment. May we please cease speaking, Miss Stanton? It is distracting me."

"Translating?" she asked in a whisper, her cheek touching his rough cheek, her head reeling from being so close to him. The vision he presented, now so real, made her gasp. His hold was tight, as if he would never let her go. She was surrounded by masculine scent, pure muscle, and *passion*. She was exerting every effort to concentrate on his words and his thoughts, to hear the quieter voices—the voices that might help her to help him—which were overpowered by the force of his attraction for her. "You are translating?" she repeated.

"Yes, yes, *yes*. Translating." A heavy sigh escaped from his lips, after which he seemed resigned to kiss and speak at the same time. "As it so happens, Miss Stanton, I read several ancient Egyptian languages, some better than others."

"Several? More than one?" she asked anxiously, suddenly sitting up so straight that he fell back somewhat.

"More...than...one." Gently he brushed his lips against hers, unaffected by her squirming, alternating each word with a soft kiss. "But I am always willing to practice. I love...to...practice," he added.

"Oh, *my*," murmured Alita in a strained whisper. "Which languages?"

"Miss Stanton, is it really necessary...?" he sighed again.

"Yes, please," she sighed. "*Yes.*"

"There is Coptic, which is Ancient Egyptian. And there is Arabic"—he nibbled her right ear—"from the Middle East"—followed by her left ear—"Arabs invaded Egypt after the pyramids were built," he murmured as he kissed her neck and moved to her throat.

Tongues, Alita thought. In the instant of comprehension, she felt a surge of uncontained energy soar through her body. "Don't you see, Lord Ravensdale?" she exclaimed as she pulled away, somehow managing to push this formidable man back against the sofa and stand at the same time.

"*Bloody hell!* What are you about, Miss Stanton?" he demanded, staring up at her, disbelieving as he rubbed his jaw line.

"That explains the tongues!" She swung around and then turned to face him again as she clenched her fists. "Oh, why did it take me so long to grasp? It was standing right in front of me."

He stared at her, his confusion startlingly apparent. If she hadn't known him better, she might have mistaken it for the look of fear.

"*That is the purpose of your life!*" She clasped her hands to her mouth, forcing herself not to scream from excitement, she who had always been so quiet and soft-spoken.

"That is...*what* is?"

"*Languages* are the connecting medium!" she exclaimed. "Lord Ravensdale, your path has something to do with other languages. That is

The Paradox: The Soldier and the Mystic *117*

how you bring people together, *which is the purpose of your life*. It is done with your knowledge of their languages."

"Actually, I was thinking that the tongue symbolism might have another meaning, Miss Stanton," he muttered. He loosened his slim silk cravat with two exaggerated movements of his hands. Promptly he placed his arms around her waist, pulled her next to him on the couch in one swift movement, and illustrated his interpretation for her consideration.

"Lord Ravensdale!" Alita exclaimed, gasping for breath, her indignation rising, forcing herself into a sitting position, her hand braced against his chest. She knew that she liked his touch, but she also knew that she shouldn't be kissing him, though she was beginning to forget why.

Gradually the reasons began to break through her clouded thinking. She placed her hand on her cheek. "No man has ever been so forward or improper toward me. And this after you have already informed me that I won't be seeing you again, Lord Ravensdale!"

"I had understood that communication was my strong point." He appeared perplexed as he studied her, his expression sultry. "And, in fact, that I was destined for greatness in that arena." His voice was low and resonant as he tenderly claimed the hand that was resting on her cheek. She felt the calluses on his hand and was reminded that she was dealing with a warrior, and no ordinary one at that.

With his touch, Alita was again bewildered to the point of light-headedness, and she didn't know how she should feel. It was the greatest mystery why this magnificent man should have the slightest interest in her. He didn't even know her.

And he *was* interested. Even though he had proclaimed they would not be seeing each other again, there was no doubt in her mind that he had a strong attraction to her. And it was just as true that he had the clear intent to thunderbolt from her vicinity. It was mightily perplexing.

Could it be that he was promised to another woman? She had never connected to that side of him, and the question had never interested her before now. She stood and moved to the velvet wingback chair, where she smoothed her gown. Shyly she asked in a whisper, "Lord Ravensdale, do you have a...sweetheart?"

"I am far too busy for such diversions." She knew that it was not in his nature to lie. He wasn't afraid of anything, so why would he lie? But he was not without his passions. He stared at her with such longing that she felt herself tremble.

"You're not too busy…*today*," she remarked with hesitation.

"Definitely not too busy today," he emphasized, his pale blue eyes penetrating hers as his fingers interlocked with hers across the table between them.

"And why don't you—isn't there…a young lady in your life?" Alita stammered, almost breathless with the light touch of his fingertips along the edge of her index finger.

"I have found a few women interesting." His lips formed a wicked smile, as if he were enjoying a memory. "Generally much older than yourself, Miss Stanton."

"*Older* than *me*?" she asked incredulously. She was a full year beyond marrying age. Oh! But she did look young for her age. "Lord Ravensdale, I am much older than you might think."

"You don't say, Miss Stanton?" He chuckled. "Let's see. I would guess you are all of seven—no, eighteen."

She pursed her lips.

"I am correct, am I not, Miss Stanton?"

"Surely you must know it is indelicate to discuss a lady's age, Lord Ravensdale." *I will not give him the satisfaction*! Suddenly his full meaning hit her, and she moved to cover her open mouth, pulling her hand away. "Are you telling me, Lord Ravensdale, that you prefer ladies older than *eighteen*?"

He roared with laughter, even to the point of taking a handkerchief out of his pocket and wiping his eyes, which served to annoy her as much as anything ever had. "Yes, one foot in the grave, as it were."

"What age do you prefer, Lord Ravensdale?" she fumed, unable to contain her interest.

"Miss Stanton, a woman under the age of twenty-four is not worth my time. But you…*you* are not typical of your age, I regret to inform you."

"I most certainly am!" she countered with indignation. "*Twenty-four*? You can't be serious." Outside of her, he was only attracted to widows and *spinsters*!

"Miss Stanton, allow me to illuminate my love life for you." Once he had calmed himself, he seemed to feel obligated to explain his depravity.

The Paradox: The Soldier and the Mystic 119

"If you feel the need to do so, I shan't stop you." She pursed her lips. If she hadn't been so curious, she would have told him not to bother!

"I feel a *burning* need to do so." He smiled at her indifferently, but she could almost hear the air crackle in truth. "Courting married women is inelegant, girls just out of the schoolroom bore me to tears, and charming widows are not as common as one might think."

"How unfortunate, Lord Ravensdale, that the supply of women meeting your elevated standards is insufficient."

"I accept your pity with a grateful heart." He took her hand again and lightly kissed the tips of her fingertips before shrugging nonchalantly. When he was amused, there was a slight tilt to his mouth on the right side, and all the ferocity in his gaze turned to intensity of another kind. He had a way of looking at one that was quite disconcerting. And she was already feeling completely lost at sea and not up to the task she had been given!

She retrieved her hand with a bit more force than was necessary. "My pity I gladly bestow, but my hand I shall keep to myself."

"More is the shame. But I will manage to keep myself occupied nonetheless," he murmured. "Thankfully, there is far more to life than idle diversions, Miss Stanton."

"Women are to you an *idle diversion*?" She felt her anger rise even as her breath caught in her chest when his eyes suddenly captured hers.

"If the intent is not marriage, yes. How could it be otherwise? But believe me, my dear, I know how to play my part. I might be rusty, but I can still satisfy. I am thought to be rather…adept."

"Excellent news! I mean…I didn't mean…"

"Do tell, what did you mean, Miss Stanton?"

Oh, what did she mean? *I don't know what I meant!* She felt herself coloring even as she attempted to suppress the memory of hard muscles underneath her palms, her skin tingling from head to toe. "I meant nothing I'm sure."

"I'm quite sure that you did."

"I only meant to ask you…"

"Yes?" He leaned toward her.

"Are you accustomed to feeling an attraction of this…magnitude, Lord Ravensdale?" she ventured, knowing she had never felt anything to approach it in her life.

He jumped from the couch and began to pace the room, affording her a pleasing view. Even in an expertly tailored, beige linen suit, she could see that his chest was muscled. His waist was slim, but it was a man's waist, gradually narrowing from his chest. He was long-legged, and his legs had form. Overall, he moved with ease within his body, which somehow complemented his unusual style of dress. He didn't dress like the British, and he didn't dress like the natives, seeming to take the best from each.

There were no tails on his suit, no flower in his buttonhole, and no watch chain dangling from a vest. Only a perfectly fitted suit in a rugged yet sophisticated fabric reminiscent of his character. His only nod to hauteur was a slim silk cravat tied in the Windsor fashion, and even that was now loosened at his neckline.

"Not generally, no." He returned his pale blue eyes to hers, and once again she felt her breath catch in her chest. In the blink of an eye, he was at her side again.

"Not generally?"

"Let me rephrase that, Miss Stanton." He seemed to reconsider his answer. "No, *never*." His voice was low, and his eyes, now a silvery liquid, seemed to pierce her soul even as his hand ran along her silk sleeve, begging her to rise and join him. "So why are we wasting it with discussion?"

"I'm s–s–simply *c–c–curious*, Lord Ravensdale," Alita persisted, swallowing hard, pulling her arms in toward her body and sinking farther into the chair. This was all so new to her, and she was having difficulty understanding the happenings around her but more so within her. "Why do you think you have this sudden interest in me? You don't even know me."

"Why shouldn't I?" Val raised his eyebrows, as if he didn't know himself, but his nonchalant mannerisms expressed little interest in resolving the mystery. "You are a beautiful woman, Miss Alita, completely unpredictable, neither insipid nor boring, as most beautiful women are. And it's been a long time for me…"

"A long time since *what*?"

"You surprise me, Miss Stanton." His lips formed a seductive smile even as he chuckled. Languidly he added, "You have great courage. I doubt if there is *anyone* who could intimidate you. Ordinarily I can manage the most frightening of adversaries. You puzzle me greatly, and I love a puzzle.

The Paradox: The Soldier and the Mystic   *121*

I comprehend that you know what you want and that we want the same thing. Frankly, I find that exciting."

"You are gravely mistaken, Lord Ravensdale." Alita shook her head definitively. "You have no idea what I want."

* * * *

Val was perplexed. He had been certain that this interlude was precisely what she had intended, and yet there could be no mistaking the immediate sadness in her large eyes, which shone like jewels against her ivory skin.

The sharpness of his disappointment surprised him. But he was not accustomed to imposing himself where he was not wanted, so he forced himself to pull away from her and to cool his approach.

"It is unusual for me, but I am having great difficulty discerning that which you wish from me, Miss Alita," he uttered, "but I'm sorry to tell you that this is the best I can offer you." He turned her hand over and kissed the inside of her wrist, attempting to communicate clearly that there was more in that vein in his repertoire.

"That is not at all true." Slowly she raised her eyelashes, startling him once again into submission. She was fast gaining the upper hand.

And he was beginning to feel like the circus lion in a cage with its tamer.

On one point she had been right, Val knew—he had no idea who he was.

He sensed that Alita was about to ask him another question. He was trying his damnedest to put an end to her inquisitiveness regarding his attributes and interests, and nothing was working. This was a new challenge for him. Generally he could squelch a young lady's interest in his viewpoints simply by opening his mouth. And yet, he was applying his not-inconsequential talents to diverting Miss Alita Stanton to no avail.

And the problem was that he was becoming intensely aroused in the process while Miss Alita continued to persist in her study of the Earl of Ravensdale as if he were the most fascinating man on earth. He shook his head in perplexity. It was flattering. She was very gifted in her Arts, he would give her that.

"Don't you think, Miss Alita"—he gazed into her eyes—"that we can find a better way to enjoy our brief time together? There is another language I would like to teach you—though I expect to find it will not be new to you—if you could cease and desist from prophesying my illustrious future for but a moment."

"It took me six weeks to arrive here, Lord Ravensdale. I was fueled only by the desire to impart to you the importance of your life. If there were anything I could say or do which would convince you, I would not hesitate to do so. However, I fear my journey has been wasted." She looked up at him with an expression of dismay. "Furthermore, you don't appear to even like me. Your attraction is of a decidedly different nature! How could I convince you of anything given your feelings?"

"Oh, that's where you are wrong, Miss Alita Stanton." He placed his face close to hers without allowing them to touch. "I like you very much."

"But you don't wish to see me again?" Her expression was distraught. "There is so much that we need to speak of."

"I have learned to recognize danger and to be cautious"—he studied her with a deep longing—"to not walk into the lion's den, so to speak. Frankly, you are much too much for me to handle, Miss Alita."

"I don't think so." Her gaze was deliciously innocent as she looked up at him. "You are capable of handling much more than myself, Lord Ravensdale."

Oh, this woman captivates me. Val burst out laughing. He knew that he had to put a great deal of distance between the two of them. *Very soon.* That's just what he would do.

"I appreciate your confidence, Miss Alita," uttered Val.

Val kept telling himself to pull back, to no avail. He was fast becoming her captive, and he was not entirely certain if she were an innocent, as she presented, or a temptress, as he suspected. She was very young. It surprised him that such a young woman should be so advanced in the language of love.

"Miss Alita, as much as I have enjoyed it, let's stop this charade. Would you like me to make love to you now?"

"No man shall make love to me until we are properly wed," she exclaimed. Aghast, she drew away, placing her hand over her mouth momentarily as she leaned back into the couch.

The Paradox: The Soldier and the Mystic   *123*

"Oh, so that is your game, is it?" asked Lord Ravensdale, both surprised and fiercely disappointed. "I had expected a different answer, Miss Alita, but you never cease to surprise me."

"This is no game, Lord Ravensdale," she remarked stiffly, a note of finality to her tone.

"And is it your wish to marry me, Miss Stanton?" He watched her with interest as she stared at him in disbelief. "Mind you, I'm not asking for your hand, Miss Alita, I'm merely asking if that is your desire."

"Do you wish me to answer you, my lord?" Finally she seemed to find her voice.

"Very much," stated Val, discomfited at the importance her answer had to him.

There was longing in her eyes, and it unsettled him that he held his breath for a long moment. Val admonished himself. It was probably just the novelty of being with a woman who actually answered his questions instead of slapping him.

"There is someone more suited to me." Her lips parted, and he watched them intently. There was a certain emotionless resolve in her eyes. "Someone of my acquaintance."

"I see." He felt more disheartened at her words than he should have.

"And yet..." Suddenly the brilliance returned to her eyes. "You excite me, Lord Ravensdale. This time with you has been rather like an exhilarating waltz with the perfect partner."

"*Exhilarating* is the right word," he muttered.

"At any rate, it is immaterial." She looked away, and her expression was wistful. "No doubt you are destined to be with someone far more exceptional than myself, Lord Ravensdale."

He laughed, despite himself. He *excited* her. He was the least exciting man alive. And she...*she* was the oddest combination of genuine forthrightness while at the same time prattling a great deal of contrived nonsense.

And she was absolutely enchanting.

"Undoubtedly, Miss Stanton, though I fear to meet her if she can out-maneuver you. She will likely take over the world." He smiled distractedly. "And I am not a supporter of imperialism. I believe in self-rule."

Suddenly, a melancholy washed over him, and the joy he had felt in their encounter began to fade. "Unfortunately, it is time to bring our meeting to a close. As I do not wish to enter into the state of matrimony, and as marriage is the only course for you, it is imperative that you leave now before I do something I will regret."

"You wish me to *leave*?"

"I do not. But it is the only course." He rubbed his hands through his hair and beheld her with appreciation, though he grew suddenly weary. "I wish the best for you, Miss Stanton. You deserve a brilliant match, and I have no doubt that you will make one." *And lead your husband on a merry dance for the rest of his happy life.* He wished he had time for this type of delightful nonsense, but there were too many important events unfolding in the world.

"Please reconsider," she asked, her expression both anxious and hopeful. "Might we not meet for conversation while I am still in Cairo, Lord Ravensdale?"

"With any other woman I would say 'yes' at the same time it would not be worth my time. With you, Miss Alita, conversation would be most enjoyable, but I could not trust myself. And again, what would be the point if it could not lead to matrimony or to other enjoyable...pastimes?" Val remembered the piles of work left on his desk and his required excursion to the south end of the city. "No, I think it is best that we part ways. I cannot become ensnared in your trap. And I have my own plans to pursue which would be out of your area of expertise, Miss Alita."

She rose timidly, her hands shaking, and her obvious distress at leaving him almost broke his resolve. He kissed her hand caressingly, memorizing her soft touch in his mind.

"I will never forget you, Miss Alita Stanton," he pronounced, escorting her to the door with a pained resolution.

Chapter Twelve

Val's prophesy was destined to come true. No matter how much he tried, the earl could not remove Miss Alita Stanton from his mind. She entered his thoughts at all hours of the day and in every state of consciousness. He began to dream of her—two could play at that game. Only *his* dreams were of a more personal nature.

Pursuing women had not been an all-absorbing or even particularly strong diversion of his lordship's. He had concluded early on to be cautious in the arena of women. His passions were too strong and his spirit too driven to be ruled by someone else.

He was exerting every effort to apply the same principles in this situation, but this woman had taken hold of his imagination, and she wouldn't release him.

Leave her to dominate another thick-witted sap, Ravensdale, he uttered to himself. *You might be without honor or conscience, but I never imagined you to be gullible.* He walked past the terrace of Shepheard's Hotel where one could see both world-renowned figures and anyone of any importance in Cairo if one dallied over coffee and pastries long enough. Since this was not a particular interest of his on any day and not a duty of his on this day, he kept walking.

Why am I here? Never mind that Shepheard's was the *only* hotel in town for the well-to-do. There was no possibility she would be staying anywhere else.

Well, a man had to have a drink on occasion. He could not help it that Shepheard's had the best bar in town—in addition to the most expensive. Ah, well. Sir Evelyn would pick up the tab if he wrote it up to local investigating.

Walking through the two-story arched entry way in the shape of a mosque dome accented by alternating stripes, a purple tassel hanging below it, he placed his feet on a Persian carpet fit for a King's processional. Even with the glass-studded dome overhead, the lobby managed to create the feeling of an opulent tent. He wondered that Aladdin might suddenly appear with his lamp and genie except for the presence of a noisy teleprinter, which rattled the ambiance and further blackened his already dark mood, the world's latest news becoming visible on paper with the pen's rollercoaster ride across the white paper.

Tap. Tap. Tap. Tickity-tap. Mary Todd Lincoln, First Lady of the United States, dies...The Royal Navy's HMS Flirt destroys Abari village in Niger...Martial law is enacted in Japan...A cyclone in the Arabian Sea causes flooding in the harbor of Bombay, India, killing 100,000 people...

A very sad state of affairs. Did nothing ever change?

...The First World Series, Chicago beats Cincinnati 2-0...Billy the Kid shot dead in Tombstone, Arizona...

Surely somewhere in the world progress was being made.

...The U.S. Congress passed the 1882 Immigration Act, giving authorities the power to deny entry to convicts, lunatics, idiots, and persons likely to become public charges...

Ah, no more admittance into America. And presumably the deportation of vast numbers of the current residents as well.

Exiled to France. They would feel at home there.

...The world's first commercial hydroelectric power plant, the Appleton Edison Light Company, begins operation in the United States...The Married Women's Property Act of 1882 in Britain is introduced into Parliament, which would allow women to buy, own, and sell property and to keep their own earnings...

He raised his eyebrows in surprise. Allowed to keep their wages rather than being required to hand over their earnings to their husbands? That would never make it into law since those voting on the act were all men.

Surely there must be some good news somewhere.

...P.T. Barnum purchases an elephant by the name of Jumbo...

There it was. A piece of news to give one hope.

He scanned the balance of the news quickly before walking past the spiral staircase toward the bar. In the background he heard the sounds of the tea-time orchestra coming from the dining room, where he glanced over to see native Egyptians dressed in crimson- and gold-embroidered jackets and

The Paradox: The Soldier and the Mystic 127

over-wide bright white pantaloons, scurrying about with dainty sandwiches and pastries and silver tea services.

Val's counter seat in the elegant bar of Shepheard's Hotel gave him an excellent view of the lobby and of everyone who came and went, while providing him with the ability to quickly remove himself from view behind a monstrous pillar.

Why am I here? Shepheard's catered to Europeans and wealthy Egyptians, not the best locale in which to mingle with the peasant population.

Shepheard's bar was known for its friendly club atmosphere so different from the seedy bars he generally frequented. None of the friendliness here today. The place was nearly empty at 3:00 in the afternoon—tea time— despite inviting, luxurious divans scattered about, piled high with cushions and a long mahogany bar.

"You're a bloody coward, Ravensdale," Val muttered to himself. There was no way to deny the fact that he was here in the hope of spying on Miss Alita Stanton without wishing to meet her face-to-face.

"It's good to see you again. What would you like, sir?" the bartender asked in very good English as he approached. He was middle-aged, and his expression was bright and intelligent. He was a short, muscular man, balding, with a long, curled moustache, strong features, a handsome face, and a broad grin which appealed to his customers—except to the brand of Englishman who thought it was presumptuous of the help to smile in one's direction. He was no doubt a good judge of character, and he knew which was which or he wouldn't be employed at Shepheard's.

Val studied the bottles of whiskey behind the bar, longing to ask for a bottle rather than a glass. After some deliberation, Val sighed heavily. "Can you make a satisfactory cup of hot tea, Zaheer?"

"Of course, sir." The bartender appeared surprised. "I make the most delicious pot of mint tea which you have ever—"

"Black tea," Val interjected. "English tea. Steeped for three minutes. With cream and sugar."

"As you wish, sir," Zaheer agreed with a smile and a bow.

Once Zaheer returned with Val's pot of tea, Val studied him with an obligatory interest. He knew Zaheer to be highly respected in the Egyptian community, and it was therefore Val's responsibility to be interested in the opinion of one who came into contact with so many from all walks of life. "Do you like your job, Zaheer?" Val asked in Arabic.

"Anyone who is lucky enough to have a job likes it, sir," he replied in Arabic, following suit.

"Why do you work here? You don't drink." He knew that Zaheer was Muslim and that it was against his religion to drink.

"But you do." Zaheer chuckled, a knowing light in his eye. "Enough for both of us, sir."

"Dispense with the *sir*," Val directed. "You know my name. And you didn't answer my question."

"Watching you increases my convictions against drink, Raven."

Val scowled at him, stirring the sugar and cream into his tea before taking a sip. "Passable," he proclaimed, even though it was an excellent cup of tea. It would be perfect with a shot of whiskey.

"I haven't seen you about here lately, Raven." Relaxing noticeably, Zaheer quizzed him, continuing in Arabic.

Val wasn't about to correct Zaheer on his name, or there was no telling what it would become. Besides, he was accustomed to everyone on foreign soil changing his name to suit them, even friends.

"I'm looking for a woman," he stated bluntly.

"Aren't we all?" Zaheer laughed heartily. "Are you certain you've come to the right place, Raven?"

"I've come to the wrong damn place, Zaheer, of that I have no doubt. And for the wrong damn woman." Val stirred the cream in his tea while cursing under his breath.

"Oh? What is wrong with the woman?" Zaheer asked, appearing genuinely interested, a necessity of his profession.

"Not a bloody thing," Val muttered. "And everything. *Damnation!* If I had to be attracted to a woman, why not an intellectual, or a woman of achievement and principle, someone who embraces the values I hold dear?"

"She's none of those things, Raven?" Zaheer asked.

"At worst, she is dicked in the nob." Val shook his head.

"And at best?" asked Zaheer.

"A sensational seductress." A slow smile came to Val's lips.

The Paradox: The Soldier and the Mystic   *129*

"I don't advise it, my friend." Zaheer hummed under his breath. "Do not become ensnared by a woman who is without virtue, as tempting as it might be."

"I can live without the virtue," Val quipped. "It's the misdirected intellect which disturbs me."

"A dangerous woman." Zaheer shook his head.

"Very." He frowned. *I should not have had any response to Alita Stanton at all.* He was drawn to this woman who embodied everything he deplored in his family. She was manipulative and possibly delusional. His father was a womanizing gambler who had attempted to exploit everyone he encountered. His mother lived in an imaginary world of her own creation. Although Alita Stanton was certainly intelligent, she did not appeal to his most deeply held values on any level. He should not have had any response to her at all.

And the fact remained that she captivated him.

"Why the devil should I even care about the lady, much less have her plaguing my thoughts?" Val asked rhetorically.

"Who is she?" asked Zaheer pointedly.

"That is the question of the century," replied Val, shaking his head in disgust. *Ravensdale, you have really sunk too low this time.*

"Egypt is home to some of the most beautiful women in the world." Zaheer knitted his brows together as he studied Val. "And I've never before seen you express more than a passing interest, Raven."

"To be perfectly honest, Zaheer, I surprise myself. Everyone has always lamented that I am the most sensible person of their acquaintance, as if it were an unfortunate trait." He was serious. He was studious. He was disciplined.

Even from a young age, he had behaved like an adult, more so than his parents had. He had not been frivolous. He never shirked his duty. Of all things, he strove to discover truth, to discern it, to speak it, to live it. Less-than-stellar personages had no appeal to him.

And now he was reacting to this fortune-telling gypsy child who hadn't put two words of sense together as if she were his last chance at happiness.

"Most unfortunate trait. The woman does you a service." Zaheer grinned while pouring more tea into Val's cup.

"Ah, now you have hit upon the point, Zaheer. This woman tells me that she wishes to *help* me," Val posed.

"You've changed, Raven," Zaheer remarked, his expression suddenly somber as he wiped off the counter with his rag. "Not a month ago you were so thin I wondered you were dying. In time, you seemed to have purpose, but still you were enshrouded in gloom. Now the light has returned to your face. Did this woman do this? Or have you found Allah?"

"Neither." Val laughed, keeping his eyes glued to the lobby, not wishing to miss her if she walked by.

An interesting thing had happened to him, Val admitted to himself. It was, in fact, as if a cloud of despair had been lifted when he first laid eyes on Miss Alita Stanton.

Now he was merely perplexed. Bewildered. Amused. Annoyed.

"Not the woman. Not Allah." Zaheer shook his head. "Why then?"

"The frivolity of my outlook is strangely out of character, is it not?" he asked momentarily, tapping his finger on his cup.

"Frivolity? You, Raven?" Zaheer laughed. Somberly he added, "And what of your former misery, Raven? Does it no longer plague you?"

"The misery is lighter somehow, but it is there, make no mistake about that, Zaheer." Val shook his head even as he searched the lobby with his eyes. "This retrieve is nothing more than an odd coincidence, my friend."

"Ah." Zaheer nodded in enlightened agreement. "No doubt. You meet the woman, the light returns to your eyes, you no longer look like a skeleton, and it is *coincidence*."

"I assure you that I have too many important things to do to be obsessed with parlor games, Zaheer. She is not for me and shall have to be forgotten."

As much as I should like to remember. Val smiled involuntarily as he recalled his encounter with Miss Alita Stanton. He didn't know how she had gathered her information, but it could have been accomplished with sources and lucky guesses. Lord knows that many a war had been won against all odds with just such a combination of sources and luck.

Val snorted. One thing was certain—he knew that Miss Alita Stanton didn't have some type of supernatural abilities. Why she would go to the trouble of presenting an elaborate pretense, knowing that he could not possibly take her seriously, he could not fathom.

The Paradox: The Soldier and the Mystic 131

"I beg your forgiveness for disagreeing with you, Raven, but I know what you do, and it is not more important than a woman." Zaheer's laughter sounded more like a whoop than a proper English laugh. The fellow had clearly become overly confident in his presence.

"I am sorry that you hold no high opinion of my work, Zaheer." Val chuckled in spite of himself. "But I assure you that it is more important than this woman. She is a merchant's daughter looking to marry a title. She wasn't the first, and she won't be the last, God willing."

"Ah, finally you acknowledge Allah's part in the whole affair," stated Zaheer. "It is a great wisdom to know that Allah has a plan for your life."

She was like stardust descending the spiral mahogany staircase. *It was her*, none other than the conjurer of this spell from which he was unable to break free, floating through the air. He caught his breath as he lowered his teacup, almost setting it on the edge of the saucer, throwing some drops of hot tea on the counter.

Zaheer busied himself with wiping the counter, his eyes glued to the staircase.

Beautiful. She was dressed to the nines in a creamy pink dress fitted to her slim silhouette. Black velvet bows accented the folds of material along her hips. A small cape of lace framed her neckline. Three-quarter-length ruffled and laced sleeves puffed at the shoulders. She wore chamois gloves and an upturned straw hat lined with black velvet and lace. Pink roses were under the brim of the hat while pink ostrich tips adorned the outside.

There was a gaiety to her expression which cast a pink glow to her cheeks. Against so much pink, her emerald-green eyes glittered, even from this distance.

As he tore his eyes from her, he saw that she was accompanied by an older woman dressed even more elaborately than she was. A large, over-decorated hat hid her face.

Bloody hell. And who was that milksop with her? A tall, blond Nordic god in English attire. Val's stomach tightened as she laughed at something he said, her eyes sparkling and attentive. *Precisely the expression she had utilized on him.*

"I would not question Allah's judgment on this." Zaheer chuckled, whistling under his breath as he followed the direction of Val's eyes. "I am sad for your burden, but you must make do with a merchant's daughter, Raven."

Val did not answer. He had *his* answer, and there was no more to be said. There was absolutely no difference in her countenance toward her new prey as she had adoringly displayed toward him.

What was she telling the fellow? *Of his illustrious future?*

Suddenly she began to look frantically about her, and Val ducked behind a post so as to be just out of her vision. She seemed to be scanning the crowd. Apparently even the blond Adonis did not have it within his power to hold her attention.

But Miss Alita Stanton had wished to help *him*, had she? Val laughed out loud.

"Clearly Allah views you with favor, Raven." Zaheer studied him with a newfound interest.

"You are welcome to your fantasies, my friend, but I have work to do. What is my bill?" Val rose from his seat, taking care that his back was to the door.

That would be the day when someone waltzed into his life not thinking of how to use him for their own purposes. That hadn't been the case with anyone in his life.

"Shall I put in on Sir Evelyn's tab?" Zaheer asked.

"Thanks for the tea," he muttered, throwing a coin on the counter.

"I hope that it met your high standards, Raven," Zaheer replied with a sly smile.

Val scowled at him. Exiting the side door, he fought the cloud of gloom that threatened to descend upon him again.

Why should I feel disappointment? The little minx had behaved precisely as suited her character.

He had thought there might be some surprises left in life when he met Miss Alita Stanton.

But in fact, everything was entirely predictable.

Chapter Thirteen

Ouch! Inadvertently pricking herself, Alita placed her finger to her lips as she considered her surprising experience of meeting the Earl of Ravensdale. The reflections transferred none too well to her needlework as she sat embroidering with her grandmother after dinner in their suite at Shepheard's.

Ordinarily she took an unexpected pleasure in the extraordinary views from the large oval windows. On one side of the suite was a view of the central courtyard and on the other a stunning view of the Nile from their balcony.

Neither view captured her attention on this evening. Nor did the Egyptian artifacts decorating the trilevel blue-and-gold suite conveniently appointed with a sitting area mid level. Even the reverent sounds of worship from the minaret of a nearby mosque failed to pull her from her disturbed thoughts.

As she studied her irregular stitches with displeasure, she considered that an explanation of his lordship's character was not as simple as it might appear. In point of fact, she had been *possessed* by this man's spirit for months—there was really no more accurate way to express it—and to meet him in person was an entirely different experience than meeting him in the spiritual plane.

And disturbingly similar.

She had encountered men who were deeply obsessed with the carnal side of life, but this was not the earl of Ravensdale. He was, instead, intensely focused on the exercise of his intellect. There could be no doubt that he was attracted to *her* in a deeply sensual way, but this was not his preferred realm of experience.

Then why is he rejecting me? She wrinkled her brow, pausing for a moment from her fatal stitching. He was attracted to her all on almost all levels, spiritual, emotional, and physical.

It was perplexing.

The dowager duchess cleared her throat, and she looked up momentarily to see that her grandmother, resplendent in a lavender Watteau wrapper as she stitched, was having considerably more success at her embroidery.

"We do not meet on the intellectual plane," she murmured.

"Excuse me?" asked Her Grace, looking up.

"Nothing, Grandmamma, just thinking out loud."

"Young ladies do not think out loud," the duchess reprimanded, muttering, "Being in this foreign land is one of the grave consequences of manners such as that."

"Of course." Suddenly grasping the reason for the chasm between the earl and herself, she nodded her head. Val Huntington was a man of deep emotions who interpreted the world primarily through his logic, and she was an equally intelligent person who experienced and deciphered the world through her emotions and her instincts. She might understand *him*, but he certainly did not comprehend nor approve of her.

She pursed her lips in self-reprimand. The purpose of her visit to Egypt was not to earn the Black Panther's good opinion, nor to fuse with him on any level, nor to procure something for herself. She had come so that Val Huntington might realize who *he* was. She had not come in order that he might comprehend *her*.

It was well known who she was—a foolish girl who had ruined her first season despite having had every possible advantage, including the ability to sense the thoughts and feelings of others.

How was it possible to fail given such advantageous circumstances?

And if she was unable to succeed with every advantage, how could she possibly succeed thousands of miles from home in Egypt where she was truly out of her element? Could there be any doubt that she was yet on another doomed mission sure to fail because *she* had undertaken it?

"Why do you have such a long face, my dear?" Suddenly the Duchess's voice broke through the string of Alita's distressed thoughts.

"Oh, it's nothing really, Grandmamma," stated Alita lightly as she stared down at her lap. Regrettably, there was nothing more she could do. She had told Lord Ravensdale what she came to say, he hadn't believed her, and he refused to see her. Possibly he would consider her words at some future point.

"Oh?" inquired Marvella. "And where were you yesterday afternoon, Alita, dear? You have seemed quite out of sorts since then."

"I went to the British Consulate." Alita took a sip of her tea and pretended to look out the window. She wished that she could forget looking into the depths of silver eyes luminous with raw pain. Defying even her own thoughts, vigilantly she searched her memory for some piece of information that might assist her.

"I see," stated Marvella. As her pale blue eyes scrutinized her, she added offhandedly, "And to what purpose?" She situated herself beside Alita, the purple satin bows of her lavender Watteau wrapper brushing against her hand.

"I went to see the garden," murmured Alita as she took up her embroidery again and set down her tea cup. "And then I had the sudden odd feeling that there might be someone there. Someone...whom I knew."

"And was there?" asked Marvella, feigning only the slightest interest.

"Was there what?" asked Alita as she lookup up from her embroidery.

"Was there someone there whom you knew?" demanded the dowager duchess.

"Yes," stated Alita as she continued stitching. "And...*no*." She saw clearly that outstanding qualities and experiences had come together to make this amazing person—the 5th Earl of Ravensdale—and he was throwing it away every day of his life.

"Child, would you please put down your needlework and talk to me?" ordered Marvella with a heavy sigh, beginning to appear most put out.

"Grandmamma, honestly, I can stitch and talk at the same time," stated Alita with emphasis.

"Then please do so," replied Marvella with exasperation, appearing to lose her patience, Alita knew not why.

"Do what?" asked Alita, a sadness washing over her. Unless Val realized who he *was*, he would never become himself. And if he did not become himself, many people would suffer and die in an unnecessary battle that he could prevent. If only she could help him, she would have done this one truly worthwhile act.

But she was at a loss to know how. Even as she attempted to foresee the circumstances, the image that came to her repeatedly was that of books. Shelves and shelves of books.

It made no sense.

The battle that he could prevent began revealing itself to her—so horrible in nature. Everything was raining down on her head at once. She was being immersed in misery, powerless to free herself.

"For the last time, child"—Marvella snatched the embroidery from Alita's hands without further adieu—"*whom* did you see at the British consulate whom you knew?"

"Well..." replied Alita, reflecting on the question as if it were open to interpretation. "In truth, I hadn't actually met him before I arrived there." *One thing is certain. I am no saint.* Alita shook her head in dismay. The man affected her. She longed, no ached, to see him again.

The Dowager Duchess of Salford began to grind her teeth even as she steadied herself on the couch. "And might one inquire of his *name*?" she reiterated in sharp tones.

"Valerius Huntington," stated Alita, feeling wounded. "Honestly, Grandmamma, you might have simply asked instead of getting huffy."

* * * *

"I do apologize, child," stated Marvella, breathing a heavy sigh of relief. Even as she patted her forehead with her handkerchief, she was gratified to learn that her granddaughter was not deliberately withholding information, merely making it excessively difficult to obtain. She was up to *that* challenge. Alita motioned for her embroidery, and reluctantly, Marvella returned it to her.

"Hmmm," sounded Marvella. "Valerius Huntington would be the sixth Earl of Ravensdale, would he not?"

"The fifth, I believe," replied Alita, not looking up from her sad designs. The girl could make a flower grow out of a rock—but no amount of practice would make her into a seamstress.

Curious, Marvella watched her. She had seen evasive behavior in her own daughter more often than not but never before in her granddaughter. This gloomy, distracted behavior was not typical of Alita. There was some significance to this meeting at the British Consulate, on that she would stake the duchy jewels.

The Paradox: The Soldier and the Mystic 137

If Alita were married—as she *should already be*—these travesties one after another would never have occurred. Alita would be expecting a baby and be deliriously happy.

Instead, Alita was moping about longing for that husband that she very naturally craved and should already have.

Eighteen years old and unmarried. The Dowager Duchess of Salford lowered her head. The saints protect us from the ignorant and shortsighted.

She remembered the chain of events with painful clarity. Alita had begun packing for Egypt, her Aunt Jane and Uncle Oroville had been contacted, responding that they would be delighted to accompany her. At the last minute—when it became clear that the child was serious about going to Egypt, unbelievable as it seemed—she had decreed that she would escort Alita, and that no one had best defy her if they knew what was good for them. The success of the venture depended on Alita's grandmamma, and if they didn't know it, *she* did.

No doubt her vital contributions would one day be known, as would the true unselfishness of her character.

It was a difficult road ahead, but the thing would be accomplished, and she would be the one to do it. She had less than no desire to go to Egypt, but to be ousted by Jane and Oroville Lovett in providing countenance to her favorite grandchild and taking the credit for same she would not allow.

Future generations would have *her* to thank for the successful match that would someday take place. It irritated her no end that this match had not taken place last year, but finally Alita would be in her hands alone, and there would be no incompetents to interfere with progress.

Well, there was nothing for it but to rectify the damage created by those less astute than herself. Marvella considered the range of possibilities. She still cherished the hope of an alliance between Alita and Lord Manchestor.

Oh, and hadn't that been a stroke of genius to arrange for William Manchestor to serve as her escort on this journey? Lord Manchestor had not been difficult to convince. Alita's father had been fit to tie, but she had insisted that she herself was Alita's chaperone and that Lord Manchestor was an old woman's escort, necessary to their safety. Alita's maid was along, so there could be no question of impropriety. That Lord Manchestor's family was above reproach and cherished their reputation above all else was evident. In the end, Elaina had actually supported the idea.

Marvella wrinkled her nose. Her daughter agreeing to a clearly brilliant plan had been a surprise.

"And what did you speak of with Lord Ravensdale, Alita?" she asked.

"His work," Alita replied with far too much emotion even as her lips formed a slight frown.

"And what does the earl do at the consulate?" asked Marvella. Was the earl of Ravensdale a suitable husband for Alita? She tapped her forehead with her index finger. That remained to be seen. Best to capitalize on every opportunity—and to play each against the other, Marvella thought with a sly smile.

"I'm not certain," stated Alita. "Something to do with translating."

"But I thought you said that you spoke of his work?" Marvella's eyebrows rose.

"Yes, we did," Alita stated emphatically, offering no further explanation.

"And did you like this Lord Ravensdale?" Marvella asked, her voice politely indifferent but her mind alert and intense. She did her best to conceal her exacerbation from her voice. It was not the facts that mattered, after all.

It was how they were arranged.

"Yes, Grandmamma." For the first time, Alita looked up, her eyes clear and her countenance present. "Yes, I think I did."

As the dowager duchess studied her granddaughter's expression, the wheels in her mind began to turn full force. It was much easier to promote a match where there was a strong attachment. And there was an attachment, mark her words, at least on Alita's side.

She was quite certain that Alita could inspire the gentleman in question to matrimony if that were the girl's wish. Alita was *her granddaughter,* after all. She smiled to herself with satisfaction.

"You're not certain about that either?" asked Her Grace nonchalantly, pretending to occupy herself with her own embroidery, which she had only just picked up from the adjoining table.

"Yes, I am. It's just that…well…" began Alita, taking a moment to consider the question. She seemed unsure of her feelings where Lord Ravensdale was concerned, Marvella reflected with interest. "It's just that when I first met him, he struck me as…*dangerous.*"

The Paradox: The Soldier and the Mystic   *139*

"*Dangerous?*" Marvella dropped her embroidery in her lap.

"Oh, *no*, Grandmamma! Not that he would hurt me, you understand." Alita smiled for the first time that evening. "But just that I had never met anyone like him before. And I suppose because he was so *different* from me, and with such a large presence, you realize, it left me overwrought." She paused, her embroidery in midair. "The fear of the unknown, I suppose."

That's all I need to know. Marvella Lancastor sat back in her chair and smiled with satisfaction.

Oh, how I miss the duke. Without warning, grief washed over her.

She sniffed. Well, there was work to be done now. There was no time for wasted days and useless tears. Honestly, these children couldn't manage anything on their own. She had been able to accomplish whatsoever she put her mind to from the time she was fourteen years old. The whole thing had been bungled badly, and now it was up to her to fix it.

"Grandmamma, could we please not speak of Lord Ravensdale anymore?" Alita sighed heavily.

She gazed upon her granddaughter, so like a fairy in a pink tea gown, a fanciful confection of sheer, ruched lace and ruffles from head to toe, ruffles framing her neckline down to her waist.

Alita was a beautiful, graceful child, everything that she liked in a female. Marvella had no doubt of the girl's ultimate success. The thing was as well as accomplished.

Now they must simply proceed through the steps. It would be laborious, but work that the Duchess of Salford was extremely capable of performing.

"Certainly, child," replied the dowager duchess. She tapped her fingers for a moment on the blue satin armrest of the couch.

Chapter Fourteen

"Alita! Are you daydreaming again? I declare, your manners are atrocious! What has gotten into you, my girl?" The duchess paused her coffee cup in midair, turning to Lord William Manchestor and remarking at just the volume that might have been heard by the entire room had the orchestra not been playing, "When she has some children to absorb her attentions, she will be just fine. All girls are this way at her"—*cough*—"*age.*" *Cough.* "It is a sure sign that they are ripe for marriage."

"Indeed." He nodded, his lower lip unable to suppress a slight quiver.

"Excuse me? I beg your pardon?" Alita's eyes opened wide in shock at the direction the conversation was taking. "I was just reflecting. Whoever would have thought of mixing...What is that?—with cucumbers?" In truth, she *had* been daydreaming, but thankfully they had not been long in Cairo, and the novelty of the exotic flavors and the exquisite dinners at Shepheard's provided her with a welcome screen.

"Tomatoes and green peppers?" Lord William Manchestor chuckled, a boyish grin lighting his deep blue eyes, sparkling against streaked blond hair. "Most unusual vegetables."

"No, silly, what *spices*?" She giggled. "Mint...and..."

"Coriander," stated the duchess. "I never cared for it myself."

"But, Grandmamma! The tomatoes are positively the sweetest I ever tasted!" added Alita. "It cannot be news to me that Egypt is home to one of the most fertile valleys in the world."

"Yes, one would think it might be applied to better use. Taking perfectly good vegetables and adding disturbing spices."

"I think the cuisine positively marvelous." She knew she had spoken her true thoughts, at least in that. The bountiful meal began with wine, a coarse wheat pita bread, tahini sauce, hummus and garlic, and the unusual but delicious salad in vinegar. These delights were followed by sautéed fish in

The Paradox: The Soldier and the Mystic 141

butter and garlic, roasted chicken, brown rice, and moussaka, a mixture of eggplant and white cheese.

As they partook of dinner, Alita gazed into vivid blue eyes framed by masculine features and sandy-blond hair, and her mind happily drifted back to a shared memory, her first moment of seeing the port city of Alexandria, her first glimpse of Egypt, a sight she knew she would never forget.

"Oh, the beaches are sparkling white," she had whispered to William, "and go on forever. One sees no end to them. And the water, so azure against the white beaches."

"The Pearl of the Mediterranean," William had murmured as his eyes rested caressingly on her instead of on Alexandria. She warmed now even to remember it.

"It is a mystery, William."

"What is, Miss Alita?"

"I was always a person so attached to home." Watching the harbor coming into view, she had reflected out loud, something she felt more and more comfortable doing in William's presence. "I never had the slightest desire to visit any place far from home—certainly not exotic lands—and here I am, coming into Egypt!"

"I feel equally astonished to find myself here."

"The surprising thing is that I am enjoying myself immensely. I did not come because I wished to come, and yet..." She had smiled at him, suppressing a giggle. It was an indescribably wonderful sensation to stifle laughter after fighting a deep sadness.

Only she knew the full reason for her journey, though her disgrace was by then well known to Lord Manchestor. She knew William to be a stickler for the formalities, but that was due more to pragmatism than to snobbery, she had learned. His family's livelihood and reason for being was politics, a field which required social approval to be successful.

She was therefore surprised that he had aligned himself with her. She had to conclude that her embarrassment was merely a source of amusement about London more than a blight upon her family's reputation.

At least she hoped so.

"I do not fault you in the least, Miss Alita." He had read the question in her eyes and answered it. "Excuse me, I beg you will finish your sentence. And yet...what?"

"And yet," Alita added, "I am having the time of my life!"

"And I also, Miss Alita." He took her hand and gently held it in his. She felt the warmth of companionship, which made her feel safe and content.

"Is it not difficult to believe that this beautiful port was the setting for the stormy relationship between Cleopatra and Mark Antony?" William had pointed to the shore and asked. She recalled his words so clearly. "And what of you, Miss Alita? Is that what you want from life? A stormy romance? Theatrical courtships?"

"Oh, no, William!" She had been unable to contain her laughter. "I seem to land myself into scrapes, but that is not what I want. More than anything, I want...Peace. Contentment. Family." *Acceptance.*

"Myself also." She remembered every nuance of his smile as he had gazed at her, so like the gaze he bestowed upon her now. Her heart quickened as his tranquil blue eyes met hers, his blond hair in striking contrast to the black formal dress he wore.

In the eight weeks she had been with William Manchestor, there was never any deviation from his dinner attire—a low-cut white vest, a white bow tie, a winged shirt, black tails and black pants, polished black shoes. His gloves were never even a shade away from pure white. His wavy blond hair was never too long or too short, always perfectly shaped. His always-clean-shaven face showed its strong lines. He had a sweet smile and a reticence to his manner, as if he were debating the appropriate thing to say.

William wore a small white rose in his buttonhole, he favored jewelry, and he always wore a watch chain. The time appeared to be of great importance to him, and he was unfailingly punctual.

This memory with William at Alexandria had given her so much pleasure and comfort.

Until now.

Since meeting Lord Ravensdale, everything seemed upside down. She was distressed, uncertain, and anxious. She didn't seem to know her own mind anymore, and her dreams were no longer clear to her.

What could have happened? Why was she so confused?

"Alita! Are you listening?" demanded Marvella. "I will not tolerate this impolite behavior!"

"I am sorry," replied Alita, feeling herself blush. "What did you say?" She glanced apologetically at her grandmamma, stunning in a low-cut red satin dress. She wore ruby and diamond jewelry of a striking quality which perfectly offset her blonde-white hair and pale blue eyes. The duchess— Alita could never really think of her as the *dowager* duchess!—was shapely, and her deportment was elegant.

Every man in the room had turned to look as they entered the room— and Alita was of the decided opinion that it was her curvaceous, daring grandmother and not she who had drawn the most attention!

She herself had modestly opted for a high-necked gown in lavender satin and cream lace. She felt uncomfortable in the plunging neckline, which was the current fashion for evening wear, and which Marvella could well show to advantage.

Yes, Marvella was hands down the show-stopper. She had been turning heads since she was thirteen, and it did not appear that the end to her reign was approaching.

"I *said* that you children are so spoiled. You have no idea how things have changed since I was a girl."

"True, Your Grace." William smiled, seeming unaware of Alita's distress. "Without your enlightenment, we might not fully appreciate our present situation."

"It is indeed exhausting to educate those who have so much to learn," admitted Marvella, smiling at him. "But it must be done."

"And we thank you." William was a most agreeable companion, Alita reflected, never a cross word. Involuntarily, she recalled with a tremor the fury in Lord Ravensdale's eyes when she had mentioned the battle of Tel-el-Kebir.

An unfavorable comparison.

"To begin with"—Marvella cleared her throat, clearly taking William's remarks as an invitation—"we certainly had no steamboats—no engines or motorized travel of any kind." Marvella scowled and glanced at Alita. "If it weren't for your father, if he hadn't invented that insupportable contraption—"

"The four-stroke piston engine," Alita offered with pride.

"There were only horse-drawn carriages at that time," Marvella continued, ignoring her. "As it should be. Why, your mother took a horse and carriage to London for her first season, as did I. For generations, people's lives were much the same."

Suzette Hollingsworth

"And how long did it take to reach London from Lancashire?" William asked politely.

"Several days, to be sure." Marvella shook her head in disbelief. "And here you are taking a steamboat to Egypt at the same age! It astonishes one."

William and Alita exchanged glances as the duchess continued with her reverie.

"When I was a girl, for entertainment, we used our own talents and our resources to entertain each other. In the evenings, we sang or played our instruments. We had dances. We read aloud to each other. We played cards. We wrote letters. We painted a picture or embroidered together." She smiled wistfully.

"I still partake in all those activities," remarked Alita.

"You aren't now, are you, my girl?" demanded Marvella. "Instead, you are traveling around the world eating heathen spices! If you have left the land of your birth—shameful!—you clearly are not spending time with the people you are not with!"

"I am spending time with *you*, Grandmamma!"

"Do not argue, Alita! It is most unladylike." Marvella sighed. "In my day, one even knew when someone lost a tooth. One knew *everyone*."

"But did you not long for some variety in your social calendar, Your Grace?" asked Lord Manchestor.

"One knew that one's neighbors could be counted on in need," the Duchess mused. "Why, when I went to my first London season, there wasn't a person in the village who didn't contribute *something* to my wardrobe or my purse."

"How delightful! What were you given, Grandmamma?" Alita sighed. To have so many people standing behind one, all wishing one well, must have been heaven in itself.

"One farmer sent eggs and a loaf of bread with me." She laughed at the memory. As if confiding a great secret that must always remain so, even these forty-eight years later, in hushed tones she added, "I traded the eggs for a cup of tea and a tart along the way."

"I shall never tell a soul, Grandmamma!" Alita teased, her spirits lifting with the shared reverie.

"An idyllic time," pronounced William.

The Paradox: The Soldier and the Mystic 145

Marvella had a faraway look in her eyes, which made her look to be a young girl. Suddenly, she frowned. "Then, machinery, and voilá! Now we have trains and steam-powered ships."

"In a very short time we have gone from an agricultural nation to a manufacturing nation," William agreed. He smiled at Alita. "Our generation never knew what it was to live in a solely agricultural nation. You know *both*, Duchess."

"I wish I did *not*!"

"I contend, Your Grace," he proposed, "that your generation and your daughter's generation have seen the most change the world has ever seen and will ever see. There can be nothing to match it."

"I have no doubt of that, Lord Manchestor!" exclaimed Marvella, scowling. "And the changes are most disturbing! All these inventions that we don't need. Ships which travel to Egypt, for one thing—"

"I, for one, am exceedingly thankful for ships," William interjected, smiling at Alita. The warmth in his gaze surrounded her like a comfortable feather bed.

Instantaneously and unwillingly, Lord Ravensdale's smile flashed in her mind, intense and hot.

"R–r–refrigeration is somewhat useful," Alita stammered, touching her cheek. "My father studied under Michael Faraday, who discovered the principle of refrigeration. Faraday found that certain gases under constant pressure will condense until they cool."

Both William and Marvella stared at her with a bit more discomfiture than she might have wished for.

"Alita Stanton!" the duchess found her voice first, which was in keeping with expectations. "I won't have a blue-stocking for a granddaughter!"

"A blue-stocking!" She giggled. "That is the last thing—"

"It is not becoming to be too bookish." Marvella whispered loudly to William, "She gets that from her father," apparently wishing to dispel any notions of excessive intelligence running in the female line.

"And did you enjoy your first London season, Grandmamma?" Alita took her grandmother's hand and squeezed it, attempting to appease her dismay.

"Hmmm, *enjoy*," Marvella considered somberly, shaking slightly these so many years later as she no doubt relived the reality that her entire life rested on her season. "It was not entertainment nor a diversion for me as it was for some. It was my *livelihood*. There was only success or failure. There was no in between. My family could not afford a second season."

She had been terrified! Alita suddenly knew her grandmamma in a way that had never been real to her before.

Marvella placed her hand at her throat as if catching her breath all over again. Her hand touched a ruby pendant nestled in expensive lace, as if they were a comfort to the resurfacing vicar's daughter who owned no jewels.

"And the men of that day. Were they very different from today's young men, Grandmamma?" Alita asked, genuinely curious. Had she more than one beau? Or was it only Richard Lancastor for her?

"Renaissance men, every one of them." She grew pensive, her lips forming a slight smile, as she remembered the elegant gentlemen of her youth. "It was a time when men understood everything in their world."

"There was less to understand," William posed.

"Far more educated than the men of today." The duchess shook her head in disagreement. "They knew Greek, Latin, Italian, and French. They were well-read in every subject, both in literature and mathematics. They played musical instruments. They were master sportsmen. They knew fencing, boxing, and all the fighting arts." Marvella smiled, and she looked as if she were sixteen again. "One doesn't meet men like that these days."

Alita considered her grandmother's words. The sounds of the orchestra drifted in and out of their words, adding weight to the nuances. She had just met such a man as her grandmamma described.

She wished with all her heart that she would stop thinking about him.

"Alita's father does not know Greek or Latin, and yet he has invented machinery which has changed the face of the world forever." William chuckled, ignoring the slight as he picked up a crystal salt shaker to season his sautéed fish displayed against crisp white linens and silver tea sets. "Surely that must count for something."

"Humph!" snorted the Dowager Duchess of Salford, raising her lovely arched brows. "There has only been one invention of note in my lifetime."

"One? You can't be serious, ma'am," stated William incredulously.

"I'll thank you not to tell me when I'm serious and when I'm not, young man." Marvella raised her eyebrows haughtily.

The Paradox: The Soldier and the Mystic

William flashed a beautiful smile at her, and the duchess was immediately placated. Alita felt herself succumbing to that heavenly smile amidst ruggedly masculine features framed by burnt-blond hair as well.

"And what is that invention of note, Grandmamma?" Alita asked, clearing her throat.

"I'll never forget the first time I walked into Mr. Cadbury's shop." Marvella sighed.

"*Cadbury's Chocolates* is the invention of note?" It was Alita's turn to raise her eyebrows.

"Do you know of a better invention than chocolate?" demanded her Grace.

"Ah, yes," stated William. "English Quaker John Cadbury opened a coffee shop after he began experimenting with grinding cocoa beans and making chocolate."

"And when was your first season, Grandmamma? When did you first make an acquaintance with Mr. Cadbury?" asked Alita, giggling. When her grandmother spoke, Alita could feel some sense of what it was like to live in former times, and it fascinated her. It felt as if she were actually engaged in time travel.

"Let's see. I was born in 1820. I was just turned sixteen, so it was 1836." Marvella tapped her finger on her cheek. "Elaina was born May 1, 1838, when I was eighteen. *Alita's age*," she added pointedly. "Girls did not waste so much time in my day," she added under her breath, her expression indicating that Alita's child-bearing years were quickly drawing to a close.

Alita stifled a giggle. "And I was born March 19, 1864. If I live to be eighty, that will be 1944." She sighed. "And yet, by talking to my Grandmamma, I can be taken back to 1820. *I am there with her* as she speaks. In reliving all these memories, my life may span one hundred and twenty-five years, utilizing both my experiences and an eyewitness account. Seeing it with her eyes, I can experience from prior to the advent of machinery to—who knows? Perhaps women will vote?"

"I hope that I may die first before I see women intrude upon a man's realm," Marvella articulated, grasping her hands to her throat. It appeared that she might choke even as William chuckled out loud.

"Your mother is well acquainted with John Stuart Mill, I believe, who has often campaigned for women's suffrage in Parliament?" William studied Alita with obvious curiosity, getting the better of his usual reserve.

"Ma-ma knows positively *everyone*." Alita smiled and rolled her eyes. "Do you realize that she was bounced on the great Gladstone's knee?"

"The duke spoiled her shamelessly!" Marvella frowned. "Elaina was allowed to converse at the dinner table with every manner of person from the time she was twelve years old."

"But you do not share your mother's zeal for women's politics, do you, Miss Alita?" Lord Manchestor asked.

She shook her head, unable to find her voice.

"It complicates one's life to hold unpopular opinions, and if complications can be avoided, all the better," he added with both undisguised affection and relief.

"There is no doubt of that," murmured Alita, longing with all her heart for a less complicated existence containing far less challenging persons— Lord Ravensdale being at the top of that list. A more complex person in more turmoil would be difficult to locate.

And yet she had come here to find him!

Some people seemed in search of trouble. She glanced at William. He was a man who avoided problems. Much wiser!

"Whereas Elaina was always drawn to people who challenge society! Most disturbing!" Marvella added, as if reading her mind.

"Long before Mill's esteemed election to Parliament, he was arrested, my mother informs me," Alita explained.

"Oh?" exclaimed Marvella as she reached for her wine. "Elaina consorts with persons who have been incarcerated? On what charge?" she demanded.

"For, let us say, distributing *controversial* literature," interrupted Lord Manchestor with a tone of finality in his voice, clearly attempting to change the subject.

"For distributing literature on birth control to the London poor," Alita stated simply.

Marvella tottered in her chair, appearing as if she might faint except that she almost hit herself in the forehead with the back of her hand in a sweeping motion, which appeared to revive her.

The Paradox: The Soldier and the Mystic 149

William likewise expressed shock at her remark, though she knew full well the content of the pamphlets were known to him.

Without wishing to consider the matter, she wondered how Lord Ravensdale would have reacted to her words.

She expected he might have simply...*smiled*. She barely knew him and she saw that smile too vividly in her mind's eye. The right corner of his mouth noticeably higher than the left, all of the ferocity in his gaze disappearing while the intensity remained.

"Alita! That is not appropriate conversation for young ladies." Marvella shook her head in grave disapproval, gasping rather than speaking her words. "I had been thinking for some time that your conversation was far too informed for a young lady. And now I see where it leads!"

"It happened." Alita shrugged nonchalantly. "I don't see how covering up the truth could possibly be of importance to anyone."

William began to chuckle, his amusement clearly overcoming his surprise. He did not seem to be able to help but be delighted by her, as hard as he might try to maintain a respectable countenance. He stated softly, "The fact that you don't see is why we are here in Egypt, Miss Alita."

Alita was pained by William's remark, and her feelings must have revealed themselves by his alarmed reaction.

"My dear Miss Alita, I am profoundly sorry if I distressed you," he offered, studying her face with mortification.

"You were merely speaking the truth, William."

"Let us speak of it no more." Marvella's expression was stern. "It is the fault of the tainted time in which we live and not of Alita's dear, sweet nature. If only ladies returned to looking and acting like young ladies, the world would be a greatly improved place," Her Grace proclaimed.

"Hear! Hear!" William agreed as he raised his glass.

The three nodded in unison. It seemed they had hit on a subject upon which they could all agree.

Their delicious dinner appeared to be coming to a close when the waiter arrived with the final course of Turkish coffee, grapes, a lightly sweetened dough filled with a mixture of dates, figs, and nuts and drizzled with honey, and, not to be overlooked, the English dessert tray. Almost in one voice they exclaimed "chocolate cake" after the dessert selection was presented.

"And now we shall show honor to Henri Nestlé as well as to John Cadbury," stated Marvella.

"Did not Mr. Nestlé develop milk chocolate for eating by mixing sweetened condensed milk with chocolate?" Alita laughed.

"May God bless his soul," stated Marvella, lowering her head as if in silent prayer.

"Ah, Your Grace, but whom do you regard more highly?" inquired Lord Manchestor. "Henri Nestlé or John Cadbury?"

"They guard the twin gates to heaven," Marvella replied without hesitation.

"It has all become clear to me now, Your Grace." Lord Manchestor chuckled as they all laughed in unison. "You place Cadbury above the great men of science for contributions to our world."

The Dowager Duchess of Salford held up one piece of the chocolate cake in Alita's line of sight. "I rest my case," she pronounced as she took a bite, her eyes closing with obvious bliss.

Chapter Fifteen

To say that she believed in magic was to stretch the truth, but Marvella certainly believed in her ability to create her world. And even if she had not, she would have died trying.

Marvella Lancastor was not a woman to accept the hand that life dealt her. She was a woman determined to be the dealer.

It didn't take too many days before she grew impatient with watching her granddaughter mope about as if there were nothing in Cairo to catch her interest. Egypt wasn't Marvella's idea of a grand holiday, but if she didn't like something, she made something better happen.

Tapping her fingers on her dressing table as she gazed into the gilded mirror, she was pleased with what she saw there. She could never think of herself as the *dowager* duchess. Who was that young upstart whom her son was married to anyway? The chit did not deserve the title.

Marvella reflected that a trip to the pyramids should respark Alita's interest. Everyone spoke of how fascinating they were. She sighed and rolled her eyes.

Whatever it took to entice her granddaughter back into the world would be worth it. She spritzed her favorite perfume, La Bud Parisienne, along the décolletage of her lavender silk gown.

Lord William Manchestor should have inspired Alita out of her doldrums, but the child was ridiculously distracted when she should be utilizing everything at her disposal to ensnare that biddable gentleman.

Honestly! Must I do everything myself? She considered her various lipsticks and chose a crimson red, which offset her pale blue eyes and blonde-white hair strikingly. It was almost never to one's disadvantage to be striking.

And certainly not today.

In the end there was nothing for it but to make a trip to the British Consulate to pay a visit to her old friend Sir Evelyn Baring, who had dined in her house on numerous occasions long before he had become a person of such importance. The duke and Sir Evelyn had been old cronies, though much of their recent communication had been through letters, since Sir Evelyn had been stationed in India for many years.

The Dowager Duchess of Salford was announced from the waiting room of the Office of the Consul General, and Marvella was sincerely touched to see Sir Evelyn's face light up with her entrance.

"Duchess, I can't tell you how delighted I am to see you," he stated with genuine interest even as his expression saddened. "I was grieved to hear of Richard's death. There wasn't a finer man alive."

"Thank you, Evelyn," Marvella Lancastor stated. "I would be lying if I didn't agree with you."

He took her hand and squeezed it, holding on before he kissed it, and there was a moment of shared, unspoken sorrow between them. He turned for a brief instant before motioning to a gray satin wingback couch and ringing for tea.

She moved the purple-blue velvet tasseled pillows and situated herself, pleased with all she saw, the room and the man. As always, his manner was studious, serious, distinguished. Sir Evelyn stood before her, immaculately dressed in a taupe three-piece suit with a satiny sheen to it. He was of average height with neatly trimmed short, white hair and a white moustache.

Egypt's magnate was well displayed in this plush sitting room furnished in gray raw silk fabrics, mahogany, and purple accents, most notably a beautiful Persian rug in blue, lavender, and gray. A masculine room befitting a man whom she understood had unlimited power. A quality she very much liked in a man.

Or a woman. As long as she was that woman.

"I am not surprised to learn that you have made a great deal of progress in Egypt already, Evelyn," she reflected.

"I am in a position to anticipate the strategies of the World Bank and the IMF." He shrugged. "And I use that knowledge to advantage, with an unwavering insistence on intelligent management, economizing, and frugality."

"Frugality I cannot like, but I suppose it is good for some," she replied with a nod of her chin.

The Paradox: The Soldier and the Mystic 153

He chuckled before they conversed happily for some minutes over shared acquaintances, followed by questions about Sir Evelyn's life in Egypt.

"Is there anything I can do to make your visit more pleasant while you are here in Cairo, Duchess?" he asked at some point. "Let us not stand on ceremony. I can assure you that the country is at my command."

"You and your wife must join us for dinner one night." She smiled warmly. She recalled that Sir Evelyn was extremely devoted to his wife, and she genuinely looked forward to renewing her acquaintance. It would be difficult to see them without her own dear Richard by her side, but let it never be said that Marvella Lancastor would forego pleasure in favor of gloom.

"Oh, most certainly we will meet, Duchess, but you will come to my home. I wish to show you some true Egyptian flavor."

"Thank you, Evelyn. That would be most enjoyable," replied Marvella sincerely. It could only add greatly to Alita's consequence when the London gossip circuit learned that Miss Alita Stanton had dined with the Egyptian head of state, she thought with smug satisfaction. She resolved to write some letters that afternoon with the appropriate hints. "Though I must say I would welcome a return to some *English* flavor."

"Oh, you prefer English cuisine, Duchess?" He chuckled. "My wife does as well. I don't think the spices agree with her constitution."

"It's settled then to the satisfaction of the ladies."

"That is all that matters. Is there anything else I can do for you, Your Grace?"

"I must admit, Evelyn, there is one small matter of great importance to myself and my family with which you may be able to assist," stated Marvella demurely.

"Anything, Duchess," stated Sir Evelyn, clearly having no objection to showing off what was within his power to do, which was just as Marvella had hoped.

"My granddaughter, Alita, has a strong desire to see the pyramids of Giza, and we need a guide."

"Is that all?" He laughed outright. "Most definitely. You cannot go without a guide. I will procure someone suitable."

"Can you keep a secret, Evelyn?" She glanced at him mischievously.

"Of course, Duchess! That's my job," Sir Evelyn stated somberly. "One could not rise to this level of government without knowing when to open and close one's mouth."

"Alita has apparently taken a fancy to a Lord Ravensdale. Do you know him?"

"Know him?" Sir Evelyn nodded, smiling slightly to himself. "Valerius Ravensdale holds a position under my employ. Most exceptional person."

"Oh? And what is his character?" she asked nonchalantly.

"His character," Sir Evelyn mused, a twinkle in his eye, almost as if he were goading her. "Difficult to put into words. One really has to meet him."

"Do try, Evelyn."

"Very well then." Sir Evelyn leaned back in his chair. "The only opinion Ravensdale is interested in is his own. His men would follow him to the ends of the earth despite the fact that he is a maniac. And he is obstinate, proud, reckless, fanatical, fearless to a fault, indomitable, passionate, heroic, brilliant...*extraordinary*."

Marvella felt great satisfaction at this pronouncement. "And is he a suitable young man?"

"As a guide or as a husband, Duchess?" Sir Evelyn's lips formed a sly grin.

Marvella did not reply but, instead, bestowed an angelic smile upon his lordship.

"As I thought," Sir Evelyn replied, breaking into an uncharacteristically hearty laugh. "As it so happens, Valerius Huntington is a language expert. He can even read Egyptian hieroglyphics, which is no small matter, I assure you, in addition to being an unusually intelligent young man of impeccable integrity. I don't know of a more suitable guide for...er...a *tour of the pyramids*." He regarded Marvella with an inquisitive expression. "But you probably knew that, my dear?"

"No, I didn't," replied Marvella truthfully. "You know how the young are. Information was sparse. But can he be spared?" she asked coyly.

"For you, Duchess, *anything*." Sir Evelyn leaned toward her, even as his expression grew pensive. "Up to now, I have seen nothing but Ravensdale's studies to interest him. I hope we can change all that, Your Grace." He had the expression of a man contemplating a desirable hold over a heretofore

The Paradox: The Soldier and the Mystic 155

elusive adversary, Marvella thought, having seen that expression on her late-husband's face many times when he was wrestling with a political problem.

"This means so much to me." And she meant that most sincerely. She leaned over to the chair in which Sir Evelyn was sitting and placed her hand on top of his. "Thank you, Evelyn."

"Yes, Marvella," he replied somberly. Sir Evelyn rose and called to his secretary. "Randall, will you please send Ravensdale in?"

The two old friends spoke for some minutes more before Lord Ravensdale arrived. He entered the room swiftly and bowed to Sir Evelyn.

Oh, my! Not at all what she expected! She almost could not contain herself from shaking her head.

He wore a tan linen sack suit without tails! Young people today were so inattentive in their dress. His shirt collar was not stiff and high like Sir Evelyn's. He wore a slim silk cravat tied in the Windsor tie. Most inappropriate. There was no flower in his buttonhole, no watch chain dangling from a vest—indeed, no vest!

He was decidedly underdressed.

His suit was well-tailored but looser than she liked to see on a young man. A suit should fit next to the skin.

But what was truly disconcerting was that, though he had no moustache or beard, he had the beginnings of both! Positively uncivilized! He looked as if he had been up all night. His hair was almost too long. Far too rugged indeed.

Yes, he would do nicely.

The man fairly emanated masculinity, strength, and a sense of purpose. Very handsome, to be sure.

If he was titled and moneyed and Alita liked him—and that she would stake her life on—who was her grandmamma to object? The children would be lovely indeed. She began to picture the offspring from the union when Sir Evelyn's voice captured her attention.

"Valerius," Sir Evelyn began as he stood, "may I introduce Her Grace the Dowager Duchess of Salford, the esteemed Richard Lancastor's widow, to you?"

"It is an honor to meet you, Your Grace." The earl bowed deeply, the pleasure and surprise on his face evident. "I am a great admirer of your late husband's. Every future generation will benefit from the Duke's reform efforts."

"Valerius Huntington, 5th Earl of Ravensdale," Lord Cromer uttered by way of introduction.

"Thank you for your kind words, Lord Ravensdale," she stated solemnly, her approval immediately increasing. She began to like the young man very much in spite of his inattention to appearance, something she generally had difficulty overlooking. "You were acquainted with the duke, Lord Ravensdale?"

"I never had the pleasure. I was at Cambridge, after which I immediately went into the army as a young man, Your Grace," he stated in low tones. "I was, in fact, on the battlefield when I assumed the peerage. I never had the honor and privilege of assuming my duties in the House of Lords."

"The duchess tells me that you are, however, acquainted with her granddaughter, Valerius," stated Sir Evelyn, resting his chin in his hand.

"Your granddaughter?" Lord Ravensdale appeared noticeably perplexed. It was well known to all present that he would have remembered the granddaughter of His Grace the Duke of Salford even if she had had the personality and appearance of a dead fish. Val shook his head, clearly certain that the duchess had been misinformed. "Possibly she had me confused with someone else."

"I don't believe so, Your Lordship. She gave me your name herself."

"I haven't been in London in years." His lips formed an enchanting smile, which Marvella had no doubt was designed to win over every generation of womankind. It was certainly working on her, she had to admit. "Even if the acquaintance had been many, many years ago within the insipid confines of London society, I can assure you that I would remember the Duke of Salford's granddaughter. I am said to have an excellent memory."

"My granddaughter did not meet you in London."

"Oh?" Politely he asked, as if merely to placate her, "What is your granddaughter's name?"

Without further ceremony, Marvella replied, "Miss Alita Stanton."

A wave of recognition immediately washed over Lord Ravensdale's face, and it was evident to both parties present that the Earl of Ravensdale both remembered Her Grace's granddaughter very well and that he had not been entirely bored in the young lady's presence.

The Paradox: The Soldier and the Mystic 157

"I see that you recall her?" stated Marvella with no small amount of satisfaction. "She is a most beautiful girl, is she not?"

"No one could deny that fact who has seen her," enunciated Lord Ravensdale in controlled tones, his voice harsher and lower than it had been. "Or the reality of her illustrious connections," he added tersely.

"Is it possible"—suddenly, yet another wave of recognition washed over Lord Ravensdale's countenance—"*could it be possible* that Miss Stanton is the daughter of Dr. Jonathan Stanton, who invented the four-stroke piston engine?"

"To be sure, Lord Ravensdale." Marvella released a single deep sigh followed by a nod. She grew weary of this connection.

"Altering the course of history forever for all of humankind," he added in deliberate tones, his voice strangely choppy.

"Are you quite all right, Lord Ravensdale?" asked Marvella.

"Quite," he replied, but there were flames shooting from his eyes, his tone carrying an edge.

"Ravensdale?" posed Lord Cromer.

"It is astonishing…" Everything else in Lord Ravensdale's countenance remained controlled and cordial. He added in the smoothest of tones, "Your Grace, how one's memory overwhelms one at times. For example," he articulated, his index finger tapping his forehead, "I believe that Dr. Stanton's wife actually works with Florence Nightingale, yet another notable?"

To a sigh and a nod, Marvella added a grimace. "You do have an excellent memory, Your Lordship," she stated flatly.

"Please pardon my slow recollection, Your Grace," Lord Ravensdale stated, clearly struggling to maintain his composure. "I met Miss Stanton here, at the British Consulate, but she did not speak of her relations. I did ask after her family, of course, but it appears that there were some…omissions…in her reply."

"Unusual," replied Marvella. "Generally that is the first thing people speak of."

"It is a fact which, frankly, perplexes me as well."

Observing Lord Ravensdale's stiff demeanor but not convinced that further quizzing would promote her purposes, she dismissed her curiosity in favor of more practical matters. "I expect that you found other topics to engage your interest. Alita is an exceptionally sympathetic girl, as I'm sure you are aware, Lord Ravensdale." She bestowed a warm smile upon him.

"Most sympathetic. It did not escape my notice."

She exchanged knowing looks with Sir Evelyn, and she was fairly certain they shared the same thoughts. Neither she nor Sir Evelyn knew the reason for Lord Ravensdale's obvious discomfort, which he was at great pains to attempt to hide, but she surmised that an attraction existed between Alita and Valerius. Whatever the meeting that had taken place, the usual formalities did not appear to have been observed, and it therefore appeared difficult for Lord Ravensdale to respond to their queries. Marvella supposed that it had been a brief meeting, though apparently memorable to both parties. Perhaps the earl had been on his way to a pressing engagement and they had merely exchanged a few words.

Sir Evelyn intervened. "You'll be gratified to know, Ravensdale, that I have offered your services as a guide to the Pyramids at Giza to Miss Stanton and the duchess."

Lord Ravensdale appeared far from pleased. "Sir, though I can think of nothing more pleasurable, and though it bestows a great honor on me, I fear that there are several pressing reports which you will not wish me to delay. Allow me to find a more suitable guide for the ladies."

"I assure you, Valerius, that I can wait another day on the reports. I desire you to accompany the ladies." Sir Evelyn's expression grew hard and his voice uncompromising, even as a wave of his hand indicated dismissal. "Call on them tomorrow."

"Yes, sir." Lord Ravensdale bowed stiffly.

"What is your direction, Duchess?" Sir Evelyn turned toward Marvella and smiled most congenially.

Marvella presented a card beautifully calligraphed with her Cairo address. Sir Evelyn's expression returned to a smile as he noted her obvious preparedness.

"That will be all, Valerius," stated Sir Evelyn with a finality to his voice as the handed the card to Lord Ravensdale.

Chapter Sixteen

What else had the little vixen not told him? *Bloody hell!* The Duke of Salford's granddaughter. Richard Lancastor, who had stood for every progressive cause in his lifetime, who had entertained every famous statesmen of his time, and whose impassioned speeches were still oft quoted. His Grace Richard Lancastor, whom he had admired all his life.

And he, Valerius Huntington, of no particular merit with nothing to show for his existence, had mauled Richard Lancastor's granddaughter as if she had been a lady selling her wares.

At the time, it had seemed a good idea. He had been sure that it was what she wanted, and it was certainly what he wanted.

Just a girl from a family with no claims to consequence, she had lead him to believe. Val was seething. He had bowed heavily prior to departing from Her Grace, attempting to erase the memory of his improper advances, a memory he had heretofore very much enjoyed reliving. Val had utilized every skill at his command to regain his composure while inwardly he was anything but self-possessed.

But the Duke of Salford's *granddaughter*? He threw his pen across his small wood-paneled office, having nothing better to throw. He moved to sit at his desk, fixating his eyes on the flow of the Nile visible from his third story window.

Oh, and let one not forget the other minor omissions, not to mention the out-and-out lies! She didn't believe he would know her parents, her father was not a peer of the realm after all.

For the love of God, she was Lady Elaina Lancastor and Dr. Jonathan Stanton's daughter! There was possibly a three-year-old in Madagascar who didn't know her parents, but even that was questionable. Dr. Jonathan Stanton was world-famous for his inventions, which had irrevocably changed the face of existence. Alita's mother, the daughter of the Duke of Salford, was active in the suffragette movement and was noted for her political prowess. People revered or despised Lady Elaina. Everyone fell on one side of the tracks. *The point was, people knew of her.*

But, oh no, he wouldn't know Miss Alita Stanton's parents. He began to pace the room consisting of a desk, bookshelves, two chairs, a Persian rug, a kerosene lamp, and a second adjoining room furnished sparsely with a bed, his clothing, a mirror, a small fireplace, and a wash basin. Up to now, he had always found his living quarters extravagantly comfortable after army quarters. The rooms suddenly seemed incredibly small.

Minor omissions indeed. It was no wonder that Miss Alita Stanton had somehow misplaced these incidental facts about her background while she found time to tell him of his greatness. *His bloody greatness.*

Val's blood was boiling. It smarted that he had been taken for a fool, but that was the least of his complaints. If there was one thing he couldn't tolerate, it was being deceived.

There was honesty even in a game if both parties knew where the stage play began and where reality ended, if both parties were privy to the fantasy. He had been forthright with Alita Stanton, and he had believed she was forthright with him, that they had entered into the pretense on equal footing. Now he knew differently, and he greatly resented her subterfuge.

He slammed the door behind him, determined to walk the extensive grounds until he had decided on his course of action. He bounded down the stairs and exited the building in record time, startling several people on the way who had the misfortune of lying in his path.

But he had not even reached the garden before he had made a decision.

He would see Alita Stanton again, with the express purpose of teaching her the error of deceit. He could be extremely treacherous when he so chose. He would instruct her thoroughly in the consequences of double-dealing.

And yet, what could be more torturous than being in her presence again? The openness in her gaze, her disarming proclamations spoken with steely assuredness, and her lack of fear or hesitation. Delicate, lovely features combined with brazen forthrightness.

Even as he was so incensed with her that he could have raged like a madman, he longed to see her again.

Devil take it! I don't need this, not now. He was a starving man in chains, watching while others feasted. There was simply no point in furthering this entanglement. This fact had never been more apparent than

The Paradox: The Soldier and the Mystic 161

now. Even if she weren't living in a fantasy land—which was a fairly large concern in his book—she could not be trusted.

Every word she uttered was a damned hum. It was one Banbury tale after the other with Miss Alita Stanton. She had done everything in her power to entice him, and he began to sweat to think of the extent of her success.

As if that weren't enough, he had no intention of marrying, and certainly not of riveting himself to Miss Alita Stanton. There would be the devil to pay. She was much more than he could handle, and he had no desire to be maneuvered by a woman for the balance of his days.

Not that she would have him. And he certainly saw no point in torturing himself on a minute-by-minute basis.

Val cursed as he punched the air, having reached the center of one of the mazes that adjoined the consul-general's offices. Unfortunately, there was no way out of his commitment short of throwing himself into the Nile. The idea began to have appeal, he thought with intense aggravation.

He attempted to resign himself to the inevitable. So be it. But the next and final encounter would be different from the preceding interlude. *Far different.*

They would simply take a tour of the pyramids. Even Miss Alita Stanton could not wreak too much havoc in that environment. She might be a sly minx, but her reign had ended where he was concerned. *He* would instigate the unfolding of all events henceforth, and she would have nothing to say about any of it.

Val considered that he had taken dozens of calculating young ladies on the tour without mishap. Without exception he had remained in charge of the expeditions. He had led a battalion of men on the battlefield who had obeyed him to the letter.

He acknowledged to himself that he could speak about the subject of Egyptian antiquities with expertise. He would oversee this next encounter with Miss Alita Stanton, and she would not step out of line or she could bloody well find a new guide. He himself would seek solace in the historical artifacts that he loved. It would be like going to a museum. Exactly like that. An afternoon of intellectual delights expressed through proper English conversation and executed with elegant decorum.

Accompanied by Cleopatra, the greatest female sorceress of all time.

Nothing like history combined with an unspecified quantity of sensuality, Val mused, unable to control the smile that was forming on his lips.

And nothing was quantifiable where Miss Alita Stanton was concerned.

Chapter Seventeen

"Grandmamma, why have you arranged a list of errands for William on the day we are to visit the Pyramids at Giza?" asked Alita, perplexed. "Surely your errands could have waited." She smoothed her green riding suit with her hands, checking her tan kid boots for scuffs. Her suit did not quite reach to her ankles, so she was feeling quite daring even though her boots fully covered her ankles. She straightened the green veil of her Skimmer hat on the table beside her.

A new day. Despite the fact that she had failed miserably at her purpose for being in Egypt—and who knew the turn her life would take as the result of an unfulfilled edict from the heavens—she had to admit that the proposed trip had lifted her spirits. Possibly the early hour had enlivened her. She always loved the encroaching morning before the sunrise. Everything was so still, and one could not help but feel hopeful as the first signs of color diffused the darkness, peeking through the mountains.

"Unfortunately, I need some medicines which are of the utmost importance," replied Marvella. "Do not distress yourself. You may go again to Giza with Lord Manchestor if he wishes to go."

"But Grandmamma, to deprive him of the pleasure—"

"Pleasure?" Marvella laughed outright. "William was relieved that he would not be required to rise in the middle of the night, though he would never deny you anything! I can assure you that he will not even be dressing for breakfast for another four hours—as any sane person should not be."

"The middle of the night?" Alita giggled. "But it is only—"

"His words, not mine." Marvella held her teacup to her lips, slowly sipping the hot liquid. Despite the heat of the desert, the duchess still maintained her morning ritual of so many years, and, to be sure, the temperature was uncharacteristically cool at this hour. "Though I am never one to complain, I agree with him. And the guide I contracted is only available today, so it could not be helped," she added definitively.

"You obtained a guide for us?" asked Alita, her spirits lifting even more at the thought of an expert on antiquities as escort.

"Of course, child," replied the dowager duchess impatiently with arched eyebrows. "We can't very well trot off to the pyramids without a guide."

"An escort certainly—but a guide? What is the extent of his training?"

"I understand him to be a most knowledgeable person on the subject of Egyptian artifacts."

"Oh, how fascinating. Who is he? Is his English good?"

"Very good, I should think."

"And what is his area of expertise? Where did—"

"Save your questions for him. I am barely awake, and I certainly did not concern myself with uninteresting details. Alita, please go fetch my ivory parasol," she commanded while pinching Alita's cheeks. Her Grace smiled at the result with obvious approval.

"Yes, Grandmamma," Alita answered as she procured the parasol. She had an uneasy feeling, but she also felt more energy and excitement than she had in some days.

No more than a few minutes later, Alita's maid shuffled to the front door of their suite after the brass door knocker was executed. Hattie's hat was on crooked, her apron was not quite centered, and it didn't appear she had brushed her hair.

"Hattie!" Marvella exclaimed. "I trust you shall be presentable and ready to go in precisely one minute?"

"Yes, ma'rm." Hattie straightened her back and her hat, nodded, and hurried to the door.

"Be sure and eat a little toast and tea, Hattie," Alita called after her. "It shall be a long journey."

The two ladies sat in the sitting room, Alita attending to her embroidery while Marvella sipped her tea. Alita sighed, attempting to quiet her odd and inexplicable apprehensions around the undertaking.

"The Earl of Ravensdale," Hattie announced as he entered the parlor. His silver-blue eyes scrutinized the room before landing on her, a frown materializing on his lips.

"Lord Ravensdale!' she exclaimed as she jammed her embroidery needle into her hand before dropping everything.

Why did he have to come here? Her work with him was clearly not yet finished. How she wished he would vanish from her life forever.

Her head was spinning, and she had no idea of the reason. True, he was breathtakingly handsome, but at that moment she would have given anything to remove his gaze from her. One did not wish to be under the Earl of Ravensdale's scrutiny. There was invariably an implied threat in his expression.

She studied him further even as her finger was throbbing. He appeared extremely dashing in...Well, she had never seen anything to match it. His clothing was loose, and he carried a straw hat. He wore a white sack coat with brass buttons, matching tailored pants, and a white shirt buttoned at the neck but with no tie! Her worries were over, because her grandmamma would never allow her to be seen in public with a man dressed in this outfit.

He could be no gentleman.

The style was almost British, except for the casual straw hat and the absence of a tie, but the colors were not, which she presumed were chosen for the desert heat.

Lord Ravensdale certainly was not afraid to set his own fashion. She kept her eyes glued to his face as she searched for her handkerchief with the other hand, kicking her embroidery under her chair. Even though it was a minor wound, she had to do something before she bled all over herself.

"I must apologize for my informal dress ladies, it is desert attire," he explained while bowing, as if to read her mind. "I strongly advise you to follow my lead and to change into looser garments yourself for your own comfort. This is not a luncheon in Paris we will be attending, and there is no one to impress—certainly not myself."

"An impossibility, I am sure!" Alita retorted, pursing her lips in anger as her admiration was quickly replaced with an awareness of the insult he offered—his undisguised annoyance at being in her company. "Though you might pretend to care a bit more for our impression of you, Lord Ravensdale."

"I never pretend, Miss Stanton—unlike some who never do anything else. And, at the moment, I am much more concerned with your well-being than with your impression of me."

"I am touched, to be sure," she purred even as she pressed the handkerchief into her finger.

"Now go upstairs, ladies, loosen your stays, and put on something not so skintight. We have no time to dally. The day gets hotter with each passing minute."

"Well, I never!" Alita gasped. She glanced at her grandmother, whom she was astonished to see was watching the earl with interest rather than distaste, a reaction she never could have anticipated from the dowager duchess.

"I won't have ladies fainting all over the place on my watch. It is absurd and a grave mistake to wear something that form-fitting to the desert! I have no reason to mislead you on this and I am most knowledgeable on the subject."

"And on every subject, in your own mind, my lord," Alita added. His unequivocal assumption of his omniscience—even to do with her under things!—was truly beginning to grate on her nerves.

She refused to tell him that she hadn't cinched her corset tight at all. Her mother had long forbidden it. She was simply thin. But she was certainly not going to discuss her corset or her undergarments with the earl of Ravensdale! She would rather have her tongue cut out!

"I am quite comfortable, I assure you. Grandmamma? Would you care to change into something looser?"

"Looser?" repeated Marvella. "I'm sure I don't have anything that fits that description!" And, in truth, Alita doubted that she did. The duchess never wore any outfit unless it was a show-stopper. On this day she was somewhat subdued in a gray foulard walking suit with wine accents consisting of a trained skirt, a long close-fitting jacket that extended well beyond her hips, and a matching Tuscan straw bonnet with a sheer wine scarf. Satin claret bows were everywhere—on her bosom, her sleeves, her hips, accenting the train, and on her hat. Faille accordion pleating accented the hem and flowed gracefully like a waterfall down her shapely hips.

As she studied the outfit, concern for her grandmother overrode her own indignation. He could be right on this one point. The duchess should change, but into what?

* * * *

The Paradox: The Soldier and the Mystic 167

As he caught sight of Alita holding a half-finished embroidery, her green silk riding dress displaying her jewel-green eyes to great advantage, his expression softened for a moment. It was difficult to believe that this delicate picture of domestic bliss was, in reality, a siren.

Oh, she is perfection. Val's eyes lingered on her silhouette. An exquisite blend of feminine sensuality and innocent beauty. He shook his head as he wondered how she had managed to achieve this divine result in her relative youth.

"Lord Ravensdale!" Alita exclaimed as she dropped her embroidery.

Val laughed involuntarily. Her acting amused him no end. It was so well done, always performed on that thin line between overacting and believability. And, here and there, just to throw him off, she would cross that line.

Surprise was her forte, and he was a man who liked to be surprised. It happened so rarely, and it took some of the boredom out of an otherwise highly predictable existence.

*What on earth...*What was she doing with her feet? Kicking her embroidery about with her feet? There could be no comprehension where Miss Alita Stanton was concerned.

Onto more important matters.

It was no surprise to him that the ladies would not change into something more suitable. On occasion someone set their pretensions aside and listened to reason, but he certainly didn't expect that from this quarter.

"You were not aware of my coming, Miss Stanton? You acted surprised to see me," he asked innocently, *acted* being the material point. Bending at the waist, Val looked up at her through his expertly executed bow. "You astonish me. It occurred to me that you orchestrated it."

"Certainly not," she gasped. She was breathtakingly feminine even in her affected shock. She arose from her seat and moved gracefully toward the earl, her expression determined. Startled, he wondered what she could possibly have planned in front of the Dowager Duchess of Salford!

"Only consider, my lord"—Alita thrust her hand in front of his face for his inspection, revealing a drop of blood on her fingertip—"I would not have pricked myself had I not been so startled by your sudden appearance!"

"I am saddened for your injury, Miss Stanton, and yet, it *is* a very small amount of blood."

"And it was apparently spilt in vain." She smiled up at him, and it was his turn to catch his breath. "I had attempted to mutilate myself in the hope that my bleeding might elicit sympathy and induce you to make an offer for me."

"Alita!" the dowager duchess exclaimed, but her expression was more curious than censorious.

"Nothing you did would surprise me, Miss Stanton," he replied matter-of-factly.

"Because you have no clear picture of my character in your mind. In contrast, Lord Ravensdale, I understand you very well. Would that you had even a glimmer of insight in return."

The dowager duchess cleared her throat loudly.

Val contained his mirth with the greatest effort. How had this happened? He had come here angrier than a hornet. He had not been here two minutes, and already she had his head swimming. He had never been in the presence of a more unpredictable woman. By the dowager duchess's reaction, it appeared that this was not her granddaughter's usual behavior.

"You seem to have forgotten your manners, Alita," the dowager duchess pronounced half-heartedly, her lips forming a pinched smile. Val thought he saw a glimmer of hope in Her Grace's eyes and a tug at the corner of her mouth, which seemed much out of place with her demeanor.

"Grandmamma!" Alita pleaded, turning toward her. "Please tell Lord Ravensdale the truth—that I had nothing to do with this meeting!"

"Most certainly the arrangement was all mine," stated Marvella, her tone of voice indicating that she considered the information irrelevant. Her eyes eagerly watched the two young people, her expression lively though her tone was subdued.

"I thank you for your confidence, Your Grace." He bowed to the dowager duchess. "And would it be too bold to inquire how you came by my name?"

"Contemptuous presumption!" Alita intonated with feeling as she glared at him, followed by a warm smile.

"Indeed," Marvella murmured with raised eyebrows. "I merely asked Sir Evelyn who was best qualified to show us the pyramids. I am sure that is no great secret."

The Paradox: The Soldier and the Mystic 169

"Do not attempt to appeal to Lord Ravensdale's logic, Grandmamma," admonished Alita condescendingly, as poised and refined as a duchess herself. "He does not conceive that anyone has anything to add to his knowledge of the world. Because I dare to pose a different reality than his limited view, he considers me to be a conniving female or possibly even a lunatic. I am neither, but he is too obstinate and vainglorious to see it."

"Your affection for me comes as a surprise, Miss Stanton, but I must warn you that I am impervious to your flattery."

"In fact, Lord Ravensdale has much in common with the ancient pharaohs, perceiving themselves to be divine." She laughed nonchalantly, still addressing her grandmother, as if she were discussing a wayward child. "He is an expert on the subject for good reason."

"Ah, you think me an expert on something, Miss Stanton? I am gratified."

She gracefully returned to her seat and pretended to study yet another half-finished embroidery, which she had expeditiously left on the end table next to her chair. Without looking up, she murmured, "Lord Ravensdale's inability to look outside his own miniscule understanding of the world will be his downfall."

"And if I am the Pharaoh"—a slow smile rose to Val's lips—"you have much in common with Cleopatra, Miss Alita."

"Lord Ravensdale, please consider your words." Alita turned scarlet red as she immediately looked up from her ill-advised sewing. In a tone of voice that was much subdued compared to her facial expression, she calmly stated, "My grandmother will construe me to have an undeserved reputation."

"There, there, child." Marvella reached across the end-table between them and patted Alita's hand. "Have you never engaged in any idle flirting before? Lord Ravensdale paid you a compliment." Marvella scrutinized him. Her expression was favorable, and she did not appear to be one bit fooled by all this hostile banter.

"Miss Stanton, I am delighted that you bring up the point of your reputation," replied Val, his voice as smooth as silk. He moved to the fireplace and leaned against it, as if he felt quite at home.

Alita's eyes opened wide, alarm and dismay evident in her expression.

"I certainly would not wish to mar your reputation, Miss Stanton," Val continued, after pausing just long enough to watch her face turn white.

There, that was sufficient. "Though it would have gratified me more than I can express had I actually been *informed* of your reputation and your illustrious family background upon our meeting."

"For the degree of familiarity which exists between you two, it *is* surprising that you know so little about each other," mused the dowager duchess.

Miss Alita turned another shade whiter, if that were possible.

"Can you enlighten me, Miss Stanton, on the reason for that omission?" He shook his head as if struggling with a puzzle. "Pray, why the secrecy? I have racked my brain, trying to discern a logical explanation for why you would wish to hide your family from me.

"Hide?" She gurgled. "I do not wish to hide anything from you, Lord Ravensdale! To the contrary! I wish to enlighten you, which is proving to be impossible!"

"Why then would you not wish to acknowledge the connection, Miss Stanton? Most young ladies would kill for just such a connection. If I had known who you were, would it have interfered with the purpose of your visit? And what was that purpose?"

The dowager duchess turned to gaze upon her granddaughter with a decided interest.

"Well I…It didn't seem important at the time," Alita finally managed.

"Didn't seem important," he repeated solemnly, gratified that she had finally lost her composure. She had discomposed him since the moment of their first meeting, and he was happy to return the favor. He added in a very low voice, "It didn't seem important to you, but to me…to *me* it was of a singular importance, Miss Stanton."

"I–I was thinking of other…" murmured Alita breathlessly.

"You found the words to tell me that I would not know your parents, Miss Stanton. It would have taken no more words to have simply told me the truth." He touched his index finger to his forehead while producing the most cordial of smiles. "Why then the omission, I ask myself?"

"I…You…We…" Alita stammered without actually creating words.

"If it was your intent to make me look the fool, I must congratulate you, Miss Stanton, for I shudder to say that you succeeded." Val made every effort to hide the anger from his expression although, in truth, he felt her deliberate deception to be a betrayal.

The Paradox: The Soldier and the Mystic   *171*

Alita opened and then closed her mouth as if she felt helpless to do anything. Val would have sworn that she was truly frustrated. But at what? He thought the game was the entire point for her.

"It's no use," she retorted faintly. "You are determined not to understand anything I say, Lord Ravensdale. I don't know whether to scream or to cry, and I no longer have the energy for either."

"Believe me, Miss Stanton, I am attempting to understand."

"Grandmamma, I am not going to Giza today." Alita turned to her grandmother. "I feel a headache fast coming on. As you must have observed, Lord Ravensdale is determined to be disagreeable and to vex me."

"I am generally not so inclined, Miss Stanton. Social games are the epitome of wasted time in my view."

"Clearly. And I would not wish you to overtax yourself, Lord Ravensdale." She turned to the duchess. "I don't find his lordship's manners to be at all appealing, Grandmamma, which he has only just indicated is precisely his intent."

"Indeed? They have a certain reckless appeal," the duchess murmured as she picked up her own embroidery and continued stitching, "and are not so different from your own, my sweet."

"Grandmamma!"

"Miss Stanton, how can my desire to arrive at the truth distress you?" he replied calmly. "*I* did not hide my identity from *you*. I was forthcoming and sincere in all of my communications with you."

"And I as well," replied Alita with a heavy sigh. "Everything I told you was the truth, Lord Ravensdale. As I told you at the time, the purpose of my visit had nothing to do with *me*."

"But that did not give you the right to mislead me as to your identity."

"Mislead? I did no such thing!" She glared at him. "I have found it to be indescribably irritating that you believe nothing I say despite my sincerity of purpose."

"If I could but discern that purpose."

"If you cannot discern that which was clearly communicated to you, there can be nothing more for you here." Her mouth formed a thin line as she returned to her embroidery. From what he could see, she had little to no talent in that endeavor. "I repeat, it is a waste of my time to go to Giza today."

"Oh, yes, we have so many pressing demands upon our time," the duchess remarked, pulling the thread a full six inches above her design skillfully executed.

Scrutinizing the scene before him, he could not take his eyes from Alita. The very thought of walking out the door pained him. On the one hand, it would be wise to leave this fair maiden's vicinity forever. His wish had come true—he was now released from the obligation.

On the other hand, Val considered, try as he might to remove himself, he truly wanted to spend the day with her.

I should have never let myself get this close.

Curiosity always got the better of him. And he had never been so desirous of deciphering a woman's personality in his life. Much as he literally lived to translate languages and hieroglyphics, he wanted to understand the complexities that made up the puzzle which was Miss Alita Stanton. He generally found people so easy to read that he lost interest in the task, and yet he was no closer now to understanding Miss Stanton than he had been at the moment of their first meeting. In fact, he was more confounded than ever!

He knew he should swiftly remove himself from this room and never look back. Alita Stanton would not come after him.

Instead, against a myriad of alarms ringing in his head, he bowed again. "I apologize most profusely if I offended you Miss Stanton. I merely wished you to make your agenda known to me, and that is still my wish. May I make it up to you and be your guide at the pyramids today?"

The duchess looked up at him with interest. Alita glared at him through long lashes, her lips quivering.

God, she was beautiful.

She was still seething, clearly livid. And yet he read in her eyes a strong desire to be with him. She was both furious and wished to be in his company. *Why*? It was perplexing.

Her mouth twisted off to one side, and she lowered her head. Finally, she sighed heavily, as if yielding to an impossible force.

The Paradox: The Soldier and the Mystic 173

"Lord Ravensdale, I have traveled far." She frowned. "Can you pretend for one brief day that you don't know everything? Without that, how can wisdom impart its gifts to you?"

"I shall do my best, Miss Alita," He shook his head in wonder at this woman, even as he moved toward her. He took her hand and kissed it. *And, successful or not, I shall enjoy every moment of it.*

Chapter Eighteen

"I never imagined," she whispered, breathless. Nothing could have prepared her for the ancient landscape coming to life before her eyes. Despite having seen drawings of the pharaohs' resting grounds in intricate detail, Alita was mesmerized by the scene unfolding before her.

They first encountered the Sphinx guarding the three pyramids at Giza. The paws alone were fifty feet in length. The magnificence of the statue with the body of a lion and the head of a king was both breathtaking and a *threat.*

This was not the first time she had entertained just such a notion. The entire trip to Egypt had been exhilarating, riveting, and frightening, causing her to reconsider all she thought she knew.

The day's journey alone had been both magically picturesque and marked by contrasts. En route first by carriage to the Nile, they had then taken a small boat with a sail called a felucca across the Nile to the west bank. Once across the river, they had ridden donkeys to the pyramids themselves! Her excitement had grown until she beheld before her a scale of monument that could not be fully assimilated by the senses.

"It is astounding, is it not, Miss Stanton?" Lord Ravensdale remarked as he assisted her in alighting from the donkey even though she was a mere six inches off the sand and he had simply walked beside her on parts of the journey. Reluctantly turning from the sight before her, she caught him scanning her face and observing her sense of wonder with noticeable appreciation.

"Oh, yes!" she exclaimed, surprised that she was able to find her voice. "It is *wondrous* and a pinnacle of contrasts!"

"I myself never fail to enter these sacred grounds without feeling awestruck. I feel I am somehow bound to a people who lived four millennia ago at the same time I stand in the present moment."

The Paradox: The Soldier and the Mystic 175

"That is precisely how it feels!" agreed Alita, startled at their accord. She had perhaps found the only point of harmony between them. "It is the most illuminating—and ambrosial—experience!"

"Even the geography embodies the spiritual, Miss Alita," added Lord Ravensdale. "Cairo is on the east bank while the sun sets behind the pyramids on the west bank, symbolizing the end of life on earth." He had begun to drop her last name on occasion, and it felt strangely tender. His eyes were intense and passionate despite the gentleness in his voice as he stared at her.

"*Heaven save me!*" Marvella groaned, even as she swatted an Arab boy's hands with her fan who was attempting to keep her from falling off the donkey. "No more speaking of the end of life on earth—which is no doubt upon us!"

Val reluctantly released Alita's waist and moved to assist the dowager duchess.

"Look! Look! Lord Ravensdale!" She giggled as she pointed, reclaiming his attention as he was placing the dowager duchess firmly on the ground.

"Are you pointing to the men on camels, Miss Stanton?"

"*Yes*! How picturesque! And what is their purpose here, Lord Ravensdale?"

"Miss Stanton, is it not obvious?"

"Nothing is obvious about this place, young man, except that it is revolting! Do address my granddaughter's overly inquisitive nature at once so we may proceed out of this heat!" Marvella patted her hair and directed Hattie to open her parasol, who almost hit her in the eye with it in her nervousness to please.

"Security, Duchess."

"*Security*? What gibberish are you spouting? Are you English? Then speak it!"

"The men on camels. They are the mighty force protecting this world treasure," explained Lord Ravensdale.

"The only remaining wonder of the seven wonders of the ancient world is being protected by *men on camels*?" Alita demanded.

"Precisely." Lord Ravensdale nodded, the right corner of his mouth rising slightly. "What else?"

"Could this trip hold any more surprises?" Alita murmured. She who had always preferred home to every other location was amazed by this most foreign of lands.

"I pray to God it does not," muttered the dowager duchess as she directed Hattie in smoothing her dress. "I am astonished that you are able to hear yourself think much less mentally transport yourself in time, Valerius, given the raucous," the duchess remarked in a shrill voice, apparently afraid she would not be heard.

"I did tell you, Your Grace, that it was not a tea party we would be attending." He shrugged, looking about himself as if he hadn't noticed the brawl. "I even went so far as to convey that your clothing was too constraining, a communication which might have gained me a slap in the face in some circles."

"As well it should! I would do so myself if I could reach you."

"Oh, no, Grandmamma! I shudder to think how we would be getting along without Lord Ravensdale!" Alita countered. In point of fact, the area was swarming with natives, both guides and beggars, including hundreds of mere children begging for candy, tobacco, and coin. Several had attempted to steal, but the earl's formidable appearance and ready command of both the Arabic and African languages created a barrier of protection around them.

"I'll thank you not to interrupt me while I am on a tirade, Alita! The truth is that Lord Ravensdale greatly understated the situation. Surely there must be houses of debauchery exhibiting more refinement than this...*this*..."

"Global treasure." A smile formed on his lips even as he scanned the pyramids with his eyes. He was clearly more at home here than he was in the British Consulate. Despite these spell-binding surroundings, Lord Ravensdale appeared to be in his element, Alita observed with acute interest. Amidst these ancient artifacts, he was focused and enthused. His mind had come alive. She felt the magnitude of his intellect surround her, she who had grown accustomed to being startled by this man.

She felt the delight of being in the presence of someone who was spiritually home. In his frequent glances she read unconcealed excitement about this ancient world, despite the fact that he had obviously been in this environ many times before.

The Paradox: The Soldier and the Mystic   *177*

"Treasure?" the duchess huffed. "I think *not!*"

"The environ is chaotic and intense, Your Grace, because a simple lady's handkerchief can bring enough food to live on for a day," he explained, motioning to a child begging nearby.

In her previous encounters with Val Huntington, Alita had experienced the full force of his attention. She felt it still, and yet his interest shifted to include their surroundings without any reduction in the attention he lavished on her, as if she were the diamond in a beautiful setting. How odd that this man who never flattered her with language could make her feel so complimented in merely being himself.

"Don't you dare, Alita!" Marvella quickly ascertained the lay of the land and exclaimed, "A lady should never be without her handkerchief!"

"The duchess is correct, Miss Alita." She began to protest when Lord Ravensdale intervened. Her hand stopped midway into her reticule, where she had, indeed, been searching for her Belgian-lace handkerchief. "Wait until the end of the day when you will likely no longer have need of it. Then dispense of it. The child will wash the handkerchief and have a sense of earning the money instead of being given charity. To further their dependence on the English decreases their sense of self-worth from the very people who took their independence from them. Always ask for some service in exchange for your gift, no matter how small. Do not deprive these people of their pride."

"All this harm from a handkerchief?" Marvella muttered, "Better to keep it, then," clearly disdainful that Alita should forego her finery.

"The three pyramids are Chephren, Cheops, and Mycerinus." Apparently seeking to divert the dowager duchess's attention, Val motioned behind them to their surroundings. "Cheops is the first pyramid constructed and also the largest. It is some 480 feet high and contains almost 6.8 million tons of limestone."

"How long ago were these pyramids built?" Alita asked, finding this new side to Lord Ravensdale very much to her liking.

"So long that it no longer pertains." Marvella remarked disinterestedly as she straightened the sheer wine scarf attached to her Tuscan straw bonnet so that it covered her face. Alita felt some guilt as she watched her, an explosion of claret satin bows remarkably visible against the beige sand.

"The Sphinx was built by the fourth-dynasty pharaoh, Khafre, who lived 2558-2532 B.C.," answered Val. "So roughly forty-four hundred years ago."

"But what of the human element, Lord Ravensdale?" Alita asked thoughtfully while staring at the Sphinx. "Can you tell us of the story behind these incredible structures?"

"Ah, so that your interest, Miss Stanton? Why does that not surprise me?" Val asked rhetorically as he placed his hand under her elbow, leading her forward. She gasped as he increased his proximity to her, lowering his lips to her ear so that she felt his breath, warm even amidst this heat. "You are interested in power and manipulation. What did people want, and how did they go about getting it?"

"N–no, Lord Ravensdale, I merely meant..." She cleared her throat, not sure what she meant anymore.

"The entire story of all of mankind lies here before you, impossible to ignore in its magnificence." He pulled away, gesturing to the sight before them with his muscular arms.

She raised her eyebrows in perplexity but did not reply. He seemed to read her expression as if she had, and it was somewhat disconcerting to have someone pay so much attention to her.

"As you can see, Miss Alita, we are surrounded by futile attempts at power." Val's lips formed a thin line as he took the straw hat from his head and fanned himself with it, a lock of dark hair falling across his forehead as he did so. "The desire to remain immortal."

"Immortality," she murmured. "Of course."

"Many died building these pyramids so that a very few might attempt to prove their divinity to themselves." He motioned to the pyramids. Lightly he added, almost under his breath, "The greater the lie, the greater the smokescreen. Behold the magnitude of the illusion."

"I suppose the irony is that the pharaohs were immortal with or without the pyramids." She considered his words. "It wasn't necessary to work anyone to death—quite literally—to make themselves immortal. God had already done so."

"Only if they had accepted Christ as their savior," remarked Marvella, suddenly interested in the conversation.

"But they lived before Christ, Grandmamma. So all of God's children who lived before Christ are condemned to hell?"

The Paradox: The Soldier and the Mystic   *179*

"We all are condemned to hell in one form or another," Val stated grimly.

"But are we all immortal? That is the relevant question," stated Alita, her eyes glued to his face.

Val shrugged, appearing to have no opinion on the immortality of the soul despite his ready opinions on every other subject.

Alita studied him intently. He was tormented with misery at the same time he functioned with extreme competence in the world. Val Huntington had the greatest capacity to hold pain of any person she had ever encountered.

"Let us begin our tour of the pyramids, shall we?" Val offered, his voice suddenly light. She couldn't help but stare at the top button of his shirt— unbuttoned! Outside of the natives, she had never in her life seen a man in such a casual form of dress! It was *unnerving*.

"Your Grace, please allow me to support you." He turned to take the duchess's arm as well, showing her the proper deference. He seemed to take everything in and to be perfectly capable of managing the entire party.

"Well, don't dilly-dally then!"

"You look fatigued, ma'am. I'll procure some water for you." He studied her face with concern as he found a place for the duchess to sit and rest, motioning to his attendant to bring water. He solicited Alita's fan, and both fanned the older woman while Hattie held her parasol over her until the attendant returned with water.

Handing the fan to his attendant and directing him to continue fanning the duchess, Val then wet his handkerchief. He handed it to Hattie, instructing her to pat the duchess's forehead while he held the parasol.

Alita was stunned that Marvella obeyed, even as she continued issuing commands. "You two take a turn about the pyramids without me," she stated. "I need to rest."

"Grandmamma, you look pekid." Alita grew puzzled as she studied her grandmother. "We should return home."

"Nonsense, child, you go on. I'll be fine here," she proclaimed with the wave of dismissal that had been perfected on her servants. Her face grew stern as Alita considered her. "Don't vex me, girl. It will do me much more harm than allowing me to rest here by myself."

"We most certainly will not depart, Your Grace," stated Val. "We will rest until we are assured that you are well and ready to proceed. In addition to our concern for your well-being, this is far too interesting a trip to deprive you of the experience."

"Young man, I shall give the orders here, do you understand? You might think you are in charge, but that is not the case." Marvella's lips formed a tight line, a warning Alita knew all too well. "You shall procure a beverage for me—do you think you could locate a cold tea or lemonade? Then you shall proceed without me. You are both provoking me beyond endurance. I am likely to have a seizure." Her voice was harsh, but Alita could see the look of approval in Marvella's eyes as she studied Val.

In general, the duchess had a highly trained eye. She could read a gentleman's interest like a bloodhound could sniff out his home territory. There was much in life that Marvella missed, but her awareness of the opposite sex and its interests was fine-tuned and second to none, Alita knew.

She also knew better than to argue with her. "Lord Ravensdale, it is truly for the best to honor Grandmamma's wishes."

"Your Grace, if I defer to your wishes, it is because I choose to. Let me assure you that I am in charge of this expedition and shall remain so." Surveying the two women before him, he spoke authoritatively in a tone of voice which communicated that he would brook no argument, "Your Grace, if you are to rest rather than partake of the tour of the pyramids, you shall rest on a bench just inside one of the pyramids. It is much cooler, and I have no intention of returning you to Shepheard's with heat-stroke. There are also some interesting hieroglyphics within view, which may catch your interest."

"There is little chance of that, you young upstart," she retorted, but her eyes had recaptured some of their sparkle.

"Are we now of one mind on this matter?" Val demanded as he scrutinized the duchess.

To Alita's surprise, Marvella nodded agreement. Val instructed his attendant to procure liquid refreshment and to meet them at an agreed-upon location. Marvella was quickly established in much cooler quarters, beverage in hand.

If the increase in her decrees was any evidence, she was much revived. She issued ultimatums to Val's guide, who fanned her energetically. Once convinced of her well being, Alita and Val announced their intent to

The Paradox: The Soldier and the Mystic 181

continue their tour. Marvella motioned to Hattie, whispered something in her ear, and the three departed for Cheops.

"Oh, look! What an unlikely picture!" exclaimed Alita as she saw guides offering rides on the camels to tourists, English ladies in bustle skirts bobbing on camels next to Khafre's four-thousand-year-old pyramid. She scurried forward to obtain a closer look at one of the camels while Hattie followed her as slowly as could be arranged without actually standing still.

The camel turned to look at Alita and gave her a look of great kinship, as if they shared a deep truth. The camel spat and, again, looked at Alita, as if asking her to spit to show her solidarity.

Mesmerized, Alita determined then and there to procure an extra treat for this unusual and magnificent animal, hoping that he understood her unspoken apology for her inadequate response. If one could not spit with one's friends, the highest form of validation, one could at least bestow gifts.

Val shook his head at the camel's keeper, speaking in Arabic to him, even as he took her by the elbow and guided her forward.

"What is his name?" She twisted to turn back and look at her new friend as she called to his owner.

"Musharif," the guide replied, apparently knowing that much English.

"Do you have any questions thus far, Miss Alita?" Val asked, clearly attempting to regain her attention. "I can assure you that I have a thorough knowledge of the area."

"Oh, yes," answered Alita. "Indeed I do!"

"Proceed."

"What do camels like to eat?" she asked. "And did we bring anything?"

Val burst into laughter. "We are in the midst of these magnificent surroundings, and you are worried about feeding the camels?"

"Worried? Not at all." Waving good-bye to Musharif, Alita remained eager for the answer to her question.

"Ah"—he cleared his throat, apparently understanding that she was quite serious in her intent—"I do not think that camels are especially particular."

"That is not my impression," Alita murmured.

"I will ask my attendant to extract a treat for the camel from our lunch. I am certain we have some satisfactory vegetables," Val reassured her.

"Thank you, Lord Ravensdale," she replied with heartfelt gratitude.

"You know, Miss Alita," he said after clearing his throat uncomfortably. His hand tightened on her elbow, which sent a slight tingle down her arm. "Many tourists to the area are convinced that the ghosts of the pharaohs still dwell here and that all the mysteries of the universe can be unraveled in this one spot."

"Do they really?" She giggled. "What an interesting study in human character these tours must provide for you, Lord Ravensdale."

"Fascinating," he replied dryly. "With your mystical *leanings,* I am curious to know if you agree, Miss Alita. I have seen many Europeans beside themselves over these tombs. Your reaction, though animated, strikes me as somehow different."

Alita watched Val intently. She knew that Val did not believe she had the sight, but he nonetheless wished to hear her answer, she felt that strongly. Ever since they had departed from Shepheard's, his interest in her had increased and warmed. It was disconcerting.

"I feel the energy here. It is…" Slowly she formulated her thoughts. "Provocative and strong. But no, none of the pharaohs were able to make themselves immortal. Or, rather, I should say, they already were. And they don't dwell here." She looked away. "Most of them don't."

"*Most* of them?" he demanded.

She laughed, attempting to divert his attention from her remark even as she hid her eyes underneath her parasol. She turned and saw that Hattie was trailing behind them, staring straight ahead without taking in the sights. "The only question of any interest to me, Lord Ravensdale, is how they impacted their souls by requiring others to die in order to glorify themselves."

"Precisely my question," Val muttered.

"Whatsoever one does in this life imparts something to one's soul, the *only* treasure transported from this life," Alita murmured quietly. "All else remains behind."

"Since you have expressed an interest, Miss Alita, I must tell you that Khufu was progressive for his time. He forbade sacrifices, making him unpopular with the religious orders," Val explained. "There is also evidence to support that he provided for his workers and was well thought of by them."

The Paradox: The Soldier and the Mystic 183

"Amazingly advanced for a person raised to believe he was a god," she consented. "And yet...he thought a pyramid was necessary to pave the way to the afterlife."

"If you remove something from the tomb, Miss Stanton, will it provide you with Power?" Val asked pointedly.

"There are no transportable magic properties." She shook her head. "There is much to be learned here, but it will not benefit me to steal one of the artifacts from this tomb. It is more a monument to folly than anything else. But a beautiful monument nonetheless of a very intelligent and gifted people."

"I am relieved to discover your viewpoint on this matter, Miss Alita."

"People are always searching for magic. And there *is* magic in the world." She surveyed her surroundings with genuine admiration and awe. The heat beat down on her, and she wondered momentarily if she might sink into the sand. Her senses tingled as she contemplated the very real mystery to unravel here. "A great deal of magic to be found."

"And where is this *magic* you speak of?" Val's expression grew suddenly apprehensive.

"Some believe it is found in fantasy." Looking up at Val, her mood was tranquil despite his disconcerting gaze. His silver-blue eyes were chilling, even in the heat. His thick eyebrows formed a small "V" over his eyes, accentuating his gaze.

"Is that what you believe, Miss Alita?"

"Oh, no." She shook her head. "Reality is as fantastic as one will allow."

"Can you explain yourself, Miss Alita?" They reached Khafre's pyramid, and Val took her arm to assist her inside. He shook his head in obvious contemplation.

"I beg your pardon, Lord Ravensdale?"

"Reality fantastic. Can you illuminate?" She found it astonishing that he actually listened to her. He never understood her, but he did *listen*. In the few seconds it took him to process her remarks, she was inclined to think he had ignored her, as most did. But, in fact, he listened intently.

Once again the air was cool. She looked around to see that they were surrounded by mysterious drawings. "With openness to the universe, one begins to manifest magic."

"I see. I am delighted for you that awareness has rewarded you, Miss Alita. My experience has been far different. I have yet to meet anyone—civilian, government, or politician—who is interested in the truth."

He ran his hand along the cold, porous stone, and, as he did so, she was, once again, stunned at the size of the blocks. He was dwarfed by them, and he was a tall, solid man, slim with wide shoulders, which tapered into a muscled waist. A man's waist.

"*I* am interested, Lord Ravensdale," she replied softly, even as she motioned for Hattie to come into the room She stood at the entry way and appeared apprehensive about the sight before her.

"Are you, Miss Stanton? That would be an interesting turn of events," he replied abruptly, turning away from her even as his lips formed a thin line. "All my life I have spoken and lived the truth, and my family subsequently cast me out, a person who had shown them nothing but love and loyalty. The last thing they wanted was the truth, and they would have sacrificed any innocent to squelch it. In the army I spoke against imperialism, which was likewise ill-received."

Something in Val's words struck a chord with her. She felt a stab of pain as she relived her social ambush at the Queen's Ball. This was indeed the greatest challenge of her life, to learn how to be genuine—and still belong. "I said to be in the truth, I did not necessarily say to speak everything you know, my lord. And yet, I feel it is somehow different for *you.*"

"It is possible for me but not for you, eh, Miss Alita?"

"It is a world run by men, after all." Her painful memories collided with her vision of him, and she sighed. "You have a commanding presence, which affords you a certain liberty others of us cannot hope for. You are one of those rare individuals for whom both acceptability and authenticity are possible, Lord Ravensdale. And you could use these talents to further the awareness of different societies and cultures."

"Perhaps, but that would require that someone were listening, Miss Alita." He grinned as he turned away from a drawing in stone, the right corner of his mouth noticeably higher than the left. His smile was almost sardonic, and yet his eyes were laughing. Oh, but he was difficult to read! "The fact remains that no one is interested in my viewpoint. Please do

The Paradox: The Soldier and the Mystic 185

enlighten me, Miss Alita. How shall I instigate this 'greater awareness,' pray tell, given this fact?"

"Don't you see, Lord Ravensdale?" There were other tourists at the opposite end of the room, so she moved closer to him, lowering her voice. Hattie remained at the entryway, appearing more frightened than interested by the sight before her.

"No, I don't, Miss Alita." Amusement was written across his face.

"Don't you see how you functioned as an officer in your army? I can see you there so clearly," Alita stated with certainty, striving to remain in the present and to avoid an uncomfortable vision.

"I thought I made it clear that we won't speak of that again, Miss Stanton." Val stiffened noticeably, his sudden frown causing her to take a step back. The other party stared at them disapprovingly before moving into the next room. Alita pretended to study the drawing in front of her face.

The pyramid might have shook in response to Val's tone of voice and the fire in his eyes, qualities that had allowed him to command a platoon of men, but Alita forced herself to continue, her voice faltering only slightly. "Only consider, Lord Ravensdale. You were an officer, but you never looked to your own glory. You were never intimidated by greatness in others, by extreme competence and capability, because it only enhanced every individual's chance of survival."

"Obviously."

"The world is mostly run by greed and ego. But an army which operated that way would quickly fall."

"Allow me to explain to you how the world operates, Miss Alita." He led her along the drawings of the pharaoh being carried into heaven, having heretofore pointed out what the symbols meant. "Evil has more power than Good because, by its very nature, Evil is going out of its way to exercise power, and Good is not. Power is Evil's sole motivation, power for money or power to inflict pain or power for self-aggrandizement. Good wants to live and allow others to live. Love, joy, creation, and so on, as I understand it. So, while Good is minding its own business, or even wishing good things for Evil, Evil is plotting how to bring Good down."

"I perceive your point, Lord Ravensdale." Alita grew thoughtful, looking straight ahead at a drawing of a woman with wings kneeling before another woman on a throne. "But you forget that love is hundreds of times more powerful than hate."

"That is precisely the point which I am disputing."

She shook her head in resolute disagreement. "Oft times, one can entice others to do voluntarily that which one wishes with love. A small child can wrap someone around her finger with love. Hate requires force, enormous outlays of energy, and constant surveillance. Love and freedom always prevail in the end."

"After Evil—or, at the very least, ignorance—has inflicted vast amounts of suffering and filled the graveyards with a great number of innocents."

"True. And hopefully one has kept one's soul intact when one departs from this world. I think the saddest occurrence is to see evil break down a good person."

"Ah, so we are back to immortality, Miss Alita." He laughed, placing his hand across his chest. "Be that as it may, we all plod along doing the best that we can with the cards stacked against us."

"You don't know your own power, Lord Ravensdale." She sighed in utter amazement at his lack of comprehension. "You have everything at your fingertips to promote peace and enlightenment."

"And if I do my part, as you advise, when will we live in this utopia of peace?" Val did not exert any effort hiding his amusement—or his disbelief—that she could see.

Staring at him intently, she considered his question carefully. Val did not receive her words, and yet she found it almost impossible to hide anything from him, a task so easily accomplished with almost everyone else in her life. The greatest mystery here was not the ancient artifacts but why she could not keep her mouth closed in his presence.

"In almost two hundred years." The words escaped from her lips.

"So...2082?"

"Earlier." She shook her head, even as she bit her lip. There. The pain would keep her quiet. If not, it would be an unfortunate necessity to cut out her own tongue.

"So specific. You have an extraordinary ability, Miss Stanton."

"I surprise myself, believe me. But I do not think of it as an ability. I merely receive. Let us say the twenty-first century, then, if that is more palatable to you, Lord Ravensdale." She pursed her lips in annoyance.

The Paradox: The Soldier and the Mystic 187

"Since you put it that way, Miss Stanton, it all becomes clear. Much more creditable."

In an instant realization dawned, and she forgot her agitation in the excitement that overwhelmed her. "Sometime prior to this there will be a great leader of nations. Oh, my goodness! In the Americas! I see that the leader is a woman."

"That the female sex will lead us, I can well believe." Val nodded his head in dubious agreement. "But an American? Peace-loving? I think not."

"Two hundred years, or even one hundred and eighty, is a long time from now, Lord Ravensdale. There are often great cultural changes in only forty years."

"The appearance of change perhaps, but no real changes. In the end, we will all die from our own hands and nothing will be left," he stated with disdain.

"It could very well proceed in that fashion." She nodded sadly. Staring at him pointedly, she added, "If no one does that which they were created to do."

"At any rate, I clearly don't have a significant contribution to make if it takes—oh, has it now been amended to a mere one hundred and eighty years?—for peace to be realized."

"To the contrary," argued Alita, wishing she could shake him until he was prepared to listen! "One step leads to another step. Everything builds on everything else. It is all important and necessary." She appealed to him by taking his arm. "Christ came almost nineteen hundred years ago, but it was an important step toward a unified world. Jesus never struck a living soul, not even to protect himself. With nails in his hands, Jesus prayed, 'Father forgive them, for they know not what they do.'"

"And yet people kill continually under the banner of Christianity. People do what Christ *did not do* under the most extreme provocation imaginable, *refused to do*, and call it Christianity." Val's face contorted in disgust. "Don't you grasp the enormity of human deception and the impossibility of love or of peace?"

"Perception is the first step. When children are taught that we are all citizens of the same world, when it's no longer *us* and *them*, there will be no more wars."

"Your perfect world will never exist, Miss Alita. There will always be evil people."

"Of course! But they are not defined by race or religion. There is a certain percentage of bad individuals in each, but labeling an entire group as evil is the general justification for war."

"I am sorry to inform you, Miss Alita, that the general view is to kill *them* before they get *us* and to fabricate some lie about why it makes us morally superior to do so. *They* are barbarians, so we must kill them." Clearly feeling the weight of his disgust, Val took a firmer grasp on her elbow and appeared determined to proceed with the tour. "Let us continue down this path, Miss Alita," stated Val, walking up steps to move into the next room.

Entering yet another chamber, her attention was immediately drawn to hieroglyphics on the wall. Alita turned to Hattie, who was stumbling up the stairs, clinging to the wall while merely glancing at the pictures. She looked back toward the opening as if moving farther and farther inside made her nervous.

"Hattie, are you quite all right?" asked Alita.

"Ummm...yes, Miss," she replied.

"You may wait in the preceding room if you don't like the stairs, Hattie. You know you should always tell me if something frightens you."

"Yes, Miss." She nodded, backing down the stairs even as she looked overhead.

"I don't think it's a good idea, Miss Stanton," Val remarked, his delivery stiff. "If someone who knows you should see you without your maid—"

"There is not much chance of that, Lord Ravensdale. It is more likely that she should fall and hurt herself." Alita returned her eyes to the hieroglyphics. "Oh, my," exclaimed Alita. "How beautiful."

"Yes." Val smiled, obviously appreciating her enthusiasm. "Hieroglyphics were both an art form and a method of communication."

"Look at this, Lord Ravensdale," stated Alita with curiosity as she pointed toward a symbol of interest to her. "It is an owl sign with a scepter. What does it mean?"

"I must say that you ask more questions than any young lady I have ever brought here, Miss Alita." He smiled.

The Paradox: The Soldier and the Mystic 189

"I don't see how anyone could not be interested!" she retorted, hating to be classified as 'different.'

"When I first met you, I believed your interest to be entirely contrived with other goals in mind." A devilish smile crossed his expression. "Now I wonder."

"Sadly, you don't know the first thing about me, Lord Ravensdale!" she remarked with indignation.

"I begin to think that myself."

"Please do continue the tour, Lord Ravensdale."

"Very well, Miss Stanton," he replied. But his smile had begun to contain a degree of affection, and it disarmed her. "Hieroglyphics were a mystery for so many years because it is a hybrid system. Some of the pictures represent concepts, and other pictures represent phonetic sounds as parts of words. Added to that complication is the vast number of pictures— more than twenty-four hundred hieroglyphs have been found. Can you imagine if there were twenty-four hundred letters in the English alphabet? Translation is therefore extremely difficult." He studied the wall. "In this case, the owl was used with a scepter to form a word meaning 'power.'" "Here." He took her hand, and suddenly heat ran through her body as he gently touched her gloved hand to lead her. "See the owl here?"

"Y–yes," She nodded, swallowing hard.

"The owl means the letter 'M' in this context used in a word 'Mar,' which means 'happy.'"

"Rather sophisticated for an ancient language," murmured Alita, feeling overwhelmed with the magnitude of the puzzle before her as well as the proximity of the man with her as she slowly pulled her hand away.

"Yes, the ancient Egyptians were an advanced race," Val mused as he studied the drawing, though he was clearly at home with the intricate paintings.

"It is so elaborately complex that I don't perceive how it was deciphered," she stated, shaking her head.

"An excellent point, Miss Alita," he exclaimed, unable to hide the admiration in his eyes. "It is likely it never would have been except for the discovery of the Rosetta Stone," he added offhandedly.

Alita swung around and stared at him. She felt that she had never truly seen Val Huntington before and that suddenly another layer had been revealed. With the enormity of the realization, she placed her hand on her mouth, feeling the room suddenly sway about her.

"Miss Alita, what is it?" Val demanded, grasping her firmly around the waist as he steadied her.

Her mouth opened, but she found no words.

"Miss Alita, answer me!" He raised his voice and shook her.

"What did you say, Lord Ravensdale?" She studied his eyes, silvery and intense. "Is the name…of…the stone?"

"The Rosetta Stone." Vaguely and hesitantly he recalled his words.

"What is it?" she asked eagerly, feeling her eyes now wide open.

"The Rosetta Stone furnished the key to decoding ancient Egyptian writing since it provided three versions of the same text. It dates from 196 B.C. but was not discovered until 1799."

"So, were it not for the Rosetta Stone," Alita stated, her voice wavering, "none of this would be translatable. Thousands of years would be lost forever."

"Very true." Val nodded. "As was precisely the case before the discovery of the stone."

"The Rosetta Stone is a bridge between both cultures and time, a single work of translation by a person who spoke three languages?" Alita murmured breathlessly.

"Correct," stated Val, surprise and appreciation crossing his face. "Very elegantly put, Miss Alita."

* * * *

Alita grew silent, which put Val in some anticipation of her next incomprehensible utterances, but she surprised him—which was the order of the day—by renewing her study of the hieroglyphics.

Val thought to himself yet again that he had never before observed a young lady express this degree of interest or intelligence. He began to wonder if he had seriously misjudged her. She was a very strange girl—of that there could be no doubt—but she was far more than met the eye.

"Hmm…" Alita reflected. "These look somehow different from the pictures I saw at the Museum of Cairo."

The Paradox: The Soldier and the Mystic   *191*

"That is yet another excellent observation, Miss Alita." Val was impressed. "The hieroglyphic texts which you saw at the museum were found at Philae and date from the fourth century A.D. Unfolding before your very eyes is the thousand-year battle between those who wished to revise the code, adapting it to Egypt's changing society, and those who insisted that the writing remain unchanged from its original creation."

"Even then, the fourth century Egyptians wanted to return to the nostalgic times of the third century." Alita laughed. "Such good times they were."

"You have the right of it, Miss Alita." Val chuckled. He couldn't remember the last time he had been so amused.

Ah, yes. It was the last time he had been in Miss Alita Stanton's company.

Val shook his head. He was absolutely dumfounded by this woman. On the one hand, she seemed unusually bright and perceptive, and at other times she seemed as if she might have been dropped on her head as a baby.

"The pictures," asked Alita, pensive again. "Even in this light they do not look Arabian."

"Very true," stated Val. "Egyptians were Africans. Later, in 641 A.D., Egypt was conquered by invading forces from Arabia. Arab-Egyptians have ruled for many years, but the majority of Egyptians are Eastern Hamites, dark-skinned Africans."

Suddenly she swooned once again, this time recapturing her balance on her own. Nonetheless, Val lunged to steady her, placing his hands squarely on her shoulders.

"Miss Alita! What is it?" He spoke more loudly. "Please, Alita! Speak to me!"

"I am fine, sir." Alita opened her eyes and looked at him. "Please do not distress yourself."

"What is wrong, Miss Alita?" he demanded.

"I was thinking of Africa as a whole," she stated wearily.

"Africa?" Val asked perplexed. "Whatever do you mean?"

"There is much trouble ahead for Africa," she stated. "And it signals a problem for all."

"And why is that?" he asked suspiciously.

"If one country is suffering, its dilemma will spread to the rest of the world."

"Ah, we shall only address the suffering of others if it affects us," he stated without emotion.

"It *always* affects us." Alita's lip quivered. "How do we deal with the poorest and most unfortunate among us? The answer to this question defines us."

"I take your point, Miss Alita." He considered her words momentarily. "However, I perceive the situation more as ignoring one's poor relations."

"Relations?" she murmured, as if she were contemplating a new idea. He wished she would stop doing that, it only led to confusion. *His* confusion.

Suddenly, a look of intense surprise crossed her features, her eyes opening wide. "Why, I believe that to be quite true, Lord Ravensdale."

"Oh? I am gratified to discover a point upon which we can agree without reservation, Miss Alita." Her eyes glistened like jewels despite the absence of any lighting but candlelight in this dark tomb. "This outing can now be deemed successful. And what is the basis for our commonality?"

"We're all from Africa," she answered gracefully. "It is the Mother Country. Everyone, in one way or another, can be traced back to Africa."

Chapter Nineteen

Val stared at her for a long while. Such an outrageously incomprehensible remark was the last thing he expected to hear uttered from those full lips the color of peaches set against ivory, translucent skin. Her emerald-green eyes looked directly at him, open and alert, without hesitation or apology.

Damn, she was beautiful. It almost made him forget that he was attempting to unravel the mysteries of her mind. Unsuccessfully at that, he thought with agitation. Val had never before been in the company of a woman who kept him in a constant state of heightened bewilderment. It continually surprised him, coming as it was from this elegant young woman who traversed so easily in British high society.

"There can be no question that Jesus was dark skinned given his nationality and country of birth." Clearing his throat, he stalled for a time while he attempted to decipher her words.

Possibly she spoke from a religious context. Since her religion was most certainly Christianity, he started there. "Whether or not he had olive skin or black skin, we do not know. We do know that Jesus lived as a child in Egypt where, presumably, his appearance did not set him apart or make him stand out while he was in hiding from Herrod. Is this what you refer to, Miss Alita?"

Alita shook her head, an expression of disenchanted surprise crossing her face, as if she had expected more from him. He felt somehow disappointed in himself, though he'd be damned if he knew why.

"No, Lord Ravensdale," she refuted with suppressed condescension. "Though I comprehend your point, certainly Jesus was Middle Eastern, Christ lived many years after the first human beings. I don't see the relevance to my supposition that Africa is the mother country."

"Not at all relevant to your supposition, it appears." *Whatever that might be*. Val cleared his throat. He was supposed to be the tour guide and in charge of instruction here. She couldn't possibly mean that all humans living today had a common ancestor whose origins were African.

"Possibly you are pointing out persons of note who were dark-skinned, Lord Ravensdale?" Her tone assumed a forced helpfulness. She smiled encouragingly at him, as if he were a child learning to read, and not doing so well at that.

"Of course, Miss Alita, I miss the point altogether," he muttered. This was like conversing with a bloody scientist. A *mad scientist*. He must likewise be mad to wish to follow her down that path. "Would you care to enlighten me?"

Alita studied him momentarily, as if she were determining if he were worthy of her knowledge. Solemnly she replied, "Not at this time, Your Lordship," her expression clearly revealing that, though she was attempting not to hurt his feelings, his performance had not impressed her to the point that he was deserving of the next lesson.

"Not even…a *hint*?" He growled, annoyed at being dismissed.

"Suffice it to say," she proposed, "do you not find, Lord Ravensdale, that almost everyone who comes to Africa feels a primal force calling to one's soul?"

"Yes…" he replied slowly. The truth of her proposition hit a deep chord, and Val was suddenly moved. "Not in so many words, but there is an inexplicable power and lure which is acknowledged."

Alita's gaze never left his face. Val did his best to regain his composure despite being intensely aware of her every movement and expression. And of the increased beating of his heart.

"Why, Miss Stanton, are you continually acting as if you have hit upon a revelation of momentous proportions? It is disturbing." Particularly when accompanied with swoons and near heart attacks.

"It disturbs me as well. I assure you that I am most unaccustomed to these constant insights."

"No doubt. Shall we continue our tour, Miss Alita?" he asked in a controlled voice.

Bloody hell. As he studied her open expression gazing upon him without the slightest reserve, it occurred to him that he wished she wouldn't say words like *primal*.

The Paradox: The Soldier and the Mystic   *195*

He took her elbow, suddenly recalling who she was and where they were.

"Miss Hattie," he called, even as he rejoined the maid in an attempt to regain his composure. "It is time to continue the tour. I'll escort you." He led her into the chamber, requiring a firm hold on her arm.

"B–b–but, m'lord…"

"It is quite safe, Miss Hattie, I assure you." She didn't look to be older than sixteen, and she was shaking like a leaf.

"Beggin' yer parden, m'lord, but no one knows how they got the stone blocks from the quarries to the pyramid. Each of 'em weighs more than a ton! No one knows now, *even these four thousand years later!* I heard you say so with me own ears!"

"True, but—"

"There's somethin' not right about this place."

"We're perfectly safe, Hattie." Alita took her hand. "No tourist has ever been hurt here. And we're safest with Lord Ravensdale."

"I'm sorry, Miss. I have failed in my duty," Hattie muttered even as Val was pulling her forward with her other hand. "I shouldn't be conversin' with the gentleman. It's just so d–d–dark in here, and what if the earth caved in—"

Suddenly they found themselves in a spacious corridor twenty-eight feet high, called the "Grand Gallery," and Hattie appeared to relax a little with the increased space. Val wondered if perhaps she was claustrophobic in addition to being superstitious. Possibly it added to her distress that they had not encountered too many other parties beyond the outer rooms. They continued onto the opening to the King's Chamber at the end of the corridor, the first sight of which was always startling to visitors.

"Oh, my!" Alita exclaimed, her amazement apparent, as she peered through the opening. "What is the stone which lines this room?"

"Solid red granite," he replied. "It is quite something to behold, is it not, Miss Alita?" he asked.

"I could never have pictured it," she murmured. Her head leaned forward, searching the room, the green veil on her Skimmer hat falling forward to cover her face. He had to admit that she looked quite the explorer in her green riding outfit with wheat-colored satin trim and buttons. Her dress did not quite reach her ankles, revealing tan kid boots, which were both lovely and serviceable. She was so slim and immaculately dressed, and yet she had not shown the slightest sign of discomfort or fatigue.

He had encountered anthropologists with less interest than Miss Alita Stanton exhibited.

Beyond a shadow of a doubt, his plan had backfired. A very bad tactical move. He had so wanted to squelch his interest in this woman, and he was far more interested now than he had been at the start to the day.

Only Hattie stood back, clearly apprehensive.

"The tomb is just on the other side of this opening, Miss Hattie," Val reassured her. This information served to alarm her more rather than to placate her, that much was obvious. There was fear in her eyes, and Alita patted her hand.

"Would you like to wait here, Hattie?" Alita asked.

"Oh, *yes*, ma'rm!" Hattie shook her head violently, indicating that she would prefer to wait in the Mediterranean Sea with a weight chained to her ankle if she had her say.

"Hmm," Alita considered. "We will be nearby. It is imperative that you call to us if you see anyone approaching on the corridor. You will lose your position with Grandmamma if I am found unattended."

"Y–y–yes, Miss." Hattie nodded that she understood. Clearly she feared the tomb even more than she did the dowager duchess, and that was saying something.

"Some of the colossal ceiling stones for the King's Chamber weigh as much as nine tons." As they entered the chamber where King Khufu was ultimately buried, a hush fell over them. It was cool and dark, and he was reminded that the ceremonies had occurred over four thousand years ago.

It felt as if they were the only two people alive in the world. He had never experienced that sensation with anyone else, and the last place he expected to experience it was in the final resting place of the pharaoh.

"This chamber, which lies ninety-five meters below the apex of the pyramid, is said to be a remarkable space in which mystical energies converge," he muttered, attempting to explain these odd sensations to himself, though he had never heretofore considered there to be any truth to the claims.

They continued walking slowly through King Khufu's tomb. In an effort to break the strange connection he felt with this even stranger woman, Val

The Paradox: The Soldier and the Mystic

drew on his knowledge of their surroundings. "Visitors come from points far and near to meditate here." He stopped abruptly and stared at her, alarmed to hear himself chattering.

"Yes, the energetic forces are very strong here," stated Alita solemnly.

"So you have an understanding of these forces, Miss Alita?" he asked, relieved to return to his familiar role of sardonic mocking and disbelief.

"It is the creative force which exists in all beings." She raised her eyebrows as she glanced back at him. "It is accessible everywhere, but it is very strong here. For people who know how to channel it, this is a powerful place. Potentially a place of great healing and life changes."

"I thought that you did not believe in such witchcraft."

"Oh, it is not witchcraft. It is simply the force of life. If you hold your hand over a leaf, or next to a tree, you can feel it," stated Alita, placing the sheer green veil atop her hat as she turned to face him, her glistening green eyes starkly vivid. "All the conditions are right here. You could run a long-distance race anywhere, but wouldn't you prefer to be running at seventy-five degrees in the early morning rather than at 100 degrees in the heat of the day? Would not your chances of finishing the race improve?"

"I suppose that is logical. I haven't ever heard it explained in quite that manner before."

"The conditions are right here to be receptive." Her face possessed a certain tranquility as she continued. "And if you bring to that an eager heart and a receptive mind, that makes this an ideal location."

"So shall you be staying?" asked Val politely.

"No, I told you, Lord Ravensdale." Alita shook her head, a sadness in her eyes which seemed to embrace him, causing his breath to quicken. "I did not come to Egypt to find the pyramids, though I have greatly enjoyed this tour."

"Why did you come then?" he whispered, barely audible.

Her lips parted and closed again. "I came to find you, *only you.*"

For a long moment, they stared at each other while standing in the burial tomb of the pharaohs, hearing only the echoes of their breathing. Val was surprised that he could find no words.

All he could do was to watch her.

"The strength of your personality drew me much more strongly than the energy of the pyramids. Mine is not a mind pulling straws out of a haystack, not quite knowing what I am looking for. My gift is strong, and my purpose is clear." Her voice grew sad, and she looked away, even as she leaned against the red granite wall. "It is you who is not receptive, Valerius."

"Please, Miss Stanton, let us not revisit my *grand purpose* and my exceptional talent again!" Val turned away, alarmed that he had been drawn in. She seemed so sincere he almost believed her.

Worse, he wanted to believe her. His weakness for flattery, for ignoring the truth, disgusted him.

Anger for his situation welled up within him. He motioned to the hieroglyphics around them, to everything that was dear to him. "It is all for nothing. No one is interested. It's a damn waste of time. No one cares about what I know."

"You have a significant contribution to make, Valerius."

"Thank you for your confidence, Miss Alita"—he laughed—"but I have no *contributions* to make. Not now. Not ever."

"Don't you see, my lord? Don't you see even yet?" she exclaimed. Alita stared at him in dismay, moving toward him. She touched his hands lightly with hers. Her voice was shaky but held conviction. "*You* are the Rosetta Stone."

Chapter Twenty

For a long moment, Val said nothing. He was no closer to understanding Alita Stanton—or, more importantly, her motivation—for all these unfathomable things she said. And he foolishly continued to allow her to pull him in despite the fact that she never uttered a word of sense! How could someone so nonsensical have reached him in such a way?

For an instant, I believed her! When she stood there in the stillness, so luminous even in this darkness, and told him that she came to find him, he had almost melted where he stood.

What is happening to me? Was he so grieved by his friend's death that he would fall for anything?

"Miss Alita, you continue to flatter me ridiculously." He forced himself to keep his voice low. "This is not the first time I have been pursued. You must know that. But I must confess that I am greatly perplexed. I beg you to enlighten me. *Why* have you taken such an interest in me? I cannot for the life of me comprehend what it is that you want from me. If you are foolish and misguided enough to contemplate marriage with me, which is difficult to fathom, I can assure you that it won't happen."

Her eyes moistened even as she touched her cheek with the index finger of her gloved hand. As he studied her gloved hand, he longed to take it in his for some inexplicable reason, but he held back from reaching out to her.

He would have given his entire estate to know why this woman was interested in him. He knew in his soul that she was.

But why? Obviously she had *not* come from England to Egypt to help him, and obviously she had *not* seen him in a "dream" before she came.

But she was in pursuit, of that there could be no doubt.

She stared at him, her eyes wide but revealing nothing.

And then her expression turned to one of desperation and powerlessness. Perplexed, he considered that the sudden sadness in her eyes seemed vividly real.

Possibly she was severely disappointed that her plan—whatever the devil it was—was not working.

How did she manage the tear? A single tear escaped down her cheek.

"My heart is breaking for you, Valerius," she whispered. "Not only do you not see me, but you cannot even see yourself."

"Rest assured, I see *you*, Miss Alita." He took a step back. "I see that you are an extremely eligible young lady, beautiful, an heiress to a great fortune, and with illustrious relations. I, on the other hand, am a respectable match, but certainly not of your caliber. My estate barely makes enough to support my extended family. My father was a notorious flirt and gambler, and we are, consequently, not of the first water. And to add to all that, I have it on good authority that I am a *bloody bore.*"

"It is true that I wish to be married, my lord, but you are not that man." Her tone held a disappointment when she uttered the words, it seemed to him. "But rest assured that I do not view marriage as rescue but as fulfillment."

Fulfillment? *A disaster, more like.* Certainly with him.

"If you would simply hear what I say rather than assuming everything I say is untrue and seeking ulterior motives, you would know why I am here." she retorted, her lips pursed.

"Ah, yes. I see." He removed his hat and ran his hands through his hair.

"No, you don't. And not because I haven't told you. I have never talked so much in my life as I have in your company. As to why I am determined to help you, Lord Ravensdale, initially I saw you as a person who could impact many lives, even to the point of preventing a terrible war." She shut her eyes momentarily as if in great pain before continuing. "I committed to help you, because I hear my directions so clearly and because I know how to obey. And, most importantly, as poor a choice as I might be, there was no one else."

"That I can readily believe."

"Someone had to care. I knew, I could feel, that *there was no one else.*" She shook her head, her wheat-colored curls shaking beneath her hat.

"Ah, so this is not personal, Miss Alita." He took a step forward and placed her small hands in his, knowing very well he should not. "It has nothing to do with your feelings toward me?"

The Paradox: The Soldier and the Mystic   *201*

"I didn't know you. How could I have feelings? But I was drawn to you. And now…" she struggled with the words, "it is…*different.*"

"I am very gratified to learn this, Miss Alita." In a low voice, he added, "I can assure you that I reciprocate your interest."

"Don't, please don't!" She pulled away from him and gasped as if struggling for air. "This is not why I'm here! I can't begin to express how much I yearn for you to realize who you are, Valerius."

"I know very well who I am, Miss Alita. It is you who has me baffled." He attempted to look into her eyes even as she looked away, leaning against the red stone.

"My heart aches for it." She placed her hand on her chest. "I keep telling you what I see in you, that which no one else can see in you and I know is there—and how the lives of so many depend on that realization—and yet you are determined to comprehend nothing. I am at my wit's end."

"Please, Miss Alita. There is no reason to distress yourself."

"If only…" Her voice became a whisper. "If *only* you were to acknowledge in your heart that you have a great purpose, that there is a plan for you. *That would be enough.* A tiny tear in the fabric which surrounds you. Things would begin to happen."

"What *things*?"

"The changes, the events which need to occur." Suddenly her expression grew hopeful. "It is so simple, so easy."

"I'm sorry, Miss Alita, but that is utter nonsense," he replied. She appeared to be in real anguish, and he was happy to push her. He was determined to end this subterfuge.

"Lord Ravensdale, if you cannot acknowledge in your mind that there is a path for you, then"—she clenched her hands—"embrace it in your *heart.* Be in the feeling. Don't you feel it on any level?"

He was suddenly touched by something in the way she looked at him, the desperation in her expression. He was as confused as ever—nothing ever made a wit of sense in this woman's presence—but she was either an even better actress than he thought, or she was seriously distressed. Against his instincts, he placed a comforting arm around her and kissed her forehead.

"I am sorry to cause you duress, Miss Alita." His deep voice became choppy as he beseeched her. "If I stand here under the apex, will this nonsense you keep spouting make any sense to me?"

"Only if you wish it," she murmured, still not looking at him. The air was still and utterly silent despite the fact that every sound and feeling was echoed and magnified in the tomb.

"Ah, then," he said as he pulled her close, "if I kiss you under the apex, my foolish advocate, will the force of it be stronger?" Suddenly he wanted nothing more in the world than to kiss her, to kiss her without reserve and to make love to her here in Khafre's pyramid.

"The draw is strong," she whispered. "I feel faint."

"On that we can agree," he whispered. His lips touched hers with a fierceness, and the softness of her lips aroused him instantly. He captured her mouth forcefully, so tired of words.

He felt a numbness from his toes to his head, being kissed in the tomb of the pharaoh. His heart was pounding, and her breath was like fire in the coolness of the tomb.

"I thought you said that we were not on holy ground," he voiced with some difficulty. "It certainly feels so to me."

"Perhaps I was mistaken," she whispered. "Experience is always the final word."

"Indeed it is." He possessed her mouth, even as she leaned her head back and accepted him.

He cradled the back of her head in his arm, his other arm around her waist, while he took a softer approach and gently coaxed her mouth. Her response was immediate.

A soft moan was released from her lips. He held that sound in his own mouth before returning it. He gingerly placed her against the wall. He continued to kiss her neck, even as he gently ran his hands along her waist and her hips. Lace covered her bodice up to her neck, but his breath was hot as his lips touched the lace along her neckline. He longed to undress her and to kiss every inch of her.

"Val," she whispered, and she held his head in her hands, pleading for something she was unable to name. His lips came back to hers, and she put her arms around him as he gently kissed her, rolling his tongue along the inside edges of her lip.

"Oh, Val," she whispered. She placed her hands on his hips and pulled herself closer to him.

The Paradox: The Soldier and the Mystic 203

Val's eyes opened wide in surprise and desire. This was not a young, inexperienced girl but a woman of the world as he had suspected. Although he had initiated this interlude—or had he?—Val began to feel as if she were the one in control and he were the pawn.

A very willing pawn.

"Oh, God, Alita," Val said. "You are driving me to madness." He held one hand on her hips as he placed his other hand at her waist. She threw her head back, and he ran kisses along her neck, her back arched.

Val did not know when he had been more aroused. He was in the temple of the pharaohs with the most intoxicating woman he had ever known. Every word, every movement, every look excited him. He could barely think of anything but her when she was in his presence.

I must be crazy. Or he would be soon if he wasn't already. Why she had this effect on him defied logic. He didn't believe a fraction of what she said.

And his head was spinning.

He pulled her toward him. What should have felt like a thrilling interlude of unthinkable liberties was frustrating him beyond measure. He hated the barriers. He detested the clothing. He wanted to feel her bare breasts beneath his hands. He wanted his mouth on every inch of her skin. He wanted...

Am I mad? Do I actually plan to make love to the Duke of Salford's granddaughter here in Khafre's pyramid? Val's head was spinning as he fell back to earth.

"Miss Alita," he whispered, his voice hoarse. He hated himself at this moment. "We can't do this here. Someone would come upon us eventually."

Val was stunned at his own lack of self-control. Discipline was the foundation of his life. To have risked ruining Miss Alita Stanton was unthinkable. A tryst of this nature would have to be in a very private location that protected her from discovery—if he were low enough to contemplate it, which he began to think he was.

How could he have lost control in a place brimming with tourists? Maybe there really was something to this apex theory.

Or maybe I am a damned fool.

Val cursed himself as he watched her regain her senses, her heart pounding and her breasts heaving against the thin lace. He had desperately wanted to take her here in this place he cherished. He had wanted to watch her fly into ecstasy in his hands. He had wanted…The devil take it, what did he want where she was concerned? And what was he thinking?

That was the problem. He wasn't thinking. They weren't married, and he had no intention of being married to this vixen. He would give that marriage about six months before she left him. Unable to curb his thoughts, Val smiled, relishing the thought of six months of making love with Alita Stanton…*Lady Ravensdale*.

Just as quickly, his mood turned dark. Val saw himself in his mind's eye, translating in front of the fire while Alita sparkled at society parties, pursuing her next conquest. She would quickly grow bored with him and begin having affairs with men who were more in the mode. She was a lively, curious woman with a great deal of charisma and appeal to men. It wouldn't be long before she responded to one of those dashing young blades. This woman was uncontainable, radiant, unhinged, irresistible.

And *dangerous*.

Val's mood turned deadly as he saw the scene play out in his mind's eye. Next he would have to duel her latest paramour to the death, along with every man who followed, until release would be afforded by the hangman's noose.

He would have lived through some of history's bloodiest, most gruesome battles only to, in all likelihood, be killed by his lust for a woman he couldn't control.

He cursed under his breath. It was one way to depart this life, and he had no objections to it, but neither did he have any wish to be desperately in love with a woman who did not and could not love him.

In love? Was he in love? It wasn't possible. He had too much sense to be in love with Alita Stanton.

She simply had control of his mind and body for a short while. It would pass.

"Miss, Miss!" As he had anticipated, Hattie began calling to them in low tones. He picked up his hat, which had landed on the pharaoh's tomb, oddly enough. Alita placed her fallen hat on her head and smoothed her curls before arranging her veil to cover her face.

She then smoothed her dress. There was no need, the blasted garment was glued to her skin.

He would forever hate that outfit. He took Alita's arm a little more roughly than he intended, and they moved to meet Hattie at the opening, appearing that they were all three just returning as footsteps approached.

"Miss Stanton, this way please." Val glanced at Alita, and even through her thin veil he could see that she stared at him in amazement, apparently equally surprised at the force of their attraction, which still lingered like the slow sizzle of a new fire on a winter morning.

Bloody hell! Why couldn't he be like other men of privilege who rode and hunted and amused themselves at pointless parties, cutting quite the dash and uttering frivolous nonsense? Then possibly he could hold onto Alita Stanton. He could devote every waking hour that he wasn't making love to her to entertaining her every whim. They would find themselves in one ridiculous scrape after another.

Just as he now found himself.

Completing the tour, they returned to Marvella without exchanging more than a few words. It seemed that each had difficulty comprehending the strong and inexplicable attraction that existed between them, and how quickly it had surfaced.

When they reached Marvella, she was conversing amiably with an elderly gentleman who was clearly quite enthralled with her.

Alita shook her head in obvious amusement.

Val smiled to himself. No doubt Marvella had been attracting men since she had escaped from the schoolroom, and it didn't appear to be something she could unlearn. Marvella Lancastor understood her time and her culture, she understood the men it produced, and she understood who had the power and how to wield it. It was second nature to her.

He considered Alita with apprehension. The ability to manipulate men appeared to run in the female line.

"Lord Falcon, may I introduce my granddaughter to you? Miss Alita Stanton. And Valerius Huntington, the 5th Earl of Ravensdale," Marvella stated.

Lord Falcon bowed agreeably and quickly returned his attentions to Marvella, talking incessantly in a jovial manner. His conversation centered on himself, and it soon became apparent that he was ill-informed on all other topics. Every subject was turned to a story about himself. Still, he was amiable and pleasant enough.

"Recently widowed," Marvella confided to her granddaughter when they were situated in a felucca sailboat sailing up the Nile River.

"You seem pale, Grandmamma." Alita studied her grandmother with obvious concern.

Val considered Alita's remark to be odd in light of the fact that Marvella Lancastor had been lit up like a Christmas tree in the company of the distinguished gentleman. But he kept his observations to himself. One had to pick one's battles with Miss Alita Stanton, and thus far she was far and away the winner.

"I overheard Lord Falcon telling you the circumstances of his birth, Duchess," stated Val. "He seemed to become on excellent terms with you rather quickly."

"Yes, apparently the family had almost lost hope of an heir," stated Marvella.

"Indeed?" Feigning interest, Alita replied courteously. "How fortunate that Lord Falcon was born."

"Proof that miracles happen," Val muttered, entering into the spirit of the day. He reassured himself that he could speak nonsense with the best of them, mentally patting himself on the back. It just took practice. And what an ideal day to practice—strange suppositions, absurd talk of magic and potential, and inexplicable forces of attraction despite his mental determination to the contrary.

"Proof that cousins should not marry, more likely," muttered Marvella under her breath.

Alita suddenly came out of her reverie and stared at her grandmother in shock.

"What are you staring at child?" asked the dowager duchess.

"Grandmamma, I thought you liked Lord Falcon!"

"Why shouldn't I?" demanded her Grace. "He's a peer of the realm. What more should he need to gain my approval?" She shrugged. "I'm simply stating the obvious. Or is that the exclusive right of you young people?"

After their sailing trip was completed, they again caught a carriage to Cairo. As the carriage pulled up to Lord Ravensdale's abode, Val felt disappointment that this bizarre day of surprises was coming to an end, when he should have felt relief.

The Paradox: The Soldier and the Mystic 207

"Miss Stanton, may I call on you on Sunday?" Against every instinct, he turned to Alita. "To take a stroll in the park?"

"Is that the park bordering the Nile River?" Clearly stalling, Alita smiled shyly at him. She seemed to be at a loss, as if she were struggling with herself. "It *is* lovely isn't it?"

"Yes, Miss Alita, it is quite lovely to stroll along the river bank of the longest river in the world. And also inexplicably charming to be transported to the river's edge in a carriage drawn by a matching team of raven-black beautiful steppers driven by a gentleman caller of some notoriety in a most elegant style of dress. I could do no less if you should allow me to call on you, Miss Alita." Val raised his eyebrows. Two could play at that game. Tapping his finger on his muscular thigh, he continued. "And your answer would be?"

Still she hesitated. For a moment it appeared that she might refuse to see him again, and the idea made his heart fall in his chest. He didn't know why, but he suddenly felt an enigmatic emptiness.

"Yes, you may call on Alita on Sunday, Lord Ravensdale." Marvella stepped in to resolve the issue to Val's relief. "But first you shall come to dinner Thursday evening."

Surprised at the command, he opened his mouth to solicit more information.

"Well get out of the carriage then, young man," stated Marvella impatiently, waving her hand. "'Pon rep, I'm tired, and I need to go home. We'll see you on Thursday."

"And the time, Your Grace? I must consult with my schedule."

"Eight o'clock in the Shepheard Hotel dining room," she commanded. In a secretive voice she added, "A word of caution, my lord. You'll have some competition. There's another gentleman of note dangling after my granddaughter, and he's making a considerable bit more progress than you are, I'm sorry to inform you." But the Cheshire-cat's grin that possessed her face told him that she was anything but sorry to be the bearer of bad tidings.

"*Grandmamma*!" Alita exclaimed.

"Some gentlemen never quite master the art of courtship and die old and lonely. I've seen it many times. Perhaps you could learn a thing or two from *that* Pink of the *ton*, your lordship." She raised both her voice and her eyebrows, ignoring her granddaughter, her expression a peculiar mix of haughtiness and sympathy. She added with a smile, "If you open your eyes, my lord."

Marvella seemed to know that her point had hit home and that she would be seeing Lord Ravensdale the following evening.

And indeed she would.

The duchess leaned her head out the carriage and instructed the driver to make haste while Val bounded onto the curve.

Val shook his head in disbelief as he watched the carriage depart while insuring that his major appendages were still intact.

That settled it. Madness ran in the family. At least in the female line.

* * * *

"Grandmamma, I am worried for you." Once the two ladies were situated at home, Marvella with her lemonade, fanning herself, Alita cautiously broached a subject of growing concern to her. "You have a health problem."

"Of course I do! I'm an old woman. I've just traveled half-way across the world to a desert where I'll probably die of heat stroke. I'm a bit tired and need more rest, that's all." She smiled at her granddaughter with pride. "Don't you worry, dear. Everything is proceeding along very well—even better than I expected. I congratulate you on finding this young man all on your own. Two eligible suitors. Nothing could be better. You see? I knew that you had it in you, my dear!"

"No, Grandmamma, it's not that. We were discussing your health. You are capable of feeling much better," she stated, biting her lower lip. "I've been thinking of it for some time, and I finally understand the cause."

"I'm sure we all do."

"Grandmamma, is it not true that you feel elevated after you eat sweets but shortly thereafter feel unusually tired? And then crave more?"

Marvella pursed her lips, refusing to answer.

"It could explain your grumpy moods, Grandmamma." Alita hesitated, her voice soft.

"Me? Grumpy?" Marvella retorted, muttering under her breath. "I'll have you know, young lady, that I don't have a disagreeable bone in my body! I have the patience of a saint, which is a prerequisite for sanity in this

The Paradox: The Soldier and the Mystic 209

family. *Grumpy!* Hmph! I am the most pleasant person on the face of the earth! I suffer without complaining. It is my way. I will punish anyone who says otherwise. And, speaking of which, I won't have you bad mouth Lord Cadbury in my presence!"

"Honestly, Grandmamma, you'd think that Lord Cadbury was more important to you than Jesus, the way you revere him."

"Certainly," stated Marvella without apology. "I have daily contact with Cadbury, and I only meet with Jesus on Sundays."

"But that is your choice, Grandmamma." Alita could not help but giggle.

"Not entirely. Jesus is welcome to come and visit with me anytime He so chooses."

"As long as he brings chocolate?" Alita's expression grew somber.

"Certainly."

"And anyway, Grandmamma, I did not say that *chocolate* was detrimental to your health—only cane sugar. I know of an herbalist in London who can assist with sweetening."

"Let us not speak of this again, Alita." Marvella's eyebrows shot up.

"Please don't take offense, Grandmamma. Many people have an adverse reaction to sugar," Alita pleaded. "It creates a cycle of dependency, requiring increased quantities to satisfy until finally nothing works. At that point illness sets in. All the organs can fail, there can be loss of eyesight and loss of limbs. It is a drug."

"That's ridiculous! Ginger cookies a drug. I never heard anything so preposterous in my life. None of my doctors have ever told me of this!"

"It is not yet known." Alita sighed heavily, putting her hand to her temple. Her head was spinning at all the images that were coming to her, impressions of the future more and more frequently and with greater clarity. Were these visions the result of spending time with Lord Ravensdale? Or was she simply changing? She desperately wished she were changing in the other direction.

"I beg your pardon, young lady! What nonsense are you driveling?"

"Grandmamma, I have the sight," Alita said faintly, her head throbbing. She closed her eyes. "I see things. I know things. I don't know why. It just happens to be my gift."

Oh, no! The words were out before she knew it. *Why couldn't she stop talking?* Just when she thought it couldn't get any worse…

Marvella fell back into her chair, fanning herself and shaking her head, talking to herself. "Oh, I knew it was too much to hope for that you could be born of that crazy daughter of mine and that…that…*laborer*…and still be perfectly normal. I *knew* there had to be something quacked with you."

"Grandmamma, I am not quacked. I know things I shouldn't know."

"Very true. Don't worry, dear. It's not your fault. It's in the blood. We'll find you a nice husband, and all will be well." She patted Alita's hand then took a sip of lemonade. She muttered under her breath, "A nice husband who is a little quacked himself. There are plenty of those to be had. You'll deal famously together."

Alita kissed her grandmother's forehead.

"This Lord Ravensdale." Looking into her eyes, Marvella asked hopefully, "He is a little odd, is he not?"

"I love you, Grandmamma. Please take care of yourself."

Marvella shook her head as if to say, *It is you who need help.*

Alita lay awake in her bed, her thoughts tormenting her. She was surrounded by people she loved, who ignored her gifts, who didn't believe anything she said, and who were headed down a path of destruction when she could see as clearly as the hand in front of her face the path to a happy, fulfilled life for them.

Oh, who am I fooling? It was her *own* life that was an absolute mess. She had destroyed her presentation when she had been given everything in life she needed to succeed. She couldn't make anything happen for herself. She had done nothing of merit and had no achievements of her own.

No wonder no one takes me seriously or believes a word I say. Alita turned her head into her pillow as she burst into tears.

Chapter Twenty-One

"Damnation!" he cursed under his breath, feeling as if he would collapse from anguish. *Would this ever get any easier?* Val's hand reached up to the door, preparing to knock. Silently, his hand dropped to his side. Tears welled up in his eyes, compounding his grief, and he shook his head. He set the packages down and leaned against the porch.

He felt the beam give slightly from his weight. *"Bloody hell!"* he exclaimed, forgetting to take care to quiet his voice. Everything was a reminder of things that needed to be done and no one to do them.

Suddenly a little face peered through the only window. The small hand-built wooden home was considered luxurious for the area, with two rooms— a bedroom where the entire family slept and a living-kitchen area—and even a window! In the cooler months the family congregated around the kitchen stove after dinner and, in the warmer months, on the porch. Although Val's estate in Norfolk had tenants with better homes, this had been a home filled with more joy than all of the rooms of his estate combined.

Had been.

"Hunter!" the child exclaimed, the variation on his name being another unpleasant reminder, even as he opened the door and beamed up at him. "What did you bring for me?" the child asked in Coptic as he ran through the door, his tan linen tunic flying past his bare legs. The tunic hit him mid calf and was shorter than the full-length version Val always wore when visiting so as not to attract attention. The boy was barefoot and wore no scarf around his waist as Val did, so the tunic flew loose. On his head was a small white hat, which Val always thought looked like a Jewish skullcap.

"Nothing, Abdul-Rashid," Val answered quietly as he picked up Rashid and swung him. "Only something for your mother."

"Nothing?" The child's eyes narrowed, his expression suspicious.

"Where is Imani?" Val placed Rashid on the wooden floor and looked around the small room.

Rashid began searching through the packages that Val had brought and pulled out a large loaf of bread. Val returned the gesture with a harsh look, and Rashid slowly began placing the bread back into the basket, keeping an eye on the large man before him in the off chance the decorated captain of the 7th Dragoon Guards decided to let down his guard. The child had been quick to learn that there was generally an opening for mischief where adults were concerned, and he clearly meant to be ready to spring into action when that opening revealed itself.

"I believe that I asked you a question, Abdul-Rashid," Val said in perfect Coptic, patting the boy's cheek.

"You did?" stated Rashid, his mind focused on more important matters. "Oh. Mama is in the garden with Jendayi."

"Will you lead me to her please?" asked his lordship. Not that he needed a guide, but this was the best way to keep an eye on Rashid.

"Yes, sir," stated Rashid as he took him by the hand.

"Look, Hunter!" Rashid pointed to the wall, and Val's eyes followed the boy's finger to see a bugle and a brass-hilted sword hanging on display. It hadn't been there on his last visit. "Father was the bugler," Rashid boasted proudly. "To warn of the enemy."

"Banafrit's position bestowed a great honor upon him," Val murmured quietly.

"I guess he didn't do a good enough job of warning himself, did he Hunter?" Rashid added somberly, his forehead wrinkled in thought.

"Abdul-Rashid, you must never forget what I am about to tell you." Val's chest heaved, but he ignored it. Instead, he got down on his knees and held the boy's shoulders. "Your father was a great bugler and a great warrior. A great man. And a great Egyptian. His blood flows in your veins, Rashid. Do you understand?"

Rashid nodded.

"Sometimes the wrong side wins, and sometimes life is not fair. All you can do is to live with courage and integrity, Rashid. And remember that your father is always with you." He patted the boy's heart.

Rashid appeared pensive, and then he smiled. "I'm gonna' be a bugler, too," he announced.

Val knew what he would be bringing on his next visit. He studied the boy's face and saw his father there. His father who loved this boy as life

The Paradox: The Soldier and the Mystic 213

itself. His father who would not see Rashid grow up or the person he would become. And Rashid, who greatly needed a father. And not just any father—*his* father.

And why? So that England had control of the Suez Canal? Was it even true that this acquisition forwarded national security when thousands of homes just like this one were growing to hate the English, a sentiment that would be passed down for generations?

There has to be a better way.

One's enemies were greatly reduced when one treated others as equals instead of as children, inferiors, or barbarians. Funny how thinking of others as barbarians allowed one to behave as one.

He couldn't laugh though. While the misery inflicted was obvious to him, almost all of his countrymen were swept up in the glory of war and nationalism.

He reminded himself that both his country and his family held him in disdain for his views. But this wasn't the time or place to feel sorry for himself for having no family that claimed him or loved him. These children had lost their father, it was his doing, and he had no business reflecting on his own grief. He was a grown man now, after all. These children had a long road ahead of them.

He followed Rashid out the back door to where Imani was tending to her garden. "Valerius!" she exclaimed, almost smiling. Being African-Egyptian, she was dark-skinned with Egyptian features and black eyes. She had been beautiful when her husband was alive. There was no light in her hollow eyes now, and Val knew that he had extinguished it.

Without warning, an image of Miss Alita Stanton, so full of life, so happy, so beautiful, flew before his eyes. And here Imani stood before him, the life taken out of her. The contrast pained him.

Imani looked up, wiping the sweat from her brow, an expression of genuine joy crossing her face for an instant, and Val felt his anguish lighten for a moment. He studied her for any hint of improvement, longing with all his heart to see it.

Her face was unveiled, but she wore a band around her head and a long scarf that completely covered her hair. An inexpensive choker of many-colored beads wrapped her neck, but there was no other jewelry visible. Her full brown cotton skirt reached the ground, and a tan scarf was draped across her torso. Despite the pleasure in her expression at seeing him, exhaustion and sadness invaded her eyes.

In the meantime, Rashid's older sister, Jendayi, moved shyly toward Val, just behind her mother. Val smiled down at the little girl staring up at him. The combination of African and Arabic blood had played out to create a strikingly beautiful child in Jendayi. She had slim Arabic features and long, thick hair. Her eyes were very large as were her lips. Her skin was lighter than her mother's, a beautiful dark olive tone. Large hooped silver earrings hung from her ears, and a circular beaded Cleopatra necklace graced her swan-like neck, accenting an ankle-length cotton tunic of many colors.

Jendayi was slim, tall, and long-legged. In the home she was barefoot and wore a band around her left ankle. The girl had a quiet, subdued manner about her, which might have been interpreted as maturity and tranquility if Val had not known it for grief.

Surprisingly, Jendayi, who was almost ten, was not recovering as well from her father's death as was Rashid. Jendayi was generally quiet and did not speak of her feelings.

"How good to see you, Valerius," Imani exclaimed as she moved slowly toward him. Though the children had Arabic names since their father had been of Arabic descent, the household had reverted to speaking Coptic, Imani's first language, since Banafrit's death.

If she only knew that I am her husband's killer. Pain gnawed at his gut. For the hundredth time, he reminded himself that telling Imani would serve no useful purpose. It would effectively remove him from being able to help the family or, at best, it would make the meeting so terribly awkward and painful for the children that he would not be able to assist to the same degree, if at all.

Revealing the pain in his soul would dissipate his own guilt—and create a situation whereby he would no longer have to fulfill his obligations. Of great benefit to him but detrimental to Banafrit's family.

Val shook his head. No, releasing his guilt was the least of his considerations at the moment.

"How are you, Imani?" Val took her hand.

"I miss him," she stated in a whisper as a tear formed in her eye. "But I am determined to find the strength to live for his children."

The Paradox: The Soldier and the Mystic 215

"You are doing an excellent job, Imani," he stated quietly.

"It is his own fault for being so political. He should have never fought the powers that be," she said with a shake to her head, pain flashing across her face.

"Imani, never think that Banafrit did wrong to fight for his people's freedom." Val fought the impulse to grab her by the shoulders. "It was a noble cause and he died bravely."

"Noble?" She sobbed. "He left us behind and achieved nothing."

"It isn't only noble if you win," Val stated with deep feeling, his eyes piercing hers. "The only thing you can do in life is to be true to your path. There is no other course."

"It was for nothing." Her lips formed a half smile, as if she were talking to a child who had offered up his small coin for the rent. She rubbed her eyes. "And it won't bring my son's father back. Let us not speak of this anymore. It is not your burden to bear."

Val winced. He wondered that Banafrit did not rise from the dead and strike him dead through the heart. He took a deep breath. "Perhaps it is, Imani. I did fight on the opposite side. I am sorry."

"You did your duty, and Banafrit did his." Imani's lips formed a trembling smile, and suddenly her expression lightened. "The seeds you brought some months ago have taken over my yard. I have such a bountiful garden that I will be able to feed the neighborhood! Come and see." With these words, her face was almost animated. Rashid bounded behind them as they inspected the garden.

Imani's garden was indeed abundant. A small amount of fertile ground could grow much food. She had lettuce, cucumber, tomatoes, leeks, beets, peas, grapes, and a pomegranate and fig tree. In her herbal garden she had cumin, coriander, sesame, and dill. Ducks roamed freely, and she had a pen with a goat for milk. Beekeeping was in another corner of the garden, producing the most common sweetener.

"We named the goat *Captain Val,*" Jendayi exclaimed.

The Earl of Ravensdale raised his eyebrows in stern disapproval.

"After you," Jendayi stated, as if to smooth the waters.

"Yes, I comprehend that fact," stated his lordship tersely. He restrained himself from further remark, with much effort. He had not yet sunk so low that he would argue with children over the correct naming of a goat.

"I explained that the goat is female," Imani interjected, embarrassed, "and that she cannot then be named after you, but they insisted."

"Ah, I am doubly blessed. Not only is my namesake a goat, but a female goat, no less. It warms the heart that such a creature would evoke my image." He bestowed a forced smile upon Rashid and Jendayi, who beamed back up at him. The goat seemed to smile as well, chewing nonchalantly, saliva drooling down her chin.

"Hmmm, possibly an improvement to the family tree," Val muttered.

"Hunter has brought something for you!" exclaimed Rashid to his mother, eager to show that he was even more in-the-know than his sister.

"Just some wine, bread, smoked fish, vinegar, and fabric for the children's clothes."

"You shouldn't have, Valerius." Imani smiled at him. "Your friendship is all that we require."

"Look! Look!" Rashid exclaimed. In going through the packages when no one was looking, he found a book. "What's this, Hunter?"

The earl raised his eyebrows.

"It's a book, silly," Jendayi announced as she moved closer, looking at the picture on the cover.

"A book?" Rashid frowned.

"It is called *One Thousand and One Arabian Nights*," he replied.

Jendayi's face lost some of its melancholy. "What is it about, Hunter?"

"It's a remarkable tale about a woman who was such a marvelous storyteller that she saved herself from a king who had vowed to kill her. He fell in love with her through her stories and married her instead."

"Did the king know that they were only stories?" Jendayi asked slowly, a look of perplexity written across her face as she considered his words. "That they weren't real?"

"But if the stories saved her life, how could they not be real?" he asked the little girl.

"Do you have anything better, Hunter?" Rashid tugged at Val's sleeve. "Swords? Games?"

"Could her stories have saved my daddy's life?" Jendayi whispered, deep in thought as she ignored her brother.

The Paradox: The Soldier and the Mystic   *217*

I killed your father. Anger and Rage killed your father, he wanted to scream. *Your father is dead because he happened to be born in a country with a resource a bigger country wanted.*

But he didn't. Val studied the girl, and he saw the grief welling up inside her, which only made his own anguish worse, even as he felt his eyes water.

"Valerius?" asked Imani. "Are you well…"

"Yes, Jendayi," Val replied in a gruff whisper. "If the right story had been told to the right people and enough people had believed the story, yes, it could have saved your daddy's life."

"Why, Hunter?" Jendayi covered her mouth with her hand, her eyes opened wide in amazement. *"How?"*

"Everything we do in life is based on a story that we believe."

"What was her name?" Jendayi asked, moving closer. "The lady who told the stories?"

"Scheherazade."

"Who was she?"

"She was an *enchantress*." As he uttered the words, in an instant a picture of Alita Stanton entered his mind involuntarily, even as he had only just forced her image out of his mind. Why she continually appeared from nowhere, he did not know. She had been encroaching upon his thoughts a great deal lately.

"She enchanted with her beauty?" Imani asked, clearly becoming intrigued.

"No," stated Val without hesitation.

"She was not beautiful?" Jendayi demanded, her eyes glued to him.

"She was very beautiful," he replied softly. "But she enchanted with her *stories*."

"Hmmm." Imani nodded. "Yes, it is so."

"Oh," Jendayi murmured inquisitively. "Will you read this book to us, Hunter?"

"Yes," replied Lord Ravensdale solemnly.

Rashid groaned. "Why? We already know what happens."

"Please stay for some bean stew with falafel, Valerius." Imani took Val by the hand, everyone vying for his attention, it seemed. "Thanks to you, our table is always full."

God, it hurt. *Thanks to me.*

Val wanted a drink. He didn't belong anywhere, and everything he touched was damaged or destroyed.

But he was not one to attempt to escape from his own pain. He had come by it through the consequences of his own actions, it belonged to him, and, *by God*, he would feel it. He would either feel it until it subsided or he would claim it as his own and live with it. To try to make it go away was the coward's way out. He was a lot of things—an idiot, a misfit, a traitor, and a bore.

But he was no coward.

"I would love to stay for dinner, Imani," Val replied. "Your cooking is second to none. First, however, I will repair the porch."

Chapter Twenty-Two

Val joined the party of three for dinner on Thursday evening as directed, whether of his own will or by design he was unsure.

Heaven save me. And then he saw her and he didn't care about the distinction anymore. Alita Stanton was beautiful by anyone's standards, but she shown to unusual advantage in the candlelight, her jeweled eyes and pale blonde hair shimmering as they caught the light.

As he was being escorted past marble columns to the reserved table in a prime location near the fountain, he found it difficult to take his eyes off her, already seated and smiling warmly at something that was said.

Miss Stanton did not display the manners of someone attempting to bring attention to herself, he reflected, and yet she held center stage in a room filled with beautiful women adorned with no expense spared.

As he grew closer, his eyes moved to the plunging neckline of a stunning emerald-green silk gown. *If her purpose is to entice, she has succeeded.* He had never before seen those beautifully formed, creamy white breasts revealed. If her purpose was to entice, demoralize, and destroy, she had achieved that goal as well.

What Da Vinci or Michelangelo would have given for the honor of painting her in the nude…

"I beg your pardon." *Umph*! Suddenly he found that he had stumbled into an elderly gentlemen, who glared at him disapprovingly through a monocle after recapturing his balance. Val apologized profusely and began his quest in earnest again.

Bloody hell! I successfully navigated the Sahara Desert in an extremely dangerous military campaign, and now I can't walk across Shepheard's dining room without injuring myself and anyone in my path.

This was what came of not ending this ridiculous alliance with Miss Alita Stanton. Val reprimanded himself that he had known from the beginning that terminating the association was the only way. He could have just as well formed a serious attachment with a gypsy or a witch doctor. Or possibly the local hospital had some mental patients of interest to him.

Becoming enamored with an opera singer would have been strongly preferable. The expectations and the rules of decorum were much less ambiguous to all parties from the outset. And an opera singer wouldn't speak a lot of bloody nonsense about his grand potential either.

She wouldn't allow herself to sink that low.

Finally he found himself within several feet of the table, and he felt a true sense of accomplishment.

Soon forgotten. His breath caught in his chest when she looked up and smiled at him.

Even that charming smile of recognition annoyed him. It was the first time she had seen him, and he had noticed her from the moment they were in the same room together.

Why the devil am I still here?

It was as if he had never seen a heavenly vision before. As her sparkling eyes rested on him for a moment, he wondered if this was the closest he would ever be to paradise.

He wished he might be a bit closer.

Admonishing himself to be aware of his surroundings, something that ordinarily was second nature to him from his military training, Val shook his head in self-reproach. If he weren't careful, Val thought, he would dislodge a waiter or, worse yet, initiate the domino effect.

Possibly Egypt would fall.

Oh, wait. I have already assisted with that outcome. One rich culture annihilated, five continents to go, and my life's work is complete.

"Miss Alita. Your Grace," he articulated, "I hope you are well this evening."

"Quite," Marvella replied. "May I present Lord William Manchestor to you? Val Huntington, the Earl of Ravensdale, Captain in the *Princess Royal's.*" Val noted the sparkling white teeth and nodded as agreeably as he could muster.

"I see that you have difficulty being on time, Lord Ravensdale," Marvella remarked with raised eyebrows, almost in unison with William Manchestor's, as he moved to be seated.

The Paradox: The Soldier and the Mystic

221

"I apologize, Your Grace. I am employed during the day, and I was detained longer than expected. It is not always possible to extricate oneself," he replied offhandedly. He smiled warmly at the duchess, quite striking herself in a pale blue satin damask gown, a white wrap, and diamonds. "I would have thought that you would be pleased to know that I was serving my country."

Rather than admiring my reflection. He glanced at Manchestor. "Besides, who will miss me beside the two most beautiful ladies in the room?"

The duchess smiled back, and he saw that he had charmed away her disapproval.

Something was definitely...*different*...about Miss Alita Stanton. *She didn't look so much the young innocent anymore.*

Once seated and assured that he was no longer a threat to his continued existence or to anyone else's, Val allowed his gaze to linger on Alita even as his mouth went dry. She wore a pearl choker and pearl earrings, further accenting her plunging neckline, and her eyes shone when she looked at him, like a beautiful emerald lodged in a snowscape. Her coiffure consisted of countless ringlets dotted with pearls cascading down her neck in an elegant but undisciplined collection of wheat-colored curls.

One could almost feast on the ambiance alone. Val swallowed hard and forced himself to study his surroundings, as was his usual regimen. It was magnificent. Marble columns, lights along every gold archway, a domed ceiling, rich crimson upholstery, delicately exquisite china, rounded mahogany furniture, and beautiful women in lace and rustling silk.

But on this evening there was an added dimension. It seemed that the mirrors and crystal reflected every nuance, every gesture, and every emotion. It was as if there were an echo attached to every word and expression.

"So you're a military man? Are you a frequent visitor to Shepheard's, Lord Ravensdale?" William Manchestor asked, probably wondering why he had had so much trouble traversing the dining room.

"I have dined many times in Shepheard's," he replied simply.

"I expect that your company has never been lovelier," Manchestor offered.

"*Never*," he stated in a low undertone, glancing at Alita.

Alita blushed, and Marvella smiled with satisfaction, while Manchestor frowned.

Amidst this feeling of being in a fantasy world, a characteristic of being in Miss Alita Stanton's presence, there was an unpalatable element to the evening.

He eyed William Manchestor with dislike, who appeared to reciprocate the sentiment though he was too bloody polite to express it. But Val had made a career out of understanding his opponent, and Manchestor was a quick study, a man who played the part and played it safe, ensuring his own comfort and success first and foremost. He doubted that Manchestor ever went out on a limb for anyone.

Analyzing the complexities of Manchestor's elegant coiffure, he found that even Manchestor's clothing irritated him. Val knew that he himself turned more than a few heads in his black evening attire—he was thankful when he found time to shave—but Manchestor had transformed evening dress into an art form with all the appropriate accessories and not a hair out of place.

Manchestor's jewelry would have done the queen proud. *Lord, is that a sapphire ring surrounded by diamonds on his finger? And the same setting positioned perfectly on his elegantly tied cravat?*

Val rolled his eyes in distaste. No doubt Manchestor had little bunny rabbits and lavender pansies embroidered on his handkerchiefs in complementary colors.

And if he didn't, it wasn't because he didn't want them.

"Nice ring, Manchestor," Val noted. "Family heirloom?"

William shook his head. "Oh, no. I recently purchased it."

"Ah," replied Val.

Even taking into account Miss Alita's elaborate hairstyle, Manchestor had probably taken longer to get dressed than she had, and that was just not *natural*. There were better things to do with one's time, and the dandy's attire was proof that he didn't know what those things were.

Miss Alita seemed to approve of the fellow, he observed with discomfort. Possibly she liked such attention to fashion in a man.

He smoothed his coat, even though it was perfectly pressed and exquisitely fitted. Like Manchestor, he wore the typical black evening dress consisting of a swallow-tail black coat, a low-cut white vest, a white cravat,

The Paradox: The Soldier and the Mystic 223

and white gloves. To this Manchestor added a white rose in his lapel, satin stripes down the sides of his pants, and a gold watch chain. For himself, his only jewelry was silver cuff links, a pearl tie clip, and a family ring.

Val knew that his only deviation from acceptability was his hair. While Manchestor's hair was perfectly cut, his was slightly overlong, considered rakish in some parties.

While there was some discomfort as the two gentlemen eyed each other with rivalry and disapproval. Marvella smiled as if things were going just as they ought.

"Oh, the scents here are divine! I think I shall never tire of the bouquet—nor forget it!" Alita remarked in her lilting, melodic voice as the duck a' l'orange was brought to the table. Everyone was served, and the party's spirits cheered somewhat as the citrus aroma filled the surrounding air.

"I shall never be able to forget it either—however much I might try." Marvella nodded in agreement as she eyed with suspicion a dish of roasted potatoes, eggplant, onions, and feta cheese.

"May I ask, are you enjoying your tour of Egypt?" Val interjected in between the presentation of one dish after another of olives, bread, and garlic hummus. "I take it this is a first trip for all."

"And, God willing, the last!" the duchess exclaimed.

"I hope not!" Alita sighed even as she partook of a salad of cucumbers, tomatoes, and balsamic vinegar, clearly savoring her dinner.

"I beg your pardon, Miss Alita," Lord Manchestor posed. "It has been a charming trip far surpassing my expectations. But you wish to come...*back*?"

"Someday." She nodded. "Egypt will be forever a part of my heart and one must revisit one's heart."

"So Egypt has found favor with you, Miss Alita?" Val pressed.

"Oh, yes! Even melancholy is satisfying in such an intoxicating setting, like a morbid poem beautifully written," Alita murmured.

"You think Egypt is morbid?" Val raised his eyebrows.

"Indeed it is!" chimed in the duchess. "Alita has always displayed a gift for clarity. She gets that from me."

"Of course I do not think any such thing!" Alita giggled, looking quite coquettish, as she leaned forward, the silk sheen of her gown and the curve of her bosom catching the candlelight.

"If not morbid, then how shall you describe this land?" After this evening, he would forever think of Miss Alita when he saw pearls and believe it to be the jewel that best suited her.

"Egypt is…too many things for words," she continued. "I was never one to long for travel, and this journey to Egypt has taught me that the world is so much smaller than I once thought. I actually received a letter from my mother today!"

"And how long was the letter in arriving, Miss Stanton?" asked Val politely.

"She wrote it from the hospital the day after we left."

"Burn the letter, Alita!" Marvella grimaced at the mention of the hospital. "There might be germs on it! A *nurse*, for goodness sake," she muttered.

"Grandmamma!" admonished Alita. "I am most proud of Ma-ma!"

"Indeed," stated William. "Nursing is now considered a respectable profession…among many."

"Aside from the fact that Lady Elaina is performing a great service to society, which is considerably more important than her perceived 'respectability,' a subjective notion at best," Val interjected as he dipped his bread in hummus and took a bite.

"There is *no* respectable profession for a woman outside of the home, perceived or otherwise." Marvella pursed her lips. "Fustian nonsense. Next you'll be telling me that being an *opera singer* is a respectable profession for a woman."

William stifled laughter at the outrageous suggestion.

"Don't ever let me hear you speak of professions for women, Miss." Marvella turned her harsh eyes on her granddaughter.

Val noted with disappointment that Alita smiled very sweetly at her grandmother as if she could be assured of her acquiescence.

"Be thankful that your maids and cooks hold a different view of things," Val observed.

"Well, that is quite different," huffed Marvella, moistening her scarlet-red lips, which made her pale blue eyes all the more striking.

The Paradox: The Soldier and the Mystic

"As I said."

"It would no doubt be better for those ladies if they were afforded the luxury of being able to stay home with their families," added Alita.

"And now you see young ladies on bicycles. *Bicycles.*" Marvella's feathers appeared to be ruffled now, and she was gaining momentum. She picked up her fan and fanned herself frantically. "Next, men will be managing the house and tending to the children while women are off on their...*bicycles*. It is beyond anything the liberty young women are given today. It will be the downfall of civilization, *I can assure you.*"

"Grandmamma, I see no reason why a woman cannot ride a bicycle and still maintain her home and her virtue," suggested Alita, running her fingers along her pearl choker, an action he found disturbingly enticing.

"Well, if you think that, Miss, you have never tried to ride one," stated Marvella emphatically. Without a pause, she continued with the evils of sporting events for women. "And badminton! I have actually seen young ladies playing badminton!"

"You can't be serious!" interjected Val, opening his eyes wide.

"I am!" She shook her head in dismay at the state of the world. Suddenly a thought seemed to occur to her and she stared pointedly at Alita. "*Never* let me see you playing badminton," she commanded. "That would be the last breath I take."

"I assure you that I shall not," stated Alita consolingly. "It looks very foolish and unladylike to my way of thinking."

"Could there be any more important criteria?" asked Val rhetorically.

"Don't you agree, William?" She bestowed her prettiest smile on Manchestor, one of her wheat-colored curls seeming to bob as she turned her head.

"I do," stated William. "Though I am quite certain that you would look charming at anything you undertook, Miss Alita."

Val rolled his eyes at the degree of insipidness to which the conversation had fallen. He was definitely beginning to feel like the third wheel. Did his highly intelligent and educated companions have nothing more important to speak of than analyzing the degree of femininity maintained while playing a variety of sports? *Who really gives a damn?* It was obvious that the three of them did.

In Zanzibar, My Little Chimpanzee. The orchestra struck up the chorus of the popular tune, more appropriate than he might have wished. As usual, his view of the world was going to lose out to a more frippery, flowery fellow.

Unless he was willing to run through a field throwing daisies and discussing the depravity of sports for women, it seemed that he was destined to be outshone by men of more scintillating conversation.

It seemed that reality was too boring to young ladies. They wished to be treated like fragile, dainty creatures and thereby perpetuate the myth.

The Manchestor fellow is a bad influence. He studied Miss Alita Stanton with no small degree of longing. The fact that she seemed to like this monkey was a great source of aggravation. She might easily become as empty-headed as Manchestor were she to remain long in his society.

A waste of a promising mind.

Val grew increasingly perplexed. There was something not right about Miss Alita tonight. She talked a great deal of nonsense ordinarily, but it was neither insipid nor superficial. *There was depth to her nonsense.* This was just petty "small talk," talking about insignificant matters of no consequence. Usually Alita spoke of things that mattered very much. She just happened to be wildly off the mark.

"Oh, and the dances!" No sooner had these thoughts occurred to him than it became obvious Her Grace's mind was now running rampant with examples of the depraved morality of the current society and its generation. "When I was a girl, they were so charming," she stated wistfully, with a faraway expression in her eyes.

"Dances are no longer charming?" Val asked in a growing state of confusion.

"In my day we weren't so familiar until after we were married." The sharpness returned to her expression.

Val's eyes caught Alita's and held her there for a moment, a slow smile coming to his lips as he studied her. Alita blushed, and Val thought that he had never seen her look more becoming. Flustered, Alita reached for another sip of her tea.

William frowned, but he politely addressed Marvella's remark. "Everything is changing, Your Grace. And who knows what it shall lead to?

The Paradox: The Soldier and the Mystic 227

Only in the last year Parliament granted divorced women the right to claim custody of their children," he stated indifferently.

Val tested the pears in wine sauce, and the dish of dates, which had been placed on the table as a dessert. He then motioned for the waiter to bring English tea for everyone. A flash of crimson and gold moved toward the kitchen, the wide, white pantaloons flapping at full speed.

"Shameful," stated Marvella. "Anyone who leaves her husband has already abandoned her responsibilities and is not entitled to her children."

"Didn't Grandfather vote in favor of that law?" asked Alita as she took a small portion of a pastry filled with dates and drizzled in honey. Marvella said nothing but pursed her lips. "Pass me the grapes, child," she finally stated.

"Yes, he did," stated Val as he selected one of the passing grapes and popped it into his mouth. "Much to the duke's credit. He understood that the lives of a cross section of women of greatly varying circumstances cannot be lumped into one moral edict. Some of these women have had terrible, painful lives, and I have no doubt that the duke would not wish their suffering to be reduced to a flippant discussion by people who never wanted for anything nor knew a powerless moment in their lives."

There seemed to be a stillness at the table for a moment.

"I agree," stated Alita with conviction. "We don't know the circumstances. We do know, however, that not all men are ethical. A woman's right to her children should not be ruled out without hearing the particulars."

Val took a sip of his wine and then thoughtfully considered Alita. Though she didn't always make sense—usually when she was talking about him—she looked outward, always outward. These other two, Manchestor and the grandmother, looked inward. And by that he was not referring to introspection. Their only concern was "How does it affect me?" He had the suspicion that, even when Manchestor engaged others in conversation, it was with the sole intent of being engaging.

"I cannot agree," stated Marvella with finality.

"Richard Lancastor is well revered as one of the great crusaders of equal rights for *all* people, man or woman, rich or poor." Val tapped his finger on the table before addressing Marvella. "I must say that I find it odd, Your

Grace, that your husband should support women's rights and that you do not support equal rights for your own sex."

"Not so odd," replied Marvella haughtily, her expression dismissing him. "You may choose to pitch the gammon, but I shall not. *Equal* rights would have given me less power, not more."

"There is nothing equal about your reign, that is true, Your Grace." Val chuckled with amusement, even while shaking his head. Despite himself, he could not help but feel some admiration for this woman who was so clear on her opinions and who, like her granddaughter, was continually surprising him with her utterances.

"Besides"—Marvella smiled, her aristocratic features revealing so clearly the beautiful young woman she had been—"I believe women are misled as to what shall make them happy."

"Irrespective of the misguided goals of other women, it is your good fortune that you hold a position in society which allows you to so freely express your opinion, Duchess. Most women do not have that privilege," stated Val.

"Indeed, Lord Ravensdale. Fortune has everything to do with it." Marvella smiled demurely. She took a sip of her tea and looked up at him, her eyes clear and blue under beautifully arched eyebrows. He smiled in return, understanding instantly the hold Marvella had had over men throughout her life.

The poignancy of the moment caused Val to turn to study Alita. He was aware in that moment the hold Alita Stanton had gained over him in such a short time.

Val was not a man to experience fear, but the picture before him frightened him. If he were not careful, he could end up as a permanent fixture of this small-minded circle.

"And, Miss Alita, what of your opinion?" William made no secret of his wish to divert control of the conversation, turning to Alita. "I comprehend that you are not particularly interested in the vote for women?"

Manchestor sought to drive yet another wedge between himself and Alita, Val surmised. The thought made his blood boil. If there were any wedges to be driven, *he* would do the honors himself.

"I have no need of it," replied Alita nonchalantly. "Everything that I want in life is a husband and a family and a home. I expect that I shall be a

The Paradox: The Soldier and the Mystic   *229*

good judge of character in choosing that husband. Nor shall I have any need to engage in employment."

"You are most fortunate, Miss Alita," remarked Val.

"I do not know why God has blessed me with so much." Alita's lips formed a quivering smile. "I am sure I do not deserve my blessings, but mine is an ideal life for my constitution and my outlook."

"Let us all be happy, then, and forget about the rest of the world." Val raised his glass of wine as if to toast.

Alita's tranquility surprised him. "If I am determined to be dissatisfied, I help no one and only hurt myself. It makes no sense to not enjoy the happiness and gifts which God has chosen to give to me."

"Some years ago I saw firsthand a woman who thought she had everything when she found that her husband was untrue to her and would remain so." Val felt a familiar sadness wash over him, and he involuntarily looked down at his hands. "The reality is that she had no options. She had no employment. No possibility of divorce. Without the vote, her concerns were consequently of no interest to the men who make the laws."

"As you mentioned earlier, Lord Ravensdale, Lady Elaina found employment in a society which offers little employment to women," William stated.

"Ah, yes. But Lady Elaina is quite exceptional and works for reasons other than support, if I am not mistaken," Val countered. "The only employment for women which pays sufficiently is being a rich man's lady-bird. The woman I speak of had been brought up on good principles. Marriage was the only option available to her. Without the possibility of divorce, what avenue was left to her?"

"And what happened to her?" Alita asked, turning pale. "She must have felt like a trapped animal."

"She had no choice but to be miserable or to enter into an imaginary world." His mood turned a shade darker as the memory washed over him. "A form of madness. These are the *only* two options available when one is trapped in a terrible situation with no hope of escape."

"Yes," agreed Alita, nodding distractedly. "To enter into an imaginary world is to separate from one's own life."

"And others are always hurt when one lives in an imaginary world, Miss Alita," he added, forcing control over his voice. "It renders one unable to address reality."

"I am sorry for the woman of your acquaintance, Lord Ravensdale, but I believe these to be the exception rather than the rule." William Manchestor made some small effort to control his agitation. "At any rate, Miss Alita has no need to enter into this dark melodrama which clearly distresses her and benefits no one. Your point eludes me."

Lord Ravensdale studied William Manchestor for some seconds before answering. He took a slow sip of wine, stretching his legs out before him. "The woman of *my acquaintance* is my mother. My point is that preserving one's illusions at the expense of supporting equality for all promotes cruelty. My point is that I am disgusted with seeing people die so that I can maintain the lie about my country's glory and Her inhabitants' superiority. Let us face the truth and correct it. Do I make my point, sir?"

"You are an officer, and you are opposed to war?" William laughed outright. "Ravensdale, if you don't wish to defend your country's interests any longer, why then do you not leave the army rather than provoking innocent young ladies over dinner?"

Impressive. He wouldn't have thought he had it in him.

Val studied William Manchestor intently. His voice was dark and deadly quiet when he replied, "I have killed many, and I could kill again."

Lord Manchestor swallowed nervously.

"I had better make damn sure I am in the right before I rip someone else's throat out." His gaze was steady, and Manchestor remained still under his scrutiny. "But I am perfectly capable of doing it."

There was complete silence at the table even as the safragis arrived with a silver tea service and began serving black tea with cream and sugar. He must have thought it odd that silence reigned and made quick business of his work.

"Miss Alita, your life is good because you are a beautiful heiress to a fortune. You will marry well." Somehow his own words filled his heart with sadness even as he sat up in his chair and motioned with his hands. "But we can never have a truly good world without freedom and equality."

"No," she agreed, nodding her head. "That is true. And it will come."

The Paradox: The Soldier and the Mystic 231

"Did you never long for anything that society has denied you, Miss Alita?" Val studied Alita intently. "Is there *nothing* that you wish for that is denied you because you are female?"

"No, Lord Ravensdale. The things that are denied me have little to do with my sex." She shook her head, appearing pensive. "However, I would have liked to see my mother in parliament. She is so well suited to it and would have excelled at it."

"God forbid!" Marvella's eyes looked upward.

"It is the greatest desire of her heart. She must content herself with influencing the men around her." Alita laughed and added, "Which she does very well."

Wonderful. It ran in the family.

"Even so, I think it is a perfectly lovely endeavor to love one's family and to have a happy life," stated Alita without aplomb.

"Hear, hear," agreed William.

"Wonderful if it can be accomplished." The muscles in Val's face tightened. "Unlikely that it can be achieved when there is an uneven balance of power."

"I agree with you on some points, Lord Ravensdale. However, it begs the issue we were speaking of. Why should *I*, in particular, join the suffragette movement?" asked Alita. "I am happy with my lot in life."

"Because," Val said, his gaze intent as he held her eyes, "you live only for yourself."

"If I only lived for myself, I certainly would not be here speaking with you, Lord Ravensdale," Alita retorted, color rising to her cheeks.

William Manchestor chuckled.

"I'm sure you've turned him up sweet now, Alita," Marvella purred.

"You have the power to make a difference, Miss Alita," Val persisted, unconcerned with the insult. "It is the responsibility of all women of advantage to promote women's rights."

"And how, pray tell, might I effect any change? I haven't any skills, and I don't have a profession." Alita was clearly frustrated.

"That predicament didn't seem to hinder your mother," he proposed.

"Ravensdale," stated William, his voice controlled. "There is no cause to distress Miss Alita. Nor does she deserve your censure."

Val kept his eyes on Alita. Reservedly he replied, "I assure you, Manchestor, that I find Miss Alita to be everything which is agreeable in a female." *And yourself as well, my fine peacock,* Val stopped himself reluctantly from saying.

But he had already hit his mark, he knew. He could see it in the daggers she was shooting at him. *Good.* He wanted her to discover why she was disassociating herself from the support of her own sex.

"I have nothing to contribute which anyone is interested in. The only talents I have are disbelieved by everyone, and I have to diligently contrive to keep them secret. Moreover, I must continually pretend to be someone I'm not just to fit in and to maintain my position in society." Alita's breathing came unevenly, her breasts heaving, and her eyes watered. *"Everything I am, no one cares about."*

Excellent. The answer had surfaced. He smiled with approval.

"I'm sure that is not true, Miss Alita."

"It is true!"

"Regardless, there is always something one can do, and feeling powerless is no excuse for doing nothing and abandoning one's sex. At the very least, change your position on the vote even if you do nothing else."

"Ravensdale, look what you've done!" William Manchestor rose from his seat abruptly. "You've upset Miss Alita with all this fustian nonsense when there is no cause for it. She is the loveliest girl imaginable, and you've brought her to tears." He sneered. "This is nothing but self-serving, insincere drama. I am well acquainted with you Lord Byron types who plume yourself on the sound of your own voice and woo young innocents with your passionate, melancholy pronouncements simply for attention. Or for more illicit purposes, which I don't care to dwell upon in the company of ladies. I've a mind to call you out!"

Val raised his eyebrows in interest. This was a promising turn of events.

"There now, dear, don't raise a fuss. Alita is fine." Marvella patted William's hand. She touched her finger to her lips, clearly knowing that which would most displease him. "We mustn't provide an on-dit for the other guests."

William's eyes were burning with anger now, but he followed Marvella's direction, either trusting that she knew her own granddaughter or not wishing to cause a scene, and sat down. Through clenched teeth he

The Paradox: The Soldier and the Mystic 233

pronounced softly into her ear, though purposely audible to all in the small party, "Miss Alita, you are perfection itself and deserve much better treatment than this peep-of-the-day fellow displays. Life does not need to be this difficult. If one but relaxes and enjoys oneself, it is the simplest matter imaginable to be happy."

Alita smiled at him.

"I couldn't agree more, dear," Marvella added.

Val studied Manchestor momentarily with some admiration. Though Manchestor surely knew that he could snap him in two had he half a mind to, the dandy persisted in defending Alita's honor in a brave, if medieval, manner.

"Manchestor," posed Val, "can you provide Miss Alita with a handkerchief? I seem to have misplaced mine." In truth, Val knew exactly where his handkerchief was but thought that Manchestor's handkerchief with the bunnies on it might be of more comfort to the young lady.

"I apologize for upsetting you, Miss Alita. I assure you that it was not my intent." While William was retrieving his handkerchief, Val attempted to console her. "And your discomfiture was not in vain. You have discovered that your skill is that you can hide who you are and get along in the world. That realization is no small accomplishment for someone of your relative youth."

"That talent is nothing out of the ordinary, I assure you, Lord Ravensdale," replied Alita haughtily. She sniffed. "All women can pretend to be someone they are not. Only men have the privilege of being their arrogant, pontificating selves."

Marvella observed Alita's defiant response with obvious interest while William was clearly still seething.

Lord Ravensdale grinned from ear to ear with Alita's pronouncement, his victory complete. He leaned toward her.

"*Bravo*, Miss Alita! Precisely my point! And why should you tolerate this injustice? When women have equal rights, there will be equal rules of conduct." Val continued, his voice warm, "You are selling yourself—and your sex—short. Let us look at this from your standpoint, since I am certainly no expert on Miss Alita Stanton, an achievement which would give me the greatest pleasure. What do *you* see as your strongest ability?"

234   *Suzette Hollingsworth*

"I am thought to be an excellent painter, gardener, and decorator." Alita shrugged, running her dainty fingertips along her pearl choker.

Marvella leaned close to Val, whispering, "She is a terrible seamstress!"

"There is more, isn't there, Miss Alita?" Val kept his eyes glued on Alita.

"I have been...*instructed*...again and again that my greatest strength is in helping others to perceive *their* gifts." She stared at Val, her eyes once again penetrating his soul. "Though I have seen little evidence of this ability myself. My successes have not been impressive," she attempted to smile, but there was a touch of sadness in her voice, even as she dotted her eyes with the handkerchief.

"Miss Alita, you are making your contribution to the world without the slightest effort, simply by being your lovely self," William pronounced.

Alita's smile was forced, but her expression grew pensive. "In truth, I do not believe one's particular activities or interests are of any importance at all."

Val stared at her, bewildered.

"Whatever can you mean, Miss Alita?" William asked.

"Quite simply, it does not matter if one practices swordsmanship or law or medicine—or even knitting." She took a sip of her tea.

"What does matter then?" asked Val with hesitation.

"It matters that one strives." She shrugged. "It does not matter if one loves science or laying bricks, it matters that one loves. It does not matter if one reaches for the stars or a rosebud, but it is vital that one questions and opens oneself to life. These talents are mere characteristics of personality, gifts, and societal times. They are all outlets for the growth of the soul and irrelevant apart from that. But it does matter that we *do* and that we do that which fulfills us. We must live fiercely with all our hearts."

Dear God, what will the woman say next?

"Hear, hear," William exclaimed, raising his champagne glass and motioning to the waiter. "Let us drink to that. Waiter, please bring champagne."

There was an immediate pouring of champagne and a clinking of glasses before Val remarked, "I must admit that I find your words astonishing, Miss Alita. You who have been insistent that I fulfill my so-called potential."

The Paradox: The Soldier and the Mystic 235

"It is a strange irony." Alita laughed. "The particular expression has no intrinsic value but is of paramount importance to the individual. It is vital that one finds one's true nature."

"And, Miss Alita, what is your true nature?" he asked softly. The room was strangely quiet—even the orchestra had ceased playing—and the sound of the water flowing down the fountain filled the background.

"Even sitting on a lace pillow and feeding the birds can be holy." She smiled, the sparkle returning to her glistening green eyes.

No doubt it would be holy if she were the angel on that pillow.

Kiss Me Good Night, Dear Love. He recognized the tune at once when the orchestra began to play again. Val's heart lightened as he listened to the melody of her voice and the poetry of her words blending with the sounds of the orchestra, her wheat-colored curls bobbing as her head moved. His eyes fixated on Alita's, and he suddenly felt they were the only two people in the room. He took her hand and kissed her gloved fingertips lightly.

"Forgive me, Miss Alita. I sought to dispense wisdom, and I am, instead, the recipient."

Chapter Twenty-Three

It is devastating to my purpose that I am clearly captivated by Lord Ravensdale, she wrote in a letter to her mother even as she resolved to do everything in her power to curb her attraction to the earl. Why had she let her personal responses compromise her purpose? And how much should she reveal to Lady Elaina?

Very little, if anything. She had always shared everything of importance with her mother, and now, at a time when she most needed someone to talk to, there was no one to whom she could tell the whole.

Taking a sip of hot jasmine tea, she glanced at the window view from the desk in her private sitting room overlooking one of the busiest streets in Cairo. The floral scent rising from her blue-and-gold porcelain cup blended with the commotion below to form a strange mixture she could almost taste.

Oh, what is happening to me? She was becoming more and more isolated, she who lived to be with other people. She forced herself to pick up her quill pen.

Alita felt the early morning sun warm her hand even as the feather from her pen brushed her cheek. A strange mix of unrealized yearnings in her heart, both foreign and unidentifiable to her, struggled to surface. Feeling an intense longing, she attempted to name it, but she could make no sense of her feelings.

I never think. I only feel, she continued writing. *You know that I have always been guided by my emotions, Ma-ma. Only this time the emotions are stronger than ever and leading me nowhere. I start each day in earnest and end up behind the starting gate.*

Is that sufficiently vague enough? She had never actually told Lady Elaina *why* she had come to Egypt—to convince a man she had never met that he had a path unknown to her, which would save lives in a manner she knew not how.

The Paradox: The Soldier and the Mystic 237

It was no wonder she had not been forthcoming. What was there to convey?

Alita threw her pen on the desk, ink making a trail down her beige parchment paper.

Crumpling the page, she sighed heavily even as she glanced out the window. Her third-story room afforded her a lovely view of all who entered and departed Shepheard's and of local artisans selling their breathtaking masterpieces as well—the beautiful papyrus paintings and elaborately designed handcrafted carpets. This private show was a favorite setting when she wished to decipher her thoughts, surprising since the noise was horrendous. Animals braying, children yelling, shopkeepers hawking their wares, and people bartering at the tops of their lungs.

So unlike English decorum, it seemed to Alita that everyone was talking emphatically at once, with much waving of arms and gesturing. Somehow watching others who did not watch back, so involved in the hustle and bustle of life, calmed her spirits.

Except today.

An awareness of her current isolation presented her with another insight. In stark contrast to her usual behavior, she had inwardly resisted setting herself aside where the Earl of Ravensdale was concerned. Almost from the moment of their meeting, she had striven to be fully present, fears and all, and to be known by him. She longed to be in the middle of the whirlwind with him, not a bystander.

She no longer wished to be the instrument. She wished to be the music.

There was a light tap on the door, and Alita responded softly, "Come in, Grandmamma."

She rose to pour a cup of tea for the duchess, a morning ritual of sorts, as her guest floated toward her in a silver Watteau wrapper.

Marvella seated herself in a chair near Alita's desk and peered out the window, shaking her head in disapproval. "It's busy this morning. I can't believe you wouldn't prefer a quieter room, my dear."

"Oh no, I enjoy it, Grandmamma."

"Indeed, you are the picture of contentment, Alita dear." Marvella raised her eyebrows, her expression stiff. "You don't seem very pleased considering you have an outing planned with Lord Ravensdale. An excursion to the park, I believe?"

"Yes, Grandmamma," she murmured, seating herself across from her grandmother.

"And what is your opinion of the earl, my sweet, now that you have come to know him better?"

"Lord Ravensdale is so unlike the perfect man I have always dreamed of, one who is amiable, dignified, and refined. A debonair and fashionable man. Caring and sociable."

"Like William Manchestor?" Marvella asked.

"Like William Manchestor. Who is perfect in every way," stated Alita, her voice beginning to fail her.

"Then what could possibly be the confusion here?" Marvella lowered her teacup.

"Why don't I long for William, Grandmamma?" She turned toward her grandmother, twisting in her seat. "And why does my heart positively burst for Val?"

"You don't long for William Manchestor, my dear?" Marvella asked disbelievingly.

Alita shook her head, giving up on finding the words.

"That must place you in a different state from all the other young ladies currently residing in England." She sniffed.

"Oh, I know!" moaned Alita. "And the life I could have with William is my heart's desire. I long desperately for it. There can be no question about that. But I don't long *for him*."

"Most unfortunate." Marvella pursed her red lips, which accented her pale blue eyes and aristocratic features. "You have won his heart, and you don't wish for it. Be careful what you throw away, my dear."

"The realization of all my dreams has been laid out before me, and I have never been more unhappy in my life." Alita nodded sadly. "I know I should be so grateful that he cares for me. And I am! Moreover, it warms my heart to think of William. I approve of him in every possible way."

"You *approve* of him? Most impassioned." Marvella stirred her tea, always practical. "And do you see a proposal materializing from Lord Ravensdale?"

"Quite the opposite," she replied in a whisper, feeling her heart fall in her chest at the words she knew to be true. "There is no chance whatsoever of such an occurrence."

The Paradox: The Soldier and the Mystic 239

Marvella set her teacup down suddenly with an uncharacteristic *clink*, liquid splashing over the edge onto the saucer. "Alita, a presentation is one thing, but this is your life we are speaking of. You have a jewel in your hand. If you don't want it, I assure you that someone else will snatch it up."

"I understand." Alita nodded. "You are saying *don't destroy your life as you did your presentation.*"

Over the past two months, ever since that dreadful Queen's Ball, Alita had begun to think of herself as the enemy. There was no doubt that she was the person who had ruined everything in her life. No one else. Only herself.

And, in the process, she had begun to separate from herself, from her feelings, from her instincts. After all, she could no longer trust her own inclinations.

Maybe the Queen's Ball was not her fault precisely, but she could have prevented that disaster. And look how she had behaved ever since she had known Val Huntington, as if her entire world lay with this man.

"Quite so! You would do well to think on that very thing." Marvella picked up a piece of toast and took a miniscule bite. "Alita dear, answer me this. Do you wish to marry Lord Ravensdale?"

Her lips quivered as she felt a battle raging inside her. A holiday was one thing, but she wanted family, home, and stability. The absolute *last* thing she wanted to do in this life was to be experiencing new lands and new people, which she knew to be Val's destiny.

If he realized it. And it would be a great loss to himself and the world if he did not.

Her head was spinning again. She who had the sight could not see her own life from one minute to the next! She felt as if she were in the middle of a hurricane, with no ability to direct the circumstances of her life and certainly no guarantees of happiness, now or ever.

"I don't know, Grandmamma. I honestly don't know." It felt like life was happening to her and at her instead of with her and through her. She had been accustomed to being present in her own life, to being an active participant who had initiated the circumstances in her life, and to being able to manifest outcomes that she desired. If an obstacle came her way, it was merely a tool toward a better end result than she had previously imagined.

Challenges, in fact, had given her the sense that Someone greater and wiser was looking out for her and giving her the next step. Now she didn't know anything anymore.

She looked out the window, and the children especially caught her notice. As her fingers ran along the fine Belgian lace—surely no one appreciated such niceties more than herself—she made a mental note to donate all but a single handkerchief to the children of Cairo before leaving.

"And I don't know that it matters what I want, Grandmamma. I believe that is quite unimportant in the scheme of things."

Out of the corner of her eye, she saw a piece of toast drop to the floor.

Chapter Twenty-Four

We have no future together.

As promised, Val arrived in a carriage of ebony and gold, depicting his family crest and driven by a handsome pair of sleek, black high-steppers.

She watched him alight from his carriage with the masculine grace of the panther. He almost leapt forward in his skintight fawn-colored trousers, black coat and bellowing white cotton shirt, unbuttoned at the neckline to reveal a small amount of his muscled chest.

He was notoriously handsome in his riding dress. Even from her window seat she could see the pale silver-blue eyes so clearly against his raven hair and the black ebony of the carriage. She moved behind a giant red hibiscus flower next to the window in the hope that he would not see her watching him.

Touching her fingers to her lips, Alita determined to remember every detail of the scene to hold in her memory. As she watched Val's purposeful stride toward the front door of Shepheard's, she felt joy at the same time she was certain her heart would break or pound out of her chest.

We will not be together. She had seen it. She might be a discombobulated mess, but her predictions were stronger than ever. Never in her life had she held the window to the future that she now possessed.

She was at her worst and at her best at the same time. Moving to the door, she took one last look in the mirror.

She shook her head as she studied her image. A perfect adherence to the fashion of the day. And yet...*I don't know what it is—but something is different.*

She wore a golden-tan damask silk, perfectly offsetting her wheat-colored hair and bringing out the golden-flecks in her bright-green eyes. The square neckline of the gown was outlined in a full frill of white point duchesse lace with a large satin bow of burnt copper-brown strategically placed below the neckline. The sleeves gathered at the elbows, also outlined in lace and accented with satin copper bows. White gloves and topaz jewelry further accented the gold in her hair and her eyes. A fringe of amber beads along the hemline revealed one-inch pleats.

Suddenly the door bells resounded through the rooms. She turned and moved toward the ringing even without willing herself to do so.

After a quiet drive in which neither of them spoke more than superficial remarks, both sensing that their time together was coming to a close, they alighted at the park. Hattie walked a short distance behind them, allowing for private conversation but nothing more.

"Hattie keeps a closer distance than she has in our previous outings. On whose direction would that be, Miss Alita?" Val raised his eyebrows in irritation as he tightened his hold on her elbow.

She turned to look at him but said nothing.

"The usual hostile glances," he muttered, his eyes glued to hers. "No change there."

No change? Everything that matters has changed.

"And yet, clearly there has been a shift in Miss Alita's feelings toward me." He continued his soliloquy. "Miss Hattie has the prerequisite gift of both understanding and obeying her mistress to the letter. Ordinarily she disappears from view as quickly as I materialize. She has been a servant of inestimable talents, holding a warm place in my heart up to this point in time."

"I am gratified to know that my maid has served you well, my lord." A pang of longing rushed through Alita as she beheld her yearning mirrored in his eyes despite his attempts at lighthearted humor. She turned away, unable to bear looking him in the eyes.

His eyes rested on Hattie again, bestowing upon her a stare which had exercised control over soldiers for years. The shy, young girl was no match for the earl of Ravensdale and took a step back involuntarily. Val raised one eyebrow, his expression resolute and hard even as he restored his gaze to Alita.

"She is an inconvenience, no more than that, Miss Alita."

"As are all women for you, I fear." She felt the seconds ticking away and swallowed hard. Each time she looked into those pale blue eyes of steel her heart was breaking for longing for this man and yet with the sure knowledge that they would not be together. It should have comforted her to

The Paradox: The Soldier and the Mystic 243

know she had been spared a life that she only reflected upon with distaste, but Alita felt her world was crashing in around her.

"I assure you, Miss Alita, I did not mean—"

"Lord Ravensdale, your purpose has come to me clearly. It was vague for a long while, but now I see it." Alita strove to keep her voice calm and clear despite the churning of her stomach.

"Should I feel encouragement or dread?" Val studied her with interest, and their pace naturally slowed, as he was holding her arm. "Miss Alita, I believe I have never beheld a more agonizing expression on a woman's face."

"Feel what you will, Lord Ravensdale. I am sure that I have no influence where your feelings are concerned."

"I beg to differ on that point, Miss Alita," he replied, astonishment written all over his face. "And won't you address me as *Val*?"

"When I first spoke with you, Lord Ravensdale," Alita continued, becoming quite accustomed to dismissing his remarks, a rudeness she would have never thought possible of herself, "I knew that your potential was great and that you could reach many people, but I did not know the specific venue for the expression of your gifts."

"And now you do."

"Now I do." A sense of excitement overcame her, even as she reflected on her discovery.

"Ah, you didn't know, but now you do. And what might account for this sudden enlightenment?"

"I do apologize, my lord, but generally I don't know future events. I only access people's feelings in the vast majority of cases." *Until coming to Egypt. Until meeting the love of my life.* Until...Her recently acquired talent for precognition might vanish tomorrow.

"No need to apologize, Miss Alita." Val arched his eyebrows in an aristocratic manner, accentuating his penetrating expression. "Having to wait one week to learn the destiny of my lifetime was some inconvenience, I grant you, but one must allow for the incomplete focus of your youth. I forgive you." He took her hand and kissed her fingertips slowly.

She wanted to slap him even as he took her hand and kissed her fingertips slowly, his touch so gentle.

"I see that I have wasted your time as usual, Lord Ravensdale. I am sorry to have troubled you." She regarded him haughtily as she pulled her hand away. She was not the Duchess of Salford's granddaughter for nothing. She turned on her heel.

"Please don't go, dear girl," Val begged, his voice husky. He captured her hand again, maintaining a tight hold.

She felt a current of energy flow through her body even as her hand was gloved in lace. She felt his skin through the lace of the glove and turned her head away, overcome by her emotion.

"Unhand me!" she demanded, but her resolve softened as she moved to see the desperation in his eyes, so like her own feelings. Alita waved her free hand in front of her face, attempting to regain her composure, unable to speak.

"I have every intention of keeping you with me for some time, Miss Alita." Val's hold on her tightened. "The only thing which would separate us at the moment is a bullet or a blade."

"Please, my lord!" Alita repeated under her breath. "Let me go at once!"

Slowly, very slowly, and clearly against his will, Val released his hold on her hand, keeping his cool, steely eyes locked on hers for one long moment before he finally released her. He offered her his arm. She could see the outline of his flexed muscles through the loose, thin white cotton fabric, tensing as he beheld her. "As you wish, my dear."

"You don't wish me to leave merely because you are not finished jousting with me," she stated as she placed her hands on her waist, her agitation growing.

"Actually, that is not my primary purpose," he replied, raising his right eyebrow.

"I am relieved to discover that you at least have a purpose, Lord Ravensdale," she mumbled. "Perhaps it can be improved upon."

"That is my greatest wish, Miss Alita."

"I hate to diminish your hopes, Lord Ravensdale, but I fear they have taken a wrong direction."

"I have so few amusements which involve any part of the currently living human race. Please don't deprive me of this, Miss Alita."

"If I stay, do you promise to be polite, my lord?" she asked with distrust as she studied him.

The Paradox: The Soldier and the Mystic 245

"I don't believe that quality is in my repertoire or that I have given any indication that it is." His voice was smooth and sultry as he answered her. "Though I shall endeavor to make the addition if it will keep you here with me, Miss Alita."

Gently offering her arm, she offered him her answer without actually finding words. They continued walking at a slow pace, Hattie having increased her distance behind them to something over five feet.

"There is something different about you, Miss Alita." He turned and looked at her.

"Oh? I'm sure you must be mistaken, Lord Ravensdale," she replied, not mentioning that she had noticed it herself but could not quite put her finger on it.

"Hmmm," he remarked, rubbing his chin as his eyes surveyed her. "You're wearing ball slippers with Spanish embroidery."

"Yes?" she stated. "There is nothing unusual in that."

"A gypsy."

"Excuse me?"

"You look rather like a *gypsy*, Miss Alita." His lips formed a slow smile. "The fringe, the gold, the sparkle in your eye—as if you are on the verge of escape.

If only it were so.

"You have never looked quite this *wild*. I do like this change, Miss Alita."

"I am delighted to have your approval, my lord."

"Miss Alita," he stated with a distinctly dangerous tone to his voice. "Might I inquire why it is necessary to have your maid follow us so closely? I suggest that we leave her at a bench, push her over a cliff, or drown her in the Nile. I desire that we should pursue a more private path. It would make conversation so much easier." Val raised his voice—quite unnecessarily as he was possessed of a deep baritone voice—when proposing his plans for Hattie's future. The girl backed up fully a foot, but she glared at him. She made no secret of the fact that she did not approve of Lord Ravensdale, which clearly mattered not a whit to him.

"Indeed?" Alita bestowed her haughtiest glance upon Val, scrutinizing him. "I am having no difficulty making conversation outside of the fact that you seem incapable of focusing your attention."

"I assure you, Miss Alita, that my attention is singularly focused," stated Val, his voice low as he put his hand on her elbow. "I find your attendant's presence intensely distracting and not conducive to conversation. It renders me positively tongue-tied."

"That is most distressing," she quipped. "Stemming from your shyness, no doubt."

"That is it," Val stated somberly with a nod of finality, the right corner of his mouth noticeably higher than the left, as if he were suppressing a smile.

"Lord Ravensdale," she said, turning to face him, her anger building. "If you are in search of other diversions, why not transport me home and go to the brothel of your choice rather than seeking out companionship among society ladies? Obviously conversation is a waste of your time."

Val stared at her, appearing to not believe her words, before bursting into laughter.

"Let me understand you, Miss Alita. You think the pursuit of intimate relations is why I have been in your company?" he asked. "And the reason why I now desire a more *private* interlude?"

"Without a doubt." She nodded without hesitation.

"Then you don't know a damn thing about me. You have lost your credibility with me, Miss Alita," he concluded, shaking his head before reconsidering her words. "But since you mention it, is there a possibility...that you...and I...?"

"No! There is not!" she emphasized, surprised at the volume of her voice.

"One merely wishes to have all the facts at hand." He smiled, his amusement beginning to grate. "But recall, Miss Alita, that it was your suggestion and not mine."

"I most certainly suggested nothing of the sort, Lord Ravensdale! And it is ungentlemanly of you to say so!"

"I would do anything to accommodate you, I assure you, Miss Alita, but the idea of a most pleasing interlude was erased from all possibility the moment I learned of your identity. I had completely forgotten the desire..." He shrugged. "And I never would have had the idea to begin with if you had not hidden your identity from me, I might add."

The Paradox: The Soldier and the Mystic

"Then why are you here with me, Lord Ravensdale? Flirting shamelessly, *I* might add."

"Although it is evident to me that you find me irresistible, my reason for being in your company is much more honorable than you contend."

"What other reason could there be?" Alita demanded as she turned to face him, now fuming. She had no patience left. She sighed, suddenly feeling breathless. "Believe me, Lord Ravensdale, I feel the force of your attraction for me."

"*Excellent*," he replied with meaning, his lips forming a sensuous smile as he took her elbow again, the palm trees to one side of them and the enormous Nile River to the other.

"Combine that unfortunate reality with the fact that you don't take me seriously, Valerius," Alita acknowledged softly as she continued walking, forcing his movement.

"Believe me, Miss Alita, I have never taken a woman more *seriously*." Val's voice softened. "And do call me *Val*."

"Lord Ravensdale, is it not true that you don't believe anything I say?" She sighed.

"For the most part, true," he agreed.

"Very well!" She turned on him full force. "At least you admit it!"

"I have no intention of lying to you, Miss Alita. This is the aspect of our time together I most value." He shrugged, aiming her forward again. "Though you are never honest with me, the surprising outcome is that I find I can be completely myself with you. It is thoroughly refreshing."

"And yet you don't believe anything I say," she accused, their pace slowing greatly. "So of what possible use could my companionship be to you?"

"Miss Alita," he replied sensuously, stopping her to run his hand along her chin as he lifted her head to look into his eyes. "I like the way you say the things I don't believe."

Alita jerked her head away from his calloused hand, which appeared to diminish his confidence not at all. "Therefore, considering that you think everything I say is either a ploy or the result of a deranged mind, I cannot think of any other reason why you would choose to be in my company other than to satisfy your appetites."

"You don't say?" stated Val, amazement revealed in his expression, unable to suppress laughter. "How good of you to inform me, Miss Alita. And might I inquire as to your process of deduction? Have you arrived at this conclusion because I have not proposed marriage after little more than a week of acquaintance?"

"*Oh, this is outside of enough!*" she barely whispered through clenched teeth as her hands tightened into fists. She stopped dead in her tracks and stomped her foot involuntarily. *Oh, this is not going well.* No matter what she did, it discredited her.

"*Breathtaking,* isn't it, Miss Alita?"

"Oh, *yes!*" They had arrived at an overview of the city, and he lured her to the lookout point. She glanced about from the hilltop, attempting to regain her composure. And, in fact, Cairo never failed to exercise a calming influence on her. She loved the combination of mosque-style buildings—domes everywhere—with tall, steeple-like buildings. Everywhere in the city there was color and texture, noise and life, movement and change. And more *color.* Camels, donkeys, mud buildings, and sailboats mixed with modern architecture and palm trees. Turbans and English clothing.

"Perhaps it is my reputation about town with women which led to your false impression of me?" he asked, moving his face in front of hers.

"*Reputation*? I was not aware that you had a reputation, Lord Ravensdale," she asked, aghast, fearing the worst.

"Precisely, Miss Alita! I know full well that I do not, in fact, have a rakish reputation, although I have many times been given the opportunity to develop one."

"How good of you to keep me apprised of your illicit invitations and tawdry affairs, Lord Ravensdale," she replied icily. "It is difficult to express the level of interest I have in this subject."

"I only just told you, Miss Alita, that there are no tawdry affairs. Well *almost* none. As to the illicit invitations, yes, I must admit those number in the—Do forgive me. I doubt that you are interested in the number, Miss Alita?" He smiled, the right corner of his lip slightly higher than the left, his raven black hair in contrast to his white teeth.

"Not in the slightest!"

The Paradox: The Soldier and the Mystic 249

"But I would not deprive you of the knowledge of any aspect of my person, however repetitious recounting the experience is for me." He ran his hands along his fawn-colored trousers, which fit him like a second skin.

"I beg you to deprive me!"

"I will be frank with you, Miss Alita."

"I have no doubt of that," she fumed.

"The material point is that if I were merely in search of a warm female body, I would have long ago achieved that end, I assure you." He gave her his most seductive glance as he turned quite serious, and she felt her mouth go dry. "And with much less aggravation than I have experienced at your hand, my dear."

"Then do not allow me to aggravate your further, I beg you!" She managed to find her voice. "Go and enjoy the hundreds of women throwing themselves at your feet—women which, I might add, never materialize in my presence but which, according to you, are everywhere to be found."

"*Hundreds?*" He shook his head, disbelief written all over his face, as he leaned against the barrier in front of the lookout point. "I wouldn't say more than a dozen."

"*How dare you talk to me like this!*" But then, he never stopped talking. He talked...and talked...and talked. Honestly, she never met a man who liked to talk more.

"How would you wish me to speak to you, Miss Alita?"

"Not at all! I wish you to *listen!*"

"I am all ears, Miss Alita." He crossed his arms in front of his muscled chest, his white cotton shirt billowing about him so unlike the starched formfitting shirts that were the fashion of the day.

"Lord Ravensdale, I agreed to meet with you today in order to speak of *your destiny.* Surely you were aware of my hesitation to even meet you." She was fully exasperated at this point. "Let me make myself perfectly clear. I will allow none of those improprieties which I so foolishly permitted in the past." Her words were clear, but her knees wobbled. She did not feel the resolution she so desperately hoped she was projecting. And she wished he would stop running his index finger along her chin, however briefly. In truth, his touch thrilled her in its roughness, so unlike any man's touch she had known or imagined.

"Believe me, Miss Stanton, I would never have presumed...But there were indications that you reciprocated my interest. In fact," he murmured as he moved his face closer to hers, their lips only inches apart, "I seem to recall that you initiated the acquaintance. Does my memory fail me?"

She could feel his breath on her lips now. She backed up, glaring at him, incensed. "Yes, but...I never...You misinterpreted..."

"There were certain signs which a man takes to mean..." He shook his head in feigned confusion. "But no, if I misunderstood, I sincerely beg your forgiveness, Miss Alita, and assure you that I have every wish of continuing our friendship in whatever form is agreeable to you."

Could I have misjudged him? No, it wasn't possible, she knew what she had felt from him. But she also knew that, at this moment in time, he was entirely sincere.

She felt her embarrassment rising, but she was determined to be resolute. "That is most certainly a change in your perspective, Lord Ravensdale."

"Indeed it is."

"And what can account for the change?"

"I have no idea, Miss Alita. But despite the fact that I cannot explain myself, you I understand completely."

"I beg your pardon! You have no such understanding."

"Oh, but I do." He bestowed his most sensual smile upon her and she suddenly felt giddy. "I am certain that your attraction to me is as strong as mine is to you, whatever you may say."

She cleared her throat, looking away. "A lady is under no obligation to respond to such inappropriate conversation."

In an instant he stopped where he stood, the momentum tossing her hat forward. "But you may have very well decided to direct your attentions elsewhere on more, shall we say, fertile ground?"

"Lord Ravensdale! Do not hinder my progress!"

"You are an excellent actress, Miss Alita. Perhaps none of this has been real." He rubbed his hand through his hair, his eyes suddenly dark. "The idea sickens me to contemplate."

Alita remained silent as he stopped where he stood and blocked her path, formidable in his resolve. She kept her eyes straight ahead, refusing to respond to such rudeness.

The Paradox: The Soldier and the Mystic 251

In one step he was in front of her, and he placed both her hands in his hands. The pleasure she felt from the strength in his hold dismayed her. Her eyes met his unrelenting gaze. She was quite certain that her determination matched his as well.

"*Release me this instant*! If you do not, I shall answer none of your impertinent questions. Not now, not ever."

"Tell me now, Miss Alita, if you have been toying with me," he replied quietly, his demeanor calm and deadly serious. "Has there been a change in your affections?"

"You assume too much, Valerius." She forced her expression to remain unchanged as she attempted to retrieve her hands to no avail. She so hoped her eyes would not well up with tears. Why oh why was she sent here to perform a function she was unable to accomplish—while being tortured in the process? Was it someone's idea of a cruel joke?

"Do I?" he asked politely.

"There was never any intent on my part toward you, so there is nothing to change. I told you that from the beginning. My purpose here has nothing to do with *us*, only with *you*." Slowly her eyes met his, and she felt intense longing there. Oh, the man would drive her to madness! "And I cannot see how my love life is any of your business."

"I am not a fool, Miss Alita, so I'll thank you not to treat me like one."

"You feel jealousy, and yet the fact is that you want nothing more from me, so how can I choose to give that which is not desired?"

She jerked her hands free and proceeded forward, opening her parasol as she walked. Val stood for a long moment before following her, grasping her parasol with one hand to hold over both of them while taking her elbow with the other. "Though you say there has been no change in your sentiment, I notice a great change in the proximity of your chaperone," he stated with a studied air. "This must communicate some information to me."

"It no longer suits my purposes to be in close proximity to you." She tipped her hat forward, attempting to keep him from seeing her eyes.

"*Damn it!*" Val took her by the waist with his free arm, holding her immobile. "I will have my answer. Stop playing your bloody games, Miss Alita! Is there is another gentleman more to your taste?"

She looked into his eyes. Oh, but he was cruel. He did not want her but he would not relent until she had given him everything she had to give.

252   *Suzette Hollingsworth*

No matter. He already had it.

"No, Valerius," she replied faintly. "There is not."

He released his breath, and she saw relief in his eyes.

"Then why are you withdrawing from me? I fail to understand, Miss Alita," he implored, not loosening his hold on her.

"I wouldn't expect you to, Lord Ravensdale," she retorted. "You never understand anything."

"That's my girl," he murmured with relief, his lips forming a seductive smile as he placed a light kiss on her forehead. She closed her eyes for a moment before pulling away. They moved forward even as Hattie retrieved the discarded parasol and closed it, all the while shaking her head.

"I am not 'your girl' by your own admission."

Alita turned to observe the petite brunette. Hattie had changed since coming to Egypt. She used to look down at the ground—now she revealed her opinion in unspoken ways at times. She was still shy—but not quite so *afraid*.

They had all changed. For herself, in ways she never wished to.

"And why is that, may I inquire?" he asked nonchalantly, but she knew that he felt some pain from her words. "Because you hold no high opinion of my understanding?"

"Because you won't hear my words if you think I am merely attempting to procure something for myself. In this case, marriage." Exasperated, she released a heavy sigh. She knew that he was determined to see her in this light.

In all fairness to him, her feelings betrayed her. "Valerius Huntington, I shall not rest until you hear that which I came to tell you about your future. I am determined that you shall know I seek nothing for myself no matter how my feelings may rebel."

"I am your obedient servant, Miss Alita." He bowed gallantly before her. Val reached for her arm, and when she offered it, they took up their stroll again. "Please proceed."

"I know the whole," she murmured quietly.

"Tell me then, Miss Alita, what is my destiny?" Val made an attempt at affecting interest. She had never seen him trouble himself before.

Alita looked up at him, his expression strangely content. He had been the most troubled person of her acquaintance—outside herself—when she

The Paradox: The Soldier and the Mystic 253

had met him. "You will write stories of other cultures for the English-reading populace."

Val laughed heartily, involuntarily shaking her arm with his movement. "This is my great destiny which will change the face of the world? Writing *stories*?"

"I do not jest, my lord." She nodded, discouraged but not surprised by his response. "Only consider. The translation of *The Arabian Nights* had an enormous impact on the English, giving them an insatiable desire for all things Eastern. A fascination with and appreciation for another people's culture and history promotes cooperation and conciliation far more effectively than can any amount of governmental interference."

"That is *true*, Miss Alita. Reality always follows perception. However, I—"

"Once there is human feeling, once it becomes an idea in our consciousness on a grand enough scale, it becomes reality." Alita's excitement grew despite herself. "Your stories will have a significant impact toward bringing the world together with a power most politicians only dream of, Lord Ravensdale."

"Very enlightening," Val pronounced with a contrived interest, which was clearly false. "A storyteller. I can indeed be proud of my noble contribution."

"Don't diminish who you are, Valerius." Alita felt the sting of his words, but her concern for him was far greater than any slight she felt. "When you discover who you are and embrace it, the impact will be far greater than you can imagine."

"Would you care to sit, Miss Alita?" She nodded, and they both sat in silence for some moments at a bench overlooking the river. The waters of the Nile were high, and Alita studied the designs formed by the current, mirroring her whirling emotions.

Alita strove to control the shaking in her hands as she observed the emptiness in Val's ice-blue eyes. Her words had not made a bit of difference. "There exists a much greater plan for you than you have for yourself. Never forget that, my lord."

"I see," Val said, his expression studious. "So *this* is my destiny, a teller of stories."

"Only partially. You have a dual purpose, Lord Ravensdale."

"I am tired already. Please do not give me so much to do."

"The translations will have a significant impact in this lifetime. But you can set the stage for other developments." Alita sighed. "You have a great ability as a diplomat."

"A diplomat? Pray tell," he said, chuckling even as he held his index finger to his mouth. "I am the least diplomatic person I know. I am astonished that this has missed your notice, Miss Alita."

"Honestly, Lord Ravensdale, you can be as dense as a doorknob for someone so intelligent."

"Perhaps you should consider diplomacy, Miss Alita. I believe you have a turn for it."

Alita sighed with irritation. "Only consider, Lord Ravensdale. You have a gift for languages and for comprehension. You understand precisely what is going on about you in the political arena. You are acutely aware. Do not tell me diplomacy has never crossed your mind?"

"Never." Val laughed, but bitterness set into his expression. "How conveniently you overlook the fact that we live in a world which is not interested in the truth. Each and every morning I begin my day with the goal of furthering the independence of Egypt."

"As you should."

"I know very well that nothing shall ever come of it."

"You will always face obstacles where persons with more power do not hold to your ideals, Lord Ravensdale," she agreed. "But it *is* possible for you to find a setting in which you could assist in uniting people of different cultures and bringing the world together in friendship."

"I hate to disavow you of your charming notions, Miss Alita, if you in fact believe any of this nonsense. Allow me to illuminate the matter. There are evil men in the world." He shrugged. "Most of them, I grant you, are in the churches, but some of them are in the queen's government."

"I am not so naive as to say evil does not exist, merely that you are more capable of discerning the enemy than most."

"Generally the fearful are the perpetuators of evil while they label those they persecute as evil."

"Precisely my point," stated Alita. "You are without fear, Lord Ravensdale. "There is generally a peaceable way to solve problems—in

The Paradox: The Soldier and the Mystic 255

many more cases than is utilized. These methods one would expect to be exhausted first."

"Unfortunately, there are those who benefit financially from war, and those whose weak egos crave the moral crusade. Tell me, Miss Alita, how shall I turn this about?" demanded Val, clearly impatient with the discussion.

"It is not clear to me how you will do this," reflected Alita, ignoring his sarcasm while smoothing her gown. "I do not see the particulars."

"Ah. That is indicative of insurmountable difficulties for an otherwise first-rate idea."

"Valerius," she asked hesitantly, "do you ever open the curtains in the morning, see the sun shining, and think to yourself, *It is going to be a wonderful day*. And then, even as you utter the words, feel a tingling in your body?"

"Are you quite serious?" He turned to stare at her in disbelief. Slowly a smile formed on his lips. "Never mind, I know the answer to that."

"Think about it the next time your mind sets upon a course, my lord," she sighed. "Verbalize your heart's desire. See if you don't feel a physical reaction."

"And if I did?"

"That is you connecting with the greater forces in the universe," she stated softly. "It is you changing. It is you receiving a greater power. It is you *manifesting*. We are all so much more powerful than we know."

"What would you have me do, Miss Alita?"

"I only see the next step that you are to take, Valerius," she replied slowly. "That is all that you need know. All any of us need to know."

He gently caressed her cheek with the back of his hand. Gingerly, he kissed her fingertips, his breath warm. He then pressed the fingers he had kissed to his lips. Alita felt herself shiver. With a slow, sensual smile he murmured, "I took the next step. Now what?"

Alita felt her breath quickening, but she looked away, her eyes fixated on the flowing waters of the Nile as she struggled with her reaction to him.

"I can see, Miss Alita, that there has not been any change in your feelings," he whispered hoarsely, his voice rough. *"Why then?"*

As they remained seated, Val studied her with obvious appreciation. He took her hand and kissed it gently. Slowly he pulled the lace on each finger of her glove until the back of her wrist was visible. He turned her hand and kissed her wrist slowly.

"And what of you, Miss Alita?" Val asked gingerly, his voice caressing her. "How do you see yourself in all of this?"

"I do not see myself in your future," she whispered, feeling as if she had been punched in the chest. "I...*am not*...in your future."

"Are you quite sure, Miss Alita?" he asked softly, his breath hot on her wrist.

"*Yes*," Alita whispered sadly.

"What can you hope to gain from this ploy, Miss Alita?" Val asked, his surprise apparent as he held her hand fixed in midair. "It would have been more effective to have told me I had no choice, that we *must* be together."

We must be together. The sound was heavenly—and torture. She turned away, unable to answer.

"Most unfortunate that you shall not share in my illustrious works, Miss Alita," Val drawled, his lips forming a slow smile, placing her hand in his lap. "And why shall we not be together, if I may ask?"

"I don't know, Valerius." She shook her head sadly. But she did know. Because he did not wish it.

"Possibly because I don't see a future for myself? So there can be nothing for you to enter into?"

"No, that's not it, I don't believe. I'm simply not a part of your future. That is all." Almost inaudibly, she added, "It is very clear."

"I see you with me *now*, Alita" he whispered. Val leaned toward her, his silver eyes seductive and full of promise. "Very clearly."

"I know you do," Alita retorted as she moved farther from him on the bench, retrieving her hand. Val told the truth. She was the center of his world at the moment. Even that was intoxicating. "But I need more than *now*."

Yes. Her answer would be *yes.* As she studied the Earl of Ravensdale, in that instant, she knew with a certainty that, despite what she told her grandmother, were he to ask her for her hand at this moment, her answer would be *yes.*

But he would not marry her—not today, not next month.

Not *ever.*

The Paradox: The Soldier and the Mystic

"If I were to marry, Miss Alita, it would be with a woman I could be of one mind with."

"And you are not of one mind with me," she repeated softly, already knowing that it was so.

"When I am with you, I forget everything that matters to me." His longing for her was evident in his every expression, and he clearly struggled with himself.

"Do not waste your charm on me, Lord Ravensdale," she managed to say. Alita looked straight ahead as she fingered the gold cross at her neck. "Assuming that it exists."

"You think that I want to make love all day with women?" He moved so that she had to look at him, and as he did so the flexed muscles of his chest became visible under his partially unbuttoned cotton shirt. "I want to make love with *you*, Alita, *only you*."

"Illuminating." *But in point of fact, people in hell want a drink of water.*

"But I can't make a life out of that." He added under his breath, "As much as it might tempt me."

"Ah, so now I am reduced to a mere temptation." She ran her fingers along the satin copper bow at her bosom. *May you always remember what you have lost and never feel satisfied.*

Oh, she shouldn't be thinking these thoughts! They were positively unkind.

"Not to mention that I have little to offer you." Val frowned, pain shooting across his tanned face.

What is it that you offer, Lord Ravensdale? It must have slipped my notice. "Let us be clear on this point, my lord. That which you have you have never offered."

"You would soon grow weary of life with me, Miss Alita." For an instant, sadness overtook those pale silver-blue eyes, starkly vivid even in the sunlight.

"I am astonished at how little you know about me, Lord Ravensdale." *Of course, you are a muttonhead, my lord, so that could explain it.*

"This is why I recommend that we at least enjoy what we have, which is an attraction for each other." Glancing at her sideways, he stretched his long legs out before him, his skin-tight fawn trousers molding perfectly to his form. "Life is so empty as it is. Why not enjoy what little is given to us?"

"Yes, that's what I'll do, my lord. I'll leave you completely satiated, so you shall need nothing further from me. I'll complete my life as a discarded, ruined woman, while you have that happy memory to hold close always, with your opinion of my virtue confirmed."

He stared at her in sudden shock before his lips broke into a smile. He took the palm of her hand and planted wet, hot kisses on her palm. He looked up at her through dark eyelashes, his eyes dark with desire. He studied her intently, and his expression was greatly pained. "We are not right for each other, Miss Alita."

"You mean that I am not right for you, Lord Ravensdale. You cannot speak for my feelings. Nor are you qualified to do so."

"It astonishes me to realize it, but I do have *feelings* for you, Miss Alita." He kissed her cheek.

"Feelings?" *Pray tell.* She raised her eyebrows in annoyance. "And which feelings might those be, Lord Ravensdale?" *Vexation, exasperation, agitation—as I feel for you?*

He smiled at her, his countenance one of wonder, his lips serenely closed. Now that she would truly wish to hear his words he was finally silent.

"Yes?" she demanded, ready to slap him for the answer.

"As if I'm not alive when I'm not with you. As if I don't want to be."

Her hands dropped into her lap even as she fought to keep her countenance. *No, don't be saying these things to me. Not now. I am barely holding myself together.* "Do not toy with me, Lord Ravensdale," she managed to murmur.

"I never toy, my dear." She leaned against his shoulder momentarily, and he bent to kiss her forehead. "I shouldn't have told you, Miss Alita. There is no point."

She nodded, biting her lip.

"I apologize. It is a fault of mine."

"Apologize for what?" she asked. "For finally saying something kind?"

"It is not in me to mislead. As for you, Alita, you have led me on a merry dance since the day we met." He chuckled.

"I have not, Valerius." She sat up and shook her head. "Quite the opposite. But you are too obtuse and pompous to see it."

The Paradox: The Soldier and the Mystic   *259*

"I see." He smiled, that incorrigible lock of raven hair falling into his eyes as he leaned forward. "And what is it I have missed?"

"Is there anything you have *not* missed might be more to the point! To help you, I had no choice but to reveal to you who I am. Believe me, if any other course had been open to me, I would have taken it! I had to speak the truth." Faintly she whispered, "When the truth is so fantastic, I suppose it does sound like a lie. I have finally fallen in love, and I am losing you because I could not pretend to be someone I am not. Because I could not lie to you."

"In love?" he demanded, lifting her chin with his hand so that she looked into his eyes, looking suddenly like they might be the gateway to heaven.

But even as joy washed across his face, just as quickly disbelief and cynicism replaced it, his expression perplexed. "You astonish me, Miss Alita. I know everything to be a ploy with you, and yet you seem to be genuinely hurting. It almost seems that you actually entertain the idea of marriage to me. Why, I still have no idea."

"I have no idea myself." She felt as if her heart would burst. "Truly, it is insanity."

He burst into laughter. "Please don't go out of your way to flatter me, I beg of you, Miss Alita."

"I was told in church that if one is kind and good, wonderful things will happen to one. It is not true." She ran her fingers along the gold cross at her neck. "Quite the opposite, in fact."

"Miss Alita," he said consolingly, "it also says in the Bible not to cast your pearls before swine."

She could not help but giggle despite her chagrin. This meeting was supposed to be about Val. Once again she had let her feelings take over.

"You know, Miss Alita, the battlefield gave me many qualities which I would give my eye teeth not to have. In retrospect, I would not have gone down this path. Not for love or money." His voice grew deadly still. "But one thing I did acquire from battle is the absence of fear. I no longer fear anything or anyone. When it's my time, it's my time. I never run from anything."

"With the notable exception of yourself, Val Huntington," she whispered.

"I am serious, Miss Alita. I fear nothing. And I'll prove it to you." He glanced at Hattie sitting on a neighboring bench some nine feet from their bench and then whispered, "As terrifying as she is, I don't even fear your maid." In a swift movement, he pulled her close and kissed her fiercely, wildly, as if it would be the last kiss they ever experienced. He pulled her tightly against his chest as he kissed her tenderly but desperately, her bonnet falling off her head and onto the bench.

Alita melted into his kiss which demanded everything from her, which she happily gave, wishing to give more. As he held her tight, his tongue plunged into her mouth without the hesitation of his earlier kisses, as if every second with her was the last. He kept pulling her closer until she didn't think she could be any closer. He ran his kisses along her cheek, and then he claimed her mouth again, breathing heavily into her own breath.

It felt indecent, as if he wanted to strip her clothes from here right there.

I wish that he would, a part of her whispered. Nothing else mattered when he was kissing her.

"Miss! Miss! Are you quite all right?" demanded Hattie, beating Val with her parasol.

"Ouch! Hattie! You've poked me with that blasted thing!" he admonished, pulling the umbrella from her hands.

"I'm f–f–fine, Hattie. You may return to your seat." She pulled away, breathless, her heart pounding, even as she struggled to replace her bonnet in her dazed state.

"I'm sorry, Miss, but he…I didn't know…""

"You did the right thing, Hattie," she assured her.

"Darling Alita." Val turned toward her, ignoring the interruption even as he rubbed his arm. "And you contemplate marriage to me? Why? What can I offer you that is worth giving up everything you want?"

"It is true. Only because I love you, Val. It makes no sense."

"You love me? Say it again, sweetheart. I love to hear the words even though I don't believe you know what they mean." Caressing her chin with his index finger, his eyes were soft as he gazed into hers. "Please erase that worried look from your expression, Miss Alita. It pains me. You shall create precisely the life you wish, I have no doubt. You'll give your love to some lucky bastard, and he'll take care of you. And you'll lead a completely predictable life."

The Paradox: The Soldier and the Mystic   *261*

Alita caught her breath. The Earl of Ravensdale was as far from predictable as a man could get.

And she loved him fiercely, completely, fully.

"Every moment with you is heavenly to me, Val. Every moment is unplanned, unrehearsed...thrilling." She almost swallowed her words but surprised herself in finding her voice.

"Give it about six months, darling, and you would be desperate to get away from me. Typically I am home in the evenings reading ancient text. I am not going to parties, taking drives in the park, dining at Shepheard's. This is not my *real* life. This is merely a special interlude for us. What would happen when you grew bored, my dear?"

"As if anyone could grow bored with you, Val!"

"There is another life waiting for you—a lovely home, a society husband, exemplary children, exquisite gowns. Your perfect life." He scowled. "You're just spouting poetry and nonsense."

"A perfect life in which I am in constant hiding, pretending to be someone else." She shook her head and whispered, "I was happy this way. But now...I don't think I can be again."

"Don't say that, Alita," he commanded, taking her by the arms, the fringe along her square neckline swaying as he grasped her. "I insist that you be happy. You were made for it."

"I had a shield to hide behind, a blind from which to view life." She shook her head. "If I could have maintained it, I would have. But it required an increasing amount of energy to maintain."

"What happened, Miss Alita?"

"It failed me on the most important day of my life. I needed a safety net which was woven from the fabric of the true nature of my being, and I didn't have one." She swallowed hard. "*I still don't.*"

"You cannot align yourself with me, Miss Alita. I cannot be your armor," he whispered hoarsely. "I am the least acceptable to society of anyone you could find."

"How can you not see, even now, why you complete me?" She looked into his eyes, locked on hers. How was it that someone so empty of comprehension had been the only one to awaken her? "You don't even know who I am, Val."

"Miss Alita, discovering who you are has been the singular endeavor of mine for some time."

It is no use. "I have been entirely honest with you at every turn. When you know yourself, you will know me in the same instant." And it will be too late.

"Miss Alita, are you well?" Val questioned with an expression of genuine concern as he observed her internal struggle.

"I came to help you, Val Huntington, but in the process, you have been God's gift to my soul, to point me in the direction of the person I was meant to be." Alita steadied her breath, striving to compose herself. "The next step for you is to focus on your translating. The progression will come naturally to you. Continue your studies, seek out the truth in all circumstances, and voice your opinion. I see that your studies have fallen by the wayside. You are not as energized as you once were. You have lost your spark."

There was no point pretending. It was all too clear that God had given Val to her to teach her how to embrace herself, to stay in her center, to speak her truth, to overcome her fear. God had given Val to her *for a short time only*, not for a lifetime, as she wanted.

Wanted with all her heart. She closed her eyes and struggled not to give into the pain of her disappointment.

"Oh?" asked Lord Ravensdale, his silver eyes filled with desire. "My *spark* as you put it, Miss Alita, seems to be in place." His jaw tensed as he clearly strove to maintain a gentleman's composure. "But, believe me, I appreciate your interest, my dear."

"Lord Ravensdale," Alita exclaimed with disapproval. "There is more that I must tell you of your future," she stated.

"Enough talk of me, I grow bored with this inexhaustible topic."

"Will you return to England?" Alita asked, hoping against hope to see him again.

"There is little to no chance of that," he stated coldly. Val scowled as his eyebrows grew close together.

"But what of your family?" asked Alita.

"My family has an elaborate system which excludes me," Val stated flatly.

"I don't understand," said Alita, bewildered. "You are the heir."

The Paradox: The Soldier and the Mystic

"Let me enlighten you, Miss Alita, on the illustrious family I am exerting every effort to prevent you from claiming as your own." Val scowled. "My father was continually feeding his wanton appetites with the maids in our employ. He even had the audacity to go after my younger sister at one point. I should have killed him then, but instead, I moved my sister to a different location in secret. I found the situation deplorable and said so. He replied by threatening to disinherit me."

"And did he do so?" Alita asked, breathless.

"I didn't give a damn, though it is not possible for him to do so. I am the heir. But that was of no concern, my father's behavior was. I told my mother of his escapades in order that she might protect her children, and she refused to believe it, despite the fact that we lost servants at an alarming rate." He shrugged. "She needed to see my father in a particular light. Possibly she took his failures to mean that she was a failure as a wife—and because she had no ally but him. Rather than see the truth about my father, she turned against me, as did the rest of my family. I became the receptacle for all the family guilt rightly belonging to my father. It was easier to hate me than to face the truth, it seems."

"Oh, it is deplorable!" uttered Alita, grief overwhelming her. "To destroy an innocent young person so in need of his family's love simply to maintain one's imaginary world."

"So you see, Miss Alita, between the lies of my family and the lies of my country, I am nothing but a damned nuisance to everyone."

She stared at him, this glorious man before her, a person so deserving of love and so easy to cherish. Deprived of an identity, of self-love, of a family.

And they will have *succeeded* in making him invisible and nonexistent—precisely their goal—if I cannot convince him of who he is, she thought.

"My father died, but the family maintains its delusions. Consequently, I have no desire to return to England. And I am not welcome."

Alita considered the man before her. Val Huntington had been betrayed by both country and family. Yet his motives remained pure, and he was, at base, a truth teller.

As was she. Heavens! She had never realized it before this moment.

And yet, they could not meet on a common plane.

Chapter Twenty-Five

"As usual, Miss Alita, I enjoyed our time together immensely." Val took Alita's hand before assisting her from the carriage at Shepheard's Hotel. He kissed her hand slowly, gazing intently at her. "You never disappoint."

"I am most gratified that I met your minimum standards, Lord Ravensdale," Alita replied, feeling anything but pleased. It was unbearable to be in his company, but it would have been worth her discomfiture if he had heard anything she had to say. "I live that you might be entertained."

"Until we meet again, Miss Alita," Val murmured as he saw her to the door. She looked into the silver depths of his eyes, foolishly allowing herself the luxury of hope.

But she saw nothing more than intense longing there. The commitment to their future—or, more importantly, to *his own*—was noticeably absent.

"And did you have a nice time, dear?" Marvella asked as she entered their suite, lounging with a cup of tea and her embroidery in a lavender silk wrapper.

"No, Grandmamma. It was pointless as always." To make matters worse, she had humiliated herself by revealing feelings she should never have let him see. Exasperated, she shook her head.

"Alita dear, if you further a young man's interest, your time is not wasted." Marvella fluffed her gown around her and poured them both some tea.

"Precisely." Alita sat beside her and warmed her hands with the teacup.

"What happened, my sweet?" Marvella looked concerned as she moved her embroidery to an end table.

"I would not have thought it possible, but I am even more of a ninny hammer now than I was when I left England." How had she gotten to this place in eight short weeks?

"Oh no, dear. I must disagree. I would not say that you are particularly clever now, but you were definitely more of a simpleton then. And besides,

The Paradox: The Soldier and the Mystic   265

beyond any doubt you are able to attract gentlemen, and that is by far the most important skill a young lady can have."

When had it happened? No longer was she possessed of the idea that she must enlighten Val in order to save the lives of others.

His was the life that mattered to her.

It was *his* future, *his* happiness, and his image that consumed her. This was the state of her heart, and it was no use to pretend otherwise.

"Do you think so, Grandmamma?" she asked absently.

"Your methods are more effective than you think, my sweet. You have the young man's attentions where others have failed. I would have preferred Lord Manchestor, myself, but Lord Ravensdale is as good as yours if you want him. Don't change what you are doing. Merely do *more*. You must simply bait the hook and draw the line."

"Oh no, Grandmamma, you see the situation in a far more positive a light than…but what if? *Possibly* you are correct…"

How could I not have thought of this before? It was a glaring truth that her spirit was intricately interwoven with Val's for some inexplicable reason. She had been so distressed by their differences—the fact that they were inharmonious where it mattered most with Val, intellectually and logically—that she had beaten a dead horse. She had ignored her strengths and their similarities.

"Of course I am!" Marvella replied, taking a sip of her tea and looking quite smug. "I always am."

Could it work? Deliberating relentlessly, suddenly an idea took possession of her mind.

"What is it, Alita?" Marvella demanded, looking at her over her gold teacup. "What is that glimmer in your eye? Whatever it is, *I like it*."

"No, I couldn't! It is nothing but parlor games!" she murmured. Generally utilized to bring glory and notoriety to oneself…

"Parlor games can be quite effective. And never forget, Alita, that where young men are concerned, one either wins or loses *everything*. There is no in between. You must ask yourself, do you want the prize or do you not?"

"True, Grandmamma. This is my last and *only* opportunity. I can feel it." She was willing to try anything.

"Good for you, my girl! But always show discretion." The duchess wagged her finger at her.

"I no longer have that luxury, Grandmamma." She shook her head.

"You *what*? Now see here, young lady—"

"Discretion has been most ineffective. I must be flamboyant! I must throw caution to the wind!"

She grew excited as she worked out her plan. Even if he only partially believed her, *it might be enough.*

Just a spark of confidence, a glimmer of belief in himself, might be all it would take to set Val on a new path. He was a person of great energy, drive, and discipline, and the smallest bend in the road might change the course of his life irrevocably for the better.

"Young lady, you answer me *now*! What are you planning? I married the greatest catch of the season—the Duke!—and I never once compromised my virtue! A little teasing here and there, yes, but *never…*"

Alita grew resolute. She must focus if this was going to work. She and Val were, in fact, aligned emotionally, spiritually, physically, and psychically. True, Val was not aware of this on a conscious level, and there was no appealing to his logic. They always came full circle back to this.

Perhaps I can change all that. She must capture his attention, even against his own will.

"Times are different now, Grandmamma," Alita murmured, tapping on her teacup with her index finger.

"Hattie, bring me my hartshorn!" Marvella commanded at the top of her lungs while waving her handkerchief in front of her face.

Chapter Twenty-Six

The devil take it, Val cursed to himself. *Why* wouldn't she see him? Each time he had called on her at the Shepheard, she refused to see him, formulating a new excuse with each visit.

It was driving him to madness. Had he done something to offend her? He had been the perfect gentleman at their last encounter

Well, perfect for him. And she was still upset for some reason.

Maybe that *was* the reason.

Was it just more of her games? If that were the case, there might be some surprises in store for Miss Alita Stanton, because he wouldn't play at this for long. It was a bloody waste of time.

"Whiskey." Frustrated beyond reason, Val parked himself at Shepheard's bar for the third afternoon in a row so that he might watch the spiral staircase from his stool. He hadn't worked much in the past three days, and he didn't give a damn.

"I haven't seen her today, Raven," Zaheer stated, knowing the question before it was asked. "She doesn't even come down for meals."

"How do you bloody know?" he grumbled, taking a sip of his whiskey without moving his eyes from the staircase. "She might have slipped your notice. You can't be everywhere at once."

"I can. And I am." Zaheer laughed. "And nothing escapes my notice. The drink has made your brain foggy, Raven."

"Enlighten me."

"Because I have friends in the kitchen, of course. She takes all her meals in her rooms." Zaheer poured him a cup of coffee.

"What's that?" muttered Val.

"It is a hot beverage made from the coffee bean. It will assist you to keep your job."

"I don't give a rat's ass about my job," stated Val, his eyes unwavering. "And I thought you held no high opinion of my work."

"We could have worse than you." Zaheer shrugged. "Probably not, but at least I know what foolishness you're up to. And you don't actually do that much work—just enough to get by. All the better." The crimson-and-gold pill hat perched on the bartender's head looked out of place against his masculine features. His long, curled moustache was apparently an asset in Shepheard's eyes, no doubt lending a touch of the exotic to the ambiance. One expected him to pull out an antique lamp from underneath the bar counter at any moment.

Val wished he would. Maybe he would stop talking then and let him drink in peace.

"Thank you for your high opinion, Zaheer. When a man is down, it's good to know he can count on his friends." Val stared at him for a long moment before took a sip of the coffee in spite of himself. He swallowed it with difficulty. Staring at the cup he muttered, "It's so *bitter*. It's bloody awful."

"Try this, Raven." Zaheer added considerable cream and sugar to the cup and stirred. "Tea is not strong enough for you at the moment, and whiskey is too strong."

Damnation! Was it that Manchestor fellow? Had she decided that he was more to her liking, despite her assurances to the contrary? Did she secretly prefer that frippery dandy and his dribble?

Maybe she is playing both sides. He wouldn't put it past her, not for a second.

Suddenly a wash of anger embraced him. Maybe the ding-dong had proposed. He couldn't blame her for snatching up what he himself wasn't willing to give.

"Zaheer, have you seen her with the blond gentleman?" he asked quietly, almost afraid to hear the answer.

"No, Raven, I told you. She has kept to her rooms."

Val returned his eyes to study the curve of the staircase. He had counted the number of stairs, and he knew the designs in the carpet so well he dreamed of them. Quietly he added, "Have you seen the tall blond gentleman in here?"

Zaheer smiled, his expression suddenly arrogant and his black eyes mysterious. At that inopportune moment one of the parties of gentlemen scattered about the room at the round tables snapped his fingers at the bartender. Zaheer seemed pleased for the opportunity to abandon his station, no doubt anticipating raising his price for the information he knew the English earl desperately wanted.

"*Greedy bastard*," Val cursed under his breath, hoping Zaheer heard him.

Returning to the bar after dispensing the drinks, Zaheer pretended to wipe off the counter directly in front of his coffee cup, already shining like the star of Bethlehem, ignoring him with aplomb. Val kept his eyes glued to that self-satisfied, pompous face even as he placed a bill on the counter. "Well? Do you know anything, Zaheer?" he demanded.

"The fair-haired Englishman would not speak with me, Raven." Zaheer shrugged, chuckling while he placed the bill in his white pants pocket with the expression of one who had just gotten something for nothing. Or just robbed a dead man of his only belongings. Grave digging suited the bastard.

"Did he seem overly happy?"

"No."

"Sad?"

"No."

"She should at least have the decency to come out and tell me instead of keeping me at arm's length." Val punched the air, sending his coffee cup down the length of the bar. "It would only take a few minutes of her time, and she could be done with me. She is entitled to spend her time with whomsoever she chooses, but I deplore a woman who keeps an honest man dangling and who can't simply state the truth."

"You deplore her. This I can readily see." Zaheer's lips formed a knowing smile as he retrieved the coffee cup, now half full, and placed it in front of him, though not quite so close.

This has been the problem with Alita Stanton along, her false façade intended for some hidden purpose. She claimed to be able to see the future and to be able to see inside people's thoughts and feelings, even *who they could be*. It was obviously absurd. But the question was, did she believe it herself?

If yes, she was a quack. If no, she had an ulterior motive. *And what is it?*

He could not stomach duplicity and manipulation in a woman. With her refusal to see him, he wondered if everything she had done and said from the minute he met her was a lie.

Then why the hell did he long to see her as much as he had ever wanted anything in his life?

"Tell me one thing, Raven," Zaheer stated, leaning toward him.

"Give me back my money, then, if you are to ask the questions."

Zaheer returned the bill to the counter, his dark eyes scrutinizing him and his gaze intense. "Do you love her?"

"Of course." Val felt a smile tugging at the corners of his mouth. "I would die for her," he pronounced softly.

"Why don't you just marry her, Raven?" Zaheer sighed heavily.

"I want her to tell me once and for all what she is about. I want her to tell me *the truth*."

"Is there anything else you want, Raven?"

He wanted to take her in his arms and kiss her, just one last time. But he had to gain entrance in order to accomplish these two goals. And it didn't appear that that was going to happen.

"None of your damn business," Val muttered. "The relevant point is that I've either fallen in love with a madwoman or a damned liar, and I can't marry either."

"Raven, why do you love a madwoman who lies?" Zaheer threw his hands into the air even as he shook his head, his crimson-and-gold jacket a flash of color.

"No, Zaheer, it's one or the other." Val frowned. "Not both."

"Yes, yes, go on with your English logic." Impatiently he added, "Just tell me why you love her."

"It's the damnedest thing," Val muttered, adding more sugar to his coffee, which was already starting to look like sludge. "I must be crazier than a loon to entertain such an idea, but I think she might actually love *me*. If she lies because she has a design on me, she has a design on me because she wants me. She is the most delusional or manipulative woman I've ever met. And she seems to love me through and through. Her eyes sparkle when she looks at me. She treats my every word like nectar from the gods. Hell, I don't think any woman has ever listened to me before, much less believed in me. The only thing she seems to want...is *me*."

"Too bad you can't love her with your heart and leave your mind to destroy other people's lives," Zaheer stated matter-of-factly, tilting his head matter-of-factly toward him.

The Paradox: The Soldier and the Mystic 271

He threw his money on the counter. He'd been here too long. She wasn't coming down today.

Val cursed under his breath. This was what came of ignoring his instincts. And this was what came of attachments. They never worked for him.

He was almost to the door when he turned back. He returned to throw another large coin on the counter and said, "Let me know if you learn anything, Zaheer."

Once out of earshot, Zaheer muttered under his breath, "And the same to you, my friend."

Chapter Twenty-Seven

"It is imperative that I see you prior to my departure from Egypt, Lord Ravensdale." Alita's hands had shaken as she wrote the missive, the words making it all seem so horribly real. *"Might you arrange a time and a place?"*

Allowing Val to be in control of the environ would grant her sure entrance, she felt. As long as the situation was disreputable, it would appeal.

"I shall meet you in Lord Cromer's office at the British Consulate at five o'clock this evening. We can be assured of privacy." His immediate response with a quickly sprawled note delivered to the Shepheard by the embassy's page confirmed her suspicions. Noticeably absent was *"Don't go, dearest."*

She threw the note on the floor. He could not even be bothered to address her by name. It was simply an opportunistic attempt at one more sordid affair—before she left forever.

Alita mustered all of her strength to see Val Huntington one last time. Striving to put her mind on anything but her sadness, she selected among her wardrobe her dullest outfit, a simple pink linen walking suit with brown velvet trim. Studying her reflection in the mirror, she frowned at the haggard image staring back at her, the fitted suit almost loose.

She was not the innocent young woman she had been only a few months ago. Though her eyes shown against the pale pink, they also revealed her exhaustion from the combined effects of sleeplessness, self-admonitions, and grief. She turned away from the mirror, striving to focus on the concerns at hand.

Upon arriving at the embassy, she instructed the carriage driver to wait for her return. She found the door to Lord Cromer's anteroom ajar. Walking inside, she motioned to Hattie to sit on the bench. Feeling considerable trepidation, she knocked lightly on the door outside Lord Cromer's office with some inconvenience, as she was holding both her reticule and a large

The Paradox: The Soldier and the Mystic   *273*

package tightly in her arms. Her maid rose to assist her, but Alita motioned with her head for Hattie to return to her seat.

"Miss Alita," he murmured, his voice low. Despite her delicate knocking, Val quickly opened the door, a slow lazy smile coming to his lips as he seemed to drink her in. She would have thought from his expression that she had worn a low-cut evening dress instead of a serviceable ensemble. He motioned gallantly with his arm. "I am delighted to see you. Do come in."

"Lord Ravensdale." She nodded, avoiding his eyes. She must see this through.

"Ah, I see that you have done some last-minute shopping. May I assist you with your packages?"

"No, thank you, my lord," she replied curtly, placing her belongings on a nearby table and smoothing her suit with her hands as she kept her back to him.

"May I ask why you have been avoiding me, Miss Alita?" His tone was polite, but it had an edge to it.

"I have been quite absorbed in a project," she stated simply, looking about the room, unable to keep herself from a quick glance in his direction. Even in his casual attire, a linen suit and tie, he made her heart do flip-flops.

"A project? It must have kept you exceedingly busy," he replied smoothly, a frown forming on his lips.

"Indeed it did," Alita agreed with as much disinterest as she could muster. Her eyes moved to his feet to see that he wore leather sandals—and no socks!

"Do as the locals do, I always say." He smiled as he followed her eyes. "Much more comfortable." It was quite annoying how he always seemed to know what she was thinking.

And *she* was the mystic! One wondered.

"Do you? I don't recall ever having heard you say it."

"You look thin. Even more so than usual." He studied her for a moment, concern creeping into his eyes. "And tired. Are you well, Miss Alita?"

"I am indeed tired," she replied simply. *And I think I shall never be rested again.*

"Shall I send out for something to eat?" he asked with concern.

"No, thank you."

"Would you care for a sherry, Miss Alita?" he asked.

He frowned at her stiff formality as she shook her head.

She felt a warmth emanating near her hand. Turning, she observed a full tea service waiting on the table, steam arising from the slender silver spout. He was prepared for her visit.

"Tea?" he asked simply, watching her deliberately.

"Hmmm," she sighed. "A hot cup of tea would be nice. Lord Ravensdale, could I trouble you to take a cup to Hattie as well?"

"Hattie? You speak of my arch enemy?" A wicked smile formed on his lips.

She smiled in spite of herself. "Hattie has nothing to do with what stands between us, Lord Ravensdale."

"*Excellent.* I shall serve her if it pleases you, my dear." He motioned to the couch, and, as before, she chose the chair next to the couch. She leaned the package against her chair before seating herself.

Val frowned, even as he poured her tea and added a little cream. He must have remembered from their dinner that she didn't take sugar.

"A touch of arsenic," he murmured almost in a whisper as he prepared Hattie's tea. After delivering the hot beverage, he poured himself a sherry and leaned up against the table, his full scrutiny focused on her.

"Lord Ravensdale," Alita began, taking a sip of the warm liquid which revived her somewhat, "there shall be no repetition of the improprieties which you have exhibited toward me in the past."

"I shall endeavor not to displease you, Miss Alita." Val moved to take her free hand and kiss it gently before sitting on the adjoining couch. He studied her intently, his expression solemn, some of his initial gaiety subdued.

Uncomfortable with his proximity, she stood to walk about the room, holding her tea cup as she walked. There were bookcases everywhere, filled to overflowing with books on agriculture, medicine, sanitation systems, and city planning. It was obviously a working office. The only sign of disorder was the scattered maps, and it appeared that the room was being wired for electricity. There were even plants in the window sill, which looked to be crops rather than house plants.

The Paradox: The Soldier and the Mystic 275

The only personal effect on Sir Evelyn's massive desk was a photograph of his wife. As she moved to the window, she observed both the Nile and a view of the maze gardens.

I will miss everything about this place—this place she never wanted to come to. And wished she hadn't. Swallowing hard, she steeled herself for the task at hand and turned to face Val.

"I brought you a parting gift, Lord Ravensdale." She motioned to the package she had leaned against her chair, even as she reseated herself. "The project we spoke of."

"Why, Miss Stanton, I...thank you." As she held the wrapped gift toward him, Val appeared immediately surprised, not an expression she had often seen him convey.

"A moment, please, Lord Ravensdale," she stated with great emphasis and yet almost in a whisper. As he reached for the package, she held up her hand. "There will come a time when you will remember this meeting with me today with great clarity and impact."

"I sincerely hope so, Miss Alita," Val said, his voice controlled. He fixated his eyes on her, appearing unable to look elsewhere.

"And when you do," Alita continued, "I want you to remember also what I have told you about who you are and what you are meant to do. Promise me," she said, *"promise me* that you will reconsider all that I have told you when that day comes."

Val stretched his long legs out before him, clearly excessively weary of the topic. "I am dismayed to disappoint you, Miss Alita, but I cannot take your remarks about my great destiny seriously, nor can I make you any promises to do so."

"Because you don't believe that I can see into the future, correct?" asked Alita.

Val raised his eyebrows. "Obviously."

"I have brought proof beyond any reasonable doubt that I can," stated Alita. She handed him the package.

* * * *

Val glanced at her, apprehensive. This was not going the way he had hoped. He was concerned for her. She was far from the vision of health and vivacity he had first encountered. And her manner toward him was decidedly reserved.

Slowly Val opened the package. Inside was a beautiful painting, executed entirely in the ancient Egyptian style. "This is exquisite, Miss Alita," Val emphasized with admiration. "Who painted it?"

"I did," stated Alita.

Startled, he returned his gaze to her abruptly, though it took some effort to pull his eyes away from the painting.

Despite his scrutiny, which he knew to be severe, Alita replied evenly, "I am thought to have an exceptional gift in both water colors and oils, but I felt the water colors were able to lend the feel of antiquities more authentically to the work."

Val felt shockingly moved and sought to control his feeling. Though his estimation of her abilities to see into the future had not changed, he was considerably impressed with her talent and touched that she had created this beautiful painting for him. He didn't recall the last time anyone had exerted this much effort on his part. "This must have taken weeks," he surmised.

"Only one," she replied reservedly.

"Remarkable," he murmured. "You had to have worked night and day."

She said nothing, but he glanced up to study her. Though beautiful as always, there was weariness in her facial expression clearly born of fatigue.

So that's what she has been doing. She was creating a gift for me. He would have loved the painting even had she been in possession of one-tenth of her obvious talent.

He examined the painting more closely. It was unlike any Egyptian painting he had ever seen before, though it was rendered in the exact style of the Fifth and Sixth Dynasties, the Old Kingdom, 2575-2135 B.C. The accuracy to the rendition was remarkable.

As he studied the painting thoroughly, another arresting feature came into play. He had never before seen this particular scene. Had she made it up? And why? It was not a scene likely to capture a young lady's imagination, and not one he would conceive of anyone, lady or gentleman, envisioning.

This is astonishing. It was a scene of hundreds of starving workers dragging the pyramid capstone. The human anatomy was consistently and realistically proportional, but the bodies were always drawn frontally while

The Paradox: The Soldier and the Mystic 277

the heads were always in profile. The figures seemed incredibly real despite the impossibility of the poses.

Val stared at Alita, stricken. "Miss Alita, your rendition is amazingly accurate. The artistic style is consistent with the period in question."

Alita's countenance displayed the Mona Lisa smile, but she simply replied, "Thank you, Lord Ravensdale."

Val was surprised at her easy acceptance of her noteworthy creation but even more perplexed at this unusual and peculiar scene she had created, apparently from imagination, as he had never before seen the original. Even allowing for her unquestionable ability, how had she been so well versed in the artistic style of the period, the equivalent of a master painter, only several weeks after having arrived in Egypt?

For the moment, his curiosity over the content overrode his marvel over her grasp of the artistic style of the time period. "I must know, Miss Alita, whatever possessed you to paint this particular scene? I have never seen its likeness."

"You will," stated Alita.

"Excuse me?" demanded Val.

"Just as I said," repeated Alita. "You will."

Val's expression grew stern. "Miss Stanton, I do not know what your game is today, but I demand that you explain yourself."

Alita sighed with exasperation. "Of course, your lordship. Have I ever held anything back from you?"

Val wished desperately to respond to that remark but was too bewildered and entranced by the painting to change the direction of the conversation.

Suddenly, his eyes grew wide as they fell on the lower left-hand corner of the painting. *Hieroglyphics.* He almost dropped the work before he tightened his hold.

Reading the words revealed that the painting paid homage to the workers themselves—the lowest caste. Why, and in what context, it was not clear.

So, she had copied the picture. But this conclusion presented him with more questions than answers. Where was the original? He had never seen it, and he was familiar with all known Egyptian art. His eyes shot to Alita's, utilizing every ounce of self-control in his possession.

"What do the words say, Miss Stanton?"

"I do not know." She shook her head.

"You do not know." Harshly he demanded, "How did you recreate the hieroglyphics, Miss Stanton?" He felt his teeth grinding as he sought to maintain the countenance of a gentleman.

"They are merely shapes to me, Lord Ravensdale."

"Obviously they were copied. Painstakingly, I might add. There are no errors, but where did you copy them? I have never before seen this exact text."

Alita's eyes shot back at him. "Since you know everything about it, my lord, why do you ask me?"

"I will not be toyed with in this fashion." Val growled through barred teeth. None of this made sense. The answer to one question provided a greater mystery with an even-more perplexing question. Was he destined to continually be in a state of disbelief in this woman's presence? As if none of the proven laws of science and logic applied to anything within her realm of existence?

She held her chin high. "I don't exactly know the meaning, but I did comprehend the shapes. It is all form for me. I am glad to know that it is accurate." Alita pointed to the painting, flippantly ignoring his justifiable outburst. "I want you to consider all that I have said when you see this picture again. You will know in that moment that what I have spoken comes from insight and true knowledge. If you engage your mental facilities in the slightest, you will learn to trust my words."

"Miss Stanton," stated Val, growing angry. "I demand to know where you have seen this representation. I find it impossible to believe that you imagined it. The very subject matter of starving Egyptians and the method with which they are dragging the capstone, believable yet ingenious in its approach, all combined with the extreme accuracy to the period's artistic style...This is a combination you would not be capable of contriving."

"I am capable of very little according to you. It is consistent with your treatment of me that you discount this talent as well."

Val leaned toward her, demanding an answer. "Miss Alita, I have not seen this depiction, so how is it that you have seen it?"

The Paradox: The Soldier and the Mystic 279

Alita's eyes grew wide, her gaze unwavering. She held his attention captive with great innocence, through lush eyelashes. "That is the relevant question, is it not, Lord Ravensdale?"

"And what is the answer?" he demanded, his eyes glued to her.

"As I said, you will see it. There will be a fall. I don't know the exact mechanism."

"A *fall*?" repeated Val, making no attempt to hide his impatience.

"Yes," answered Alita. "Someone will fall. I don't know how this will instigate the discovery of this scene, but it will."

"Discovery?" questioned Val. "Stop toying with me, Miss Alita. I am speaking of this painting." Why, *why* must she always be playing games? Why couldn't they, *for once*, have a genuine conversation? What was this illness of the mind that continually required her to lie? It pained him to see her, to love her, and to continually be reminded that they could not be together.

"As am I," she replied calmly.

"I see," articulated Val slowly, seething. But he didn't see. He didn't understand any of this. "And where will this 'fall' occur?"

"South of the Great Sphinx," answered Alita. She smiled sweetly at him. "Is that specific enough for you? Or perhaps a lucky guess on my part? Shall I give you the exact number of paces? I am sorry, my lord, but I do not know."

Val was fuming now. "Miss Stanton, I find your antics unamusing to the extreme."

"I was not sent to amuse you, Lord Ravensdale," Alita replied evenly, her anger matching his.

He ground his teeth, even as he closed his eyes momentarily. He wished he had kept them closed.

She smiled with a certain unbecoming arrogance. "I have heard you speak of women's equality, and yet it does not occur to you to take me seriously." She sighed. "However, as long as I have come this far, I might as well tell you the whole."

"By all means, tell me everything," growled Val. This interview was not going in the direction he had hoped, but he would not let her out of this room until he knew the entirety of this outrageous ploy.

280   *Suzette Hollingsworth*

"Since I know you to be a quantitative person, I will let you know that some forty-eight hours later—after the fall, that is—there will be a pair of eyes."

"A pair of eyes," Val repeated, controlling his voice with effort. "Do tell."

Alita nodded. Suddenly she sighed, exasperated. "I am sorry. I can tell you no more than that on that score."

"Quite enough. Indeed more than enough. But your story fascinates me, Miss Alita, and I require to hear the whole," retorted Val, his gaze intense as he studied her.

"Very well," acquiesced Alita in deliberate tones. "I bow to your wishes *as always,*" she emphasized, appearing more than a bit impatient. What in Hades did she have to be impatient about? She was the one who was always concocting some fantastic scheme to set his world on end when they had merely to be happy and enjoy each other's company. But, no, that would be too straightforward for her.

Alita frowned before continuing. "The last piece ties in with your life. There will be a message in it for you, a personal message. A message which relates to your storytelling and its importance."

"Excuse me?" asked Val. "I don't see how that concept fits in with this picture." He pointed to her painting.

"You will," she repeated. He was beginning to get irritated with that phrase. "Remember what I have said. I have said it now, in advance, at a time when I could not possibly know it."

Val tapped on the armrest of the couch. It appeared that he had to humor her in order to obtain any information. He was damned tired of this woman always having the upper hand with him. He had controlled whole battalions of men, but where Miss Alita Stanton was concerned, there was nothing to be done but to allow her to roll the dice.

Val knew well that, in some instances, the only way to win was to bow to another's will and to pretend defeat. "So, Miss Alita, we have this painting, a fall, forty-eight hours, a pair of eyes, and a message which pertains to my storytelling. Is that it?"

"Yes," answered Alita. "Is that not enough?" she asked, flabbergasted. "It seems to me to be quite enough for even the stupidest and most unaware

The Paradox: The Soldier and the Mystic

of persons, and you are neither. Well, at least you are not stupid. Not entirely."

"Miss Alita," Val said slowly through clenched teeth, feeling extreme agitation, "I have heard a great deal of nonsense from you in the short time I have known you, but this surpasses even my vast expectations. You never cease to amaze me."

"Thank you," Alita said as she rose from her chair. Her expression turned immediately sad, and her face was pale. Her bright-green eyes glistened against opaque ivory skin. "Good-bye, Val," she said longingly.

He rose with her. He wanted to strangle her, and yet his heart fell in his chest as he comprehended that she was leaving. Suddenly the anger he had felt evaporated.

"And shall we kiss before you go?" he asked, putting his strong arms around her waist.

Her lips trembled. She seemed to struggle with herself.

Before she could answer, he pressed her close to his chest. He looked into her eyes. Slowly, his lips met hers, each second anticipation. He savored each moment. Gently, he parted her lips and moved his lips along hers. Time was stopped for him. He alternated with soft kisses and deep kisses. "Alita, dearest," he whispered.

Suddenly, he pressed her close against his chest, placed his hand at the back of her head, and kissed her fiercely, frantically.

He picked her up and moved her to the couch in one sweep, placing her in his lap. Gingerly, slowly, he planted soft kisses on her shoulders, her neck, and across her bodice.

He watched intently as her breathing increased. She placed both hands on his head and brought his lips to hers.

"Oh, Val," she exclaimed.

He ran his hand along her cheek as if to memorize the contours of her face.

"Alita," he managed, his breathing uneven.

"Oh how have I let this happen again?" she whispered, struggling to sit up. "It happened so quickly."

"*Stay.*" His voice sounded heavy even to himself. He ran his hands down her slim arms. "Don't tell me that you don't see us together at this moment. I know I do."

"I want more than anything in the world for us to be together. If I could have willed it, I would have done so." Her eyes fell. "We will never be together. You don't wish it."

"Funny," he replied. "I had a different impression of my wishes."

"You have no intention of marrying me, Val," her voice was calm and sure. "And what's more, you *never will.*"

She stood up and turned to leave, and his heart fell.

Before she could reach the door, he took her arm and pulled her against him. "I have nothing to commend myself to you. I cannot believe that this is more than a passing attraction on your part."

"Unhand me, Lord Ravensdale." She would not face him, which he found singularly annoying. "And, in point of fact, you will recover from my absence much more easily than I shall recover from yours."

"Tell me, Alita, just to satisfy my curiosity." Slowly he released her, wanting to keep her in his arms forever. "Would you be happy being leg-shackled to a man whose family wants nothing to do with him? A scholar with no taste for the gaieties of social life?"

"*Happy?*" she asked. She looked up at him, and her dismay turned to a genuine expression of surety, her green eyes clear and deep, as if she had realized her own heart for the first time. "I would be *deliriously* happy."

She turned and walked out of Val's life. Val had the sinking feeling that she would never return to Egypt again.

Chapter Twenty-Eight

"Grandmamma, it's time to return to England," Alita pronounced faintly, lowering her embroidery momentarily. Why she had picked it up, she did not know. In fifteen minutes she had executed one stitch.

One very crooked stitch.

"But your young man? What of him? Are you keeping something from me, Alita dear?" Marvella smiled smugly to herself.

Alita looked up, and her eyes rested on a painting of a snake charmer and his dancing serpent, flanked by candle sconces, strangely perfect in this ornate room decorated in gold, blue, and crimson. In the evening the lights would flicker on the wall, making it appear as if the snake were truly moving inside the picture.

She wondered if the twisting reptile enjoyed executing his graceful, artistic movement or if he hated his captivity but felt compelled to perform. She glanced through the archway to the window where the Nile, free and powerful, flowed through Egypt on its journey to the Mediterranean Sea.

I wish I had never come. She had seen a glimpse of what her life could be, might have been.

And she wished she never had.

Val didn't see it. He was living in that place of being invisible and unrealized. *And that's how everyone wanted it*. Her eyes rested on the blue, lavender, and rose threads moving across the linen fabric like a meandering brook going nowhere.

It would have been better for her to have lived in ignorance. She was happier in that state.

It was so different where Val was concerned. Sighing, she picked up her needle again. She wished she could create some semblance of order out of this cross-stitch. Then there would be something in her life that was in place.

"Ouch!" She pressed her pricked finger to her lips.

Suddenly something shifted. The room seemed to move, and she braced herself in her satin wingback chair. Something changed in the patterns of the universe. She didn't know where or how, but something was altered. Just when she thought despair would overtake her, peace washed over her instead.

"*Heavens to Betsy*, child!" Marvella huffed, exasperated. "Why don't you wear your thimble! It is clear that you cannot learn to keep the sharp part of the needle away from your hand and are determined to mutilate yourself!"

Val will fulfill his destiny. She felt it clearly, strongly, as surely as she knew that she loved him. *Something* had happened or *would happen*, a new thought, a small action, which would lead to other actions, a word of kindness shown by another, a release in Val's soul or a healing, and Alita knew beyond a shadow of a doubt that Val *would* find himself. It would take time, and he might plod inefficiently and laboriously through it, but Val Huntington *would* discover who he was.

"My handkerchief! Oh, *where* is my handkerchief!" she sobbed. She burst into tears of happiness, and the relief made her chest heave.

"HATTIE! Bring the Hartshorne!" Marvella screamed as she moved to her chair and shook her. "A washcloth! NOW, girl!"

With Hattie's near-immediate arrival, having been trained by the duchess, Marvella patted Alita's face with a wet washcloth even as she continued to sob convulsively.

Would she and Val be together? As joy overwhelmed her, Alita asked her subconscious this question she had asked a thousand times. The answer was clear and resounding.

No.

This only managed to increase her sobbing. Her heart was breaking, and yet she was deliriously happy at the same time.

"Get the sherry! What are you waiting for?" Marvella screamed to Hattie even as she waved the Hartshorne under Alita's nose.

"No, Grandmamma! Please!" she gasped, the fumes agitating her further.

This trip to Egypt had depleted her of everything she had. But it had not been in vain. She had accomplished precisely that which she came to do.

"Breathe, Alita! Breathe at ONCE, or I'll shake you until you do!"

*The Paradox: The Soldier and the Mystic*285

She had made a difference. A significant difference. Possibly for the first time in her life. She had utilized her gift, and something good had come from it. And not just in one person's life, but in all the lives Val would save.

She, an imperfect person so lacking in experience and knowledge, had succeeded!

Her personal life might be a shambles, but something good had come from her existence.

What more might she do?

"Thank you! Thank you!" she whispered, closing her eyes and saying a prayer of thanks to the universe, to God, the angels, and every event that had anything to do with this shift. Alita clutched her heart in relief.

"You're welcome, child! Now drink this sherry immediately!"

Cough. "Really, Grandmamma"—*cough*—"I only just want some hot tea."

"Hattie! Get the hot tea! Hurry, girl!" Hattie spun around, almost moving in circles, switching course with each new command.

The tea arrived shortly, which no doubt would have been forcibly poured down her throat as well except that Alita stopped crying and began to talk. She thought she had best before her grandmother poisoned and strangled her in earnest.

"There, there, dear." Marvella sat next to her granddaughter and patted her hand as she spoke in quiet, consoling tones. "It will all be well. Many people suffer at least one heartache before they find their true love. *I didn't,* but many people do."

"I have found my true love, Grandmamma," she replied quietly. "But he has not found his."

"Pish tosh! He must be an idiot, or he would have chosen you, my dear. And an idiot cannot be your true love!"

"I assure you that Lord Ravensdale is not lacking in intelligence, Grandmamma!" She almost giggled in spite of herself.

"He can be no concern of mine if he is not marrying you, my sweet. All I say—because I have that caring, sensitive temperament which is my curse—is that I pity the poor, stupid children he shall inevitably produce. You, on the other hand, shall have everything you want and dream of. I promise you," she pronounced with determination. *"So help me God."*

Alita did not reply, but a new calm descended upon her as she pursed her lips. She was loved. That she knew. Her grandmother would go to the ends of the earth for her. She nodded, striving to avoid bursting into tears again.

"Now, dear." Marvella appeared to interpret Alita's silence as grief. "I know it seems like he is the only man for you. But it is simply not true."

"No, Grandmamma," Alita murmured, "not the only man for me but undoubtedly the *best* man for me. He completes me."

"And what of Lord Manchestor? He could make Adonis himself jealous."

"I like Lord Manchestor very much," agreed Alita hesitantly, shaking her head. "And...I know everything that William will say before he opens his mouth."

"And how is this a bad thing?" Marvella demanded, raising her eyebrows. "It is ideal! Speaking as one with experience in these matters, I can tell you that to know one's husband inside and out is to be able to wield him, to predict him and to acquire that which one desires. I defy anyone to produce a more perfect man than Lord Manchestor!"

I don't want a perfect man. I want the Earl of Ravensdale.

"You shall improve upon the journey home, my dear." Marvella patted her hand. "A few days closer to God's beloved England, and all will be well."

The duchess's expression carried more conviction than Alita felt.

Chapter Twenty-Nine

As the *RMS Imperial* pulled out of the bay at Alexandria, Alita felt her eyes swimming, wondering if she should jump overboard. Along with a respectable sampling of the other one hundred and sixty-six first-class passengers, she and William were seated in the first-class dining saloon, their eyes glued to a large porthole, which afforded them a beautiful view of the magical city while sparing them the smoke exhaust generated by the twelve boilers. As the *Imperial* strove to separate herself from exotic lands and return to civilization, it was as if she protested violently, spitting streams of black smoke fifty feet into the air from each of two huge cylinders.

Once the ship was underway, standing on the deck would be idyllic, the four masts of sails sharing more of the burden of travel, but for now the saloon on this most elegant of ships held the most romantic ambiance even as champagne was poured, smiles reflecting a vacation never to be forgotten. Crystal glasses toasted, ignorant of two hearts meant to be together distancing themselves from each other.

"Miss Alita, I hope that you can forgive my awkwardness." William took Alita's hand and kissed it gently. He was dressed impeccably in a black morning suit with vest, crisp white shirt, maroon-and-white silk tie, and gold-and-ruby tie clip, seated across from her at their private table positioned next to a porthole. "I have never done this before. Would you do me the honor of becoming my wife?" he asked, his expression full of hope and promise.

"Oh, William," she whispered. Her lips trembled, and she felt her eyes tearing up.

"Dearest, whatever is wrong?" He took her hand and kissed it again.

"I cannot marry you, William. *And I love you so.*" Alita felt a sadness wash over her.

"I–I don't understand, my love." He moved back in his seat, his confidence obviously waning.

"*I love you so*, William. With all my heart. But not as a wife should love you."

"Miss Alita…" His expression was one of having been taken to the heights of heaven and the depths of despair in an instant. "Whatever can you mean?"

"William, to be your wife is what dreams are made of. And you are so kind, so valiant, able to provide everything a woman could want."

"Forgive me, Miss Alita." He stared at her in wonderment. She kept waiting for his expression to turn hard, but it didn't. "I don't understand the problem."

Alita shook her head in dismay. She was not like Val, who, when everything he wanted came knocking at his door, turned it down. He had only known a life of hardship, and happiness was so unfamiliar that it could not be trusted.

But this wasn't her situation, she knew, one who is unable to receive happiness.

Oh, I hope with all my heart it isn't. She was never going to marry Val, she was sure of it. She didn't see him in her future, and *she had the sight!* It was inconceivable that someone would come along who was more exemplary than William Manchestor. He was the best she could hope for— and a very good "best" he was.

Panic rising up inside her, she felt as if she were suffocating.

And yet she just could not form the words to agree. Her heart rebelled in every way. *It just wasn't right.* It wasn't right for her, and it wasn't right for William. And she always took the right course, even when her logic rebelled.

Especially when her logic rebelled.

No longer could she act out her fairy-tale life anymore, Alita knew. It didn't feel authentic for her any longer.

"William, I don't know how to explain. I'm…*different*. I see things."

"You see things? I don't take your meaning, Miss Alita," he inquired, his expression patient.

The Paradox: The Soldier and the Mystic   289

"I know what people are feeling. And recently I've developed the ability to know of events before they happen." Alita replied quietly. "I am changing in ways I do not understand and for reasons I cannot conceive."

"Miss Alita, I can't fathom what you are speaking of"—William gazed upon her with affection, his expression resolute—"but I'm sure it doesn't affect us."

"How can who I am not affect *us*?"

"Everyone has their eccentricities." William's expression was resolute. "As long as you present your most charming side in public, which assuredly you will, your *purported* odd propensities should not be a problem. We won't speak of it."

"We won't speak of *what*, William?" Alexandria was getting smaller and smaller in the window. She folded her hands in her lap even as she could still hear the glasses tinkling.

"Miss Alita, it truly doesn't matter to me what you *see*." His face turned momentarily hard, but his eyes caressed her tenderly. "I know in my heart that in twenty years you won't be having affairs outside marriage, as many of my friends' mothers do, some of whom have approached *me* for God's sake. Forgive me for speaking of it, but I feel it is necessary to make my point." His expression revealed his disgust.

"No." She shook her head, speaking softly. "I would *not*."

"Don't you see, Miss Alita? I want to marry a woman of character, someone *true*." He grasped her hand, the action conveying to Alita his desperation despite his natural gentleness. He rarely did more than merely brush her hand. As she looked into his eyes, she saw genuine longing there. "A woman who has a kind heart and who will be a loving wife and mother. You are all this and so much more, my darling. The fact that you are the most beautiful woman of my acquaintance is simply icing on the cake."

"We would do nicely together, William." She nodded in agreement, almost tempted beyond endurance. Maybe he was the right match for her...

"And to all that, your charm and goodness would be a great asset to my career. You are a perfect politician's wife. And perfect *for me*." His eyes searching hers, he added, "Tell me what you require from me. Do you desire that I should support women's suffrage? To not support women's suffrage? I can accomplish either and manage public opinion. We can manage it together. Or is it something else?" He loosened his hold but took her hands, love in his eyes.

She heard the blaring of the ship's horn, startling her. She tipped her large white velvet hat trimmed in forest-green feathers, hiding her eyes for only an instant before returning her eyes to his.

"William, I do love you. Deeply. But not as my one marriage partner through life. We're not on the same journey."

"Journey." William stared at her. "But, dearest, what journey is that?"

"Before I came to Egypt, I followed a script. It wasn't my script, but it seduced me." Alita struggled to explain what she doubted he could understand, but she owed it to him to try.

"Seduced you?" He appeared alarmed.

"I lived inside the painting with no hope of new colors or scenes being added." She sighed. "I do not belong there anymore. Not now."

"*Lived inside the painting?*" he repeated. Agitation replaced longing on William's face, an expression she had rarely seen him exhibit. "Sounds like a line from Byron's poetry. It's that damned Ravensdale fellow, isn't it? He filled your head with all kinds of melancholy, tragic nonsense. *You wanted to live inside a painting, and now you don't?*"

"It is an analogy, William. Surely you take my point."

In an instant he regained his composure, his expression pleading. "Miss Alita, I implore you to leave behind lachrymose thoughts and embrace the real world of happiness which is available to you. For my sake and yours. I'll move heaven and earth to make you happy, my love. Alita, I *love* you," he emphasized. "How can anything be more important than that?"

"Nothing, William. Nothing is more important than that."

"Then *why...?*"

"William, you have fallen in love with a type of woman. You haven't fallen in love with *me*." How she wished it were not so.

"Miss Alita, I will accept your refusal as a gentleman, no matter how much it pains me, but I will not allow these untrue words to pass. You are my angel, and I do love you. You are the only thing I have ever truly wanted in my life." His blond hair framed his perfect features, and his expression was distant.

"Please believe me, William." In that moment she would have given anything to help this dear man understand. "I may appear to be the right

The Paradox: The Soldier and the Mystic 291

match for you, but, in essence, I am not." She reached out and squeezed his hand. "Do you recall Charlise Sinclair?"

"Of course," he replied softly. "She introduced us, in effect."

"Charlise has all these qualities you desire in addition to an unequaled purity." She sighed. Charlise was never conflicted. She knew precisely what she was about.

"Now is not the time to console me with matchmaking, Miss Alita," he implored with an uncharacteristic gruffness.

"Oh, I am sorry. It was very unfeeling of me." She never seemed to say the right thing. The ship was now well underway, and she stood, needing to move in order to dispel some of her despair. Inadvertently she smoothed her moss-green velvet traveling jacket from which emerged a flow of white ruffles from her neckline to her waist. He stood without speaking, and she picked up her velvet muff and straightened her hat even as he offered her his arm. On some level, they understood each other so well, even without words.

"Shall we take a stroll about the ship, William?" She placed her hand in his, and they began to walk the ship's deck in silence, the view of Egypt becoming smaller and smaller, both of them devastated with lost love and a lost life. They saw nothing else in their futures as yet, and it pained them to be in each other's presence.

At the same time, their shared love for each other provided some comfort, and it was difficult to be anywhere but together.

Chapter Thirty

"Whiskey," Val muttered, throwing his money on the counter and motioning to the bartender. The hour was late, and the swank bar was almost empty. His preferred drink was being poured even before the words left his mouth.

"You look miserable, Raven." Zaheer eyed him with obvious concern.

"You are nothing if not a reader of people, Zaheer. How you picked up on that astounds me." Val was worse than miserable. A month ago he had rarely been a customer of the bar at Shepheard's except when he was with notables of state, and now he found himself in here frequently.

And he knew why. The surroundings reminded him of her. The familiarity both comforted him and tortured him.

Val looked about him. Possibly it was time for another plan other than torture. He had sat in this bar for something approaching a week, and he didn't feel a damn sight better.

"What are you doing here again? Don't you have somewhere to be? Do they pay you at your job to drink all day?"

"It's nice to see you, too, Zaheer," Val muttered, replying in his native tongue.

"I like you, Raven," Zaheer stated. "You know both Arabic and Coptic. I have never met an Englishman with a greater sympathy for the Egyptian people."

"Why don't you have a drink with me, then, if you like me so well?" Val replied absently.

"I don't drink," answered Zaheer, shrugging. "You are familiar with my religion, Raven."

"I would have to find another religion."

"Besides, the tongue becomes too loose when one drinks. I prefer to listen than to talk." The short, wide man with the large grin made a welcoming gesture. "It is much safer."

The Paradox: The Soldier and the Mystic 293

"Safe?" Val quizzed. "Ah, that explains it. I don't require safety. Quite the contrary. I wish to put a period to a worthless existence."

"You have studied the Holy Quran, Raven." Zaheer shook his head. "Surely you now know of your importance in the world."

"A far lovelier person than yourself tried in vain to convince me of my importance. I beg you to let that subject lie," Val muttered under his breath, recalling a sweeter delivery of the same words.

"Your English friends have left for England." Zaheer stated the obvious, breaking into Val's silent reverie.

Val stared into his glass and said nothing.

"Why do you stay if you miss them so much?" Zaheer asked.

"Miss them?" Val laughed. "You must be mad, Zaheer. Let me explain the appeal of your country to me, Zaheer. Muslims believe in one God, in the Day of Judgment, in life after death, and in angels. Same sex relationships and killing one's unborn child is forbidden. Saved souls will experience the bliss of heaven and unsaved souls the torture of hell. Last but not least, you subjugate your women under the pretense of cherishing them." Val shrugged with indifference. "Just like being home."

"You state these truths as if they mean nothing, Raven." Zaheer frowned.

"They don't mean a damn thing," Val muttered. Heaven was a place he had never known, and he was on familiar terms with hell. He had never been so lonely in his life. He was, in general, a solitary person, but his solitude had been a peaceful haven and afforded him pleasure up until now. He had found refuge in his studies and in his intellect, and even that didn't help him anymore. It was as if the sun had departed from his existence.

Val pictured Alita before him, her hair the color of wheat and her crystalline green eyes, which took on hues of gold in the light and gazed upon one with a calm stillness. Val's lips formed a smile.

And she had looked at him as if he were a prince. No person had ever gazed upon him with such admiration. Most people wouldn't give two quid for his existence.

Steady, sir. Val's heart tugged at him for an instant. It had been a pleasant fantasy, nothing more.

And yet, when she had looked at him like that…

Damn! She was the most irresistible woman he had ever met, and he had let her go. He was a bloody fool for wanting her and a bloody fool for letting her go as well. It was that simple.

He was simply a bloody fool.

"The Englishwoman was very beautiful," Zaheer commented.

"Very." Val agreed, taking another swig of whiskey. "And almost as talkative as you are, my friend. An annoying habit."

"Tell me one thing, Raven," Zaheer remarked.

"What?" Val growled.

"Why did you let her go if it torments you to be without her? Enlighten me on this," Zaheer inquired.

"Torment?" Val cursed under his breath. "She torments me whether I am with her or without her, so letting her go is irrelevant. The woman is insane, so why should I miss her? She is as crazy as a loon. I am a sensible, intelligent man, and yet I miss this woman who never put two logical words together in the time I knew her."

"Intelligent?" Zaheer laughed loudly as he began wiping the bar with his rag. "You are about as intelligent as this dirty rag I am wiping the bar with, Raven."

"Exactly my point, Zaheer." Val glared at him for but an instant. "She told me that I was destined to help bring the world together. That I had *a great purpose.* There is your proof that she was insane. And I could not marry anyone who was insane. There might be children."

Children. Lord, he missed her. Even though he had never taken a single thing seriously that she had said, he loved the fact that she said it. Most of all, he missed how badly she had wanted him.

He motioned for the next glass of whiskey but only toyed with it.

"Do you have children, Zaheer?"

"Of course. Do I not seem happy? They make everything else seem like a waste of time."

"It wouldn't have lasted." Val swirled the whiskey in his glass. "Crazy or not, she would have left me just inside six months, and then where would I be? On the outside again." There was something larger than life about her, though he couldn't quite put his finger on what it was. She was small and delicate and...*filled his whole world.*

The Paradox: The Soldier and the Mystic 295

She acted as if she were trying to save his life. Val swore under his breath. He saw through her act, but it had been pure bliss to play along.

"The blond Englishman did not find her annoying. He treated her well." Zaheer interjected into Val's thoughts. "You should try being polite, Raven. It might work for you."

"So the blond gentleman spoke of her, did he?" Suddenly Val felt as if his eyes could bore a hole through the wood, even his forced amusement fading.

"The Englishman drank a bit too much one evening, and his tongue became loose," he replied, nodding, his white teeth gleaming.

"What did you overhear, Zaheer?" he demanded, placing some coins on the countertop without hesitation.

Zaheer shook his head, motioning to Val to keep his money. "For you, my information has no cost. Except possibly to your heart."

"All right then," Val replied evenly, his fingers forming a fist. "How about you tell me what you heard, and I won't bash your head in?"

"Yes, the other Englishman loved her, too." Zaheer frowned, stepping back. "But he was not afraid to follow his heart. Unlike you, he was not a coward."

Val slammed his fist on the counter. "Would you mind to get to the point, Zaheer?"

"Her dreams did not worry him." He shrugged. "She had a dream of a black panther, and the people of England thought she was crazy. As do you?"

"Yes, yes, I know all about the dream. She told me that preposterous story herself, I—" Val stopped in midsentence. In a split second, Val jumped up, his stool falling backward, taking Zaheer by the throat, across the counter. Val placed his face very near to Zaheer's. "Do you mean to tell me that Manchestor knew of that dream *before* they left England?" he demanded, his voice deadly.

One of the footmen looked into the bar, and Zaheer waved him away. "It is not she who is mad, but you, Raven."

Val muttered between barred teeth, "Simply tell me the whole." There were other people in the bar at that time, who quickly departed.

"Have I ever withheld anything from you, Raven?" In low tones he emphasized. Val released him, but he did not sit down.

"Yes, all the time."

"She had a dream about a black panther, she went to a party, the other Englishman was one of the party, he heard it there. But he was not overly concerned with the story. I believe even then that he loved her." Zaheer took a step back and added, "Personally, I hope he wins her. You don't deserve her."

Val felt his head spinning. She had not made up the story when she arrived in Egypt and saw him. There had been a dream, and it had occurred *in England*. Since it was to her great disadvantage to recount the dream, it was thus very likely that she believed the dream to be true. Could it also be that she truly believed he was the black panther of her dream?

Zaheer afforded him the general greeting reserved for Islamic men of the region, touching his fingers to his lips and kissing them, touching his heart, and then opening his fingers toward Val, murmuring in Arabic, "Peace be with you, friend. May Allah preserve your soul, Raven." Then he turned to another customer.

Val's thoughts were gaining momentum. He didn't know why it afforded him pleasure to finally learn that she wasn't lying—that she must therefore be crazy—but it did. She had wanted to be happy, and she had thought that being with him was happiness itself.

That very fact had been reason enough to marry her if he had been possessed of even an iota of sense. Two crazy people together might have been happy.

Alita Stanton was the most amazing mix of seductress and saint that he had ever met, and he had let her go.

Why, in God's name, he was starting to wonder.

Chapter Thirty-One

"There has been a discovery," Mr. Mariette, Curator of the Museum of Cairo, explained, his voice elevated. "A very important discovery," he emphasized. His strong Egyptian features clean shaven of facial hair further revealed his excitement.

Val was working in his private office the following week when he received a personal visit from Mr. Mariette accompanied by Sir Evelyn. It was highly unusual to receive the attention of two such notables in his Spartan quarters.

"Would you care to be seated, Sir Evelyn? Mr. Mariette?" He stood and offered the only two chairs in the room, one of them his desk chair. He didn't offer sherry, as he knew that Mr. Mariette did not drink.

Lord Cromer took a seat on the room's one comfortable chair, situated centrally on a crimson-and-navy Persian rug. Mr. Mariette abandoned his customary subdued, intellectual manner and continued pacing the room with uncontrolled energy, each of his words emphasized with the creaking of the ebony wood floors.

"Sir Evelyn has graciously agreed that I might have use of your hieroglyphic interpretive services, Lord Ravensdale," Mr. Mariette continued, clearing his throat. He straightened the dark silk tie of his three-piece suit, his expression suddenly humbled and pleading. "If you can spare the time, of course."

"Believe me, it will be worth your while, Ravensdale," Lord Cromer added, crossing his legs, a suppressed smile on his lips as if he knew something of great importance.

"What have you found, Mr. Mariette?" Val asked, unable to wait politely for the information any longer, beginning to wonder if it would ever be forthcoming.

"It appears to be a burial ground," stated Mr. Mariette, barely able to contain his excitement. Val knew him to be very serious about his work and

Egyptian heritage, but he had never before seen this level of emotion from the scholar. "It is an extensive discovery."

"Fascinating. And where is it?" asked Val.

"In the low desert margin south of the Great Sphinx," stated Mr. Mariette, motioning his arms in the direction.

Val raised his eyebrows. Something about that direction struck a familiar chord.

He looked at Lord Cromer, who nodded his approval. "I'll see you in a few days, Valerius."

"By all means," Val answered with anticipation. "Let's commence immediately."

"Tomorrow morning then, Lord Ravensdale." Mr. Mariette shook Val's hand, smiling broadly.

* * * *

Part of the journey to the site was in a felucca on the Nile River, followed by travel on horses to the site. While in the sailboat, Val had more opportunity to speak with Mr. Mariette. "And how was the discovery made?" he asked.

"It was an accident!" exclaimed Mr. Mariette with a gurgling laughter, making no effort to hide his amazement. "It was the most extraordinary circumstance! The discovery was actually made by a man falling from his horse!"

"Falling?" Val focused all his attention on Mr. Mariette.

"Ravensdale, what is it?" Mr. Mariette appeared startled by Val's expression.

"Nothing. Continue, please," Val barked, realizing too late that it sounded more like a command than a request.

"Is something disturbing you, Lord Ravensdale?" asked Mr. Mariette.

"No, of course not. Tell me the whole, Mr. Mariette," implored Val impatiently.

"To be sure. A find of this magnitude makes everyone behave uncharacteristically. I find that even in myself." Mr. Mariette smiled warmly.

The Paradox: The Soldier and the Mystic   299

"You were describing the fall, Mr. Mariette?" Val asked with all the charm he could muster. Which wasn't much.

"A rider's horse stumbled into a hole, revealing a mud-brick wall," began Mr. Mariette. "Digging into the sand, we first uncovered a cemetery of mud-brick and stone tombs. It appears to be a burial ground for the lower castes—the workers themselves—by the number of tombs crammed into the space."

"Excuse me?" Val uttered. He reached for ship's rail, his head throbbing, feeling as if he were suddenly seasick. "You did not mention, Mr. Mariette, that this was a burial ground for the workers."

"Oh, didn't I? Well, only the first level. We're not sure about what lays beyond. That's why we need you, Lord Ravensdale," Mr. Mariette added, taking a step back. "Do you need a doctor, Ravensdale?"

"I'm fine," he replied briskly. But he didn't think that he was. He used every ounce of strength available to him to tighten the muscles in his strong arms and to steady himself. He had seen and partaken in every gruesome act a person could experience. He had been covered in blood and barely able to walk. He had suffered great physical and emotional deprivation. And he had never lost his ability to function at his best.

It was no doubt an odd coincidence. He vowed to consider all this later, and, for now, to do the job he came to do. "In fact, never better."

Chapter Thirty-Two

"It is astonishing that all this has been covered by sand." Upon arrival at the archeological site, Val investigated the markings on the walls.

"For thousands of years." Mr. Mariette nodded, a man with no laugh lines unable to stop smiling. "What is your opinion, Lord Ravensdale?"

"As you suspected, Mr. Mariette, this is the burial ground of the workmen and laborers who built the pyramids."

A narrow flight of steps led from this cemetery up the cliff face to larger tombs, partly carved out of the rock, to which they then proceeded.

"These are the tombs of the artisans and the overseers," Val explained. Softly, he added, "This is the greatest find in a thousand years, Mr. Mariette."

"And here we are, Lord Ravensdale," Mr. Mariette replied giddily.

As they walked together, Val stopped in front of one tomb which had a small hole in the mud-brick wall, revealing a pair of gleaming eyes created from jewels and paint. The eyes were vividly real and seemed to follow one.

He stopped dead in his tracks as the realization hit him.

"It can't be," Val whispered, wondering if he had died and was being tortured for his sins. If so, his punishment was aptly chosen.

Nothing was worse for him than to doubt his logic and its conclusions, the basis for his entire life.

"Fascinating, isn't it?" asked Mr. Mariette. "We only recently discovered this."

Val stood still for a very long time, frozen, staring at the eyes. His voice empty of all emotion, he asked, "How long did it take you to unearth this second set of tombs, Mr. Mariette?"

Mr. Mariette shrugged, calculating mentally, before answering. "About forty-eight hours."

"Bloody hell." *Impossible.* Val's head was in a spin, but he continued forward as if sleepwalking. He wished he might awaken, never having seen

any of this. Ordinarily he would be completely focused on the artifacts before him, but he was in a daze. This was the find of a lifetime—thrilling beyond compare—and the most horrifying moment of his life. He would rather be shot in the head. It felt as if he had been.

"Are you all right, old chap?" asked Mr. Mariette. "You're usually quite a fellow for conversation, and you seem almost speechless."

"I have never been so awestruck in my entire life, Mr. Mariette. This is so stupendously unexpected that I almost feel as if everything I have ever believed is in question."

And as if he, very possibly, had lost the one love of his life unnecessarily.

"I understand. To be in the presence of magnificence. It is beyond anything I have ever personally experienced."

Val nodded without speaking, his brain contemplating all possible explanations.

Of which there were none.

As they turned the corner, suddenly Val was entranced with that which lay before him, momentarily setting aside his extreme disorientation to study the hieroglyphs. His brain had saved him at every point in his life, and surely this was no different.

"These chambers are the king's," Val uttered, his excitement rising. "King Unas."

"The last king of the Fifth Dynasty?" Mr. Mariette asked.

"Precisely. King Unas apparently instructed that the walls of the internal chambers be covered with vertical columns of hieroglyphs."

"What do you see, Ravensdale?" asked Mr. Mariette impatiently.

"Magical spells and incantations stemming from solar and Osirian religious beliefs, the intent of which was to solidify a prosperous afterlife for the pharaoh." Val's heart began to pound faster, if that were possible, his curiosity overcoming other concerns. He smiled at Mr. Mariette, beginning to feel himself again.

"Astonishing! It keeps getting better and better."

"You are quite right, Mr. Mariette. This is a major discovery. These hieroglyphics will open a new chapter in the study of Egyptian religious beliefs."

"And it was written here to record the spells for posterity?" asked Mr. Mariette.

"I don't believe that was the purpose, no." Val contemplated, reading as he spoke. As an afterthought he murmured, "It is, essentially, to invoke power."

"I don't follow you precisely, Lord Ravensdale," considered Mr. Mariette.

"Keep in mind that, in the ancient Egyptian's mind, all one had to do to make the story real was to write it down."

"Of course." Mr. Mariette nodded. "Not a mere recording of events."

"Not at all. Writing transforms reality. It was to the ancient Egyptians the power of creation. The storyteller is the magician. It was believed that the act of transferring a thought to a visual—in this case a picture, but in modern times the equivalent would be the written word—would magically make the story happen." Val caught himself short, not believing that which he had just uttered. His world was spinning out of control around him. Everything he believed was standing in line at the guillotine. Val leaned against the pyramid wall to steady himself.

"Ravensdale?" asked Mr. Mariette. "Surely you must need a doctor?"

"I've been better," muttered Val, shutting his eyes. The words played again in his mind. *So magical is the act of writing that doing so transforms not only thought into word but thought into future reality.* He had uttered them himself. The prophecy had come out of his own mouth.

"Is there anything further, Mr. Mariette?" he asked reluctantly. Ordinarily he would have been drinking all this in like a man dying of thirst, but he was forcing himself to complete the task at hand. He feared that his legs would collapse from under him and that there was some possibility his heart might give out in the middle of this investigation.

"Yes," stated Mr. Mariette with apprehension, clearing his throat. "We found the temples. But I seriously contend that we should go back. You need to sit down and rest. Possibly you need a drink of water?"

"It wouldn't help." Val's lips formed a crooked smile. "Let's finish the tour. I've the balance of my life to rest."

Which probably wouldn't be that much longer. Unless he was already dead and didn't know it.

The Paradox: The Soldier and the Mystic   303

They continued toward the temples, Val forcing himself to observe the points of interest as they walked and to lend his interpretation.

"We have cleared away the sand from these temples and found decorated blocks from the causeway," Mr. Mariette explained.

"Astonishing," Val murmured. "Quite exceptional—and beautiful to behold."

"Indeed. We were surprised at the beauty of the treasures. As you can see, Lord Ravensdale, the temples are richly decorated with wall reliefs and adorned with statues of the gods and the king."

As they viewed the carved scenes on the decorated blocks, Val stopped short. There, before his eyes, was the scene Alita had painted for him weeks before in excruciatingly identical detail.

Chapter Thirty-Three

She had been right about everything.

The location. The fall. The eyes. The forty-eight hours. The message.

The *painting.*

He felt dazed as his mind automatically reevaluated his entire life. Everything he believed was now in question.

There was no possible way she could have known. Unless...*she has the sight.*

Impossible. *And the only explanation.*

Back in his room that evening, Val's head was spinning. Pacing the room, he ran his hands through his hair. He had never been more shaken in his life, despite the fact that his life had been destroyed and rebuilt more times than he cared to recall.

Kicking his chair away from his desk, he sat down, taking his pen in hand. The pen simply slipped through his fingers as he stared at his notepad.

She couldn't have sneaked into the tombs with her pink silk parasol. The burial tombs hadn't been discovered at that point, much less excavated. They were still underground and covered with earth while Alita painted the rendition of the altar.

And if she had been right about the picture, to exacting detail, could she have been right about the content of the message?

The message that had been uttered from his own lips.

The storyteller is the magician. All one must do to make the story real is to write it down. He threw his head into his hands and closed his eyes. *The power of creation.*

Damnation! That was precisely the point of all this. That was the only thing she wanted him to take from this elaborate show.

Stunned, he opened his eyes and shook his head. Alita had once said to him that his translations possessed the potential to bring the world together with a power most politicians only dreamed of.

The Paradox: The Soldier and the Mystic 305

He stood up and began pacing the room again.

Bloody hell. Cursing under his breath, his mind's eye was captivated again by the image of Alita's painting as his eyes followed suit and wandered to rest upon the unusual rendition. He leaned against the wall of his study, one shining black Hessian bracing his weight against the wall.

He shut his eyes as if to shut out this unwelcome invasion into his well-ordered philosophy of the world. Instead, his mind betrayed him, picturing and juxtaposing the canvas against the carved face of the altar, every detail so vivid to him, even from memory.

Val opened his eyes. *It is no use to pretend any longer.*

A lucky guess? He laughed out loud at his own supposition. He knew that his mind was grasping for straws now, desperately trying to contradict the truth he could no longer escape. The subject matter of the painting was unique and unusual. And never before seen.

Alita Stanton has the sight. Val whistled to himself. He hadn't believed in the sight. He still couldn't wrap his mind around it. *And yet she has it.*

He could tell himself it wasn't possible to see into the future. But he would have to ignore the evidence in order to come to that conclusion.

She was half touched in the attic, he had thought. And all the time Alita had been seeing things clearly. Possibly it was the rest of the world that was a bit skewed.

I need a drink. He continued to hold himself up against the wall of his study. He needed to sit down. He needed to *run.* His mind was racing, and his heart was not far behind. He was utterly exhausted, and it was an impossibility that he should sleep tonight.

Val walked to his mahogany cabinet and poured himself a glass of whiskey. Slowly and gingerly Val picked up Alita's painting, setting the onion-skin wrapping on his desk. With a deliberate fastidiousness he lowered himself to sit at his desk, drinking the glass of whiskey in one swallow. He took off his boots, keeping his eyes glued to the painting, and kicked them out of the way.

He had lost the only woman he had ever loved because of a lie. A lie he himself had construed.

And she had loved him, he reminded himself. Had she? He was too dazed and shocked to know anything. He felt as if his heart might dissolve into nothingness right then and there

Very lightly he ran his fingers along the surface of the image as if he would find her there in the picture. He studied the painting he now held in his hands. He shook his head in disbelief. It was an exact replica in every detail.

Unbelievable. Unfathomable. A beautiful work.

He propped the painting on his desk, leaning it against the wall, and stared at it for a long while.

He didn't know how much time had passed. The clock chimed once. 1:00 a.m. or 1:00 p.m.? *It must be a.m.* Should he try to sleep? No, it wasn't possible.

Alita Stanton had seen the future. The thought kept repeating itself round and round in his head.

She had said that he was capable of impacting the world, of bringing about positive change. He had thought her words were all foolish flattery.

What if...*What if* there were some use for his abilities? Val let out a deep breath. What would it feel like to be able to do that which he loved and to influence policy?

For just a moment, Val closed his eyes and let himself be immersed in the feeling. The idea that his interest was also his purpose, that he could follow his heart and would someday find success in it, thrilled him beyond all description.

"You'd better come back to reality, Ravensdale," he muttered.

Laughter sprung from his lips. He wasn't sure what reality was anymore.

If Alita had been right about all these events, and she had been, could she be right about *him*?

Val shook his head in response to his internal argument. He was an out-of-work soldier whose information assisted Britain in running her colony. When he spoke of his translations, people's eyes rolled back in their heads.

Unable to remove his eyes from the painting, his lips formed a very slight smile. The first amusement he had felt in some time. Since Alita left for London, in fact.

Alita Stanton had certainly managed to get his attention. And she wasn't even here.

He did not believe in the idea of Val Huntington. *But he was starting to believe in Miss Alita Stanton*, the glimmer of a thought in the midst of so many, as yet, unformed worlds.

Forcing himself out of his daze, he studied the hieroglyphics more intently. Hieroglyphics which *she drew*. She had spoken her prophecies in *his* language, a language he couldn't ignore, *a language she did not know*. She had spoken to him in a manner that she knew he could hear.

Reluctantly he turned his head to stare at his book of translations, which he hadn't opened in weeks. Then he looked at Alita's painting.

Val Huntington, the Earl of Ravensdale, opened the book of translations and began to work.

Chapter Thirty-Four

I know that I owe this newfound sense of value, still both strange and intoxicating to experience, solely and exclusively to my darling Alita. Val paused, looking up to stare at the now-framed painting that was his prized possession and a reminder of so many forceful words once spoken to him, the memory like an otherworldly Dvorak melody that only he could hear.

And why don't I go after her? He laughed out loud, the answer obvious as he stared at the painting. She who had been remarkably prophetic, who had shown herself to be a seer of incredible accuracy, *had said it would not be.*

What more did he need than that?

She must have seen into her own heart or the future. By her own admission, she was either already spoken for or no longer cared for him. Probably both. He had to thank God for the time they had had together and let her go.

He had written her a hundred letters. And mailed none of them. How could he? What would he say? *I love you, return to Egypt and watch me work.*

He had nothing to offer her, now more than ever. The earl of Ravensdale was floundering...and *unfinished.* He was only now beginning to have the slightest idea what he wanted to do with his life, not knowing if it was feasible or possible. He was in no position to take a wife.

A wife. She was probably married to that Manchestor fellow by now. Val let his pen trail off the page as he clenched his fist.

He didn't know where this path would lead him. He was only now, at this seasoned age, just starting out on a new journey.

A man who asked a woman for her hand in marriage had to know what he was about and be firmly established.

Especially with a woman like Alita Stanton, granddaughter of the Duke of Salford, and heiress to the Stanton fortune.

The Paradox: The Soldier and the Mystic   *309*

For six months, he had been applying himself to his work, making a point of recording his feelings as well, something he had never undertaken before he met Alita. *I can no longer escape the fact that I embraced the view of diminished worthiness and disposability with which both my family and country beheld me and, on a deeper, unspoken level, viewed myself in the same light.*

I am determined that I shall live. Possibly for the first time. Val paused, formulating his thoughts, attempting to put words to his strange experiences.

"As for the fact that my dear friend died by my own hand, leaving his children fatherless, I can never excuse that act. Nor will I ever again be the man who performed that murder. I pray for Banafrit's soul, and I pray that I shall have an opportunity to redeem my own. I can add nothing more on that score. Val knew that he could kill in self-defense or to protect his country or his loved ones, but he would never again kill, unquestioning, at someone else's orders, for greed, self-aggrandizement, or for the pleasure of revenge.

Val glanced again at the beautifully rendered painting. Strange how such a terrible scene of suffering was so dear to him, warming his heart merely to look at it. On the surface, it meant one thing, but it represented something entirely different through the artist's execution.

A found life.

Transformation.

As for Alita's claim that I possess a propensity for diplomacy, the very idea remains preposterous in my mind. But it was also preposterous that he had written a book slated to be published. Which was, in fact, the case.

Translating an ancient story of particular interest, he had submitted the idea to a British publisher with his own variations, aiming the story toward older children. A young Egyptian warrior who served the pharaoh deeply longed to be an artisan and to paint the sacred hieroglyphics in the pyramids, which would ensure the pharaoh's entrance into eternity. This desire burned inexplicably in the young man's heart although his family was of the proud warrior class and belittled his ambitions.

The narration told of the young man's visions, which taught him the art of hieroglyphics though he had received no formal training. Were the visitations from the dead, the angels, or a product of the young man's imagination? This was for the reader to decipher, in the same way that hieroglyphics must be interpreted and translated. Val included examples of the hieroglyphs in the book to fuel a child's curiosity.

Centuries later, a man on horseback fell from his horse and discovered a hidden pyramid, magically hidden beneath the sand. The fallen rider views the young warrior's paintings on the walls of the pyramid of Unas, the last king of the Fifth Dynasty, revealing to the reader that the young man had realized his dream, the creation rather than the destruction of life.

The publisher was enthusiastic, writing that Lord Ravensdale's book drew on the intense interest the English-speaking public had for ancient Egypt, adding that most submissions in a similar vein did not have the legitimacy and scholarly aspects of this fascinating tale of fiction.

"Or is it fact?" the publisher added with humorous intent.

Val held the letter in his hand, dated six months after Alita Stanton's departure from Egypt. *The Immortal Warrior*, by Val Huntington, 5th Earl of Ravensdale, to be published. The inscription...*To Abdul-Rashid and Jendayi and to their father, Banafrit, who gave his life for his beloved country, Egypt, and for the freedom of his people. He lost his life but not his honor.*

The Earl of Ravensdale with a published *children's book*. He knew that his family would be embarrassed rather than proud.

Val shrugged, dismissing the thought. For the first time in a long time, he had a sense of purpose.

I feel as if my life is a canvas upon which a beautiful dream is unfolding, as if some fantastic imagining crossed over from the realm of dreams to the realm of reality, and the only thing that it wants is a qualified painter to apply the colors. I am a color-blind painter who is grappling for the paints and throwing them everywhere, dropping and misapplying them.

Val's lips formed a half smile as he recalled telling *The Immortal Warrior* to Rashid and Jendayi, watching intently for their reactions and then returning to his private study to make changes accordingly. In subsequent stories that he was developing, he started with a direct translation of hieroglyphics and then embellished them with his own imagination before running the stories by Rashid and Jendayi.

For a short time they could all forget their pain in traveling to another world together. The children craved his companionship, while he looked to

The Paradox: The Soldier and the Mystic   *311*

their responses. Somehow, visits that had been so difficult became mutually rewarding.

For the thousandth time, he desperately wished that he could give Rashid and Jendayi back their family instead of a book. Banafrit had been reduced to a single phrase. It took an adult mind to understand that their father was merely a *casualty of war.*

It was a child's heart which knew the truth. He rubbed his forehead, but it was his heart that ached.

Val set his notebook aside and stared at the letter from The Gresham Publishing Company in London for the hundredth time, turning the formerly crisp and elegant paper round in his hand. When he began the translations, he had been acting on blind faith—blind faith in Alita, not in himself—and she had been correct on every point.

He moved the kerosene lamp on his desk to improve the lighting. Alita had seen another reality that could be, and because he had believed her, that possibility had been realized. And even though he didn't believe in even the next step, he did believe in Alita, making him determined to take that step.

God, he missed her.

His view of the Nile out his window had faded, replaced by the stars in the vast Egyptian sky. But he could still hear the flow of the longest river in the world though he could not see it.

She has never left me. She is with me every day, and I remain irrevocably changed from having known her. The torturous longing that fills me when I think of her is almost a comfort to me because it keeps me close to her. The slight smile at the corner of her mouth, which was scintillating in its simplicity. The twinkle in her eyes and the utter lack of pretense in her nature. Her steady, unflinching gaze, ethereal and translucent. Her bravery and determination, which met me equally in all matters and faced my attempts at intimidation squarely. Her quick intelligence and constant observations.

So many observations. He had dreaded her pronouncements, and now he played those precious reminiscences round and round in his head as if they were whispers from angels.

I was an imbecile. As he had done hundreds of times before, he picked up a pen to write a letter to Alita. The pen stopped in midair. But what would he say? *Forego your dazzling London life, leave your suitors, and marry me?*

Or *Renounce Manchestor and marry me. Return your trousseau. You won't need it here.*

He threw his pen across the room.

The Devil take it, why did he torture himself like this? What did he have to offer Alita Stanton? How could he possibly hold on to any woman's love, much less Alita's?

She is beyond my reach now. Val let his hand fall.

No, this is where I belong, and Alita Stanton does not belong here.

Even he was not that much of a bastard. It was that simple. She had told him so herself. Marriage to Alita was out of the question.

Marriage to Alita. Val felt the words reverberating throughout the room. He shut his eyes and savored the words. Yes, that was what he wanted. With all his heart. For just a moment his mood lightened. His lips formed a slow, sweet smile as he set down his notebook and leaned back in his chair.

You're a damned fool, Ravensdale. He didn't need a soothsayer to tell him that. Miss Alita Stanton, beautiful, vibrant Alita, the wife of a storyteller and a washed up soldier. She was possessed of every desirable quality, beauty, parentage, wealth, intelligence.

And the ability to *captivate a man for the rest of his life.*

He returned to his translations. He needed something more demanding to occupy his mind. When the brain was engaged, somehow the heart didn't hurt so badly.

Val didn't know what the future held. He didn't have the slightest idea. He simply knew what he needed to be doing at this moment. That was as far as he could envision for now.

The Paradox: The Soldier and the Mystic 313

Chapter Thirty-Five

Val groaned as he looked at the clock. Nine o'clock. He had overslept. When had he finally fallen asleep? 2:00 a.m.? 3:00 a.m.?

You're an uncivilized heathen, Ravensdale.

He surveyed the books strewn all over his desk and the half bottle of whiskey prominently displayed. *It is no accident of fate that you are a bachelor.*

And likely to stay one.

"Hell!" Val uttered as he threw himself out of his too-small bed, kinking a muscle in his back in the process. "Damn bed is made for a midget," he mumbled.

Gliding across the wood floor barefoot, he still savored the fact that he wasn't wearing heavy boots—not to mention trudging through sand in the desert heat, each step one step closer to departing this world. Enjoying the feel of the wood beneath his feet, he wondered if he would ever be able to forego his leather sandals, hand-crafted for him, and return to traditional British shoes.

He hoped not.

Splashing his face with cold water left in his basin from yesterday, he picked up his razor, examining the beginnings of a beard in the mirror hung over his basin. Beaded renditions of ancient Egyptians in the hieroglyphic art form encircled the mirror, staring at him disapprovingly.

He had to agree with their assessment.

He glanced at the half-empty bottle of whisky and his notebook on the small wooden desk. Six months ago the bottle would have been empty. And he wouldn't have had a filled notebook in the morning.

Val's stomach began to growl as the smell of fresh bread wafted up through his third-story half-open window as he shaved. Hurriedly he dressed and sliced a sausage, spreading it on stale bread with a generous portion of mustard. His eyes searched the fruit bowl for something to wash it down with.

Empty except for a few shriveling orange peels.

I need a woman. And since the one he wanted was out of the question, he was inclined toward a native woman. A beautiful Cleopatra look-alike, perhaps...If only he could find one whose language he didn't know.

He slammed the door behind him. He would get a cup of hot tea on the way, possibly with a fresh pomegranate or Valencia orange.

He would be working that evening, playing host to an acquaintance of Sir Evelyn's. In the meantime, he could pass away a couple of hours at the Cairo library. He would head for the sacred-writings section in the far confines of the library. Since it was comprised mostly of books written in the original ancient languages it was the quietest place in Cairo.

Not too many minutes later, Val was sitting in the library when he observed an elderly English gentleman, whom he recognized immediately, having a heated argument with a muscular, middle-aged Egyptian.

"Disrespect of Quran is *haraam* and greater sin. It is most holy book."

"Get out of my way, Arab."

"Insult me, but not insult Quran." Suddenly, the Egyptian drew a sword.

Val leapt from his seat and lodged himself between the Englishman and the Egyptian, drawing his own knife toward the Egyptian. The Egyptian was speaking loudly and waving his sword, even as his language changed to Arabic. Standing his ground, Val calmly conversed with him in Arabic, inquiring of the source of his agitation.

"Lord Falcon, it is most unfortunate that you have thrown a sacred text onto the table." Keeping both eyes on the Egyptian, Val spoke with equal humility to the English gentleman. "You have blasphemed against God in this man's eyes."

"Don't be ridiculous! It's just a bloody book!" sneered Lord Falcon, even as the Egyptian raised his sword higher. "It isn't the Bible."

"No doubt you did not know, Lord Falcon, that God's word is uniquely important in the religion of Islam. Religious art is forbidden, so all artistic expression is in God's word. The formation of the letters themselves become an art form, the Word is that important." Val's eyes moved to the book on the table, his voice calm but authoritative. "Apologize to the Egyptian, please, sir, and we'll be safely on our way."

The Paradox: The Soldier and the Mystic 315

After a long silence Val stonily commanded, "*Now*, please, sir."

"I shall do no such thing. The whole thing is absurd." Lord Falcon laughed. "I'll take out my gun and shoot him first."

The Egyptian raised his sword and moved forward. In one swift movement, Val surprised both parties by turning toward Lord Falcon and relieving him of his gun, throwing it on a nearby table. As Lord Falcon began to walk toward the table, Val pulled Lord Falcon's right arm behind his back, easily turning Lord Falcon around like a top before he held him immobile in front of him with a knife to his neck.

"Have you gone mad? Who are you? I'll have you court-martialed!" Lord Falcon screamed. Soon library patrons circled them, some holding weapons.

"Apologize to the gentleman, my lord." Val spoke again under gritted teeth, not feeling it to be germane to the situation to tell his lordship that they had met before. "We're not having any bloodshed here because you are too self-important and ignorant to respect someone else's viewpoint."

Lord Falcon twisted his neck with difficulty to stare at Val in disbelief, sputtering saliva on Val's hand as he twisted. "You want me to apologize because I didn't pick up his bloody book the way he wanted me to?" He glanced at the Egyptian, shooting him a look of disdain. "He's an uncivilized savage."

"Pretend it is your Bible, sir," Val suggested with steel in his voice, even as he kept his eye on the Egyptian and the portion of the circle that he could see, all of whom seemed to be growing angrier instead of calmer. He wondered if this would be his last minutes on the earth. Of all the places he might die, he didn't expect it to be in a library. "That should allow you to see it as he does."

"You can go to bloody hell," Lord Falcon muttered.

Pinning Lord Falcon's arms behind his back, Val held him at a gridlock, his knife blade now touching Falcon's throat, a few drops of blood materializing. Unfortunately, he had to make this real to the skeptical. He noted a few smiles developing on the faces surrounding them, as well as a few weapons lowering. Speaking in soothing tones, he replied "If you will pardon my candor, sir, I might remark that you are something of an ass. You keep your mouth shut, or I'll slit your neck myself, I swear it."

"Unhand me, you f–f–fiend!" he stuttered, having some difficulty with his breath. "You're an officer of the q–q–queen! You're supposed to p–p–protect me!"

"I surmised when I met you before that you were dull-witted and slow to comprehension, Lord Falcon, and now it is confirmed. Let me spell it out for you. I promise you that I won't kill *him* to protect *you*. Protect yourself by shutting your mouth." Val's voice was raw as he applied more pressure to Lord Falcon, which he hoped would direct his attention to the pain and thereby curtail his incessant meanderings. "I won't be privy to an uprising only because you have no regard for anyone's life but your own. You will die at his hand and without my interference, I assure you—and possibly with my assistance."

More weapons were lowered. Slowly he began to turn in the circle, pulling Lord Falcon with him, desiring to be facing the most explosive of the lot. Returning his eyes to the Egyptian, Val motioned to the book on the table with his eyes. He then spoke in Arabic, directing the Egyptian to kindly remove the book from those not appreciative of its holy contents, to return it to its place, and to avoid the British in future. The Egyptian gentleman appeared to be as shocked as anyone, and Val knew that he had to have recognized that he was a British officer since he was dressed in full regimentals for his dinner with Lord Cromer.

"You wouldn't d–d–dare," whispered the elderly gentleman. "I'll have you court-martialed and hanged."

"Do you think so?" Val laughed. Lord Falcon might be a nincompoop, but he was always good for a laugh and there was never a dull moment. "How do you propose to do that once separated from your body, sir? Furthermore, I'd be gone by the time they found your body. Look around you. We're the only two English in this section of the library. No doubt the door to this room has already been locked. Your body would never be discovered. The Egyptians have less than no love for the English, and anyone here would help me escape."

There was a general round of laughter and shared camaraderie, and all but one or two of the weapons were returned to their sheaths. Lord Falcon's eyes darted about him, the only part of him that could move, growing more frightened.

The Paradox: The Soldier and the Mystic 317

"Believe me, sir," stated Val, his tone deadly. "I don't wish to kill you. But I would do so without hesitation before I would allow you to cause another war in which thousands of young Britons would die because you cannot admit when you're wrong."

But the damage had already been mostly rectified, as Val had hoped it would. The Egyptian had picked up the book and gingerly returned it to the shelf. He spat on the elderly gentleman, put his sword away, tilted his head in deference to Val, and walked majestically away.

"Let me go, you bastard!" exclaimed Lord Falcon. Val had to give it to him. He made up for in spirit what he lacked in intelligence.

"I will when you are no longer a danger to yourself or to the rest of us," Val said, his tone harsh, his grip on the man severe. "Now, you listen to me, and maybe I'll leave you alive. Remember that you have no claims on this country. You are merely an unwanted visitor. You may not value your own life, a sentiment which has considerable merit, but I'll not have you taking down innocent people by sputtering your importance about." Val held the knife closer to his neck, drawing another drop of blood.

Val released the gentleman, who stared at him in fury.

"You'll pay for this!" Lord Falcon threatened.

"Go back to England and tell someone who cares," Val muttered with a polite bow, returning his knife to its sheath and pocketing Lord Falcon's pistol before leaving the room.

Chapter Thirty-Six

Damn the luck. As he entered the room, his heart sank. Arriving for dinner at the British embassy one minute past the appointed time, Val joined Sir Evelyn in his office as planned.

"The ace of spades again," Val cursed under his breath. How did he manage to draw the winning hand every time?

"That's him!" the elderly gentleman seated across from Sir Evelyn screamed when he saw Val, almost dropping his sherry with his now-shaking hand. "That's the idiot who accosted me! I want him court-martialed immediately."

"Valerius, it appears that you have met Lord Falcon." Sir Evelyn's expression was devoid of emotion, and he paused only for an instant. "Lord Falcon, Valerius Huntington, the Earl of Ravensdale."

Val bowed but stood his ground calmly. "Sir, I don't wish to correct you. But I saved your life today. And"—he cleared his throat—"if it's any concern of yours, I forestalled a bloody massacre of many innocent people."

"He held a knife to my throat, Evelyn!" Lord Falcon jumped out of his chair and began flailing his arms about. He turned to Sir Evelyn, thumping the bandage on his neck as if he had a tick. "A *knife.*"

"I am most gratified to see that you are still in good health and fully functioning, Lord Falcon." Val suppressed the corner of his mouth from forming a smile even as he felt some regret. *I am going to miss Egypt when they deport me.*

Lord Falcon's face turned red as he turned to face Sir Evelyn, who said nothing as he scrutinized the situation. This had the effect of aggravating Lord Falcon even further, if that were possible. He bellowed, "If you won't take action, Evelyn, I'll find someone who will," and he departed the room hurriedly.

"You are most welcome, Lord Falcon. It was a pleasure to ensure your continued existence," Val muttered under his breath after the door had

The Paradox: The Soldier and the Mystic   *319*

slammed. It was an odd twist of fate that he should be the one to be punished for saving the lives of everyone involved.

Sir Evelyn studied him, his expression ominous. *I never wanted the position anyway. It is a damned nuisance.* He hoped that Sir Evelyn didn't ban him from the country and return him to England, which was fully in his power to do. He would prefer to remain here and translate his discoveries.

England. His heart skipped a beat as he thought of Alita. *Now is not the time, Ravensdale.* He forced her picture out of his mind, surprised that it should present itself at this inopportune moment. He wondered if he would ever be free of her.

Sir Evelyn tapped his pencil on his massive oak desk, everything about him from his starched three-piece suit to his hair in perfect order. A painful reminder that, despite Sir Evelyn's lofty position, he was a pencil-pusher at heart and a stickler for the legalities.

I will not submit. If Sir Evelyn chose to press charges, he would be a fugitive from the law. Not the course he wished for, but he wasn't seeing out the rest of his days in a jail cell. His hand moved closer to the pistol he always kept at his belt. He wouldn't kill Sir Evelyn, but he would have to immobilize him momentarily. *A definite black mark on his record to have shot the King of Egypt in the arm.*

Quickly he surveyed the room without moving his head and found what he was looking for—a half-open window.

Wasn't it just his lucky day? The window was behind Sir Evelyn. He glanced at his own feet, feigning a humble stance. It wasn't going to be easy to run in sandals. Possibly he should rethink his preferred footwear.

If he lived.

Sir Evelyn motioned to Val to sit down.

Ignoring the implied command, he moved slightly closer to the window as he awaited the verdict.

"I think I have pieced the story together pretty well," stated Sir Evelyn. "Is it possible that you found no other way to handle the situation, Valerius?" he asked pointedly.

"There were many other ways to handle the situation, Sir Evelyn, all less dramatic in nature. However, Lord Falcon did not choose any of the other options available to us." Val pretended to pace in agitation, allowing him to move closer to the window. He was not in the mood to waste much time explaining that which should have been obvious. Even so, he truly hoped he didn't have to hurt Sir Evelyn, and the closer he got to the window, the less likely he would have to. "There was only one option left which did not involve bloodshed. I chose that option."

"Was it that serious?"

"We were circled by Egyptians with weapons." Val laughed. "You be the judge, Sir Evelyn. I, myself, did not feel the stakes high enough to warrant blood on either side."

"And what stakes were those, Valerius?"

"No gold, no territory, just one stupid peer of the realm who didn't know when to keep his mouth shut."

"You should be sensitive to that malady, Valerius, if I may say so. Please be seated. I require more information," Sir Evelyn commanded.

"Lord Falcon is no doubt unskilled at weaponry. He is nonetheless ignorant, ill-mannered, and exceptionally skilled at offering insult."

"Surely you must have felt a loss of face to have deferred to the Egyptian." Sir Evelyn frowned, touching his index finger to his chin reflectively.

"Irrelevant, sir. Never occurred to me. Possibly the Egyptian was angrier than the situation warranted, no doubt bringing to the table anger over foreign occupation of his country." Val ran the scene round in his mind as he considered Sir Evelyn's question. "Maybe the Egyptian lost a son in the wars. We do not know. Everyone has lost *someone*."

"So you sided with the Egyptians?" Sir Evelyn demanded, his tone devoid of all surprise but not without annoyance.

"Not at all. Regardless of my opinion of either party, it was necessary that I address the situation." Val quickly regained his composure, leaning against the wall next to the window while keeping his feet firmly on the ground and ready to move, his hands at his waist and near his weapons. Sir Evelyn now had to turn in his chair to look at him. "If the Egyptian had continued to be unresponsive to our apologies, I would have had to take him in hand. I would not have killed him. I merely would have disengaged him of his weapons."

"If he had not killed you," stated Lord Cromer evenly.

"True," stated Val nonchalantly. "That is a risk I had to take, Sir Evelyn. I am a soldier for the Crown. My life is secondary to my duty. It is my job to

The Paradox: The Soldier and the Mystic

321

preserve the peace now that Egypt is English-occupied, whether or not I agree with the occupation."

But I will not die to further a lie. Nor will I be a scapegoat for politicians who only ever put their own interests first.

"We are at peace. And still you risk your life, Valerius," stated Lord Cromer stated impatiently. "You could have easily killed the Egyptian, and it would have been ruled as self-defense."

"And how many lives would have been lost in retaliation?" demanded Val. "As it is, we have no loss of life and one arrogant peer who goes about mostly as he did before, pontificating and attempting to impress his importance on others. He will likely be killed before he leaves Egypt, but hopefully he won't take any young men with him."

"You feel a strong bond to your countrymen, it seems," stated Lord Cromer, deep in thought.

"Of course," stated Val, running his hand along the windowsill. "To be British is to be for Britons."

"And also for the Egyptians," proposed Lord Cromer, his expression contemplative.

"Why shouldn't I be?" asked Val. "The Egyptians are a great people with a great heritage."

"I'm sending you back to England," Sir Evelyn stated conclusively in that tone he used when his decision was final.

"You're dismissing me?" Val asked forcibly, staring at the window. *Good, there is a ledge.* Second floor, no tree to climb down on.

"No, Valerius," Lord Cromer replied somberly.

"You're pressing charges and sending me to trial," Val stated coolly, wondering why someone who was generally so direct was having the devil of a time getting to the point. He fingered his pistol. He never acted until all the information was in hand, though there was always a situation that warranted breaking the rules, and he had a sinking feeling that this was it.

"Neither. Your skills are not fully realized here, Valerius. I'm recommending you to the Foreign Office. You have the language abilities in addition to all of the other rare qualities which are needed, I now see—a level head and a respect for the indigent population. Not to mention bravery, intelligence, and a willingness to die for your country."

"Diplomacy?" Val stared at Sir Evelyn in disbelief, moving away from the window in search of a chair. "After the scene that just passed in here?"

"Don't tell me my business, Ravensdale, or I'll send you to the brig to learn some respect. You're going to the Foreign Office." Sir Evelyn nodded his head, thoughtful as he stroked his beard. "Falcon might be angry, but no one died. He will live another day to be angry at some new imagined foe. In diplomatic circles there is rarely a perfect solution, merely a *best* solution."

Val stared at Sir Evelyn for a long while, as if he had seen a ghost. Or possibly an angel. Finally he replied, with all the voice he could muster, "Thank you, sir. I will endeavor to be worthy of this honor." He walked to the door in a daze and left, hoping he wouldn't wake up.

But despite the fog he was in, he no longer doubted his path, and he knew precisely what he would do.

Chapter Thirty-Seven

"Hartshorne! Hot water bottles! Extra blankets! Hot tea and toast! *Immediately*!" Lady Elaina exclaimed, assisting her daughter out of the carriage while Jon took Alita's other arm. It had taken Lady Elaina all of two seconds before she regained her wits and began issuing instructions right and left to the servants and her family, demanding precise and absolute obedience in defiance of their efforts to calm her.

"*Heaven help us*!" she had gasped in dismay when she had first laid eyes on her daughter an instant earlier. Far from appearing refreshed from a holiday, Alita's face was drained of all color, and dark circles accented her eyes. How emerald-green eyes could appear dull was yet a mystery to her, but there it was! Alita's frame was almost skeletal.

Lady Elaina turned in shock to gaze upon her mother, desperate for an explanation, who only shook her head from side to side. She had never before seen such an expression of helplessness on the duchess's face. Her Grace had heretofore always believed that nothing was beyond her power to solve, placing herself somewhere alongside the Messiah and natural disasters, depending on the circumstance.

"Lita! Are you sick?" asked Julianne. "What is wrong?"

"Hello, Julianne, dear," Alita murmured, reaching out to touch her sister's cheek.

"Don't ask so many questions, Julianne!" hissed Harvey. "Can't you see that Alita is not well?"

"Take my arm, sweetheart," Jon commanded. "Let us go inside."

"Yes, Papa."

Lady Elaina sat with Alita daily, limiting both her work at the hospital and her political and social activities. For a woman who had been likened to a cat on hot bricks, the picture of domestic tranquility that she presented as she painted, embroidered, played music, and had tea with Alita surely gave pause to those who knew her well.

But now her daughter needed her.

"Alita, won't you paint with me?" Lady Elaina asked quietly, pretending to consider her canvas when she would have far preferred to toss it in the fireplace, which was where it belonged.

Sitting on a lilac satin fainting couch while staring out the window, Alita's face was pinched and her mouth down-turned. Her buttercream velvet robe, which used to look so well on her, only served to amplify the sallow shades of her skin. Lady Elaina wouldn't have recognized her if she hadn't been her own.

"No, Ma-ma, not just now." Without moving her gaze, Alita ran her fingers along the delicate leaves of the blue hydrangea in a vase next to her couch even as the lavender chiffon curtains moved slightly in the breeze.

"Why don't you wish to paint, Alita?" Lady Elaina asked, attempting to keep the worry out of her voice. This was unprecedented. Alita had drawn and painted since was three years old! She had always before found pleasure, and even solace, in painting, and her parents couldn't have stopped her from producing art if they had wished to.

"I believe the last picture I painted may indeed be my last," she stated simply.

"Whatever do you mean, sweetheart?"

There was no answer, and Alita would not even look at her.

"Alita, please answer your mother. You are worrying me." Lady Elaina sighed heavily, even as she managed to splatter green pain on her artist's frock. "What are you staring at so intently?"

"Just a little hummingbird. He's going to tire himself out with all that activity."

"A little activity might do you a bit of good, my dear."

"Those poor little birds are so busy, and then they die."

"Hmmm...I see." But she didn't. "Alita, I do need some assistance. What do you think I can do to improve this painting?"

Lady Elaina could see that Alita was not going to budge, so she took the painting to her, smearing paint on her hands in the process.

"Oh, *my*. If you...if only there was a touch of..."Alita stole glances at her mother's poorly executed renditions and sought to offer gentle suggestions. Lady Elaina knew herself to be a terrible painter. *Most fortunate, indeed.*

Even in her exhaustion Alita could not help but offer assistance. She was so kindhearted that she was unable to view *anyone* as a hopeless case, which Lady Elaina knew herself to be but was remiss to divulge.

After several weeks of this exercise, at some point Alita picked up a tablet to illustrate her point.

Lady Elaina knew herself to be a gifted musician and an educated nurse and mathematician, not to mention an astute politician. And yet, on more than one occasion, it served Lady Elaina's purpose well that she was thoroughly untalented in the arena of Alita's interests.

"Oh, Mother, *no*! Don't cut the flower *there*!"

"Here then?" Lady Elaina asked, moving the sharp scissors closer to the precious plant.

"*Stop!* You'll kill it, Mother!" Slowly Alita moved toward her across the dark walnut floor, concern written all over her face. "Allow me to do it. *Please.*"

"Of course, dear. It wouldn't do for a nurse to kill anything."

While Alita painted, embroidered, and arranged flowers, she began to speak, the activities apparently freeing some of the suppression her mind had self-imposed. "Did Papa know that he loved you from the first? 'There was never anyone for me but Elly,' he always says."

"Yes, I believe so." Lady Elaina set her embroidery down in a wad momentarily, uneven stitches producing an odd mix of design, even as the familiar pain resurfaced. "But I didn't know that I loved *him*. Well, I knew, but I couldn't allow myself to know what I knew. If that makes any sense."

"Not truly. How could you hesitate, Ma-ma, from the first moment of knowing him?" Alita asked, perplexed. "His character, his intelligence, his looks—all remarkable. He is a world-famous scientist! You are so *perfect* for each other!"

"I know it seems nonsensical now, and it was. But recall that I was the daughter of a duke. Your father was the son of a tenant farmer, with no other profession eminent. Our being together was, frankly, ridiculous. It was unheard of. Much of his education began with the books I provided."

Lady Elaina sighed. "I should have been able to see beyond societal expectations—I did with everything else—but I had aspirations. It was my gift and my curse."

"Aspirations?" Alita sighed, her lip quivering. "How could *anything* possibly be more important than true love?"

"I was not like other girls, Alita. I completely rebelled against having no identity of my own. Unfortunately, I allowed the most undesirable aspects of society to blind me to true love."

"When did you *know*...that you loved Papa?"

"When I met Jon next, he had obtained respectability though not fortune, having completed his doctorate at King's College. I would have married him in a heartbeat. There was no hiding from my heart any longer," stated Lady Elaina as she retrieved the embroidery and sewed another uneven stitch, shaking her head. "However, it was too late."

"Why, Ma-ma? Why?" Alita asked anxiously, moving forward in her chair, her eyes recapturing some of their glow. "Why was it too late?"

"I had hurt him so badly that he didn't want me any longer."

"So why didn't you marry someone else?"

"I didn't want anyone else." Lady Elaina raised her eyebrows as she looked up, somewhat startled by Alita's expression. "I don't know how to illuminate you on the workings of my mind, Alita. I was never practical. The only time I was practical was the worst mistake I ever made."

"Not choosing Papa?" Alita whispered.

Lady Elaina nodded. "If I couldn't have precisely what I wanted, I never stood for second-best. I had my profession, I had dear friends, I had wealth, and I had no intention of giving all that up to revolve around a husband who did not engage my heart." She laughed. "And who would want such a wife, anyway?"

"No one except Lord Phillip Manchestor." Alita stared at her mother wide-eyed, giggling in spite of herself. "Only the catch of the season."

"Oh, *that*." Lady Elaina Stanton shrugged. "Phillip didn't love me, so that can't be counted. That marriage would have been all about promoting Phillip's success without regard for my aspirations."

"I believe that you misjudged the depth of Phillip's love," Alita replied softly. "And, anyway, couldn't they be one and the same?"

"For you, I expect so." Lady Elaina smiled warmly at her daughter, patting her hand as she contemplated her. She wondered. Had something happened between Alita and William Manchestor? Alita refused to speak of

The Paradox: The Soldier and the Mystic 327

it, and his visits were strained, though he always brought flowers and obviously cared for her. What had happened in Egypt?

"You, I think, are different, dear heart. You want to be married and to have a family. You might be happily married to any number of gentlemen, I expect."

"It is not a *gentle* man whom I want," Alita whispered, almost inaudible. Elaina caught her breath as she heard the pain in her daughter's voice, and there was a dead silence between them.

"Whom is it that you want, dearest?" Lady Elaina forced herself to ask, unable to control the shakiness in her voice, as she took her daughter's hand.

"A bewildered, broken soldier who wants to save the world."

"There is a young man who is *perfect* for you, Alita. Perhaps you simply haven't discovered him yet."

"I have," she insisted. "I'm just not perfect *for him*." Alita pursed her lips, obviously trying to control her emotions as tears began to form. "Mama, I don't know what is wrong with me."

"Nothing is the matter with you, my dear." Lady Elaina put her arm around her daughter. "You are simply in love and feel just as you ought."

"But it hurts so much," stated Alita.

"Of course." Her mother nodded. "If the love were not so deep and not so real, it would not hurt so much."

"Did it ever stop hurting when you were apart from Papa?" asked Alita while intermittently dotting her eyes with her handkerchief.

"Not truly, but much of the time I was too busy to feel it. And if I was lonely, I tried to find someone else who was lonely and reduce their pain. Then it didn't hurt *as much*." She shrugged. "I had to either accept my fate and live with it or marry someone else. I chose the former." *And the pain kept us united so that we might one day be together. But this is not a recommendation I can make to you.*

Lady Elaina smoothed her daughter's hair and kissed her forehead. She knew that Alita would come to a solution that was acceptable to her, but she hoped that her precious daughter didn't have six years of suffering ahead of her, as she herself had. Or worse, *a lifetime.*

Chapter Thirty-Eight

The small hand poured the water, peering between the green leaves to ensure that the soil was properly fed. As she poured, a droplet of water landed on the blanket, and the child almost lost her balance from dismay. But Alita caught the glass of water and gently secured it.

Julianne covered her mouth in alarm, causing the old lady to laugh. Tears formed in the old woman's eyes, but they were tears of joy. "You girls brung so much joy into my life. I don't have hardly anyone else. No family, only a few friends left, and I don't own nothin'."

"Now you own this plant." Julianne straightened the pink bow on the potted plant and asked shyly, "Did I get you wet, Mrs. Mulroney?"

"No, dear. Ah've nevah' been bettah', Miss Julianne."

"Can I tell her?" Julianne glanced up at her sister, her eyes wide with wonder. "Can I tell her the *secret*?"

Alita nodded.

"Mrs. Mulroney, may I tell you a secret? A very, very big secret that you can't tell anyone?"

"Yes, dear! I luv secrets!"

"If you put your hand just above the leaves"—Julianne placed her lips very close to the old woman's ear and whispered—"you can feel the plant talk to you."

"You don' say, Miss Julianne?" Mrs. Mulroney appeared quite entranced with this information. She turned to stare at the beautiful begonia, bursting in pink, with a matching pink ribbon. Mrs. Mulroney addressed the plant. "I'm pleased to make yer acquaintance, Elmira."

"Mrs. Mulroney! What's the matter? Why are you crying?"

"It warms my heart that you girls thought of me, a dying old woman, when you saw this beautiful plant." She sniffed.

"This beautiful *talking* plant," Julianne corrected her. "Do you like the flower, Mrs. Mulroney?"

The Paradox: The Soldier and the Mystic   *329*

"I *luv* the flower, Julianne." Tears welled up in Mrs. Mulroney's eyes. "I'll think of you and Miss Alita ever' time I look at it, and I'll never feel lonely agin'."

"Julianne…?" Alita nudged her sister.

Julianne beamed. "We brought you another present, too!"

"Besides th' beautiful pink flower?" Mrs. Mulroney appeared shocked. "It's too much for the likes of me. I don' deserve you two."

"You deserve far more than we could ever give you," Alita whispered sincerely. Alita bent down and kissed the old woman's cheek, and their eyes met.

"Well, then, I'm sure I'm not one to argue with quality!" Mrs. Mulroney smiled shyly, looking like a schoolgirl despite wrinkles and white hair.

Excitedly, Julianne pulled a large basket from the other side of the bed, containing apples, pears, cherries, cheese, dried meat, and even a box of chocolates. Mrs. Mulroney eyed the chocolates with longing, having eyes for nothing else in the basket. Her hand clasped over her mouth, and she looked as if it would be a sin for her to take it. "Ah've never had a box of chocolates in m'life! That's only fer the rich!"

"Now it's for you," Alita said as she opened the box for Mrs. Mulroney's selection. "Take one, Mrs. Mulroney, or you'll hurt our feelings."

"Oh, I couldn't do that!" she exclaimed, shaking her head vehemently. After some deliberation, she selected a candy. As the chocolate melted in the woman's mouth, she looked as if she were in perfect bliss. Alita offered to procure a cup of tea for her, which Mrs. Mulroney refused, closing her eyes momentarily. "I want to taste the chocolate in my mouth and nothin' else," she said simply.

After Mrs. Mulroney was snoring softly, Alita and Julianne moved to their next regular patient, Isabelle, a girl a little more than Alita's age who was dying of diseases of prostitution. Alita held Isabelle's hand, so cold and clammy that it was difficult to believe she had ever been warm. Possibly she hadn't. Alita propped Isabelle up against her pillow and assisted the young woman in drinking hot tea.

Alita could see that the warmth revived Isabelle, even as she glanced at the miniature rose bush now vibrant with red roses.

"Can you read to me, Miss Alita?" she pleaded, her eyes not meeting Alita's for apparent fear of rejection.

"What do you wish to hear, Miss Isabelle?" Julianne asked.

Isabelle smiled at the polite inquiry. She had clearly not been accustomed to being treated respectfully.

"The same as las' time," Isabelle replied. Her powder-blue eyes were large in her sunken head, her long black hair thinning.

"Sweet Princess, my gift to you is this..." Alita began to read, and Isabelle was intensely attentive, as if it were the first time she had heard the story. "I weave this magic into the evil spell cast unjustly upon you."

"Who is it, Lita? Who is it? The fairy Merryweather?" Julianne demanded, as enthralled as the woman over ten years her senior.

"Yes." Alita nodded, resuming Merryweather's voice. "If you should prick your finger and enter into death—"

"Under the *evil* spell of the *wicked* witch..." Isabelle completed the sentence.

"*My* spell will change that death to sleep," murmured Alita.

"Because the good spell is stronger than the evil spell," Julianne interjected.

"And if, while you sleep"—Alita pulled the covers up over Isabelle, her voice soft—"true love's kiss should find you—"

"And it will. It *will!*" promised Julianne.

"You will awaken from your slumber—"

"*And be happy forever more.*" Isabelle finished the sentence, drifting off to sleep.

"Lita, is it saying that the prick to her finger is the gift?" asked Julianne.

"Sometimes it is, Julianne," Alita answered quietly, closing the book.

"Can true love break the spell and awaken you from sleep?" Julianne persisted.

"Definitely." A slow smile came to Alita's lips. "Sometimes even if you're the only one in love."

Julianne's expression was perplexed, and she started to speak again, but Alita put her finger to her lips, motioning to Isabelle. "Let her sleep, sweetheart. She's a princess when she sleeps."

Julianne nodded in understanding, whispering, "That is why she loves the book so much."

The Paradox: The Soldier and the Mystic   *331*

"They're going to die, aren't they, Lita?" As Alita and Julianne were exiting the hospital to return home, Julianne appeared somber.

Alita nodded.

"It's too sad, Lita. I don't want to come back."

"You don't have to come back, Julianne," stated Alita. "I'll come by myself."

"But it makes you sad," Julianne said.

"It doesn't make me sad." Alita shook her head, feeling her lips tremble. "It makes me happy to take some of their sadness away. They have so little happiness compared to mine. I can spare a little."

"I guess I can, too, then." Julianne nodded.

At this moment a carriage of young ladies in the first stare of fashion drove past them, all laughing. Alita felt a pang of sadness and longing to be one of their number. But if she focused on that, it would keep her in their world.

"Do you miss your friends, Lita?" Julianne asked.

"Yes," Alita admitted. "But I'm learning to create my own world rather than entering into everyone else's."

"What do you mean, Lita?" Julianne asked, her expression puzzled.

"Without us, Isabelle was in a horrible world. Now she is a princess sometimes. And she truly *is* a princess, she just didn't know it before we painted that world for her."

"It's like we paint a picture and people step into the frame!" Julianne covered her mouth with her hands, astonished with the realization.

"I find that I paint a better picture than most." Alita giggled.

"Are you happier now, Lita?"

"I think I was happier then," she answered truthfully. "But I'm in between paintings now. I have the dream of something...*magnificent*. I just can't see it yet."

"Oh, Lita, you'll never guess what I heard!" exclaimed Julianne.

"What, Jules?"

"William Manchestor and Charlise Sinclair. *Engaged*!"

"A charming couple, don't you think, Julianne?"

"Indeed *I do*," exclaimed Julianne with a coquettishly affected expression. "Who could not?"

Alita nodded in agreement. Effortlessly she added in a whisper, "They shall be gloriously happy together."

"What does it mean to be *gloriously*?" asked Julianne hopefully.

"It means that she shall ground him in a genuine love and spirituality, and he shall adore her and provide her with a sense of gaiety and light-heartedness she never knew. And a family of her own."

"That is glorious in excelsis!" Julianne nodded triumphantly.

"*Deo*." Alita smiled.

Chapter Thirty-Nine

"How odd that your birdsong should mimic your sworn enemy. To honor your bravery, here is some buttercup and chickweed for you. Now shall you sing for me?" She waited for the soothing, purring song of the turtledove, sounding more like a cat than a bird, to the chagrin of its species, but no music was forthcoming. "I believe I shall name you *Buttercup*. If not for those tortoise-like markings on your wings..."

She watched more of her feathered friends alight on the nearby stone birdbath, two sculpted angels holding a wide-rimmed bowl. Birds grew quickly accustomed to a young lady who came often with a veritable feast of seeds, fruits, and cereals.

It was the first days of spring, the garden soon to be bathed in color. Sitting on the whitewashed stone bench in her garden, an arbor of lilac bushes hanging overhead, Alita was saddened by the lack of anticipation that she felt.

Eight months had passed since she had returned from Egypt, and it still felt to her as if a part of her would never return from that faraway land. She attempted to authoritatively place her yearnings into a mental box that she might examine and transform, but instead, her longings placed her in the box, and she became their toy.

Closing her eyes, she forced herself to breathe in the blend of roses and lilacs shyly entering the air like a young girl at her first dance. The scents revived her, playing a tug of war with her melancholy.

"And shall you sing for me then, little nightingale, or shall you merely steal my berries?" She turned to search her shrubs for the movement where the nondescript bird was rummaging. "You might be plain and brown in appearance, but *when you sing...*"

She reminded herself that the glimpses of joy were coming more frequently. She was deeply grateful, and yet she felt dismay that these occurrences were primarily when she was removed from herself.

"You brought the babies! Oh, they are so *cute!* You have the funniest walk of any creature!" Giggling, she hurriedly reached into her white straw basket lined in gingham for poppy, wheat, and barley for the quail. The mother bird's crown bobbed forward as she moved toward the feast without hesitation.

"Shall no one sing for me? Or shall you only eat at my table without thought for my pleasure?"

Possibly the exclusive focus on others was necessary for a time in order to heal, she reflected, but she longed once again to know the pleasure of her own companionship and to embrace the life that was her own rather than wishing for an altogether different life.

"And my favorite of all! For you, Jennie, fruitcake and coconut cake." She reached inside her basket, placing the cake crumbs in her left hand. Not for the first time, the robin ate directly from her hand. She murmured, "I have no doubt that you fly with the angels. Your song is so melodic—light, wistful, even...elevating. Shall I hear it?"

Each time she faced her internal captors, she felt the balance of power shifting slightly. As the ripples in the pond flowed, caressing the lily pads, she felt her soul joining with the water, and a moment of tranquility filled her heart.

Amused with their playfulness, she watched the fish swimming in her pond when, with an abrupt suddenness, she turned away from that peaceful endeavor and looked into the eye of the storm.

The Earl of Ravensdale stood just outside her arbor, completely absorbed in intently observing her, his expression so stark as to almost be a frown.

She felt a wave of shock rush over her as her breath caught in her chest. His coal-black hair waving over his ears—still too long, ever in need of a haircut—his ice-blue eyes the color of a rain cloud resting on her. As she stared back at him, the right corner of his mouth slowly rose to form that half smile she had wished to have forever forgotten, and she thought she might melt right then and there despite the morning breeze.

Clenching her hands in her lap, cake crumbs scattering everywhere, she wondered if she deceived herself. He had the look of a man who had been dying of thirst and had finally found water. Val moved slowly toward her as

The Paradox: The Soldier and the Mystic 335

if he had never expected to see her again and was drinking in every instant of the moment.

"L–Lord Ravensdale!" Struggling to find her voice, she only managed to stammer. Hurriedly she brushed the crumbs and seeds off her lap. She was simply dressed in her lightweight green wool suit. Thankfully she had tied a peach silk scarf around her throat, which might have cast some color into her otherwise pale complexion. Her hair she had pinned hurriedly atop her head, and no doubt a curl or two had come loose. "What are you doing here?"

Oh, that didn't come out as she intended. But she had never been so surprised to see anyone, and her head was spinning.

"Miss Stanton." He bowed abruptly. The frown returned to Val's face, his disapproval apparent. "Would you prefer that I left?"

But the Earl of Ravensdale did not have the look of a man who had any intention of departing. As always, he was in control of their encounter, and she was merely present to observe and flounder.

"Oh, no, my lord. I would not," she managed, shaking her head while struggling once again to find words. "But…w–why are you here?"

Once again, a slight half smile formed at the corner of his lips, and again it soon faded into the austere expression.

"I know I shouldn't have come, Miss Alita—his hands fell to his side— "but I was in London anyway, and you traveled two thousand miles to see me. It struck me as rude not to travel five miles to pay my respects and to thank you…" He ran his fingers through his hair as if he had no idea what to say next, or even why he was here. She felt the usual sweet attraction that he had for her, but it was so much stronger than their last meeting that she began to tremble. She clenched her hands in a failed effort to keep her world from spinning.

"I am delighted to see you, Lord Ravensdale," she whispered, barely breathing. Still dazed but slowly returning to earth, for the first time she realized that he was actually dressed appropriately. He wore a morning suit consisting of a starched white dress shirt, black pants, a maroon silk ascot tie, a pearl tie pin, a black jacket and a dark gray striped vest. He even wore a boutonnière! Despite the severity of his gaze, for the first time in their acquaintance, she sensed in him a desire to please her and a concern for her opinion, startling and further enhancing her state of confusion.

He breathed heavily, as if he had more to say. He seemed to be caressing every inch of her with his eyes, and she felt dizzy under his scrutiny. She stared at him patiently, awaiting an explanation. And then, without warning, he blurted, "I have a proposition for you, Miss Alita."

"I beg your pardon?" She swallowed hard.

"I need an artist for my book. My first publication, that is." He spoke much more rapidly than she remembered. "I reviewed the work of the artists recommended by my publishing company, and the paintings simply did not meet my criteria of excellence nor of style." He seemed to stumble on his words, as if he were uncertain of what to say. His austere and logical manner did not fit with the raging emotions she felt emanating from him. For the moment, she could think of nothing to do but to follow his conversational lead.

"Val, that is wonderful." And, in truth, the news filled her with delight, so much so that she quickly regressed from formal address. "You have a book about to be published. I am thrilled. It will be such a gift to the world."

"Will you do me the honor of illustrating my book, Miss Alita?" he asked. "After all, the work never would have been published were it not for you."

Could that possibly be a good idea? She felt a genuine delight as she contemplated being able to see Val again. But it might teach her to hope where there was none.

But to paint for the world to see? A sudden guilt at her own anticipation overtook her. Was it vain and immodest? Her mother would say, *No, of course not. How could it be, to cultivate one's gifts, be one female or male?* As she glanced back at him, she saw that he had immediately responded to her apprehension.

"I confess that such an arrangement would provide me with an opportunity to be in your presence, which I have already been informed would not otherwise be my privilege. Does this aspect displease you?" He kept his eyes glued to her face.

"You are always welcome to call on me, Lord Ravensdale," Alita replied shakily, "in respectable circumstances. As to the painting, I appreciate your thinking of me, but I do not think I shall be able to assist you." If his intent were reputable, that was one thing, but she was feeling

The Paradox: The Soldier and the Mystic 337

something far different from him—raging desire! And to simply be in his presence with no hope of a respectable marriage?

She had been devastated by the unattainable nature of his love, and she would not traverse down that path again. She didn't deserve that pain again. No one did. She had helped him to the best of her ability. That was where it ended. She was not obligated to service his whims.

His expression plummeted, and he appeared to be burdened with weighty concerns. His commanding presence was in stark contrast to the deeply troubled state he displayed.

"What is it, Lord Ravensdale?" she asked, concerned. "Why are you distressed when you have so much cause for celebration?"

"I'll get straight to the point then." He stared at his hands for a moment before capturing her eyes. "Miss Alita, forgive my intrusion. But might I ask if I am to wish you happy?"

"Whatever would give you such a notion, my lord?" Alita stared at him blankly, her annoyance building. Of what possible interest could it be to him? But she well knew the answer to that.

He had not changed. He did not want her, and he wanted no one else to have her either. She so wished she might flash an engagement ring before his pale blue eyes.

"While socializing in my club over the past week"—Val cleared his throat—"the fervent high praises and obvious partiality which several outstanding young men of my acquaintance held for you was inescapable." A dark gloom passed over his features, as if it were ripping his heart out to speak the words.

"And, if I may be so bold as to ask, how can this possibly be any concern of yours, Lord Ravensdale?" She pursed her lips. *As if it were any of his business after these eight months.* Why on earth did she not tell him so or play him as he had played her?

To what purpose? What would she gain? The knowledge that she had hurt him as he had hurt her?

It wasn't possible to hurt him to that degree.

"I have received an offer." There. She said it. It did give her pleasure to see the jealousy cross his face. But what difference did any of it make if they were not to be together?

None whatsoever.

"And did you accept that offer, Miss Stanton?"

She looked down at her hands. She felt her lip quivering and bit it in order to control herself. "I have not answered." That was something of a lie. She knew that the answer would be *no*.

Especially now. With all these feelings resurfacing in Val's presence, the notion that she should contemplate marrying someone who could not illicit even a fraction of these emotions was suddenly all too ridiculous.

Val released his breath, as if he felt a surge of relief, which caused her to return her eyes to his. He stared at the ground momentarily even though he stood frozen before her. He bowed stiffly, turned as if to leave, and then returned to stand before her.

"Dare I to hope, Miss Alita, that I might once again engage your affections?" His expression was anything but hopeful.

Oh, no! Please, not this. Alita studied him with a stark attentiveness. She couldn't bear to have her heart broken again. She was not yet recovered.

She began to wonder if she would ever be.

She loved him heart and soul, and she had seen that they would not be together. She did not know the purpose of the earl's inquiry, but she had no intention of being a feather in the wind again at his request, responding to his almost simultaneous invitations and rejections. She had grown up since then, she had a life now, and she could survive on her own.

"Don't, Val, please don't." As tears filled her eyes, she shook her head. She had not seen him in her future, and she did not need to be tortured anymore in the present.

"My sincerest apologies, Miss Alita." He turned to face her one last time, his expression sincerely remorseful, bowing as he spoke before turning to leave. "Forgive me."

Even without looking at him, she felt the genuine sorrow in his heart, and it overcame her, welling up inside her chest. Despite the grief that filled her own heart, she could not bear the pain he was feeling.

No, no, never again, stop it! Just this once, I must stay inside myself! My compassion will be the end of me! Just as it ruined my presentation to society. She summoned everything in her power to ignore his feelings.

He began walking down the path, slowly exiting from view.

A little while longer and he would be gone. *Forever.*

The Paradox: The Soldier and the Mystic 339

Don't say a word, she admonished herself. Just a little while longer. The sound of leather shoes meeting pebbles—a sound which she knew she would remember forever—grew fainter and fainter.

Val, her mind screamed. *Val. Come back. I shall listen.* But where her heart would not be contained, her voice failed her, protecting her when she most needed it.

His expression was fiercely resolute as he turned abruptly and returned to her side though she was unable to speak. "Miss Alita, though you refuse me, I will not leave until I have stated my case. I am prepared to be kicked to Hades and back, and I am prepared for my heart to break—if there is anything left of it—but I will not give up without a fight."

"Refuse you...*what*?" she managed to ask. "I am very sorry, Lord Ravensdale, but I cannot paint your book cover. And I will not be your mistress."

"Bloody hell!" He waved his arms in the air, his expression menacing. "Are we destined to never speak the same language? You might know the future, Miss Alita, but from the beginning, you have comprehended not a damn thing about me in regards to yourself!"

"Odd that you should say so, Lord Ravensdale. I always considered that it was *you* who did not understand *me*."

"That is true, Miss Alita. But now that I comprehend your gifts, I might have thought we would reach an understanding. You are still the most infuriating female of my acquaintance!"

"We are incompatible, it seems."

"That possibility has occurred to me as well. And the fact remains, Miss Alita, that you are the love of my life, and I would be an idiot not to fight for you with my last breath." His expression softened, and he fought the smile that begged to form on his lips.

No, it cannot be. Alita stared at him, not believing his words. *I did not foresee this.* It simply was not possible.

"Won't you sit down on the bench with me and tell me the whole, Lord Ravensdale?" she barely managed in a whisper.

"No thank you, Miss Alita." As he turned to face her, a new resolve seemed to fill his steely blue eyes. He fixed his full attention upon her and she felt somewhat dizzy by the impact. "I am done with this nonsense."

"I see." Just as she had known. He would never cease playing with her feelings! Oh, she was an idiot. An instant ago she had wished him gone, and now she couldn't bear to see him go. Just as he had orchestrated. "So you don't have the time to sit for a few minutes and to tell me of your life of the past eight months?"

"I have all the time in the world for you, Miss Alita," stated Val as he went to one knee beside her on the bench and took her hand. "But I prefer to kneel. I have another proposition for you, Alita."

Alita could not fathom nor believe the indisputable conclusion. As Val's intent became inescapable, tears rolled down her cheek, which turned quickly to uncontrollable sobs. She attempted to quiet herself, waving her hand in front of her face, but to no avail.

"Miss Alita, have I upset you?" His resolute expression turned to dismay. He seemed not to have the heart for this after all. "It is deplorable on my part after all you have done for me to want yet something else for myself. I should never have presumed...It is just that I love you *so dearly.*"

Presume. Please presume. She clutched her free hand to her chest. *Am I dreaming? Or am I mad?*

This could not be happening, she knew that with a certainty, so any minute she would surely awaken. Or, *if this were real,* beyond a doubt she would do something to destroy and undo it, with the end result being just as she had foreseen.

"I know that I don't deserve you, Miss Alita, but I am an old soldier." He kissed her hand, still on his knees, now trying desperately to comfort her rather than woo her.

I far preferred the wooing, she wished she could voice. Comfort she could obtain, comfort from cook's lemon tarte, her childhood doll, or a windowsill plant. But only Val could make her heart skip a beat and her voice fail her.

"I was trained to advance against impossible odds. It is deeply ingrained in my nature. I was born a soldier, and I will die a soldier. I will never give up until I have given my last and best effort."

Please do so. She began to hiccup through her tears. Mortified, she anticipated each hiccup and resolved to swallow. The rhythmic convulsing of her body she could do nothing about.

The Paradox: The Soldier and the Mystic   *341*

He moved to his feet even though he still held her hand. "I shall remove myself from your company immediately."

Still unable to speak—largely because she had to swallow in a short staccato rhythm—and still sobbing, Alita shook her head, holding tightly onto his hand. She could not fathom what she was hearing, but she must hear him out. She took both hands and enclosed them around his one. He attempted to move away from her, but he was unable to disembark from her grasp.

"Miss Alita, forgive me if I misunderstood," he began apprehensively, "but, do you wish me to continue with my proposal?" Val's despondency turned to hope as he searched her face.

Alita shook her head violently up and down as she gasped for air, tightening her hold on his hand. The one time in her life when she most strongly desired to behave as a proper lady, the moment she had often dreamed of and rehearsed, and she was positively a sniveling idiot.

"Miss Alita, I will—but only if you release my hand. I fear that your fingernails will soon draw blood."

Yes, yes. Of course. I mustn't make him bleed. It exhibits no decorum in the slightest. And I must, I simply must compose myself. She searched desperately for a handkerchief with her one free hand, refusing to let go of Val's hand with the other. She managed to quiet herself and to reduce her sobs to tears trickling down her cheeks, but despite her self-admonitions, she could not find her voice.

She dared not for fear it would awaken her.

An expression of hope flashed over Val's face, quickly replaced by concern as he watched her, obviously perplexed, as she waved her free hand wildly. Val's silver-blue eyes twinkled with sudden amusement, even as he chuckled. "It has been so long since I have laughed. I have only just arrived, and already you are casting your spell on me, my love. *God, I missed you.*"

Hiccup. "But...*how?*" Her lips formed the words, which came out louder than desired, as if the flood waters had burst. "I didn't see you in my future." *Hiccup.* And she never would. He no doubt would run for his life at any minute.

"I decided to change that prophecy," Val replied resolutely, grinning. He moved to sit beside her, kissing her cheek gently as he put his arm around her, his breath so warm and sweet, lingering on her neck.

He hadn't left yet, and she resolved to enjoy every sweet moment.

"Oh, Val," she pleaded. *Hiccup.* A moment ago she had been overcome with melancholy, and now confusion threatened to destroy her. Oh, she hoped her nose didn't start running. She would remember this day for the rest of her life—and possibly into several future lives—and for all the wrong reasons.

"I was certain"—Alita stared at him in shock—"I was certain that we would never be together"—*hiccup*—"and that you did not *wish* it. I did not see it. How can this be?"

"Can it be that you look with favor on my suit?" he asked forcefully. Hope crossed his face, and it seemed that he might become delirious along with her. "I need to know if this foray into madness on your part has anything to do with me—or is completely removed from my proposal."

"Is this a jest, Val?" *Hiccup.* Alarm filled her as a sudden thought occurred to her.

"I never jest, Miss Alita," he muttered with a voice that could have cut steel. He kissed her fingertips. Involuntarily, he moved his hand to lightly stroke her cheek.

"Do not you realize how visions and predictions work, dearest?" Val asked.

"Please tell me, Val," she whispered. *Hiccup.* "I confess I am at quite a loss."

"No outcome is predetermined, my love. Any future outcome can always be changed." Val shrugged and stated matter-of-factly. "We are all in possession of free will."

"I am aware of that fact, but..." Alita uttered, swallowing hard, barely audible.

"You predicted my future given the path I was proceeding down." Val continued with his explanation, speaking slowly, as if to further her limited understanding. "Suddenly, I can't tell you exactly when, my heart rebelled violently, and I knew beyond hope that I must do all within my limited power to prevent that end result."

"Your heart...*rebelled?*"

"You gave your heart to me, and my heart became *yours.*" Val's eyes caressed her as he continued. "So I changed my actions, willing to exhaust all possibilities, willing to suffer or die to create a different outcome."

The Paradox: The Soldier and the Mystic 343

Alita gasped and swallowed hard. It seemed that her physical malady was in remittance, but could she ever wrap her mind around this?

He made it sound so simple. And yet she had never been so wrong before, and on such an important matter of so much significance to her. How could she enter into something of which she had no knowledge?

"Let me try a different angle, Miss Alita." Val shook his head, beholding her with eyes of longing, clearly aware that he had not reached her. "When Moses went to pharaoh and told the pharaoh of his dreams and his visions, Moses said, 'Let my people go.' If Pharaoh had listened to Moses and complied, a far different outcome would have occurred, saving the pharaoh from the plagues, floods, and the death of his firstborn son. None of Moses's visions would have come true."

"And God would not have sent Moses to Pharaoh if there weren't the possibility of a different outcome," she murmured. "God does not toy with his children."

"As you say." He shrugged.

"Or, rather, possibly it proves once and for all that I cannot trust myself." She clasped her hands to her face.

"I trust you more than any other person alive, Alita." He placed an arm around her and kissed her forehead. "Without your vision, I would have never become myself. I am living proof that you can trust yourself."

Alita felt her head spinning. Everything she thought she had known...

"Most of us do not realize our own power to shape our lives." He stared at her with eyes of love and longing. "I didn't before I met you. I changed. I changed a great deal."

"Yes, I see that, but—"

"I had the gift of seeing into my future, which you provided. I knew it to be an accurate prediction based on the verification of your qualifications. Having had the unusual gift of seeing into my future, I decided to change my path and to thereby bring into existence a reality more to my liking."

"Do you mean, Val," she implored, "that having a true prediction of the future was the tool which enabled you to change the future? It sounds almost *nonsensical*. Like a paradox."

"And it makes all the sense in the world. Common sense. Change your behavior, change the outcome."

"And how did the change occur?" Alita persisted. "Was it sudden?"

"The initial shock to my system was dramatic. When I found the painting. I realized in an instant that you could be right about me. Something snapped inside me, and possibilities which had never before occurred to me tempted me...teased me...*became* me. After that initial jolt, everything was gradual, progressing naturally. I went about simply pursuing my interests. I submitted my book. It was accepted for publication. I performed an action which should have elicited a court-martial. Instead I was given a desirable promotion. I now have a post as a diplomat for the British government."

"A diplomat?" she almost squealed. "I knew it, I saw it, I—"

"My outlook is considerably changed as well. I perceive everything so differently, my darling, dear Alita." He took both her hands in his. "Is it too late for us, sweetheart? Can I regain myself in your eyes?"

"I did not foresee this." She smiled up at him in shock. "I do not see it yet."

"Believe me, my love, that limitation and lack of vision comes entirely from you and not from me." To prove his point, he took her in his arms and kissed her passionately, as if to bring her into his world. And it did. His lips were hot on hers, and his desire was raging. She felt the full impact of his absolute need of her.

"Alita...Alita..." he implored desperately. "Marry me, my love."

Her body molded to his, she felt her soul intertwining with his, and her disbelief collided with her longing in a way that made her body shake. Could she be a good wife to him? She could ever forgive herself if she disappointed this amazing man? Her heart was racing, but she pulled away from him, staring at him in confusion.

"But Val," she countered. "What of your diplomatic post? What of your *future*? How do you see me in all this? I could not bear to damage your life as I have my own." She shook her head in confusion, her chest rumbling in trepidation. She desperately attempted to compose her thoughts. "Your profession is everything to you, Val. Your intellect is the expression of your spirit. It defines you. You need a help-mate of a certain presentation."

"I don't give a bloody damn about my profession." He turned to her, his voice fierce and terrifying. "It means nothing to me without you. And I don't require a 'help-mate.' I need only you, Alita, only you.'

"You are *grateful*," she murmured.

The Paradox: The Soldier and the Mystic

"*Damnation,*" Val muttered as he surveyed her expression. "Though I owe you everything I am, missing you doesn't have a damn thing to do with your sight, your gifts, or what you can do for me or can't do for me. I have no further need of an advocate or a healer. I am irrevocably on my path.

"I miss you desperately, Alita. I desire you with every fiber of my being. I am a transformed man, and I owe it all to you, but none of that matters to me now. All that matters is that *I love you.*"

"Oh, Val. And I love you. *So much.*"

He covered her mouth with his own, effectively putting a stop to her protestations while he tightened his hold on her, his hands holding her face firmly to his.

As she recalled the love in his eyes, which engulfed her like a bed of rose petals, Alita allowed herself to release her confusions for the moment and to float in his love. Suddenly her imperfect union to the wisdom of the universe seemed secondary to the fact that she was bathing in love.

Or possibly that was the wisdom of the universe.

"Where will we live? She leaned her head on his shoulder. "What will we do?"

"Alita, I cannot tell you how ready I am to stop talking about life and to begin experiencing it. With *you.*" There was an invitation in his eyes, which were now as blue as the heavens to Alita despite the steel that she saw there. He teased her lips with his soft, warm mouth as he whispered, "God save us, Alita! Come into this life with me!"

The steamy look in his eyes assured her that he intended to fulfill his prediction or die trying. He put his arms around her waist and kissed her violently, deliberately, desperately, as if he never wanted to let her go.

"Oh, Val, it broke my heart to not see us together. And yet I could not marry another." She placed her hand on his cheek, whispering, "I wanted a pretend life in a perfect setting. And then I met you. And suddenly it became much more appealing to actually live."

"Marry another? Who asked you?" Val demanded, his eyes suddenly fierce.

"That's not important now," she murmured.

"I must not lose you again, Alita." He frowned, his face darkened before he returned to his purpose. His arms were around her waist as he whispered, "Marry me. Marry me, my love."

346   *Suzette Hollingsworth*

She smiled, looking deep into his eyes, so full of love for her.

"You're going to be traveling the world, darling. And not always in the most comfortable of conditions. Your children will speak many languages, in all probability. We will have our home in the country and in London, which we will return to, but our lives will be uncertain at best, with every day unpredictable." Val whispered in her ear, "Travel the world with me, dearest. Let us take a little magic everywhere we go. Let us share a small spark of hope for a better world, plant a seed in every port. Let us envision something better and set the wheels in motion. *Marry me*, my love."

She knew that, though she had given up the picture-perfect life she had always envisioned, somehow, the life she would take on would be far more glamorous and exciting than anything she could have imagined. What had seemed to be the most frightening was now the most natural and joyful existence possible.

She simply had to take the first few steps.

Her Creator had been knocking at her door all along, wanting to give her that which would make her happiest. But she was going to have to break the eggs and stir the batter to make the cake. God wouldn't arrange for a delivery. Every change had to occur *through* her life.

She had to take the steps herself. And she had. She had gone to Egypt, she had done what she felt was right, she had experienced the pain and still made the ethical choices, and when the time was right, fulfillment came.

She smiled up at him through her confusion and her tears, feeling no reservations despite the picture of her future life that Val had painted. "Oh, yes, Val," she whispered. "*Yes.*"

Val took her into his strong arms and kissed her with a passion which told her that marrying her was the thing he wanted more than all else in the world.

Tsweep. Tsweep. And then she heard the birdsong—the robin, the turtledove, and the nightingale. *Turr-turr.* The sweetest of all was the Meadow Pipit, whose song always corresponded with movement. He sang as he flew from a perch, flying upward as his song ascended into a crescendo, then gliding downward on half-spread wings, followed by a trill to finish.

How peculiar. She smelled the orange blossoms, though she had none in her garden. She smelled sweet frostings, strawberries and almonds, and rice.

The Paradox: The Soldier and the Mystic 347

She smelled the clean soapy scents of lavender and roses, of lotions and powders, and the smell of a baby's clean skin.

She heard other sounds blending with the birdsong. The rustling of silks. Harps and trumpets. Church bells ringing. Crystal clinking. And the cheers and words of love from well-wishers.

The vision came, and she saw honor guards forming an archway with swords and sabers just outside a cathedral church. Rice was landing everywhere, and she and Val moved through the archway into their new life, joyous in each other's love.

Alita came back to the present, so much better than the sweetest vision, as Val's lips brushed hers.

I can trust myself after all. She had just needed a little fine tuning. She had gone forward, trusting in something bigger than herself and, in the end, had found herself.

With Val, the sounds and the colors and the visuals came alive from the still-life painting that had been her existence.

Suddenly it was no longer a painting, and the scene had come to life.

Chapter Forty

"And how long will you be in London before you assume your diplomatic post, Lord Ravensdale?" the brunette purred, her eyes saying something entirely more suggestive than her words.

The raven-haired temptress was particularly beautiful in a daring pink satin gown, her eyes shining and eager, her advances pronounced. She seemed like a young lady who might overstep the line in search of adventure.

Exactly my type.

Val removed his eyes from her exceedingly low décolletage and took another sip of sherry as he scanned the ballroom. Slightly less interesting than the last time he was in London, if that were possible.

But that was all about to change.

"Long enough to find myself in a scrape or two, one hopes," he replied, allowing his lips to form a slow, wicked smile, even as he continued scanning the room. He knew beyond a shadow of a doubt that she had not entered, and still his eyes searched for her.

It wasn't like him to give into anxious feelings. He knew what he had seen and not seen, he knew everyone who had entered the elegantly appointed room and where they were, and he knew not to waste his energy unnecessarily.

"I love a scrape," she replied breathlessly, displaying her abundant cleavage to advantage.

"Surprisingly, I find that I do as well, Miss Kristine. I haven't for some time, but now I find that the idea...*appeals*."

The devil take it. He wanted to announce their engagement. How much longer would he have to wait? Alita had asked for just a little time to prepare her mother, whom she knew would be distraught with the news of her oldest daughter traveling so far away so soon after her return from Egypt.

A few more days...

The Paradox: The Soldier and the Mystic 349

Stunning. His breath escaped as his intended glided through the entryway in an iced-lavender silk, as if illuminated by a backdrop of spun silver. If ever a woman seemed to command stardust, it was his fiancée.

Soon to be his *wife.* In an instant she glanced around frantically while still in conversation, nodding perfunctorily, as if she had lost something. He smiled.

It is her sense. She knew he was here.

Her obvious agitation thrilled him.

"What has you so preoccupied, Lord Ravensdale?"

"Stardust. Beauty beyond compare. Moonbeams. That type of thing. It's frequently on my mind these days." Damn poetry filled his mind whenever he saw her. He was growing more insipid by the day.

He moved so as to be out of the range of Alita's direct vision. He had stationed himself so as to watch the entry door from a distance, and his current entourage had materialized without any effort on his part, providing him with a useful screen. Who would have thought that military training could have its useful applications even at a tiresome London ball?

"Lord Ravensdale, are you hiding from someone?" the brunette asked coyly, following his vision even as he observed a frown forming on her lips out of the corner of his eye.

"In a manner of speaking, yes," he replied.

"What deliciously naughty thing have you done, my lord?" she asked, her voice now displaying something of an edge though her expression remained confident.

His lips formed the slightest smile as if to say, *Wouldn't you like to know?*

And, indeed, it appeared that she did. "I haven't done it yet," he admitted. "But I shall. *God willing.*"

"Ah, does God speak to your actions, Lord Ravensdale?" She giggled in a very inviting way, to which was added the nervous laughter of her court of young ladies, who rarely spoke and whose main purpose seemed to be to accentuate whatever remarks Miss Kristine made with the appropriate sighs, giggles, and expressions of hauteur.

"Not directly, but I have an angel," he murmured with feeling. "And God speaks to her. So I suppose the answer is *yes.*"

The brunette cleared her throat, a gesture that lacked her characteristic poise. Suddenly there was complete stillness in the group. "Do you intend to dance, Lord Ravensdale?" she pressed, angling her body in an inviting pose.

"Yes I do," replied Val. "And I shall. Very soon." He forced himself to maintain a cool demeanor, but he felt anything but cool inside. Even while he continued to entertain the young ladies around him, he kept his eyes glued to his true object.

He couldn't have looked anywhere else if he had had the slightest inclination to do so.

And then she glanced in his direction. She couldn't have seen him, but *she knew.* Her hand moved to her mouth, and she sought to suppress an exclamation. With resolve she walked toward him, her gait an uneven staccato movement.

He chuckled. The proper thing for a young, unmarried lady was to wait for the gentleman to approach her.

That would never do for Miss Alita Stanton.

She was all that was feminine wrapped in the heart of a lion. *I love everything about her.* He had rejected her, the idiot that he was, and had somehow won her back. He sighed at his inexplicable good fortune. Everything he could want from life, and so much more, was his.

"My lord," Alita murmured breezily, holding out her hand to him. "And are you well?" she asked hopefully. She seemed surprisingly shy, as if his entourage of young ladies disturbed her. Surely she couldn't think that he had the slightest interest in any of them…

"I am now, Miss Alita," he stated deliberately as he touched her gloved hands to his lips, holding it possibly longer than was permitted. He looked up at her through his eyelashes as he kissed her hand.

God how he had missed her. He had not seen her in several days, and before that, eight interminable months. He longed desperately for their marriage.

Val studied her. The smile on her face was somewhat frozen, and she was oddly quiet. Alita had never been short on conversation in any of their interactions—a propensity that he had at times regretted in the past—and yet she simply stared at him awkwardly.

"And your mother, Miss Alita, how does she carry on?" Val asked, striving to convey his true meaning with his voice.

The Paradox: The Soldier and the Mystic 351

"Better than I had hoped, my lord," Alita replied, her countenance instantly blissful. "She finds herself suddenly very busy, which has always agreed with her."

"Busy with the hospital? Political reform?"

"No"—Alita shook her head, her eyes suddenly glowing—"with dressmakers, musicians, menu selections, and silly decorative touches, which she finds utterly absurd."

Val felt his heart sing. *She had told her mother.*

"A party?" The seductress took the direct approach, which did not surprise him. "So you have reemerged into society. Let us hope you have more success with this attempt, Alita." Whispers and giggling ensued.

"I shall do all within my power to ensure that she does *not*, since she is betrothed to *me*," interjected Val, making no attempt to hide the aggravation from his tone. He would not allow anyone to speak to the future Lady Ravensdale in that fashion.

"To...*you*, Lord Ravensdale?" Kristine's jaw dropped, acrimony spreading across her expression.

Odd, he thought. What could anyone find to dislike in Alita? He had a vague recollection of difficulties in Alita's first season—no doubt inspired by jealousy—but it was yet inconceivable to him that her sweet, unselfish nature should find disfavor with anyone.

"Miss Kristine, I take it that you are acquainted with my fiancée, Miss Alita Stanton?" He bestowed his most gracious smile upon the Faustian she-devil, though he knew that his expression dared her not to cross him.

"Does Lord Ravensdale know of your search for the black panther, Alita?" the little strumpet persisted. There was a murmur of voices and self-satisfied chuckles surrounding them.

"She found him." He kept his gaze steady on Alita, and he found no difficulty in fixing his most seductive gaze upon her as he took her hand and kissed it again.

Alita's smile filled the room, her joy palpable.

In contrast, he could sense Kristine's anger rising, her plan serving to elevate Alita rather than to diminish her.

"So you and Lord Ravensdale have already met, Alita," Kristine barely sputtered. "Possibly while you were *away*? How interesting. I would love to hear the circumstances."

Val caught Alita's eye and shook his head ever so slightly. He knew that Alita's genuine nature compelled her to answer every inquiry truthfully, but she did not owe information to one who would deliberately hurt her if given the opportunity.

Alita's expression was pained, but her sudden restraint indicated a new direction in her thinking. "If you ever choose to be my friend again, Kristine, we shall speak of it."

"It is you who were never my friend, Alita," Kristine retorted venomously.

"I was and I am," she replied. "Though I do miss the woman who won Colin O'Rourke's heart. And mine."

"How dare you speak of Colin, Alita Stanton!" Fury grew in Kristine's eyes, as well as tears. But the truth of the implication seemed to impact her, if only for an instant in time. "You never entered into my feelings and were preoccupied with more important *fantasies* when I lost him." Soft murmurs of agreement accentuated Kristine's remark.

"I can assure you that your loss was uppermost in my mind and that it pains me to say hurtful things to you now when you have suffered so much. But I must before the friend I cherish is gone forever." Alita closed her eyes as if to compose herself.

"You are too late, Alita Stanton!" Kristine hissed.

Val raised his eyebrows and took Alita's hand, trembling in his.

"Lord Ravensdale fought beside Colin in his last moments," Alita managed, her voice shaking. "He can tell you much."

"You were with *Colin*?" Kristine turned on Val.

"So, you were Colin's fiancée, Miss Kristine." Val studied Miss Kristine with an elevated interest. Sweet-tempered, hilarious Colin had loved a fire-eater. He felt a sudden compassion for her, knowing how much she had lost.

But if she was successful in hurting Alita, that's where his compassion ended. He glanced at Alita, who appeared to be holding up well. "If I can tell you anything about Mr. O'Rourke which might prove to be a comfort, I would be most happy to. Colin O'Rourke died with honor, lived with honor, and loved you as life itself."

"What difference would it make?" Kristine clenched her fists.

The Paradox: The Soldier and the Mystic 353

"With the fire in your heart, there are unlimited possibilities, Miss Kristine." He bowed.

"*Unlimited?*" She laughed. "There is positively nothing myself nor anyone else can do. *Nothing.*"

"There is no greater pain than losing a loved one. Being alive without him is the greatest torture. You feel in every moment that you wish to die," he replied somberly. "How well I know. But you might start with being the woman whom Colin loved."

"You have no *right!*"

"You are mistaken. I have earned that right alongside you, Miss Kristine. You and I have suffered much—war has done that to us—but attempting to inflict that suffering on others will never heal you. Express it, state your truth, but use the fire in your soul for warmth rather than destruction."

"Val, look, *look!* An old friend!" Out of the corner of his eye, he saw Alita waving happily at a couple who had just entered the ballroom. He turned to see Philip Manchestor with a glowing platinum blonde boasting the same sublime blue eyes as her companion's.

No doubt she was his equally irksome sister. They were of the same cut—polished, appropriate to a fault, revoltingly friendly, pleased with everything they saw, and *gorgeous.*

And exultant to see Alita. *Damnation!* They were moving this way.

"Delighted," he murmured. Definitely not *his friend.* He surveyed the dazzling Phillip Manchestor. Indeed, someone for whom he had nursed no small amount of resentment these many months.

Ah, his advice so easily given to the heartbroken was soon to be tested. Never a moment's respite. He took Alita's hand in his, holding onto it possessively. "Alita, my love, if I might beg the pleasure of a dance? I particularly like this tune."

Light she was and like a fairy... The words to the tune circled in his head as his eyes rested on his petite angel. *His* angel. They could call on the flawless Philip Manchestor and his unblemished sister after the wedding.

Good. A tall lanky gentleman had waylaid the couple, and they were chatting politely with him, even as Manchestor glanced in Alita's direction.

Alita looked up at her soon-to-be husband quizzically, disbelief written across her face.

Oh, my darling, Clementine?

And her shoes were number nine.

"One of my favorite tunes." It was becoming uncomfortably clear that married life with Alita was going to require more honesty than he might have bargained for.

Herring boxes, without topses,

Sandals were for Clementine.

He loved sandals. And how many songs even mentioned them? He did adore this melody, whatever his insightful fiancée might mistakenly believe.

Alita nodded in strained acquiescence, but she returned her gaze to Kristine, her expression compelling.

"An honor to meet you, Miss Kristine." He bowed to Kristine, born to be Mrs. Colin O'Rourke. "I am truly sorry for your loss and ours."

Alita waved her hand awkwardly, as if she wished to take Kristine's hand but knew better than to stick her hand in the lion's cage. "Take care, Krissy," she murmured.

"How are you, sweetheart?" Her hand was shaking in his as he led her to the dance floor. Looking into Alita's eyes, he worried for her.

"I hope that Krissy allows herself to feel love again." Her lips formed a shaky smile. "She has the potential to be such an amazing person, more real to me than the person she now is."

Oh, no, the dreaded *potential.* Placing his hand firmly around her waist, he shook his head in disapproval.

"You cannot live another's life, my love. All you can do is to state the truth. She will make her own choices."

"Like you did, my lord?" She smiled up at him, her eyes full of love and promise.

"Not a bit of it," he refuted. As he whirled her onto the dance floor, holding her near to him, her shimmering pale-lavender gown with a silver spray glimmered in the candlelight. Her emerald-green eyes glowed as they alighted on him.

"Whatever do you mean, Val?"

He pulled her closer, knowing that, if he should die in this moment, he would have known pure bliss. "I could never have chosen anything this wonderful for myself."

Chapter Forty-One

It was the morning of the ensuing nuptials of Miss Alita Jane Celeste Lancastor Stanton and Valerius Gregory Christopher Huntington, the 5th Earl of Ravensdale. The preparations were complete, and the couple's much-anticipated wedding was to be that evening. Already seated at the breakfast table were the groom, Dr. Stanton and his two younger children, and Her Grace, the Dowager Duchess of Salford, who wore a very self-satisfied smirk indeed.

Lady Elaina advanced directly to her daughter's bedroom, and the two embraced in unconcealed anticipation before proceeding to the breakfast table.

"Such a lovely complement to your eyes!" Lady Elaina exclaimed, examining Alita in an aquamarine silk tea-gown with a small train and three tiers of ruffles along the hem. "It looks more like a ball dress than a wrapper on you, my love!"

"Whoever could that be?" Alita asked her mother. Midway down the spiral staircase as they proceeded to the breakfast table, the butler opened the door in response to some truly obnoxious knocking and shouting.

"Whom do you think?" asked Lady Elaina, her eyebrows raised in mirth.

"Uncle Oroville! Aunt Jane!" Alita exclaimed. Alita bounced down the remaining steps, throwing her arms around them.

"*Blimey*! Ain't you a fetching sight, Lita!" Oroville exclaimed, hugging his niece while smiling from ear to ear as he gazed at all the ladies present in astonishment. "I never saw so much beauty in one room 'afore!"

"Your timing is impeccable, Uncle Oroville, as usual! We're all just sitting down to eat," interjected Lady Elaina, smiling broadly, in stark contrast to their frowning butler, who had the expression of one who had only just swallowed a glass of vinegar water following indigestion.

"Oroville has a gift for arriving minutes, sometimes seconds, before meals are served," explained Jane, laughing even as she spoke. Jane was slim but shorter than Marvella and even a touch more fashionable if that could be imagined. She wore an elaborate satin traveling suit in alternating rose-cream-brown stripes with a cuirasse bodice which reached to the thighs and satin bows all along the bustle flowing into a train. Her blonde-white hair formed a braided loop in the back of her head, and she wore a rose-pink satin hat, which stood a good eight inches above her elaborate coiffure.

"When did you arrive in London, Aunt Jane? It's quite the journey from Somerset," mused Lady Elaina. "I shall never forget the happy times I spent with you in Bridgewater on the Bristol Channel."

"Nor I, my dear. We arrived in London yesterday afternoon, to be sure. We stayed at the Dolphin & Shakespeare last night and awoke early, as is our custom. I told Oroville we should eat first, they have a nice breakfast, but—"

"Oh, I'm so glad you didn't, Aunt Jane!" interrupted Alita, hugging her.

"Whoo-whee, Elaina! If this house don't just take the biscuit!" Oroville looked around the entryway, whistling as his eyes alighted upon a medieval knight's armor centrally displayed. "It sure looks to be Notre-Dame's naughty younger sibling!"

Oroville Lovett, in contrast to Jane's fashionable presentation, wore a hunting costume of sorts, a red coat, gilt buttons, blue stockings, white breeches, top-boots, and a black top hat. His long white moustache was curled at the ends, and his short white hair was slicked back on his head. Mischief was permanently etched into his pale blue eyes.

"I presume that you refer to the gothic influences, Uncle Oroville?" Lady Elaina giggled, even as she directed the servants to transport their luggage upstairs.

"Oh, *no*! This ain't a decorating style! It's a moral code by which all who enter must live!" Oroville pronounced. "Or be banished to the dungeon!"

"Come into the dining room, Uncle Oroville," managed Lady Elaina, laughing. "Everyone will wish to see you immediately."

"*Well, almost ever-one,*" Oroville muttered under his breath with a grin on his face.

The Paradox: The Soldier and the Mystic   357

"You've growed up into quite a beauty, Lita!" Oroville remarked, beaming from ear to ear as he took Alita's hand and allowed her to lead him into the dining room. "But she still don't look old enough to be married, Janie."

"Tell your husband to be quiet, Jane," Marvella commanded curtly as they entered the room. "Or he shall have to eat with the servants."

"Now don't throw a wobbly, Velly! I'd rather eat wif' you, bein' as how ye're me favorite sister-in-law, but if they's eatin' what we're eatin', I'm sure I'll enjoy me breakfast either way!" The inviting scent of Alita's favorite dishes wafted to add credence to his words—salmon and cream-cheese omelet with fresh chives, strawberries with almond meringue, chilled asparagus in dill, cranberry-orange scones, bacon, fresh-squeezed orange juice, and Turkish-roasted coffee and cream.

"I don't think Orv is ever quiet," considered Jane, clearly having no need to maintain a ladylike solemnity free of laughter. "Even when Oroville sleeps he snores, talks, chuckles. Sometimes he even sings!"

"Hardly appropriate conversation, Jane Celeste," Marvella remarked under her breath, as if she were the older of the two.

"Is that coffee I smell?" asked Oroville, clearly undaunted by the insults to his person, possibly to the point of enjoying them.

"Alita acquired a taste for Turkish coffee on her recent journey to Egypt," Lady Elaina explained. "We also have tea if that is your preference, Uncle Oroville."

"Tea? Naaah! That would destroy me digestion if I wuz' to start drinkin' tea."

Dr. Jonathan Stanton stood at the first glimpse of his wife, as was his custom, claiming her hand to kiss it. Lady Elaina felt her heart warm as she beheld the love in her husband's eyes.

"Good morning, Elly," Jon murmured as he held the seat next to him for her. They did not hold to the custom of sitting at opposite ends of the table. Elaina looked about before being seated to observe a smile on Val's face as he watched them, as if he were seeing his future play out before him. Her own children paid no notice, and Marvella's eyes remained fixated on Alita.

"Good morning, Lady Elaina and Miss Alita," Val offered cordially before turning his eyes to his affianced bride. Marvella smiled approvingly.

Introductions were made, and all were quickly seated.

"Glory be!" exclaimed Oroville, studying the dining room. "Stone floors, an oak table as big as the Loch Ness hisself, even a circular iron chandelier with candles. When will Sir Lancelot be joining us?" He looked down at the leather chair he was sitting in. "I hope I don't have his chair. I'm too old to fight him for it."

"Uncle Oroville, you and Jane don't look but five years older than you did at my wedding!" Lady Elaina observed.

"Clean living." He winked, pulling from his jacket a gold-filigree and blue-Chinese-porcelain whiskey flask, hand-enameled, proudly displaying an intricately designed gold dragon and the initials "OWL."

"Oroville! Not in front of the children!" Marvella exclaimed, aghast.

"Jus' for flavorin'." Oroville returned the flask to its padded home but not before adding a touch to his coffee. "That black sludge is bitter without it an jus' right with it!"

"As I consider the matter, I do believe you are wearing the same...um...*outfit* that you wore to my wedding, Uncle Orv!" Lady Elaina considered, attempting to distract her mother.

"Ain't it just tickity-boo? But don't you worry, Elaina! I know what is expected of me! I have a proper suit for this London weddin'! Jane made sure o' that."

"He'll be the handsomest man there"—Jane nodded to the tea service that was being offered—"with the possible exceptions of the groom and your husband. But he will draw more attention than either of them, I daresay."

"Without a doubt," Val agreed, inclining his head as he gracefully conceded to his vanquisher.

"I even brung fancy men's perfume to cover up the smell of the whiskey. Purchased at Harrods of London, so you know it must be good."

"You're wearing perfume?" demanded Julianne, disbelieving.

"I thought smoked fish would do just as good. Either way it's coverin' up one bad smell with another, as I told the showy department-store lady and the two managers who came to assist me with me selection, which I thought was tolerable nice to have three people helpin' me when everyone else just had one store clerk."

"They are exceptionally *helpful* at Harrods," Lady Elaina agreed.

The Paradox: The Soldier and the Mystic   359

"Ain't they?" reiterated Oroville. "Well, I suppose they would have to be when they don't have nothin' anyone in their right mind would want. I couldn't find where there was any fishin' poles or worms, even mousebait. Or liquor," he added in a whisper audible by all.

"And what men's cologne did you decide upon, Uncle Oroville?" Alita asked.

"What? Oh. Well, first I wuz shown Eau Du Coc, that means water of cock, don't you know, in French, no less."

"*What?*" Harvey demanded. "Water of what? Is that like saying—"

"Harvey!" Lady Elaina warned her son.

"Uncle Oroville, I don't think it means—" Alita managed.

"Well then why did they name it what it don't mean? And that's what it smelled like. So that must be right! Didn't it, Janie?"

Jane nodded in agreement as she stirred her tea.

"Don't you know your French, Lita?" Oroville asked with concern, directing his attention to the bride-to-be.

"Well, it's not perfect..." Alita appeared unable to answer.

"Marvella isn't much for educating the girls, Oroville," Jane cautioned in a whisper. "And Alita never took to her studies."

"Yes, I know, lovey, but I thought French was acceptable. We've a strange relationship wif the French," Oroville considered, shaking his head. "Always talkin' bad about 'em, wanna t' be just like 'em."

"Uncle Oroville, that's not right!" interjected young Harvey, appearing somewhat inflamed. "Alita is *smart*. She just don't try!"

"Now don't get your feathers in a ruffle, son! Lita's like me—smart but not edeecated! 'An I ain't nobody's fool! We're right proud of her."

Harvey nodded happily, glad to have vindicated his sister, while Alita placed her hands quietly in her lap.

"And if other people want to waste a lot of time gettin' formal learnin', and it makes 'em happy, I don't pay no never mind. Though I can assures ye, there is a bucket load o' gormless educated fools out there. I'd rather spend that time makin' money and enjoyin' meself. You have to learn, son, don't get me wrong, so takes yer pick. But I kin learn ever thing I need to out in the world."

360   *Suzette Hollingsworth*

"I take it that you did not select the Eau Du Coc, Uncle Orv?" Elaina cleared her throat, presuming this display was something akin to what occurred at the perfume counter of Harrods.

"Oh, no! I smell bad enough without *that*! That's when the first manager came to help—was his name Mr. Hancock, dearheart?"

"Mr. Palmer, I believe," Jane replied. "A nervous sort."

"Yep, that's 'im," agreed Oroville. "Terrible case of the nerves. He seemed all right, and then he started talkin' wif' us, and the next thing you know—" He slapped his hands together, sending one of his spoons flying, which just missed Harvey's head.

"Mr. Palmer struck me as a perfect candidate for nerve tonic," Jane continued, sliding a spoonful of strawberries with almond meringue into her mouth, a blissful expression crossing her face. "Possibly we should pick up a bottle of Pastor Koenig's Nerve Tonic Remedy for him, dearest?"

"Naaah! Mr. Palmer is not the sort who should have an indoor job. It's that simple," Oroville pronounced. "A full day's work would do him a world of good. Now this young fellow here who Lita is soon to make an honest man of—he's known a day or two of work in his time."

"*Work?*" Val repeated. "Unlikely. Physical labor, yes."

"And he looks right calm."

"You mistake my calm for intrigue, Mr. Lovett," Val suggested.

"You see?" Oroville replied as if Val had agreed with him. "Where was I?"

"It doesn't matter, Oroville. It's not important," offered Marvella, waving her hand. "Eat your breakfast."

"Mr. Hancock, that's it! Now who was *he*?" Oroville's lit-up face was quickly replaced with confusion.

"Well, let's see," considered Jane. "You spoke at length to the hotel clerk, the carriage driver, the policeman on the sidewalk, the doorman at Harrods, the ladies' lingerie salesclerk—it wasn't her!—but she was almost as nervous as Mr. Palmer, the proprietor of the chocolate shop—divine!—all of whom you invited to the wedding, the—"

"Excuse me?" Val asked, appearing to choke on his buttered scone. "You invited...*all* of...whom?"

"All those what we met, of course," replied Uncle Oroville. "I don' wanna' to go through life bein' no Billy no-mates. Oh, I remember! That

The Paradox: The Soldier and the Mystic

jars me memory, love! Mr. Palmer was the *doorman* at Harrods. Nice fellow. He has a son what is wanting to be a seafarin' man. Hope he breeds, we need more thinkin' people in the world. And so's I told 'im. Yessir, I made me fortune on the seas, startin' as an underseaman until I ran me own ship."

"How did you make your fortune, Uncle Oroville? Killing pirates?" asked the ever-eager Harvey even as Val drank an entire glass of water and motioned for another.

"Well, I did that fer sure, but there ain't much money in it. You have to be able to sort the good from the bad to make any money in this world, son. Isn't that right? You ask the knob, 'an he'll tell ye. Military man, too, he's seen it all."

Oroville clearly did not intend to continue the conversation, or to allow anyone else to, until receiving Val's dazed nod and murmured response, which was barely forthcoming. "I thought I had. Seen it all, that is."

"Nope, it wuz in findin' stuff people don't need in other parts of the world and bringin' it back to England. So's I shouldn't a' had to buy that men's perfume at Harrods, but I made a few new friends, and you can't have too many in this life. Are you good at cipherin', son?"

"Sigh fer...what?" asked Harvey.

"Mathematics," explained Lady Elaina.

"I sure am!" replied Harvey proudly.

"You gets that from me!" Uncle Oroville winked at him. "Be good at cipherin' and knows people and you'll go far in this life, young Harvey. Ye don't get 'oowt fer nowt."

"And Mr. Palmer showed you another selection of *cologne*?" persisted Alita.

"Hmm? Yes, he did. Didn't like it either."

"What was it called, Uncle Oroville?" asked his nephew, his countenance hopeful.

"Oh, I don't speak French that good. I can talk on and on in English, so it's kinda funny how no other language comes easy to me. What was it, love?"

"Mouchoir de Monsieur," Jane replied with a sniff. "By Guerlain, very exclusive and expensive."

"Handkerchief of Monsieur?" Julianne asked, perplexed, buttering her cranberry-orange scone.

"Yep, that was it. Glad to see at least one of the girls is getting' some book learnin'. Mister's Handkerchief. Anyone who has seen my handkerchief—Well, that's the last thing me or anyone else would want to smell like, as I told them two and that lady in the purple ostrich hat who wuz almost as pretty as my Jane."

"She was much prettier, Oroville." Jane blushed. "Even in my youth, I could not have competed. I was never known for my beauty." As a young woman Jane had been too thin, which had served her well as she aged. Like her sister, Jane's hair was blonde-white, and her eyes were sky blue and open to the world. But where Marvella's expression was determined and regal, Jane's was joyful and warm. Jane was not in possession of Marvella's classic beauty, but she had a warmth and exuberance, which bestowed upon her an approachable and magnetic persona.

"*Style.* You always had style in spades, Jane. And *class.* Can't be taught. Everyone is drawn to ye." Oroville smiled at her, warmth etched in his sun-lined face. "Well the lady in purple were some competition, I grant ye. She were a right-fit bird. But, no, she weren't as pretty. Even so, a sin to hide all that loveliness under such a big hat. A broad-brimmed hat like you wouldn't believe! Almost like she didn't want to be seen! A raven-haired beauty she were, and so I told her. Mrs. Stone, I believe it were. Invited her to the weddin'."

"Mrs. *Glad*stone," Jane corrected.

"Ohhhhhh!" moaned Marvella. "Please, dear Lord, *not* Gladstone as in the Prime Minister?"

"There, there, Velly. I know politics is not a respectable profession for a decent man what wants a day's wages for a hard day's work, but Mr. Gladstone is not as dodgy as most."

"Did Mrs. Gladstone *accept?*" asked Marvella, her eyes glued to Oroville.

"She didn't say yea or nay," answered Oroville with a shrug.

"Indeed," repeated Jane. "But Mrs. Gladstone *is* acquainted with Elaina."

The duchess covered her face with her hands. "You made the connection known…"

The Paradox: The Soldier and the Mystic 363

"If I'm not ashamed of the connection, why should you be? Now that we know *her*, we have to claim *him*—he's her other half—even you can see that, Velly. Anyhoo, he's done a decent job fer a fellow who don't do no real work. The *People's William* they call him, and so they should. 'An I agree with him, leave the Irish to rule themselves. Leave 'em alone! Do unto others as ye would have them do unto you. There's the answer to almost every question. And so I told her, but there's a few more things he needs to know, so I invited them to the weddin'." Oroville chewed his food dramatically, his moustache bobbing. "I'll tell him there."

"Not the connection to *him*, you imbecile! The connection to *us!*" Marvella barely sputtered, furious.

"We ain't ashamed o' you, Velly, so never think it! I married Janie, and you came with the beautiful package, like a sticky piece o' glued string what holds the bow and the gold wrapping together. You might act all hoighty-toighty, but you're a woman what makes things happen, always has been, and you stand by yer family no matter what," Oroville reassured her, reaching over to pat her hand, which now resembled a claw. He turned to Alita and added with a smile, "Janie's father was a vicar, a man of God. But Velly aims higher than God. Always has!"

"And I presume this is when the second manager came to assist?" Lady Elaina smiled to herself.

"It was! How did you know?" asked Oroville, stabbing some omelet with his fork.

"Whom you also invited to our wedding, I presume?" asked Val.

"I did! He was skinny. I don't think he'll eat much, so don't order no more food." He placed the omelette in his mouth with obvious pleasure, waving his fork about. "But sometimes the thin ones will surprise ye."

"And did this second manager assist you?" asked Lady Elaina.

"He tried," replied Oroville, studying his coffee cup as if it had a foreign substance in it. Taking out his whiskey bottle, he added a short tablespoon of flavoring.

"He tried and *failed*," remarked Marvella, rolling her eyes. "As we all do."

"In the end, the missus picked the perfume. No one has better taste than my Janie. Though they're all welcome at the wedding, I ain't going to let no stranger decide how I'm going to smell!"

Harvey nodded in agreement, this apparently making a world of sense to him.

"Not *the* wedding, *our* wedding," corrected Val, a half smile now forming on his lips as he rested his gaze on Alita. "Miss Alita's and mine."

"Not so, young man!" argued Oroville. "You've already chosen each other, anyone can see that, you're arse over teakettle fer little Lita. The weddin' is fer the family!"

"I hadn't quite thought of it that way, sir," replied Val, making it clear that he still didn't, taking Alita's hand.

"I wonder that you won't let Aunt Jane dress you, Uncle Oroville, if you trust her sense of smell." Alita giggled. "Surely you must trust her taste."

"Oh, *no*," he emphasized. "I ain't *daft*! Not for ever-day wear! I'm a seafarin' man, not a dandy! Never pretend to be someone ye ain't. That's a code to live by, Lita."

"Indeed it is," Alita murmured. "And what scent did you decide upon, Aunt Jane?" she asked, a course she clearly should have taken from the beginning.

"Vol de Nuit," answered Jane.

"Night Flight!" exclaimed Julianne.

"Yup. Because I'm a fly-by-night affair. Fly by the seat of me pants, fer sure!"

Marvella glared at him as if she wished he would take flight.

"Vol de Nuit is a partially ambered chypre with leather overtones," explained Jane. "One almost wishes to say *green* leather, if you can envision such a thing."

"Easily," murmured Marvella. "I feel quite green since Oroville's arrival."

"That means it smells like you is eatin' an orange while wearin' your leather chaps. After fallin' off your horse into the grass on your—"

"It doesn't sound like you, Uncle Orv," Alita interrupted.

"No, but they didn't have anything what smelled like you had been thrown overboard, wrastled an octopus, and been in a bar brawl."

"And what would you name it if they did, Uncle Oroville?" Julianne giggled.

"What would you name it, Jules? This *is* the smart branch of the family, whatever they might say." Oroville studied his grandniece.

The Paradox: The Soldier and the Mystic 365

"Grandmamma, may I name it?" begged Julianne, looking at her grandmother, who was seated beside her, her aquamarine eyes pleading.

"*If you must*, Julianne—say it to family," replied Marvella reluctantly. "That will save you from saying something inappropriate in public."

"Hmmm…" considered Julianne.

"Now don't fanny around. Give us a name." Oroville smiled encouragingly.

"It is true that all of the children in my family line are far too intelligent. Especially the girls," added Marvella as she dabbed her mouth with her handkerchief, at last finding something she and Oroville could agree upon. "It's not surprising, I suppose."

"I should name it," contemplated Julianne, "L'eau avec le poulpe."

Water *with* octopus. There was a general burst of laughter, even as Uncle Oroville grinned from ear to ear with pride. "She takes after me."

"We all do, Uncle Oroville," Alita agreed, standing to kiss him on the cheek.

"As long as we are giving credit"—Lady Elaina patted Marvella's hand and announced—"this beautiful match between these two young people so perfect for each other would not have been possible without Her Grace."

"Most assuredly." The duchess's expression bore little humility, looking about as smug as a cat with a full bowl of cream. "Never have any doubt on that score."

"Would you care for some tea, Elly?" Jon asked, pouring the cup as he spoke, knowing her preferences as well as his own.

Elaina looked into her husband's sapphire-blue eyes, intense against black hair, now graying at the temples. His expression was sultry, and she was certain she had never beheld a more handsome man of *any* age. As the sound of melodic chimes filled the house, she glanced at the mahogany grandfather clock, which had been a wedding present from her Uncle Oroville and Aunt Jane.

It was moments like this that gave her the most joy. A shared moment of anticipation for a member of their clan, all of one mind in wishing happiness for the one despite the unhappiness it would bring to them all upon her departure. Elaina felt that pang of pain enter into her joy but did her best to brush it aside.

Even Harvey grinned from ear to ear. Though Julianne and Harvey did not fully understand the proceedings, they felt the anticipation.

"Harvey," stated Dr. Jonathan Stanton. "Will you be coming to the laboratory today with your tutor?"

"Oh, yes, sir!" Harvey's face lit up.

"Jon, surely you won't be going to work today?" asked Elaina, surprised.

"Only for a few hours," he replied, motioning to the two lovebirds with his eyes, engaged in some private conversation. "We are not needed here until this afternoon. Better to leave these proceedings to the ladies." He winked at Julianne.

"To be sure, Papa. I am sorry, but I cannot go with you to the laboratory as usual. Alita might need me," apologized Julianne.

"Indeed I will, Papa." Alita emerged from her conversation with her intended long enough to nod. "Julianne is indispensable to me today."

It seemed to Elaina that Val had no previous concept of what it was to be in a loving family. He watched everyone so intently and with such amazement, even as he conversed with Alita.

"And what are you working on now, Jon?" Lady Elaina asked somewhat mechanically.

"Magnetism." Jon gave his wife his sultriest look.

Elaina wondered when she would cease to melt in the spot where she stood when her husband gazed into her eyes in that manner. She cleared her throat. "Magnetism," she murmured, attempting to regain her composure. "Would you care to elaborate, Jon?"

"I would." He kissed the tips of her fingers as he looked up at her through dark eyelashes. "I would very much care to elaborate." He leaned near to her, whispering. "When would be an acceptable time for you?"

Elaina felt a current shoot through her body. She parted her lips in an attempt to answer him but was unable to vocalize her response. Looking about her, she saw that Alita and Val were still engaged in a private conversation, Julianne offering advice at intervals.

"Father," stated Harvey. "Why don't you answer mother's question? What are you working on in the laboratory?"

Jon turned to look at his son, whose expression was inquisitive.

The Paradox: The Soldier and the Mystic 367

"I apologize for the delay in satiating your curiosity, son," stated Jon, smiling at his son. "I did not realize that you were still listening. I am profoundly sorry that I underestimated your powers of concentration, Harvey, though I hope you will forgive me based on my prior experience with your discriminating interests."

Lady Elaina suppressed a giggle as she watched her son nod agreeably at this remark, which he clearly presumed to be a compliment. She felt the sudden interest of all three of their children, their eyes glued to their parents.

"I'm working on a new theory," Jon stated matter-of-factly, clearing his throat.

"What's a theory?" asked Oroville, munching on a strawberry.

"It's an explanation for an existing fact," replied Dr. Stanton.

Oroville raised his eyebrows. "And this is what you call 'work'?"

"Shall this theory change the face of the world as we know it, Dr. Stanton, in the same manner as your two-stroke piston engine?" Val studied the world-famous scientist with obvious interest.

"If I am correct, yes," replied Jon simply.

"What theory is that, Papa?" asked Julianne, her eyes wide.

Jon's expression grew pensive as Elaina could almost see the wheels in his mind turning. She was accustomed to those long pauses as her husband's mind unraveled the secrets of the universe in a matter of minutes.

"As you know, children," Jon began, "if a moving, charged particle experiences a force always at right angles to its direction of motion, then it is moving in a magnetic field."

There was a less-than-unanimous show of understanding on the faces of his listeners, despite the fact that they had been assured of their prior understanding.

"I am interested in the individual atomic dipole moments of the transition metals," Dr. Stanton continued, "which, I am proposing, can be determined by examining the unfilled interior electron shells and executing a simple addition of which even young Julianne would be capable." He smiled at his daughter.

"Adding what, Papa?" Harvey asked. "I want to do it!"

"Adding the electron spin and the orbital moments in those unfilled interior electron shells. *Why?* you will ask, I am sure, being blessed with both intelligence and curiosity. Because, as I have discovered, those unfilled third shells are the source of paramagnetism in the transition metals. Harvey, which are the transition metals?"

"If it ain't gold or silver, I ain't got no use for it," stated Oroville, adding a bit more flavoring to his coffee.

"Uh, earth—" began Harvey.

"Rare earth," corrected Dr. Stanton.

"Yes, sir. Rare earth, platinum, palla..."

"Palladium. Very good, Harvey. And actinide groups. Almost all exhibit paramagnetic behavior at high temperatures but undergo phase transitions to the magnetically ordered states of ferromagnetism and antiferromagnetism at sufficiently low temperatures. This has enormous implications for the field of physics."

"What does it mean, Papa?" Harvey asked.

"It means, son, that altering one particle on one side of the laboratory alters her sister particle instantaneously on the other side of the laboratory faster than the speed of light. And yet the speed of light is the fastest possible form of communication between them."

"B–b–but how does the sister know, then?" asked Julianne.

"No one knows. It's scientifically impossible. And yet it is. There is no form of communication, and yet *they know*. That is where the theory comes in. This has enormous implications for time and space, reality and non-reality. But the fact remains that she *does know*. The data confirms it."

"Oh, Papa, you academics make everything so difficult! You let your minds get in the way of knowledge!" Alita glanced at her betrothed accusingly. "It is quite simple really."

"It is? I know some who might argue with you," quizzed Dr. Stanton, clearly interested. "Explain it to me, dearheart, please do."

"It simply means that we are connected. How does a mother know that something has happened to her child halfway around the world? Or to one's loved one? How do you explain it? You have the scientific evidence before you, and yet you persist in being confused and in contriving elaborate theories. Scientists encounter a nonquantitative concept and become utterly derailed."

"Yes, but it also implies—" Dr. Stanton began.

The Paradox: The Soldier and the Mystic 369

"No, you diminish it to attempt to make it something further, Papa. It is quite profound and magnificent in its simplicity. That is the paradox of it." Alita smiled.

"I told ye she was the smart one—and even without her book learnin'." Oroville grinned from ear to ear. He winked at his sister-in-law, who rolled her eyes.

"Alita! Wait until *after* the wedding to discuss your odd notions!" The dowager duchess frowned. "Julianne! Please serve your grandmamma some asparagus—and some hartshorne!"

The children stared at their sister for a moment and then resumed their conversation between themselves, suddenly inexplicably losing interest in both their parents and their sibling.

Lady Elaina observed a self-satisfied smile form slowly on Jon's lips, and she felt somewhat queasy. He captured her eyes with an expression that said that the morning's business was not yet complete.

"Son, is there anything you wish to say to your older sister today?" Jon asked quietly, tearing his eyes from his wife for a moment.

Harvey stared at Alita with a blank expression on his face. "Pass the raspberry jam?"

"Har! Har! Har!" Uncle Oroville laughed, his food not quite chewed.

"You are deplorable, Harvey!" Alita exclaimed, watching her brother with suppressed laughter. Val raised his eyebrows at his soon to be brother-in-law.

"Yes, aren't I?" Harvey asked, swelling with pride.

"Give your sister a kiss on the cheek and tell her how exceptionally lovely she appears this morning, Harvey," Jon stated authoritatively. As he did so, his eyes caressed his wife's face before returning to glance at his son.

"But, Father," Harvey protested, his expression of mirth replaced with one of confusion, "Alita looks the same as always."

"Indeed she does," Jon pronounced gingerly, studying his eldest daughter, the slightest expression of melancholy entering his eyes. Though not evident in his countenance or his voice, it was enough for a mother to see. Lady Elaina knew well the mixture of joy and remorse to observe one's children growing up and leaving home.

"Harvey," Jon proclaimed as he struggled to regain his composure. "This is a very special day for your sister, a fact which I am certain has not escaped your astute notice after these months of preparations. If you do not care for the wording of my compliment, please devise one of your own, the purpose of which is to lend encouragement and well-wishes."

"Praise her beauty and pass the scones, son," directed Uncle Oroville in uncharacteristic succinctness, placing a heaping serving of eggs onto his plate.

"I know! I know!" exclaimed Julianne, grinning from ear to ear, clearly impressed with herself and her earlier success. "Lita, let me say that your cheeks look very cute this morning. Like a chipmunk's."

Alita burst into gales of laughter as Val watched her, smiling.

"Harvey, can you think of any other compliments to render your sister, apart from comparing her appearance to that of small, furry animals?" Dr. Jonathan Stanton raised his eyebrows with intense disapproval.

Harvey appeared thoughtful for a moment before formulating his calculated compliments. "Alita, my dear, sweet sister, I am very happy all this wedding nonsense has finally got here so that we can get back to our lives. And so that you are not moping about like a love-sick puppy."

Alita gasped, covering her mouth, but her eyes danced.

"And congratulations on nabbing a gent!" Never one to do anything halfway, Harvey got up from his chair and bowed to his sister, his black curls flying about his face. "I know for a fact it's all you have thought about these past three years!" He beamed at his father in awaiting a signal of approval.

"May the saints preserve us!" Marvella beseeched, looking upward.

"He's so much like you," Jane murmured as he nudged her husband. Uncle Oroville nodded proudly without slowing his consumption of the breakfast spread.

"Papa"—Alita gurgled with laughter—"I believe my confidence would be best served if Harvey and Julianne were to refrain from complimenting me further." Val could contain himself no longer and burst into a roar of laughter.

"And Uncle Oroville cannot be allowed out of the house," added Val, "or all of London will be invited to our wedding."

"I have to take my after-breakfast walk!" argued Oroville. "Otherwise I won't be hungry for lunch! An' you can't expect me not to talk while I'm out takin' the air!"

The Paradox: The Soldier and the Mystic 371

"It might kill Oroville to keep his mouth shut," Marvella muttered.

"Aunt Jane, how long do Uncle Oroville's walks generally last?" asked Lady Elaina.

"It depends," Jane considered. "At home in Bridgewater, where people know him and know the time of day when he walks, he can run into surprisingly few people, but here in London where there is never any shortage of people *anywhere...*"

Lady Elaina turned to their butler, standing in attention beside the table. "Mr. Arnold, please tell cook to add food for fifty additional guests. The wedding is tonight, so that should be quite enough. Some will not come, I daresay."

"Yes, m'lady. I am also asked to inform you that the dressmaker is here for Miss Alita's final fitting along with the tailor for his lordship," the butler announced.

"Thank you, Mr. Arnold. Grandmamma, would you care to supervise?" Alita addressed her grandmother.

"Jane and I shall attend you." Marvella appeared most pleased as she rose from her chair. Elaina thought it was a most fitting symbol of the dowager duchess's contribution to the union that she should supervise the last stitches of the wedding dress.

Alita blew a kiss to Val, who seemed to drink in everything she did, and the two exited the dining room, glancing at each other just as their paths placed them out of view of each other.

Lady Elaina Stanton looked to her husband, who indicated that everything was well in hand. Before departing, he stated to his wife in a low voice only audible to her, "It is imperative that I explain the theories of magnetism to you at your earliest convenience, Elly." He touched her cheek lightly, bestowing upon her his most seductive glance. "I flatter myself to think you will find my explanation...*enlightening.*"

Elaina took a deep breath. *No doubt I shall.*

Chapter Forty-Two

"Goodness' sakes!" Alita exclaimed as she stared in dismay at her new baby, only just placed in her arms. Lady Nicolette Huntington was not born in a sterile London hospital as her Grandmother Elaina had wished. Instead, Lady Nicolette was born in Tibet with the aid of a Sherpa, screaming at the top of her lungs with a voice that shook the small hut in which she found herself.

"Wha—" Val's eyes were filled with alarm even as he placed his hands on his ears and looked in turn from his wife to his tiny newborn.

"Heavens! Did you ever hear such a set of lungs, Val?" Lady Ravensdale exclaimed in raised tones, over the fray, to the father of this monstrosity.

"*Not blooming likely!*" Val blasted in his military voice. "There are some now-scattering goats on neighboring mountain tops who have never heard the equal either." Despite his consternation, Val's eyes were filled with pride as he gazed at his beautiful baby daughter and then at his wife. A pride which competed with pain, as no reduction in the volume of his offspring's vocal performance was forthcoming.

"When it comes to vocal ability, there is volume, and there is the ability to project, and Lady Nicolette has both to her credit," Alita stated, but her words could not be heard by anyone but her Maker.

On April 5, 1884, some ten months after Alita Stanton became Lady Ravensdale, a baby daughter was born, christened Nicolette Genevieve Marvella Stanton Huntington. Nicolette claimed both her grandmother's and her great-grandmother's names, a lifelong reminder of the women whose love made her existence possible.

In addition to a healthy set of vocal chords, Nicolette was also in possession of a full head of hair, as if she knew to prepare herself for the altitude. It was coal black, like her father's, and her eyes were aquamarine

The Paradox: The Soldier and the Mystic 373

like her grandmother's. From the beginning, she had her own mind about everything.

"Pardon me?" Alita yelled, unable to hear Val's request over the baby's cry.

"I said," Val exclaimed, putting his lips very close to his wife's ear, "can you not persuade her to stop?"

Suddenly Alita came out of her state of shock at the unexpected lung capacity of her baby daughter and realized what she was supposed to be doing with a newborn. "Oh! Yes! Of course!" she exclaimed as she hurriedly proceeded to nurse her firstborn.

The worry that had overtaken her dissolved as she beheld her beautiful baby daughter partaking of her first meal in the world. Her eyes filled with tears of happiness, amazed that this special being could be hers. Now that quiet reigned, she felt her spirit melding with that of her daughter's.

Her curiosity was almost unbearable. For a person who was accustomed to exercising clairvoyance toward persons of far-less importance to her than this baby, she was unable to resist discovering that which was within her ability to ascertain.

"You are far too quiet, my love," Val interjected suspiciously. "May I ask why?"

"Am I?" she asked, embarrassed. "I suppose I am quite tired."

"Ah." He nodded, his expression one of confident assessment. "Funny, you look quite intent for one so tired, dearheart. In fact, you look to be deeply in thought."

He knows. She couldn't quite get used to someone knowing what she was doing.

It was an unfair turn of events.

"It's so amazing, Val, this new life in my arms," she replied flippantly with a light laugh. "How can I not wonder?"

"Unless I miss my guess, Lady Ravensdale, you are doing far more than *wondering.*" Val's hard expression softened a little, and his eyes alighted on his baby. "What do you see, Alita?" he asked tenderly.

"I see," she stated reverently, "that she has a strength and independence to match her father's." She paused in amazement as she felt the intensity of it. "Most impressive. She will also have your discipline and determination. I see much of you in her, my lord."

"I would not wish that on her, love," he mused, concern evident in his voice.

"Everyone has lessons to learn in this life, and the detriments are also the attributes," Alita assured him. She did not add that she also saw an ego and confidence to surpass that of both of her parents.

"And what does she carry of her mother, Lady Ravensdale?" He ran his hand along her cheek. "I would much prefer she took after you."

"She seeks her pleasure"—Alita sighed contentedly—"but her heart is kind. She will not be shy to follow her dreams nor to give her opinion."

"Two in the same home?" Val laughed. "I shall not be allowed an opinion of my own."

Under her mother's scrutiny, Lady Nicolette began to fuss, giving the impression that she felt all this attention was well-deserved and very nearly insufficient.

Val raised his eyebrows. "She is clearly demanding that there be faster service in the future."

"Yes." Alita chuckled. "Otherwise these two hovering about her will regret not having paid immediate heed to her kindly given instruction and condescension."

* * * *

Val asked himself if he had ever experienced a happier moment. His beloved wife had made it through childbirth and was in glowing health. She was the center of his entire world. If anything had happened to her, his grief would have been too much to bear.

And here was this amazing little person, *his* child. Since he had married Alita, every day of his life was like a heavenly dream.

His life was now more fascinating than he had conceived in his wildest imaginings. The business of countries communicating with each other and establishing policy through single individuals—knowing that every day he held the lives of tens of thousands of people in his hands—was a heavy responsibility.

But he had never felt more in his element. Rising to the level of his ability and performing within that context was far easier than attempting to do a job that called on a limited number of his skills.

The Paradox: The Soldier and the Mystic 375

His career wasn't about pretending to be someone he was not, he had learned. His job was about service to people, pure and simple. And if he didn't know it, his wife did and told him so.

The Earl of Ravensdale was filled with so much joy that uppermost in his mind was being a part of the circle of love that filled this cabin in the Himalayas. He preferred to leave philosophical considerations for another day. Val moved his chair closer to the bed and took his wife's hand with one hand while he stroked his baby's head with the other.

Chapter Forty-Three

"Your Holiness, you honor me and my family greatly," Lord Ravensdale offered humbly as he bowed low.

Lady Nicolette Huntington was six months old when she received her first visit from the most notable of personages in Tibet, Thubten Gyatso, the thirteenth Dalai Lama. Oddly enough, the Dalai Lama's appearance at the humble log cabin occurred in a little-known moment during which Nicolette was not screaming or demanding attention. Val could not help wondering if Lady Nicolette possessed some of her mother's gifts and understood the importance of her visitor.

The Dalai Lama bowed in return and then approached the child. He stared at the beautiful child for a long while, the household remaining in perfect silence. After some moments he spoke in perfect English. "She is very spoiled."

"You are most astute, Your Holiness, particularly since she is on her best behavior of many weeks today." Val bowed again. "However, though I would not suppose to argue with superior knowledge, in my wife's and my defense, I find it necessary to point out that much of Lady Nicolette's behavior stems from her own character and not from our encouragement."

Lady Ravensdale smiled, quietly standing by and attentively watching the Dalai Lama with obvious interest. She had met him several times before, but he had never before honored them with a visit to their home. Since Val was the British representative to Tibet, a country of much interest to Great Britain due to its proximity to both India and to Russia, he had audience often with Thubten, who was both the religious leader and the governmental leader of Tibet.

The Dalai Lama, however, did not smile, carefully considering Lord Ravensdale's words. He gazed at the child again, who looked back at him with large sea-green eyes, her black hair thick around her head.

The Paradox: The Soldier and the Mystic 377

"*Coo! Ahmm! Bllllb!*" Lady Nicolette began to coo at the holiest of leaders.

"She does not make these sounds because she likes me." His expression unmoved, the Dalai Lama returned his solemn gaze to Val again.

"Oh? What other reason could there be?" Val inquired politely.

"Merely to add me to her entourage of admirers."

Val nodded his agreement, his eyes shutting midway through his nod and opening again. *One does not argue with enlightenment.*

"I shall explain to her that her methods will not work on me." Thubten turned back toward the child. "It is in her best interest."

"You might as well be speaking to the moon, Your Holiness." Val shook his head in a hopeless gesture. "She will hear nothing but compliments. Everything else is ignored by her."

As the Dalai Lama watched Nicolette, kicking her feet now and cooing, a smile tugged on the right corner of his mouth.

"She has a kind heart and a great passion for life. But a very high opinion of herself." He nodded his head in sadness. "She will not follow the Buddhist way. Do you agree, Lady Ravensdale?"

"Most assuredly." Alita suppressed a giggle. "There is only the *Nicolette way* for her."

"Do not distress yourself, Your Holiness," Val interceded. "My wife and I plan to someday have another child. We hope to be luckier with the second."

"In the meantime, we must do all we can to maintain discipline and to channel her energies into constructive outlets," Alita added somberly.

"It is on such matters that I am here, Lord Ravensdale." The Dalai Lama nodded. "May we speak?"

"I would be honored," stated Val, placing a cushion on the floor for the Dalai Lama. Of all the world leaders he could be speaking with, to have the good fortune to speak with one of supreme honesty, ethics, and a genuine servant's heart for his people was of the greatest honor Val could imagine.

Alita situated herself next to Nicolette and maintained her baby's attention through a variety of methods learned over the last few months in order to ensure a quiet conversation for her husband. At the same time, the presence of the Dalai Lama filled her world with an awareness of peace and goodness, Val knew.

"I intend to restore discipline to the monastic life." Thubten addressed Val.

"Ah," remarked Val. "And how will this be accomplished, Your Holiness?"

"I will increase the number of lay officials in order to avoid excessive power being placed in the hands of the monks."

"Of what assistance can I be?" asked Val, fully approving of the plan but not knowing why it was being discussed with him.

"What do you see as the first steps toward modernization, Lord Ravensdale?" Thubten asked pointedly.

"Introduce electricity, the telephone, and motor cars to Tibet," Val replied without hesitation.

The Dalai Lama nodded and sat quietly for a few moments. "Can you help Tibet with this?"

"Indeed I can, Your Holiness. I would never propose to introduce anything into Tibet which you did not ask for, but if you ask for it, it can be done." He paused. "It will require English workers to be here, of course."

"You will educate the workers on our customs and on appropriate behaviors?" asked the Dalai Lama.

"I can maintain order, I assure you." Val called upon his military training at that moment, and his resolve grew hard and cold. He would not be disobeyed when it came to the respect due to another's country's people.

"I will," Val answered with a definitive fierceness. It felt intensely satisfying to be assisting people of different cultures rather than to be subjugating them.

"Let us begin then," stated the Dalai Lama. He stood up, bowed to Lady Ravensdale and to her daughter, and left.

"He is a great man," Alita said simply, watching her sleeping baby while she spoke.

"Yes," stated Val faintly. "I believe he will go down in history as a great reformer."

"Darling," he whispered, putting his arms around his wife and pulling her to him. "Have I ever thanked you for this life I have?" he asked.

The Paradox: The Soldier and the Mystic 379

"Once or twice." Alita's inviting eyes shown like green emeralds against ivory silk. "Have I ever thanked you, Val?"

"No need to," Val countered, his voice low. "The credit is entirely your own, Lady Ravensdale."

"Oh, Val," Alita implored shyly. "Don't be silly. It is because of your talent that we are here. People rarely speak to me." She placed her hands delicately on his muscular shoulders as she searched his eyes.

"Sweetheart," Val replied, his lips against her temple, "let me tell you what you have done for me, if it is possible to put into words. I once asked you what your greatest gift was, and you said that you helped others perceive their gifts."

* * * *

"That is true." Alita felt her lips trembling as she looked steadily into the silver reflections of eyes, his gaze intense.

"Others become their best selves in your presence," Val stated tenderly. His lips formed a half smile. His silver-blue eyes fixated on hers, and she felt, situated on this mountain as they were, that they were the only people in the world, along with their daughter. He took her hand and kissed her fingertips in a romantic gesture.

"Oh, Val," Alita implored, her eyes tearing. "You don't have to play the diplomat with me. I am so happy. I don't need your flattery. And anyway, you exaggerate. Whatever gifts I have are from God. I did nothing to earn them. They simply are."

Val swung her around so that her torso was parallel with the ground, his strong arms supporting her. His silver eyes turned dark, and his expression fierce. "I never...ever...play at anything, Lady Ravensdale." His expression grew sultry as he reiterated, "I advise you to take everything I say and do *very* seriously."

Alita met his gaze, her countenance serene. "With the greatest pleasure," she replied alluringly.

He returned her to a standing position and added, his voice dark and contemplative, "If someone said to you, 'You can have your greatest dream come true, and you *will* have it, how energized would you become?"

"True." Alita smiled. "When people have absolute confidence in their dreams, they are working around the clock."

His expression appeared pained. "But it is rare to have that kind of confidence." Tenderly he added, "That's what you gave to me, Alita, my love."

Chapter Forty-Four

Val turned to observe that their baby was sleeping. Slowly his head lowered, and his lips touched hers ever so lightly. His breath was hot in her mouth, and he pulled her very close to his body, now hard with desire for her. His hands stroked her buttocks through a soft velvet, pulling them closer to his body. As he held her hips, he lowered his mouth to kiss her breasts through the lace on her bodice.

"I detest French lace, Lady Ravensdale," he whispered in a low, masculine voice. "Always in the way. Please wear no more of it." His mouth formed slow, hot kisses along her neck, tantalizing despite the barrier. She understood his frustration, as she would very much like to feel the hard muscles in his arms absent the stiff linen beneath her palms. He took those arms and pulled her hips closer to his.

"And why can't you wear lower-cut dresses?" He lifted his head to gaze appreciatively at her breasts. "The style would become you very well."

"Lord Ravensdale," she murmured, her voice coming in short gasps, "if you desired me to wear lower cut dresses, I wonder why you shall have procured an assignment high in the mountains."

A slow smile came to his lips. Without warning, he moved her against the wall and braced her there with one thigh, freeing his hands to unhook her stays. Skillfully, he released her breasts from her bodice. He smiled as he beheld her beautiful bosom before him and methodically set about teasing her nipples with his tongue. He took both hands and massaged a breast in each, pleasuring himself as much as he was her from the expression on his face. He seemed ravenous for her, and that knowledge thrilled her all the more. He placed one hand in the small of her back while he quickly lifted her dress and stroked her, still bracing her against his thigh.

"Are you still feeling 'quite cold,' as you put it, my lady wife?" he asked, his gaze intense with desire. "Shall it be necessary to move to a warmer climate? Say the word, my love, and I shall make the necessary arrangements."

"Oh, Val," Alita whispered, desperately wanting him. "Please do." She moved to stroke him in such a manner as to procure his immediate attention.

In one swift motion, Lord Ravensdale picked his wife up and carried her to their bed, removing her undergarments almost as quickly, her bare breasts visible over her skirt. He then quickly removed his own pantaloons and undergarments.

She watched him, admiring the tall, muscular form before her, fully aroused as he stared down at her.

Not allowing her as much of a view as she might have liked, he quickly joined her on the bed. He suckled her breasts while stroking her between her thighs, until Alita was gasping for air. "Val, Val," she whispered, her mouth reaching for his. He gave her short, sweet kisses, teasing her, not letting her partake fully of his mouth. Instead, he lifted her skirt and teased her with his now-erect manhood, prodding and caressing her. Val massaged her lower body, moving slowly as she gasped, while he held her hips firmly.

Finally she could stand no more. He would be sorry he had teased her so mercilessly. Now it was her turn. She grabbed the back of his head with both of her hands and pulled his face to hers, forcing him to kiss her fully. Val obliged her, delving his tongue deep into her mouth. Whereas he had kissed her lightly before, she now felt that he would swallow her whole.

Definitely more to her liking.

In one swift movement she rolled him on his back and held his erection near her entrance, rubbing it against her while her breasts caressed his chest. She took her hand and stroked him, enticing him in every way possible.

"Damn," Val groaned with obvious surprise and gratitude. "It's always the prim and proper ones. Alita," he pleaded, "I must caution you. You are torturing me."

"Would you prefer that I cease these activities and inform you instead about your illustrious future?" Alita asked sweetly, barely maintaining her control, as she moved her body to massage him. "I have foreseen...certain...events."

He quickly rolled her to her back and entered her, planting his mouth on hers as he massaged her breasts. He whispered, "Not unless it has something to do with our future children. On second thought, *no*, under no

The Paradox: The Soldier and the Mystic 383

circumstances, no." But before she could answer his mouth was on hers again.

In that same instant, he entered her, his rhythm immediately desperately fast-paced, as if he were mad with desire for her.

As she was for him. She ran her fingers through his hair, shaking her head back and forth, craving the release at the same time she hoped it might never come.

But it did, even as she arched her back in pleasure

Softly Alita moaned as she was transported to a place where nothing but love existed.

Chapter Forty-Five

Val lay satiated after their love-making, but he knew he had not told his wife everything. Other thoughts broke their way into his blissful state.

"Do you recall, my love, our conversation before you distracted me?" he asked.

"Begging your pardon, my lord, but I did not distract you. I asked you to improve the climate, and you obliged me." She smiled at him. "Very well, I might add."

His lips formed a half smile, but his voice was stern. "Lady Ravensdale, I grow weary of your minimizing your contributions to the situations in which I find myself. I shall brook no more false modesty nor pretense of innocence." His smile grew seductive. "Particularly of innocence, which I find to be the greatest deception."

"A woman must have some secrets, even from her husband. *Particularly* from her husband."

"As you well know, my lady, I abhor hypocrisy and deception of every kind." He ran his fingers gently along her neckline and followed this movement with light kisses.

Alita sighed contentedly, but her expression held a slight concern to it. "And what would you have me do, my lord? What is it that weighs heavy on your heart?"

"Merely a thought," Val answered distractedly, but his expression indicated that it was not minor at all but of paramount importance to him. "What would the world be like if we were one country, motivated by concern for others instead of by fear?"

Alita studied her husband intently. Could this man ever stop thinking in terms of the world and of mankind? "I think you know the answer to that question, Val. It would be a completely different world." She shook her head. "But the world is not ready for that yet, dearest."

The Paradox: The Soldier and the Mystic 385

Alita grew pensive as she recalled their trek to Tibet through the mountain passes. An isolated herdsman wandering with his flocks of sheep and goats encountered the last thing he expected to see 12,000 feet above sea level, an Englishwoman on foot carrying a parasol, accompanied by a tall Englishman, a Sherpa, and a donkey carrying their belongings. The dainty, pale woman wore a peculiar but serviceable outfit consisting of woolen puttees, fur-lined gloves, a riding habit of thick English tweed, a leather coat, a gauze veil, and, he was clearly astonished to see, *goggles.* Beneath the gauze and goggles, unbeknownst to him, were her swollen and sunburned cheeks and lips—and an unmatched joy in her heart with an unswerving belief in her husband.

She who had been dressed by the grand modistes of London had counted herself fortunate to don an outfit that would have brought tears of laughter to any European!

Alita had never imagined that she could be happy in a cabin high—very high—in the mountains. And yet, she loved and embraced her life. She adored her husband and her daughter. She cherished the mountains of Tibet, so immense that one could not imagine them until one saw them, breathtakingly beautiful in their magnitude. A peace washed over her every time she beheld their majesty.

She revered and admired the people of Tibet. Nothing was false. There was a tranquility, a purity of intent, and a spirituality that she had never felt anywhere else. Strangely enough, she felt more at home here than she had ever felt.

She was pleased to exist in her world, in her small realm, and yet Val Huntington never ceased thinking in terms of the entire earth. A small smile tugged at Alita's lips even as she cupped her husband's face with her hands.

At the moment it was enough for her to experience perfect bliss.

But her husband needed more, she knew that. She opened her mind to the universe, searching for something that might give him the hope which he craved.

"Val," she whispered between kisses, "do you remember—in Egypt— when I told you of a great leader, a woman, who will bring peace to the world in the twenty-first century?"

Val lifted himself on his elbow, and his expression was one of great interest and attentiveness. "Yes, yes, I do recollect...."

She smiled. "I know that you didn't take me seriously at the time. But you take me seriously *now*, don't you?"

A slow, sultry smile came to his lips. "*Very* seriously."

Simply Alita stated, "She will be a descendent of ours."

"A direct line from you and me?" asked Val, excitement crossing his face.

Alita nodded. "When I first saw her, I had no idea that she had any relationship to you and me. Lately, I have thought of this leader more and more."

Val spoke quietly. "She will carry some of our values with her, passed down from parent to child."

"You will do much in this lifetime to lay the groundwork for peace," Alita added serenely. "This future child and her ideals is only one of your many contributions."

Shaking her head, she sighed as she realized her husband's brain was again contemplating some perplexing problem. The idea that they might set the groundwork for world peace was not enough to satiate him.

"And what of Nicolette? Shall she do anything besides scream at the top of her lungs and demand our absolute and total allegiance and adoration in every waking moment?" Val nodded in resolution, looking intently at his wife. "Yes, I am sure of it. Lady Nicolette will be the dictator of some unsuspecting country which she will rule by alternating between tyranny and irresistible charm. Her country will adore and worship her at the same time she abuses its people."

"Oh, Val." Alita giggled.

"She is laying the groundwork for this profession now." Val looked into his wife's eyes with complete sincerity, his expression one of his growing conviction in his offspring's diabolical plot. "Is this what you see in Nicolette's future, my love?"

"Lord Ravensdale," she said. "Why do you always ask so many questions? Why must you always be thinking of something other than the present?"

"It is my path," he replied slowly and with conviction, his silver-blue eyes intent on hers. Suddenly, with resolution, he added, "We must produce another line. A line which lives by the principles of democracy and humanitarian values rather than by dictatorship, manipulation, and torture."

She remarked off-handedly, "There is no stopping Nicolette from her destiny, so it is pointless to presume to deter her," she remarked off-handedly.

Noticing that unmistakable gleam in her husband's eye, she saw no need to inform him that the future leader of such importance to the world was a descendent of Nicolette's and therefore already taken well in hand.

And then it happened. He opened his mouth to speak again.

She sighed heavily, interrupting him. "Cannot you think of anything we might do in the present moment, my lord?"

He smiled back at her, a slow, deep smile that started at the corners of his mouth and made a woman shiver to behold, revealing to her that he was thinking very much in the present. "Indeed I can," he replied in a low, masculine voice. As he lowered his lips to hers he murmured, "Give me time, Lady Ravensdale. Give me time. You loved me into being, but my life is, as yet, an unfinished dream."

"Oh, no, Val. You are a dream come true," she whispered, smiling as his lips approached hers. "*My* dream come true."

THE END

WWW.SUZETTEHOLLINGSWORTH.COM

ABOUT THE AUTHOR

Suzette Hollingsworth grew up in Wyoming and Texas, went to school in Tennessee, lived in Europe two summers, and now resides in beautiful Washington State with her cartoonist husband and five cats.

Suzette has written the *Daughters of the Empire* trilogy in which the daughter of each union is the heroine of the sequel novel, encountering along the way a British officer in Egypt, a Spanish prince in Madrid, and a World War II spy in Italy. The author believes that time travel is the most magical gift a writer can impart.

Suzette loves the elegance of language and subtle wit utilized by Georgette Heyer and Jane Austen and the personal connections and slower-paced lives of former times. Her favorite writer's loop is the *Beaumonde*.

Suzette's hobbies are theatre, opera, and ballet as a viewer and snorkeling, belly dancing, and tropical vacations as a participant. She loves playing the flute and traveling with her husband. Her favorite music is opera, Little Richard, and bluegrass. She admits to being a little bit country and a little bit rock'n'roll with a passion for all things Jane Austen. Suzette also loves her Seattle gal pals and Girls' Beach Party weekends with her Texas SHS graduating class.

Also by Suzette Hollingsworth

Bookstrand Mainstream: Daughters of the Empire 2:
The Serenade: The Prince and the Siren
Bookstrand Mainstream: Daughters of the Empire 3:
The Conspiracy: The Cartoonist and the Contessa

Available at
BOOKSTRAND.COM

BookStrand

www.BookStrand.com

CPSIA information can be obtained at www.ICGtesting.com
Printed in the USA
LVOW1306050607/2

288826LV00002B/222/P